THE VENGEANCE TRAIL

Lady Fan Mysteries
Book Nine

Elizabeth Bailey

SAPERE
BOOKS

Also in the Lady Fan Mystery Series
The Gilded Shroud
The Deathly Portent
The Opium Purge
The Candlelit Coffin
The Mortal Blow
The Fateful Marriage
The Dagger Dance
The Unwanted Corpse
The Hanging Cheat
The Killing Cave

THE VENGEANCE TRAIL

Published by Sapere Books.

20 Windermere Drive, Leeds, England, LS17 7UZ,
United Kingdom

saperebooks.com

ISBN: 978-1-80055-865-6

CHAPTER ONE

July 1796

A welcome breeze from the river fanned Ottilia Fanshawe's cheeks. Conscious of a feeling of tedium, she moved unobtrusively away from the coterie of males sitting on rugs placed under the trees.

Her husband, Francis, attended by the Barbadian Hemp Roy, and Francis's brother-in-law Gilbert Fiske, were engaged in desultory discussion of scant interest to Ottilia. They were all in the deshabille of shirt-sleeves, having discarded their coats in protest against the weather. Not that the heat of early July was unwelcome after the severe winter early in the year. Ottilia's mother-in-law, Sybilla, the Dowager Marchioness of Polbrook, had already sauntered back towards the mansion, declaring the day too hot. She was accompanied by her daughter Harriet Fiske, their hostess for this prolonged visit, as well as Miss Henrietta Skelmersdale, the young companion who had, much to Ottilia's secret satisfaction, rapidly made herself indispensable to the dowager's comfort.

Ottilia had declined an invitation to join the ladies, all of whom were clad in the lightest of muslins, even Sybilla donning a gown of lutestring, although she flatly refused to appear as did the younger set in what she decried as "these new-fangled fashions with a waist where no waist ever was".

Harriet was kindness itself, but Ottilia's endurance of her sister-in-law's inconsequential chatter was beginning to wear thin. She enjoyed the stimulation of Henrietta's company, but as she considered herself to be at Sybilla's beck and call, opportunities were scarce.

The excursion to Dalesford Hall had provided, Ottilia reflected as she strolled towards the riverbank, a welcome diversion from the untrammelled domesticity of the past months. Not that Francis could be brought to own as much. Her husband had groaned at the necessity to attend his niece's wedding.

"It was bad enough we had to uproot to see off Candia last year. I suppose I must be thankful there are no more nieces of marriageable age once Maplewood has taken Lizzy off our hands at last."

The trip to London for the nuptials of Lady Candia Fanshawe and her betrothed, Sebastian Davidge, Lord Ledbury, had been unavoidable. On that occasion, Ottilia was able to plead an excellent excuse for cutting their visit short, as she was still breastfeeding. This time she had appeased her husband by insisting upon bringing the children, together with their entourage.

"After all, Fan, according to your description, Dalesford Hall is huge. They can well accommodate both nurses as well as Pretty and Luke."

"And the rest of our household too, no doubt."

"Don't be absurd, my dearest. You know well who will come with us and —□

"That is all very well, but if we take the children we will have to stay for an age, Tillie."

"We cannot rush away immediately after the wedding. Besides, it will do Pretty good to meet her cousins —□

"Who are all a deal older than she is."

"— and Luke is toddling now, so they may well enjoy his company too."

Her spouse had remained unconvinced until his favourite, appealed to by Ottilia (in a most unscrupulous fashion, as her dear lord informed her), proved unshakeably enthusiastic. As Ottilia had known it would, that decided the matter. Francis could never refuse Pretty anything.

"It is of no use to protest that I spoil her to death, my dear one, since you saw fit to broach the business in the first place."

The accusation had elicited a giggle, but Ottilia had in truth felt uplifted at the prospect herself. Not that she yearned for excitement, but she found herself with time on her hands once Luke was weaned, and life at Flitteris afforded little in the way of stimulation for a mind too used to being exercised by baffling puzzles. At first, Dalesford had provided just enough distraction to keep her engaged. However, once the married pair had departed upon their honeymoon trip, with the Lakes as their declared goal, followed in short order by members of the bridegroom's family heading for home, there was little to hold Ottilia's interest. Within a very few days, the sensation of a lack in her life again made itself felt.

Ottilia chided herself as she walked, enjoying the cooling waft of air coming off the water. It would not do. She had much for which to be thankful, as indeed she was. Luke was a constant source of joy, and Pretty of amusement. She had a husband she adored and who loved her in return. Her household ran like clockwork even without her intervention. Nor was she purse-pinched, nor subject to the whims of others. Her situation was enviable in every way. And yet...

A little sigh escaped her. Guilt lodged in her bosom. Why could she not settle in the way Francis had? He had become quite the country squire, grudging only those duties that drew him too long away from his home environment. Admittedly, these were few. He seemed content to follow at a distance the progression of hostilities with Spain and France, which looked to be forming an alliance against Great Britain. To Ottilia's mind, her husband's interest was but cursory in anything outside the concerns of his immediate family.

Her meandering led her to a little jetty protruding out into the river and Ottilia stepped onto it, moving to stand right above the fast-flowing water. It was pleasant to feel the breeze and she breathed in freshened air. Her gaze wandered across the water to the bank beyond.

Trees abounded on the other side, which likely accounted for the cooler atmosphere. The estates extended across the river and well beyond. Gilbert Fiske, the Earl of Dalesford, had been explaining to Francis how the land on the other side of the forest was occupied in the main by cottagers, employed by his agent to work the fields and the farm, maintaining its buildings.

The Great Ouse at this point was wide, its waters running fast, eddying around the bend and rolling along a downward slope on its way south. It split the Dalesford estate, which ran for some way in both directions.

Ottilia shaded her eyes as she looked along its course, her gaze catching on the distant posts just visible beyond the next turn which she knew to be the start of the bridge that took the main road across. Gil had spoken of his three young sons' enthusiasm for fishing, saying how the jetty had been built to accommodate their hobby. Were the fish abundant here, then? Ottilia looked down into the water. She caught a flash of silver beneath the blue and leaned closer. Yes, there. A big one too. It was gone in a second, but another soon followed and she amused herself with spotting them as they passed below.

"Take care, Tillie!"

Ottilia briefly straightened, turning to acknowledge her husband's shouted admonition with a wave. As she leaned over the water once more, she felt her ankle seized. Instinct made her look down. A tug on her leg unbalanced her. A shocked cry escaped her lips, silenced as she lost her footing and plunged headlong into the depths.

Lord Francis had turned his attention back to his brother-in-law when he heard his wife's cry of alarm and the subsequent heavy splash. He just caught sight of her dipping beneath the waters.

"Tillie!" He was up, only half aware of the shouts and motion around him as he ran.

"She's fallen in!"

"Milady!"

"Damnation, it's deep there. Quickly, man! Before the current takes her."

Reaching the jetty, Francis scanned the river. Where was she? Why did she not surface? "Tillie! Tillie!"

"There, milord!" Hemp Roy's pointing finger registered. Francis followed its line. A long shape cut out of the water. Downstream already. Floating. Too fast.

As the thoughts swept through his mind, Francis left the jetty and raced down the bank, his gaze fixed upon the vague shape, his heart hollow with dread. When he thought he was level with it, he leapt.

"Milord, wait!"

Cold engulfed him, briefly welcome to his heated limbs and torso. He pushed up, surfacing, treading water as he looked again for the tell-tale shape. It had vanished. Where was she? Lord help him, where was she?

In a strong crawl, he swam towards the spot where he had last seen the shape, took a breath and dived beneath the water. He thrust his eyes open, ignoring the smart as the water hit. He could see only mistily in the gloom, but a long shape ahead of him materialised. Surfacing again, Francis followed, his progress hampered as his boots became heavy.

"Milord!"

Francis ignored Hemp's call, intent upon only one thing: catching his wife. He thought he saw the shape again and dived, pushing with the current. He had to reach her. He had to find her. She could not be far.

All but his need retreated from his mind. Again and again he sought the shape, thought it was there and swam, then dived. Looked and looked at hazy shapes beneath the water, eyes hurting, heart in shreds.

Surfaced, dived. Surfaced, dived. Where was she? *Where, my loved one?* Where? Where?

Hands seized him. Tugged as he struggled to keep on, out of breath, out of time, out of life if he could not find her.

"Milord, enough! Stop, milord! She is gone. You can do no more. She is gone."

He tried to speak, refuse the words. Some sort of hoarse noise came out, he knew not what. His throat ached with the effort to refute it. *She cannot be gone. She cannot be gone.* "Must … find…"

"Enough, milord! Enough now. Come, or we will lose you also."

The voice was warm, thick with grief. Recognition hit. The words echoed in his head … *lose you also.*

Exhaustion overcame him and his struggles ceased. Strong arms encircled him. Francis allowed them to take him where they might. The weight of the unthinkable hovered over his chest, waiting to descend.

"Help me, Ryde! Take him!"

More hands, dragging at him, pulling him up.

"I've got him, Hemp. Get yourself out, man."

Weight returned, his body heavy with past effort where it lay. Still the other weight had not yet descended, kept at bay by denial.

"We'll find her, Fan." Gil's voice. It registered only vaguely in the hollows of his mind and heart. "I've sent Charles running for more men. My fellows are already hunting along the bank. We will find her."

Find her? The brutal thought thrust up from nowhere and he spoke it aloud. "You may find her, but she will be dead."

CHAPTER TWO

Ottilia must not struggle, that she knew, understood. Her clothes would drag her down if she did, even the light muslin petticoats now heavy with the wet. As well it was summer. Inconsequential thoughts floated as she allowed the current to pull her along. The water was colder than she would have expected. More peaceful than it looked. It was not unpleasant once the coughing had ended. If this was death, it was easier than she would have supposed.

Was she going to drown? Probably. The only effort was to keep her head above water. Had Francis followed her? He could swim, couldn't he? She ought to have learned. Did she hear him call her name?

The notion brought sadness. How would he manage? The children too. Regret washed through her and she lost control, slipping under.

But then instinct took over and she thrust into the water with her hands. Like oars. It ought to work. Her face broke the surface and she saw the sky. She drew in air, realising she had been holding her breath.

Shadowing trees? She must be close to the bank.

She tried to look, her head too immersed to take in much as she turned it from side to side. A mass of green, closer on one side. If she used one hand only, opposite to the bank, could she shift closer? You turned a boat that way.

She tried, tentative at first, then more strongly as it seemed to work in her favour. Then she was turning too much, sideways on to the current. Her body dipped and she had to snatch a breath and hold it. She kicked without thinking and felt herself sink.

No, that was foolish. She did not want to end up head first in the current. Ottilia went still, her pulse leaping a little. Gradually her body shifted with the swell of the water and she was once again floating free.

Not yet ready to die, then? Amusement trickled in. *What, Ottilia? In this extremity?* Well, she had rather die laughing than weeping.

She watched the drifting sky. It was extraordinarily peaceful. Her hearing was muffled, but for a deeply muted rippling sound. The water itself, calling to her. Wishing her under.

She would not succumb, not yet awhile. She could still think, still feel. She must be alive. A strange lethargy possessed her. Acceptance? The inevitable would overcome her soon enough. Would there be discomfort? Best if she sank first into unconsciousness, perhaps. Let the river do its worst then. It could not hurt her if she was asleep.

Time ceased to exist as she drifted, a kaleidoscope of past images wafting along with the blue above, peopled with those she loved. Something crossed her vision. A bird? Or was that Pretty running after little Luke? Poor children. Poor Francis. They would be sad.

On the thought, she became aware of bumping to one side. Had she veered into the riverbank? An obstruction cut into her view. Something sticking out. Not a bird, then.

Without conscious thought, Ottilia reached up as she came level with it. Even as she seized hold, she realised it was a branch. The will to live surfaced and she clung, aware of how much she must struggle to keep hold of it as the water tugged at her limbs, trying to dislodge her.

Ottilia grunted with effort, her little strength threatening to fail. She took hold of the branch with her other hand and tried to pull herself up. If she could drag herself onto the bank...

But the bank was out of her reach. Would the branch give way? Was it anchored? She could not hold on for much longer.

"Da! Da! There's a leddy in the water!"

The youthful voice penetrated. Ottilia squinted up and found a boy's face leaning over her. She tried to call to him, but her lips were stiff, refusing to form words.

"Da! She seen me, Da!"

"What you say, Jem?"

"The leddy, Da! She's drownded."

Heavy footsteps. Then a man's voice. "Out the way, Jem!" A face. "Here, missus, hold on! I've got you." Hands, blessed hands catching under her arms. "I've got you now, missus. You can let go."

Ottilia released her hold on the branch and felt herself sink at once. But the arms that held her were strong. She was being lifted, dragged, her body heavy again and cold, so very cold...

The squelch of his boots was the only sound that registered as Francis trod where he was led. The sound that kept reality tight against the hopeless wish of erasure. Long-ago words of hers surfaced in his mind. *It is natural to look for ways in which the worst should not have happened.* But the wet in his feet proved otherwise.

"Nearly there, milord. You must change out of your wet clothes."

Was it Hemp holding him thus strongly? "As well," Francis said aloud, only half realising he spoke, "or I would fall."

"Milord?"

Francis turned his head and found Tillie's steward's face. A thought occurred. "You are drenched too, my friend. Did you see her?"

"No, milord." The words were uttered low, the thickness still there. "The river runs too fast."

Swirling water in his mind's eye, in his true eyes, blurring the solid building in his sight. Running figures.

"I will take him now, Roy." The valet's voice. "You'd best change into dry clothes too. Come, my lord, I have sent for jugs. We must get you into a hot bath."

"No time, Diplock. I need to change, and then I must search."

"No need, my lord. Lord Dalesford is arranging everything. They will not give up."

Francis allowed himself to be ushered into the mansion, aware of an inordinate number of persons milling about the spacious entrance hall. "Ill news travels fast."

"Yes, my lord. Come, if you will. Pay no heed."

An urgent notion surfaced. "The children? Where are the children?"

"The nurses have them in charge, my lord."

"They were playing there. Did they see?"

"I cannot say, my lord."

Francis was pushed through an aperture and heard the door close, aware of a bustle of noise becoming muted. Numbness possessed him. His head felt woolly. Yet the dead weight in his chest remained heavy.

He made no protest as Diplock stripped him of his clothes, wrapping instead a bedgown about his person. He watched a procession of footmen bringing huge jugs, emptying them into a bath that had materialised in front of the fireplace. "A fire? In midsummer?"

"You are shivering, my lord. We don't want you going down with a fever."

Francis had not been aware of the tremors, but he felt them now they had been drawn to his attention. Intermittent, involuntary, shaking his torso for seconds at a time, like a body caught in an eddying river.

The dread image sprang into his inner vision, that long shape under water. His throat seized up, his breath choking as the sobs forced their way out of his chest. All thought suspended as the grief burst through in painful, gasping breaths.

In a moment, or an hour, he could not tell, a voice cut through. "Out, out, all of you!" Then arms enfolded him and his head was pulled against a woman's breast. The voice, softened now, spoke in soothing tones. "There, my son, there now. Mama is here. Hush, my dear boy, hush."

At length, the murmuring succeeded in its mission. His breath eased, the tight ball in his chest relaxed and he wept no more.

When he was able to raise his head, Francis found himself looking into his mother's face. She was lined, grey, old. Not like the strong creature he knew as the dowager marchioness. Strangely, he was able to speak from the heart in a way he could not habitually do in her presence. "I could not save her. She is lost to me. I tried, God knows I tried! Yet I am to blame, Mama."

Her black eyes regained a little of the old fire. "Don't be foolish, boy! How could it be your fault? You were not even on the jetty by the account I was given."

Francis tugged in a heavy breath and sighed it out. "I distracted her. I called to her to take care. The very next instant, she fell."

Sybilla let out an exasperated sound. "If you mean to add to this disaster, you will continue in this vein, but I beg you to desist, my son. Ottilia is a capable woman. If she slipped, it was purely accidental. It is nobody's fault."

Before he could answer, a knock at the door produced his valet, fussily anxious. "I beg your ladyship's pardon, but the bath will be growing cold."

His mother moved away. "Very well, very well, I will leave you." She turned back to Francis. "When you are ready, come to the family parlour. We must decide what is to be done."

She left him then, and Francis followed Diplock's directions as he threw off the wrapper and stepped into the bath. The water was still hot enough to be welcome, and he sank into it as his valet repeatedly dipped a jug and poured warmth over his shoulders. As he threw water over his aching eyes, his mother's words came back to him. What was to be done? Was there anything to be done? Tillie was lost to him. What possible use had he for doing anything without her?

By the time Francis was again dressed, a measure of common sense had returned. His valet had produced fresh clothes, which he donned without paying the least attention to what he was doing. Diplock, perhaps in a praiseworthy bid to distract his mind, kept up a gentle running commentary throughout.

"The shirt, my lord, if you would. No, no, pray allow me. There, my lord. Let me straighten it. You have only to step into them, my lord, and I will do the rest. Will you tie the neck-cloth, or shall I? Your waistcoat, my lord. Be seated, if you please, while I ready the boots. Now pull, my lord. It is fortunate we brought your second pair, for I hardly think the others will be dry inside of a week. There, my lord, the coat and we are done." The valet flicked at the coat lapels and declared himself satisfied.

Francis thanked him, drew an unsteady breath and left the bedchamber. He still felt defeated, but the creeping hope would not be suppressed. In the family parlour, one of the few informal apartments in the mansion where visitors were never encouraged to enter, he found both his mother and his sister. Harriet, though some years his senior, closely resembled him in both countenance and their rich dark locks, inherited from their long-deceased father, so it was said. She had evidently been weeping, but their mother remained dry-eyed. The reason readily became apparent.

"Ah, in good time, Francis. We have news. Brandy, Harriet! Pour him a generous measure."

He ignored the bustling as his sister went to a side table inlaid with marquetry on a rosewood ground, where a tray had already been set. "What news? Is she found?"

His mother, who was seated in a comfortable cushioned armchair close to the open windows, waved a hand. "Nothing so encouraging, I fear. But Gilbert came in briefly. He is driving at once to Buckingham to call in the militia to aid in the search."

Harriet hurried across, holding out a glass half-filled with golden liquid. "Meanwhile, the men are continuing. Take this, my dearest brother! They are working their way along the bank. There is no saying how far the current may have taken Ottilia."

Francis accepted the glass and threw a swallow down his throat. The liquid burned a fiery path, but it warmed the icy regions in his chest. "Even if they find her..." He did not finish the sentence, but his sister took it up at once.

"Don't say that, Fan! You cannot know but Ottilia may have managed to drag herself out. She could have swum to shore and —

"I don't even know if she can swim. The matter has never before been raised."

"Well, but we must hope for the best, Fan. We must not despair."

As of instinct, Francis made for the fireplace and leaned against the mantel. It was a stance that gave familiarity and helped him to think. He watched Harriet sink into the wide chintz-covered sofa, this one placed to catch the air from the windows while a chaise longue, similarly upholstered, stood by the opposite wall. Her dark eyes were fixed upon Francis in a look of acute anxiety.

He attempted a smile. "I am all right, Harriet. For the moment, at least." His gaze found his mother's. "I'm worried about the children. They were there. If they saw what happened…

Sybilla cut him short. "They were too far away. I have spoken to the nurses. They had the sense to hurry the children off as soon as they realised what was happening."

"Besides, Fan, even if Luke had seen, he could not understand what was afoot."

"But Pretty could. She is a sharp child. One does not easily fool her."

"Do not fret, my son. I sent Henrietta to see what she may do to entertain the little ones. At the least she may make herself useful in this. She is pledged to distract Pertesia."

An image of his adopted daughter's face assailed Francis and a groan escaped him. "What am I to tell her, for pity's sake?"

"Nothing." His mother's dark eyes were snapping in their customary fashion. "Tell her nothing until you know more. Of what use to distress the child before you need?"

"She will ask, I know it. The moment she sees me, she will bombard me with questions."

"Then let her not see you."

Everything in him balked. "Do you suggest I keep out of Pretty's way? That would be bound to raise questions in her mind. I have never gone a day without taking my time with her. Except when we have been from home. She expects her story every night. What am I to do, ma'am? Refuse to read to her?"

Harriet emitted a sigh. "He is right, Mama. Disturbing her routine is the worst Fan could do." She leapt up suddenly. "Gracious! I must see my own brood at once and warn them not to say a word of this to Pertesia."

She flitted from the room on the words and Francis turned to his mother. "Gregory and the others know?"

"They were playing at bat and ball, it seems, and rushed to see when you, as I understand it, leapt to the rescue."

"Much good was I!" He tossed off the rest of his brandy and set the glass down. "I could wish the young ones had not witnessed it."

"Take heart. Gilbert ordered them back to the house. You will not have been aware of it, I dare say, but according to Gilbert, it was near chaos. Servants flying at his orders, that fellow of Ottilia's jumping into the river after you, and heaven knows what besides."

"All to no avail."

His mother wafted an impatient hand. "You don't know that, Francis. I forbid you to lose hope!"

He uttered a sigh and moved to drop into the sofa, raising his gaze to hers. "How can I help it? The current took her so fast, Mama. I kept thinking I saw a shape beneath the water that must be Tillie, but I fear I was mistaken. Imagining it because I wanted to save her. If she survived, it will be a miracle."

"Miracles do happen, my son."

He shook his head. "To tell you the truth, I dread the moment they find her."

"Because you fear they will find her corpse?"

Francis winced. "Must you put it into words?"

"Yes, because you must face your fear. Only then will you conquer it. Ottilia herself would say so."

A faint laugh escaped him. "Pray don't quote her. I don't think I could bear it."

"But that is just it, my Fanfan. She will expect you to bear it, whatever comes. Ottilia will rely on you to take care of those children and to carry on with your life."

"Do I have a choice?"

CHAPTER THREE

Even under the generous quilt, Ottilia was racked with uncontrollable shivers. She had not supposed she could feel so cold on a day still so hot. The little casement window was wide open. To let in the air, as the elderly dame declared.

"You'll stifle otherwise, dearie, and it's enough you have to deal with getting them limbs warmed up." The woman tucked the quilt well in on either side and shuffled off, calling down to someone below stairs. "Fetch me up them bricks I put on the fire, Samuel! They oughter be hot enough by this."

Ottilia opened her eyes as the shuffling tread returned to the bed. Her benefactor had given her water when she'd woken with a raging thirst, commanding her to sip. She had obeyed, but even the little effort involved in lifting her head had exhausted her.

She dredged up a voice to speak with. "You are very k-kind, ma'am."

The woman's face, considerably lined, creased in a smile. "What do we live for, dearie, if not to aid our neighbours, eh? And I ain't no ma'am. Meggot's my name, and you be free with that. Or Meggotty. It's all one."

Ottilia managed a smile. "It is good of you to t-take care of me, Meggotty. The man who s-saved me, is it your son?"

"Samuel, aye."

"I d-doubt I even thanked him, and I m-must."

"Time enough fer that, dearie. You was nigh half gone by the time he got you here."

Ottilia clutched the quilt to her, trying to still the tremor in her fingers. "I remember very little."

Meggotty tutted. "That ain't no surprise. Least Samuel had sense enough to bring you straight."

Straight to where? Ottilia had no notion where this place was. Nor indeed of much after she'd let go of the branch on to which she had been holding. A vague memory surfaced. "Was it you who stripped me of my clothes?"

"Me and Bridget managed it betwixt us. Had to get you dry and warm, dearie, speedy as we might."

"Who is Bridget?"

"Married to my Samuel, she is. A good girl, but don't have no nouse, if you know what I mean, dearie. She'd have put you to bed in all your wet, she would, left to herself."

Footsteps on the stairs took Meggotty hurrying off to an opening above them. "That you with them bricks, Samuel?"

The grunted response was incomprehensible to Ottilia. For the first time she took in a little of her surroundings. She was lying in a cot bed in a tiny accommodation under wooden eaves. An attic room? Was that why there was no door? Had Samuel carried her up the stairs to reach it? She could not remember walking. She must be in a cottage somewhere. But where? How far had she drifted before she'd caught that branch?

She was still shivering as Meggotty returned. The old dame set down a load at the far end of the bed.

"This oughter do the trick, dearie," Meggotty said as she lifted the coverlet and set a thick package, well wrapped in coarse cloth, at Ottilia's side.

An immediate sensation of warmth in that spot made Ottilia gasp.

"Too hot, is it?"

"No, no. It is very welcome."

"There now, I thought it would do you good. Here's one for t'other side and I'll set another to your feet. Keep the extremities warm, that's as I allus say. Can't beat a good pair of thick socks, but a brick'll do the job just as well."

The warmth at either side spread slowly, bringing balm. Presently Ottilia's feet began to prickle. Feeling returning? She had not realised they were numbed.

"There now, dearie, that should get you warmed up proper. Bridget's making up a wholesome broth. We'll get that down you and yer'll be right as rain in no time, that you will. Take another sip of water now, dearie."

Ottilia had no notion of how long it was before the chill in her bones began to subside at the onslaught of the creeping warmth. It made her drowsy and she lost track, unsure whether she dozed or merely daydreamed.

Blue skies. Children's voices raised in protest and laughter. Fish flashing in the blue. Masses of shadowy green. Fan's voice calling. Luke at her breast. But he was weaned. It must be a dream. She ought to wake, tell them. How would they find her otherwise?

"Open your mouth, dearie."

Ottilia flicked her eyes open instead. They fell upon a spoon held to her lips. The old woman was a silhouette above. She obeyed the command and a dribble of hot liquid made her cough. The spoon vanished as Meggotty tutted.

"Well, that weren't too clever now, was it? Let me clean you off first." A hand wiped at her mouth with a cloth. "We'd best raise you first."

Ottilia tried to push herself up but she was too weak. The old woman proved surprisingly strong. She lifted Ottilia's shoulders and slipped a fat pillow behind her, settling her back with her head and shoulders now raised a little.

"We'll try it again, dearie." She presented a spoonful and this time Ottilia was able to swallow. The broth was thick and good. Made with lentils, she guessed, pungent with onion and the distinctive flavour of bacon. Nevertheless, she was unable to consume very much and Meggotty thankfully realised when she had taken sufficient.

"That'll do for now. We'll get more down you in a while. A sip of water first. There, that's enough. Rest now, dearie." A hand felt her forehead. "You're a bit hot for my liking. Hope you've not taken a fever."

Ottilia's core knowledge took over. "If I have a fever, you must cool me down again. Take away the hot bricks."

"They're long cold, dearie. Been asleep for hours, you have."

"Hours?" Ottilia's gaze went to the casement. It was almost shut and skies of dark blue showed beyond the leaded panes. Only now did she take in that the bulk of light in the room came from a lantern hanging upon a hook near the open stairwell. Alarm crept into her breast. "We should have sent to them long since."

"Sent to who, dearie? We'd no notion of where you come from, see."

"I live at Flitteris." Even as she spoke, Ottilia realised her error. "No, not that. I am not at home, am I? Lizzy's wedding. Dalesford, that is it."

"Dalesford Hall, you mean? That's a ways, that is. My, you drifted far, dearie. We'll send our Samuel in the morning. He and Jem went back to the forest. He's back from his labours but too late fer him to go now. It'll be full dark by and by."

Anxiety gnawed for a while, but Ottilia realised it was futile. There was nothing she could do to change it. The children must be asleep. Did they know? Her heart ached for the little ones, ached more for the torment she must have caused her husband. The family too. Had they sought for her? Fan would have done all in his power, that she knew. Heaven send he had not abandoned hope.

Sleep eluded him, tired as he was. Despite all protests, Francis had been unable to wait for news. Even though he went on horseback, by the time he caught up with the searchers, they were hunting a couple of miles downriver. His groom was among them and had only failure to report.

"Nothing, m'lord. We've asked round about, accosted everyone we saw."

Dismay had gripped Francis. "Somebody must have seen something of her, Ryde. If the current brought her this far, I can't believe she was not spotted."

"To my mind, m'lord, it's more hopeful than not."

"How so?"

"As long as her ladyship ain't been seen, there's a chance she made it to the bank."

If she was not languishing at the bottom of the river. But Francis did not say it, the possibility too crude and painful to be spoken aloud. In his need, he was ready to drag the river, but the Great Ouse was both too long and too deep, so his brother-in-law had asserted when he returned from Buckingham, bringing the militia in his train.

"The sluices and locks cannot accommodate the volume of water, Fan."

Truth be told, the notion of dragging the river, even were it possible, only to find Tillie's lifeless body on its muddy bed was unendurable.

"Besides, Fan, you know as well as I that a corpse will wash up eventually."

Brutal. It hit hard. His brother-in-law seemed to realise it. His features, stronger but very similar to the piquant face of his daughter Lizzy, showed a trifle of colour. He spoke in a tone which sounded falsely encouraging. "Not that I am expecting that outcome. It's my belief Ottilia will be found safe and sound."

Francis did not answer this directly. "What are the militia doing?"

"I've set them to hunt across the river," said Gil, his voice dropping back to normality. "They'll begin closer to home. It's more forest in our section. Easier for them to comb through there. If she's found her way into the trees, she'll spot a redcoat faster than one of us."

It had not occurred to Francis that his wife might have ended up on the other side of the Ouse. He had clung to that thought as well as any offered by well-wishers and searchers. Anything to drive away the hideous conviction that the image haunting his breast was the right one.

True to his expectation, when he went to tuck Pretty up, she had questions impossible to answer.

"Where did Auntilla go? Why did she swim away, Papa? Does she not like us any more?"

He had struggled as he reassured her on each point, holding to the tale that Tillie would soon come back to her family. How could he burden the child with the loss of a second mother figure? Francis did not know if she had any recollection of her real mother, but he shrank from the task of explaining the loss of *Auntilla*.

Yet it was the sight of his little son, asleep with his cheek pillowed on his hand, that proved his undoing. Luke, sublimely unconscious, had no inkling that his small world might be broken apart. Francis could not prevent the tears that trickled from his eyes.

Worse, as he turned away, Luke's nurse, Dorote Gabon, handed him a pocket handkerchief.

He took it with a nod, managed a wan smile, and left the nursery. He barely made it to the bedchamber allotted to himself and Tillie before the storm broke. He had only just managed to master himself when Diplock arrived to inform him that the company were gathering for dinner.

"One must eat," was all the comment his mother made, though her sharp gaze clearly took in his condition.

The meal was subdued, Gil speaking briefly of his reluctance in calling off the search. "Pointless, however, to continue through the night. If we could find no trace in daylight, we will certainly see less with torches."

Francis said nothing, but his mother applauded the decision. "Quite right, Dalesford. Make the best use of the resources you have."

His sister Harriet was less enthusiastic. "I do think you might have kept on, Gil. Suppose Ottilia is out in the open somewhere?"

"If she was, the militia would have found her, my love. The captain assured me they combed every inch of the land round about. Depend upon it, if she is alive, she will have found shelter somewhere."

"If she is! How can you, Gil? Fan, pay no heed! Ottilia will be found, I know she will."

"Of course, my love. We are all hoping as much."

"Enough!" The sharp admonition came from Sybilla. "Less talk, more eating. Francis, I insist upon you finishing that plate. No good ever came of starving oneself."

He had made an effort, but his usual hearty appetite had deserted him. Every mouthful felt as if it must choke him. He maintained a cool front but did not remain to drink port with Gil, pleading fatigue. In the privacy of the bedchamber, once Diplock had assisted him into his night attire, he gave way to his emotions for a while. The bout left him with a corroding sense of futility. He slept but fitfully, plagued by unquiet dreams, distorted images of the day together with remembered fears of the past.

The irony could not but strike him. At every turn, during these infernal investigations into which his wife had been thrown, he had feared for her life. Yet she was taken from him instead by a mere accident of fate. Had he not called out, had she remained on the bank and not stepped onto the jetty, which must have been slippery, she would be beside him at this moment.

Tillie would decry such reasoning, pointless as it was.

A shaft went through him. Was this to be his life now? Snippets of how Tillie would have thought? What she might have said? How she would have teased and gurgled at his response? *My dear one, my dearest love, be not lost to me.*

It had not occurred to Ottilia that the bed she was occupying was Meggotty's. She woke to dawn creeping in at the window and found the elderly dame lying beside her, covered only with a blanket.

Guilt rose up as she recalled snatches from the night hours. She had been fed again with the soup at a late hour. Once, when half asleep, she had tried to rise from the bed and had almost fallen. Meggotty had been at her side on the instant.

"What is it, dearie? Lay you back down. Don't want you keeling over."

Ottilia had made known her need and caused the old woman to emit a cracked laugh as she hunted under the bed.

"Should have thought of that for meself. Here you are, dearie. Come, I'll help you."

Only then, as she was assisted to make use of the chamber pot, had Ottilia discovered she was clad in a voluminous nightgown. It was made of thick cotton and must have been Meggotty's own. That she had only the one became apparent now as Ottilia took in that the woman sleeping at her side was fully dressed, folds of her calico chintz gown visible where the inadequate blanket did not reach.

Touched by the kindness of her hostess, she vowed to find a way to repay these people. Mere money would not serve, although it might be welcome. One could not show true gratitude only with coin.

These thoughts could not long occupy her mind, which turned again to her loved ones. She had no need of second sight to know how her vanishment must affect her dearest lord. The sooner she could set his mind at rest, the easier would be her own.

Delay began to chafe her as she gazed at the greying square of light beyond the window, trying to gauge the time. This was a working household. Surely they would rise with daylight. Even now, perhaps Samuel would be waking, readying for his day's labour. What if she missed him and he was already gone? Who would take the message then?

She took some comfort from remembrance of Meggotty's promise that Samuel would go this morning to Dalesford Hall. Yet had the dame so advised him? Would he think of it?

"Awake, are you, dearie?"

Ottilia turned her head to find Meggotty had pushed up on her elbow and was regarding her with a critical eye.

"Fretting, is it? No need, dearie."

A tiny laugh escaped Ottilia. "How did you guess?"

A wry grin, almost toothless, came. "By my time of life, dearie, you get to know the signs."

Throwing off the blanket, the elderly dame shoved herself to her feet with an agility that pricked at Ottilia's conscience. She was growing spoiled, to be thus weak at the slightest setback. She could wish she might have half this creature's strength.

But the urgency of her need came through and Ottilia pushed up on her elbows. "Will Samuel have time to go to Dalesford Hall? Will it keep him too long from his work?"

Meggotty was folding the blanket, neatly attaching corner to corner. "It won't come to that, dearie. Leastways, it won't if I don't miss my guess." She looked across, a snap in her eyes all too reminiscent of that in Ottilia's formidable mother-in-law. "You'd not credit the noddy I give birth to, dearie, and that's a fact."

"Samuel?"

"Aye, Samuel, though he's nowise as wise as his biblical namesake."

"Why, what has happened?"

Meggotty set down the blanket on a chest under the window that Ottilia had not before noticed, and turned back, setting her arms akimbo. "There was redcoats hunting the forest yesterday."

Hope leapt in Ottilia's breast. "Militia?"

"Aye, them. Samuel seen 'em, for as he's one with the other foresters as coppice the trees and stack the wood. 'Did you tell 'em as we had missus here?' says I. 'No,' says he, for as he didn't know as they was searching for you. Would you credit it?"

Ottilia ignored this last. "They might have been. It is possible Lord Dalesford called them out. But your Samuel could not know that, Meggotty."

"Could've asked, couldn't he, but no. Noddy didn't think to." Meggotty came around the bed towards the stair. "I'll fetch hot water and we'll get you ready. Samuel ought to be on his way by this. Told him to look out fer the redcoats, for as you ain't been found and they're bound to be out again first thing. If we've the luck, dearie, they'll tell your people at Dalesford quick and you'll be fetched home straight."

Hope leapt, tempered with question. "But will Samuel be willing to approach the militia?"

"He'll do as he's told, or I'll know the reason why. Not that I don't know it already. Too scared, for all of me. I'm guessing he kept hid of them. 'Fraid they was looking fer crim'nals. There's been talk of thefts roundabout, and even a killing. Leastways, they say it weren't no accident, nor it ain't locals as done it. Think there's a gang of them operating out of Newport Pagnell."

Ottilia's senses prickled. No accident? How could she have forgotten so readily? She had not fallen from carelessness. That grip on her ankle! It must have been intended. What if there had indeed been a killing already?

Did someone want her dead too?

CHAPTER FOUR

The captain of militia saluted smartly as Francis reached the hall. Alerted by Hemp Roy, who knocked on his door just as he was tying his hair into a queue, he had seized his hat and left the bedchamber at a run, hurtling down the stairs into the large wood-panelled hall, Hemp right behind him.

"You have news of my wife?"

The captain, a stocky fellow who looked to have a few more years in his dish than Francis himself, gestured towards Gil. "As I have just been telling his lordship, I can't be sure of the woman's identity."

Impatience rode Francis. "But you think it may be she? Where is she? What did you find? Tell me, for pity's sake!"

His brother-in-law, dressed for riding as was Francis, ready to resume the search, came across and set a hand to his shoulder. "Patience, Fan! Let the man tell his tale."

With difficulty, Francis refrained alike from retort and throwing off the soothing hand. "Well, sir?"

"One of my men was accosted by a fellow who says he is a forester. He picked a woman up out of the water yesterday."

Francis's heart dipped. "Alive?"

"Alive, but exhausted."

His pulse awry, Francis again pelted his questions. "Where is she? What happened to her? Did he think to —? □

"Hush, man!" Gil in his ear, the hand on his shoulder gripping hard.

The captain glanced from one to the other, but resumed. "He carried her to his cottage, sir. It seems his mother took charge of her."

Francis could no longer contain himself. "Where? Where is the cottage? Can you take me there?"

The captain jerked a thumb towards the door. "I've got the fellow here, sir. Thought it best to come here at once rather than waste time going to the cottage, since I couldn't verify the lady's identity myself."

"Very wise," said Gil. His hand on Francis's shoulder prevented him from dashing out on the instant. "You go, Fan, and take your fellow Roy here with you. It'll be quicker on horseback. If this unfortunate proves to be Ottilia, you can send Roy back for the coach to bring her home. I'll have everything prepared meanwhile."

"My thanks, Gil. Hemp! With me!"

"At your service, milord."

Already on his way to the back door that would lead him through the house to the stables, Francis was stayed by Gil's voice. "One moment, Fan!"

He turned with impatience. "What is it?"

"I'll call off the hunt. The men are already out."

From somewhere, common sense surfaced. "No, don't. Not yet. Not until we know for sure." Francis turned again, calling to the captain of militia. "We're for the stables. We'll meet you out front."

Once the cavalcade had crossed the road bridge, the way soon became circuitous. The forester, mounted behind one of the militiamen, had begun to lead. Francis turned his head to speak to the steward, riding beside him.

"I hope you are taking note of this passage, Hemp. I could not swear to finding my way back."

"If necessary, milord, I will commandeer the services of that forester fellow."

"Well thought of. I will have to compensate him for his trouble. I dare say he is supposed to be at his work."

He spoke without paying any real attention to his words, his whole mind focused on what he might find at the other end of the journey. Hope had sprung up, giving him the first glimpse of averting disaster since the instant he had seen Tillie drop below the surface of the river. As time went on, however, doubt set in.

If it was indeed his wife, why had she not sent to them immediately? Unless she was too debilitated by her ordeal, Tillie would not dream of leaving him in suspense. Which gave rise to the dread thought that the forester had rescued some other woman altogether. It was not beyond the bounds of probability that another woman had also fallen victim to the river's current, although it did seem unlikely. Needing reassurance, he canvassed Hemp's views.

"What do you think? Is it her ladyship?"

Hemp gave a grunt, of what significance Francis could not fathom. "Of what use to speculate, milord? We will know soon enough."

"Not soon enough for me."

"Milord Dalesford bid you to patience, milord. We cannot be far from the place now."

"Could she have drifted such a distance?"

"We searched even farther yesterday, milord. The current is strong."

Francis said no more, the dread rising up to torment him. No longer dread of finding a corpse. Instead he dreaded now the discovery of a different face from that he sought.

From where the captain was riding ahead, there came a call. "It is but a matter of half a mile, my lord, so this fellow claims."

"Thank the Lord!" Francis put spurs to his horse and caught up with the captain. "You will wait, I hope, while I go in to see if my wife is there?"

"Certainly, sir. Small point in my leaving you until we are certain. My men are ready to resume the search at need."

"I thank you. Though I pray it may not be necessary."

Washed, but not dressed, Ottilia remained in the attic, propped up with a bolster and pillows against the wooden backboard of the cot bed. There was no hope yet of resuming her clothes.

"Bridget had 'em hanging all night in the kitchen, dearie, but they're still damp and we don't want you taking a chill. I told her to put 'em out, for the sun's up and they oughter dry out soonish."

Ottilia thanked her, saying naught of her preference to be ready and dressed in anticipation of her husband's hoped-for arrival. As well, perhaps, for even the effort to wash had exhausted her. Nevertheless, her mind ran wholly on her desire to be reunited with her dear ones.

What if Samuel failed to find the militia? She felt sick with anxiety, unable to do justice to the bread and cheese her hostess brought up, even though it was her favoured Cheddar. The bread, clearly from yesterday's loaf, was tough and the cheese hard but she did the best she could, aware this meagre fare was costly for her hosts. Meggotty offered ale to wash it down, but Ottilia, who longed for coffee, took only water from the jug on the bedside table, which was refilled at intervals.

At length the older woman nodded in a decisive fashion. "Well, if you can't get it down, dearie, you can't. Here, I'll take it away and you can rest."

"Pray leave the water, Meggotty, if you will."

Her hostess picked up the jug and refilled the glass she had supplied, tutting the while. "Ale would have done you good, but water'll do. Drink as much as you can, dearie."

Left alone as Meggotty clumped down the stairs, Ottilia sank back against the pillows with a resigned sigh. She seemed doomed to be a trouble to everyone. If it was not a murder on her doorstep, she must needs fall victim to some malevolent individual hiding under the jetty. Her imagination painted for her the panic and confusion caused among the onlookers. With the militia on the hunt, there had clearly been a concerted search undertaken, the entire Dalesford household no doubt dragged into the business. So much bother and all for what? Who had it been? Why was she a target?

This last occupied her thoughts for several painful moments. The realisation that it could not have been random chilled her blood. Someone had intended her death. A flitter of images crossed her mind as it came to her that there were all too many persons who might wish her ill. Her activities these many years had been for justice. Yet justice might readily have meant a terrible loss for the families of those affected. Could one such person be bent upon revenge?

Before Ottilia had an opportunity to sift possibilities, the sound for which she had half-consciously been waiting came to her ears. The clopping of horses' hooves.

They were muffled by the turf, but unmistakeably heading in this direction, growing louder by the moment. Ottilia's pulse picked up its beat and hope bloomed in her breast. Fan! It must be. Could it be? Unless it was merely the militia?

Her ears strained to hear the jingle of the harness, the murmur of men's voices, a thud as boots hit the turf and the clopping ceased. They were here.

Thought suspended, she listened for the voice she longed to hear. It came.

"These stairs? I thank you, madam. I will find my way."

Ottilia pushed forward, her gaze fixed upon the open space above the stairwell. The sound of boots climbing fast. Then a head appeared, the beloved features under a beaver hat.

"Fan, it is you! Thank heaven!"

He paused on the top stair, dark gaze raking her face. Then he moved, throwing off the hat. Within instants, Ottilia was in his arms, crushed to his chest, anguish in his voice.

"I thought I had lost you forever! My darling, my loved one…"

Ottilia could not speak, her throat too thickened. His murmuring words, only half heard, were nevertheless balm and she wept.

At length, Francis loosened his hold and Ottilia found herself looking into the strong-boned features, ever attractive to her, framed with lush hair, the dark eyes damp with emotion. The marks of the past four and twenty hours were visible.

She brought up a hand to caress his cheek. "You have suffered, my dearest. I am so very sorry."

He leaned in to kiss her briefly, releasing one hand and stroking her hair, which was loose and dry now, though lank from her sojourn in the river. "Don't be. I am only too relieved to find you alive."

"I would not be, I think, if not for Samuel."

"The forester?"

She nodded. "His son saw me. I was clinging to a branch. Samuel got me out and brought me here. They have been kindness itself, Fan."

His gaze seemed to devour her, and he spoke absently. "We will reward them, never fear. But are you well? You look perfectly washed out."

A tiny gurgle escaped her. "An appropriate term, Fan."

"Don't be facetious, sweetheart. Only tell me. How do you really do?"

She managed a smile. "I am fatigued, but Meggotty managed me so very well that we avoided a fever."

"Who is Meggotty?"

"Samuel's mother." Ottilia laughed then. "She reminds me of Sybilla. She is just such a tartar, I fear, ruling the roost in this cottage."

To her joy, he laughed. "Lord help you then!"

"No, indeed, she has been my saviour. She acted fast to get me out of my wet clothes and into this bed, with a quilt and hot bricks, and later a sustaining broth. She took the greatest care of me and I have thus avoided the worst of consequences."

He drew her hand to his lips and kissed it. "Then she is my saviour too. But could they not have sent to us at once? Did you not tell them where to go?"

Ottilia fetched a sigh. "Fan, I had not my wits about me. I cannot even remember being brought here. By the time I was able to think of it, Samuel was back from his work and I was obliged to concede when Meggotty said it was too late to set out. I might have spared you the worry otherwise."

A grimace crossed his face. "Worry? That is the understatement of the century, my loved one."

"Oh, Fan…" She crumpled into his arms again.

His embrace was tight, his words gentle. "No matter, sweetheart, it is over now." Presently, he put her away from him and looked searchingly into her face. "Are you certain you have suffered no serious ill? We will have a doctor to you as soon as we are back at Dalesford."

"There is no need, my dearest dear. He will only tell me to rest, and that much I know for myself. But tell me, is all well? The children?"

He let out a sigh that sounded overcharged to Ottilia's ears. "How could it be well? The whole household has been turned upside-down."

"Oh, no, Fan."

His smile was wry. "Well, not quite that. But all the men have been out hunting along the bank. We only gave up when the light failed. They began again this morning, and I was about to join them with Gil when the captain of militia arrived with this forester fellow."

Impatient of this divagation, Ottilia persisted. "But the children, Fan? I have been so anxious. Did they see? Were they troubled?"

"Pretty was, yes. She asked me all manner of impossible questions. At the time, however, the nurses had the sense to hurry them away to the house. The Fiske children also, though they were aware of what had happened. I knew nothing of it, Tillie, until later. I was intent upon finding you. I would not have stopped but that Hemp dragged me out of the river."

The agony under the words moved Ottilia to throw herself back into his embrace. "My darling lord, I wish I could have prevented you from suffering so."

Francis held her close, his voice warm in her ear. "It was an accident, my loved one. My fault too. I distracted you."

At that, Ottilia pulled away, looking into his face. "But you did not, Fan. I was not in the least distracted. Nor was it an accident. Something seized me by the ankle."

His brows snapped together. "What? What thing?"

"A hand. A person, I should say. It tugged and I lost my balance. Because I was bending over, I think. I was watching the fish."

Francis looked incredulous. "How in the world can that be? Who would do such a thing? Tillie, it can't be so."

She seized his hand and clutched it. "I did not imagine it, Fan."

"I am not suggesting you did, but —□

"I was perfectly safe. I would not have fallen otherwise, I promise you. I can't remember much about what happened afterwards, but that I could not forget."

For a moment he said nothing, the brown gaze intent. Ottilia waited, a trifle of anxiety rising. Did he not believe her? If Francis doubted, she might begin to doubt herself. When he spoke at last, his words were disappointing.

"We will talk more of it. I must leave you for a moment. Hemp will return to Dalesford for the coach Gil is preparing, and the militia captain is waiting for his dismissal."

A brief peck on the lips and he was gone, his steps thumping on the stairs as he hurried below.

Ottilia sank back against the pillows, dismay creeping into her breast. Had she imagined it after all? The notion caused a flash of irritation. Had she not this moment past anticipated this danger? She must hold to what she knew, no matter who might scoff. At once she chided herself. Her spouse had not mocked her, but he was clearly disinclined to take her words at face value. What, did he think her so deprived of her senses she had woven such a fantasy in her head?

In common justice she was obliged to admit she had lost her senses indeed — afterwards. Yet the clarity of that fateful instant was total. If she thought back, she could almost feel the grasping hand about her ankle and the yank that had tipped her into the deep. It had been real, deliberate. The aftermath was something else. The act itself she recalled as if it had only just occurred.

Feet on the stairs indicated her husband's return. Ottilia prepared for battle only to have the wind taken out of her sails, for Francis spoke as he reached the attic.

"That Meggotty of yours is seeing about your clothes, my loved one. If they are dry, she will help you to dress." He plonked down on the bed and took hold of her hands. "Now, tell me precisely what you remember."

CHAPTER FIVE

The journey back to Dalesford Hall had not occupied very much time despite the slow progress made at Francis's orders, but Ottilia was chagrined to find that it tired her unduly. She was relieved that her arrival caused less bustle than she might have expected, for which she had Gil to thank, as her husband informed her.

"He instructed everyone to stay away until you were safely bestowed in the bedchamber. Even my esteemed mother obeyed."

Ottilia managed a laugh, though she was relieved too. "I don't think I could yet tolerate an invasion, my dearest."

"Nor shall you. We will institute a strict rota for visitors until you are recovered."

"Which may not be for some little time," Ottilia said, rueful. "I fear I am more fatigued than I knew."

She felt even more exhausted as her personal maid helped her to change out of the clothes in which she had nearly drowned, eager to be rid of that reminder. Besides, the muslin petticoats had suffered several tears and acquired stains from their sojourn in the Ouse.

"Ruined these are, my lady," Joanie complained. "Nor this under-petticoat ain't fully dry. You oughtn't to have worn it, my lady."

"I had no choice, Joanie, unless I were to arrive in Meggotty's nightgown."

She had been all too aware of the musty smell and slight dampness in the garments. Unwilling to repay the kindness of her hosts with complaints, however, and mindful that she would not be wearing the clothes for long, Ottilia had said no word of it while she donned them with Meggotty's assistance. Joanie insisted upon rubbing her down with a towel before enveloping her in one of her own lawn nightgowns while a housemaid passed a warming pan between the sheets despite the growing heat of the day. Ottilia was glad enough to slide into a warm bed, banked with a number of pillows.

She sighed with relief, glancing about the spacious bedchamber allotted to the Fanshawes' use for the duration of their stay, as if she saw it for the first time. The contrast with kind Meggotty's attic could not but strike her. The four-poster with its high tester took up prime position, but there was room enough for a large japanned press, a washing-cum-dressing table with an adjoining stool for Ottilia, a gentleman's shaving stand for Francis, equally well equipped, several chairs, both with and without arms, set against the walls, and a standing long mirror.

The massive sash window gave onto pleasant prospects towards the rear of the mansion, and the walls were papered in the same delicate Chinese design of humming birds and flowers as the bed-curtains and the coverlet. Harriet's work, Ottilia was persuaded. One could not fault her hostess's taste. Thinking of the tiny room at the top of her rescuer's house, she could not but reflect upon her good fortune. Which led inevitably to a flurry of guilt. How had she dared to decry her situation, and thus make herself vulnerable to attack?

Before she could fall into a threatening melancholy, Joanie re-appeared at the bedside, armed with a voluminous shawl. Ottilia was no longer feeling the cold, but as the article was of tabbinet, more silk than wool, she made no protest when her maid set it about her shoulders.

"You keep that tucked nicely about you, my lady. I know it's hot out, but your skin is chill as chill and you need warming up."

Aware that her maid's gentle bullying concealed the deep-seated anxiety under which she must have laboured, Ottilia produced a wry grimace. "What I chiefly need, Joanie, is coffee."

The maid tutted. "Do you suppose I hadn't thought of it, my lady? Of course I remembered. It'll be here directly."

Ottilia caught her hand and squeezed. "Thank you. It is such a pleasure to be safe home with you to look after me. What would I do without you, Joanie?"

At that, her maid's eyes sprang tears and her voice became husky. "What should I have done without you, my lady? I ain't never been so scared in my life!"

"Hush!" Ottilia shook the hand she held and let it go. "It is over now. We will go on just as if it had never happened."

Joanie sniffed and dropped a curtsy. "Yes, my lady. Not that I'm likely to forget, nor any of us."

Fortunately for Ottilia's peace of mind, a knock at the door produced a servant with a tray upon which reposed the makings of her favourite beverage. Joanie recovered as she busied herself in pouring a cup, laced with sugar and cream just as Ottilia liked it. For the maid's benefit, she made a great play of enjoyment as she took a first sip, but in truth it was indeed nectar on her tongue. She was into her second cup by the time her husband reappeared, ushering in her mother-in-law.

"What is this Francis has been telling me?" began Sybilla without preamble. "Some rigmarole of a hand pulling you in? I never heard of such a thing!"

Ottilia exchanged a glance with her spouse, who cast up his eyes. "I am very happy to see you too, Sybilla."

The dowager halted on her way to the bed, brought up short. She raised delicate brows. "What do you say?" Then she flapped a dismissive hand. "You may take my relief as read, child. Do you suppose I have not been anxious?" Arrived at the bedside, she pointed to one of the straight chairs by the wall. "Francis, bring that over. Since you have allowed me a limited time, let me not waste it."

"Just don't tire her out, ma'am, that is all I ask." Francis set down the chair and Sybilla sat, magnificently ignoring this admonition.

"Just what did happen, Ottilia?"

Repeating her tale, Ottilia found she was able to think more fully, details coming to light that she had not before recalled. "I heard someone speak, but not clearly. It must have been just as I hit the water. I was too shocked at the time, I believe, to take it in."

"What was said?"

Ottilia took another sip from her cup before responding. "Something *you*? No, I can't be sure I heard any specific word."

Sybilla tapped a hand on her knee for a moment. "Did you see anyone?"

Francis had plonked down at the end of the bed and took this. "How would she, ma'am? She was underwater in an instant. She could not have had time to see anyone."

Ottilia set her cup down in the saucer. "I might have done when I surfaced, but I cannot remember. I coughed up water, I know. In any event, I think I had already drifted beyond the jetty. I was concentrating on staying afloat. I knew not to struggle, for that would have taken me down. I cannot recall seeing anything very much, except the sky and the trees."

Her mother-in-law seemed intent upon pursuing the search for a perpetrator. "What of this voice? Was it a man or a woman, do you think?"

Ottilia tried to hear again the sounds she was only half convinced were a voice. "I could not say."

"Surely a man." Francis was frowning. "Would a woman have the strength to do it? Pull you in, I mean. How many women can swim, indeed?"

"Ha!" Sybilla struck her hands together. "That is a fair point, Francis. Man or woman, this person must be capable of swimming." She gave a little shudder. "Horrible to think this evil person must have been hiding under the jetty, waiting his moment."

"Not only that." Ottilia sipped the last of her coffee and put the cup and saucer down on the bedside table. Then she looked from her mother-in-law to her spouse.

"Well, Tillie, what?"

"He, let us say for the sake of simplicity, must have been lurking in these parts for some time."

Sybilla gave a gasp. "Watching you, do you mean?"

"Just so."

"What a perfectly unsettling notion."

"Yes, I find it so too."

Francis became brisk. "Have you had any idea of anyone watching you before? Did you notice anything untoward?"

Sybilla tutted. "With all the fuss and pother of the wedding? Of course she cannot have noticed anything."

Something leapt in Ottilia's mind. "But I did!"

"When, Tillie? Where?"

"Here?"

"In Newport Pagnell. Remember, Fan? We went there to purchase a gift for Pretty to give to Lizzy."

"Because we forgot to provide for it. Yes, I remember."

"While you were convincing Pretty that the haberdasher's doll model to show off her materials was not for sale and I was looking at the silk bags and muffs…"

Sybilla became impatient. "Yes? What happened?"

Ottilia sighed. "Nothing very significant. Not at the time. I had that sensation of being under observation. You must have experienced it, Sybilla."

"I cannot say that I have."

"Well, I made nothing of it then. After all, I have on occasion been pointed out as *that Lady Fan*. But here? Who would know me in that capacity?"

"Yes, but what exactly happened, Tillie?"

"I felt eyes upon me, as I say, and when I turned to look I just caught a glimpse of a person leaving the shop."

"A man?"

"I cannot be sure. He, or indeed she perhaps, was cloaked. I have an impression of green, but that is all."

There was silence for a moment. Then Sybilla gave herself a little shake. "Too eerie, my child. Depend upon it, that was mere coincidence."

Ottilia drew a breath. "I am not so sure. Meggotty mentioned something about a gang operating out of Newport Pagnell."

Francis had been leaning against the slim gilt and white bedpost, but he sat up straight. "What sort of gang?"

"Thieves, it would seem, although I understood her to say there were rumours of a killing." She struck her hands together. "Why did I not think of it before you let that captain go, Fan? You might have asked him."

"I can still do so. In fact, I shall ask Gil to send to him."

"You go too fast, the two of you. What should a gang of robbers have to do with Ottilia? It is not as if she has an enemy among such."

Ottilia emitted a mirthless laugh. "I may well have such enemies."

"Poppycock! Who could possibly have a grudge against you, my dear?"

Francis took this, rather to Ottilia's relief. At least he understood. "Think, Mama. How many individuals has she sent to the gallows?"

"Or whose reputations I have ruined." Ottilia sighed. "I fear there may be a number of persons who might well harbour a desire for revenge."

Sybilla remained sceptical. "Such as?"

"Such as relatives, for one. I have not as yet had an opportunity to sift possibilities, but offhand I can think of two cases where a wife has been left without a breadwinner. Who is to say what family might deem themselves disgraced by what they perceive as my machinations?"

"It is preposterous, Ottilia. You pursued justice."

"Where possible, yes. In some instances, justice was never served since I could not bring the crime home to the perpetrator."

Francis was up, beginning to stride about the room. "This becomes serious. I will have that fellow immediately begin upon a hunt."

"The captain of militia? Oh, no, Fan."

"I must, Tillie. If this person discovers he did not succeed, he will try again as sure as check."

Ottilia sat up, ignoring a wave of dizziness that at once afflicted her. "He will never believe it, Fan. You do, I thank heaven, because you know what we have been through."

Francis halted in his perambulations. "Not only that. I admit I was incredulous at first, but I know you, Tillie, and your ability to notice things."

"But this captain does not know me, my dearest. He will suppose me to be a hysterical female whose mind has been addled by my experience."

To her surprise, Sybilla backed her up. "She is perfectly right, Francis. Unless this fellow had seen Ottilia in action, he would pooh-pooh the whole affair."

"Just as a number of officials have done in the past, Fan. We must solve this ourselves."

"And in the meantime expose you to this lunatic's villainous schemes? I won't do it. You need protection."

"You are all the protection I need." Ottilia held out a hand to him. "You have championed me from the outset and ever been my shield, my darling lord."

He came across and took the hand, settling onto the bed beside her. "That is all very well and flattering, my loved one, but I will not be satisfied until I know the militia is at least alerted. Besides, we need to know if there is any connection with this gang you mentioned."

"That, by all means. But if he takes my story of being forcibly dragged into the river as other than feminine ravings, I shall count myself astonished."

By the time Ottilia had sustained visits from her sister-in-law, her excited adopted daughter and her little son, she was altogether fatigued. Harriet, who rustled into the room with her figured muslin petticoats swishing about her, was volubly horrified.

"To think such a dreadful thing could happen in our grounds! It is quite shocking, Ottilia. I have told Gil he must post men to guard the entrances to the house. There is no saying what might happen if some fellow is indeed bent upon attacking you."

Ottilia tried to soothe. "I doubt he, if it is a man, would be so bold as to attempt anything in the house, Harriet."

"I wish I might share your opinion, but a fellow who could lurk in secret in broad daylight —

"In the river, Harriet," Francis pointed out. "He could scarcely have remained unnoticed had he been wandering around on land."

"You may say so, Fan, but there might be any number of strangers walking about, for all we know."

Harriet's spouse, entering the bedchamber in time to hear this, raised an objection. "We don't keep servants who cannot use their eyes and ears, my love. But you need be under no apprehension. I have put the word about that everyone must be upon their guard." With the smile so reminiscent of his daughter Lizzy, Gil turned to Ottilia. "Forgive the informality of us foregathering in your chamber, my dear Ottilia. I came to find Fan, but let me say that if there anything you need, you have only to ask."

At that, Harriet, reminded of her duties as hostess, immediately reiterated his words. "Yes, indeed, my dear. Everything is at your service. It grieves me that such a thing should happen while you are with us. Pray don't hesitate to make known your needs." She turned to Gil, continuing without pause, "Did you send to that militia captain? I declare, it is too bad he did not think to inform you of these robbers operating in the vicinity."

Gil held up a hand. "Give me leave, my love. I was just about to tell Fan that I have heard from Captain Dalby. He will present himself upon the morrow."

"I trust you did not tell him of my having been tugged into the river," Ottilia cut in.

"I only said there was some question about your accident and suggested he might be able to assist."

"Thank heaven. I cannot but suppose he will dismiss the notion out of hand."

Harriet entered a caveat. "But you will tell him surely, Ottilia? How is he to keep you safe if he does not know?"

"I do not need him to keep me safe, I thank you. I have Fan, who is more than capable of ensuring my safety."

"How can you say so? After yesterday's fiasco?"

"Harriet! Be silent!"

Ottilia, glancing at her husband's tight-lipped countenance, was glad of Gil's intervention.

Harriet's colour rose, but she spoke up again nevertheless. "Well, I am sorry, Fan, but it is true. Although you could not have prevented Ottilia from falling in, of course."

The conciliatory tone proved too much for Francis. "I thank you, Harriet, I am well aware of that. However, I have no intention of allowing my wife to go off investigating without me, so you need not —"

"Investigating?" Harriet interjected. "Good heavens, Ottilia, you cannot mean to begin one of these hunts of yours. Not when you are in danger yourself."

Gil, who was of a slighter build than his wife but had nevertheless the mastery of her, emitted an exasperated sound. "I do wish you will be quiet, Harriet! Ottilia is the best judge of what she may do, and you may rely on your brother to ensure she does not run her head into danger."

Ottilia might have refuted this, aware of too many occasions when she had been foolish enough to run risks that had sent her husband up into the boughs, but she held her tongue.

Harriet was only brought to desist when Francis assured her at last that he would enlist Captain Dalby's assistance, should there prove to be anything he could better manage. "If we need his authority, I shan't hesitate. What we want for this present is to find out from him what he may know of these robbers."

"But why, Fan? What have they to do with Ottilia?"

Gil added his mite at this point. "Yes, I should like to know that too, Fan."

Francis exchanged a glance with Ottilia, but she gave a brief nod to indicate he might answer on her behalf.

"We may be able to fathom whether there is any connection with past incidents."

A frown creased Gil's forehead. "You mean to imply that the perpetrator is after revenge?"

"Just so, Gil," Ottilia said. "But who it may be is a mystery at this present."

As Harriet showed signs of wishing to discover whom she might have in mind, Ottilia was relieved when her host made it his business to remove his wife, saying she had no doubt overstayed her time.

"Do you forget that Fan imposed a limit? Ottilia needs her rest. Besides, I have it from your steward, Ottilia, that the nurses wish to bring in your children."

At this point, Ottilia bethought her of something she did need, and perhaps it would give her sister-in-law's thoughts a different direction. "There is one thing you could do for me, Harriet."

"My dear Ottilia, you have only to name it."

"I am anxious to repay Meggotty's kindness. Fan has proffered money, I believe?" She turned an enquiring gaze on her husband.

"I slipped the forester several notes, Tillie, don't fret."

"Yes, but perhaps we may do better than that. Harriet, could you arrange for a basket of provisions, do you think?"

"An excellent notion! I shall see my housekeeper at once. I am sure Cook will have a plethora of tarts and jellies that —□

"I was thinking more of a ham and some cheeses, my dear, if you can spare them. Food that will be of use for several days. A jug of ale, perhaps, and a fresh loaf or two with butter. Or a large pie. Include tarts if you wish, but —□

"Have no fear, Ottilia. I know just how to do."

Harriet flitted off, full of new intention and clearly pleased to be able to make herself useful. Ottilia could only hope she would not load the basket with frivolous items. Gil followed in short order and she was granted a period of rest, Francis refusing to allow the children in until Ottilia had a chance to recover from the annoyance of his sister's visit. She took the opportunity to send for her maid and consume a light snack together with a fresh cup of coffee before the onslaught.

In the event, after the briefest of acknowledgements from her little son, Luke chose to potter about the bedchamber in a spirit of exploration. Pretty, who at six years of age was looking quite grown-up, was wont to play the elder sister. She was clad in a muslin dress not dissimilar to those worn by the adults, though adorned with a sash, but she had evidently removed her pins and left off her cap, her blonde locks curling onto her shoulders and down her back. She looked as pretty as her name and far too much so, in Ottilia's eyes, for the mischievous spirit she had proved to be.

She spared but a few words for her adoptive mother, instead choosing to instruct the toddler in the accoutrements of the room, lifting him so that he might see himself in the standing glass and plonking him on the dressing stool, where she proceeded to seize Ottilia's hairbrush, take off Luke's cap and stroke at the soft dark down on the child's head.

Ottilia had to laugh, remarking to Dorote Gabon — the erstwhile slave girl now employed to care for Luke, but who had on this occasion accompanied both children — that neither child appeared to be a penny the worse for missing their mother. The Barbadian nurse, her strange blue eyes growing luminous, set a hand on the bed. "They forget readily, milady, but the rest of us do not."

Ottilia drew a breath. "Was his lordship severely disturbed?"

"Can you doubt it, milady? Milady Polbrook had to comfort him, so Diplock told us."

Ottilia's heart squeezed in her bosom. "I wish I might have spared him." Recalling what Doro had said, she added with a smile, "All of you too. I could not wish anyone to be distressed on my account."

Doro's smile was wide. "How will you help it, milady? You are beloved, you must know it."

"Oh, stop, Doro! You will have me in floods."

"But it is true. Only I was permitted to witness it, but Hemp was…" She faded out, an odd look in her eye, and then resumed with more energy. "I have rarely seen him thus. He values you greatly, milady. I believe he was almost as distraught as milord."

Ottilia knew not how to answer, aware of an undercurrent in Doro's voice she could not identify. Or perhaps she preferred not to do so. She considered Hemp her trusted friend and she knew the fondness was mutual. But on neither side was it an affection to threaten Doro's place in Hemp's heart.

Before she could think of a way to phrase her thought without delving into deep waters, her attention was claimed by the children as her son chose this moment to climb onto the bed, assisted with voluble instruction from his adoptive sister. "Careful, Lukey! Up you go. Now, don't go jumping on Mama, you hear?"

Once satisfied that Luke was secure, Pretty herself proved quite as fatiguing a visitor as Harriet, pelting Ottilia with questions and comments. "Did you get all wet? Was it cold? Doro says you nearly drownded. Did you see a crocodile? You swam with the fishes! I wish I might swim with the fishes."

Ottilia's responses were punctuated with cries of delight from her little son, who made free with his situation on the bed and took the opportunity to bounce and roll, the baby gown he still wore twisting around him.

"Careful, Master Luke! Don't fall on Mama. Shall I take him off, milady?"

This last as Luke threw himself bodily onto Ottilia's stomach. "No, I have him, Doro."

She reached for the child, but he eluded her, scrambling off and away. In a moment, he had dropped off the bed and begun chasing about the room. Pretty promptly followed suit, threatening dire consequences when she caught him, and a cacophony of high-pitched laughter and shrieking ensued until Francis arrived on the scene.

Order was restored in a very few moments and the children were bidden to kiss their mother farewell before being despatched about their business.

"Take that boy outside, Doro, for pity's sake, and let him run off his excess energy. As for you, Miss Pertesia Fanshawe, shouldn't you be practising your letters? If you want a story tonight, you'd best have something to show me first."

"Papa, I'm on holiday! You said so."

"Until the wedding was over, I said. Back you go to Hepsie. One hour of lessons, and not a minute less. You can tell her I said so. Doro, see that Hepsie knows, will you?"

The children left at last, Pretty under protest, and Ottilia was able to let out the laugh she had been holding in. "She will outfox you somehow, Fan, and you know it."

He grinned. "Little monkey. We ought to think about a governess. She is growing beyond poor Hepsie's ability to teach her."

"Well, I may take over that duty, Fan. There is no need for a governess yet."

"I won't have her rely upon you, my dear one. Especially after this episode. Your health is far too precious."

Ottilia sighed. With the best will in the world, she knew she was not strong. The miscarriage of several years back had damaged her constitution. She had discussed the matter with her doctor brother, and Patrick had been less than sanguine.

"It happens sometimes, my dear sister. You may never be as robust as you were. Take heart, however. You are still a good deal healthier than my unfortunate Sophie. A little care, eat well and keep exercised with walks that are not too strenuous."

She had abided by his dictum as best she could, particularly during her pregnancy with Luke. She knew, however, that her misadventure in the Ouse was likely to have debilitated her more than it might another.

"I am glad to be alive, however, Fan, so I must not complain."

"Yes, but you must rest. You know what Patrick said."

"I will be good, Fan. But I am not so badly off that I cannot undertake Pretty's education. Indeed, it would suit me to do so. I need a project of some kind."

"I should have thought you'd had projects aplenty," said Francis, his tone a trifle disgruntled. "As if we have not now enough on our hands with this vicious individual wishing you harm."

"That may be true, but I might not have fallen victim so easily had I not been musing about my current state of discontent."

Francis had been standing in a casual pose in the middle of the room, but at this he straightened, casting her a narrowed glance. "Discontent?"

Ottilia inwardly cursed. That was careless. She hastened to disclaim. "I don't mean that, quite."

"Then what did you mean?"

His voice had dropped a notch, and there was that in his face which caused Ottilia's heart to miss a beat.

"Fan, pray don't take a pet! It is only that it seems a long time since we had one of these problems to solve."

"A long time, yes. A time which I supposed had been as welcome a respite to you as it has been to me. It seems I was mistaken."

"Fan!"

His shoulders shifted in a way Ottilia recognised was wont to indicate discomfort. The conviction seized her that she had inadvertently hurt him, and deeply. She held out a pleading hand. "Fan, no! Pray don't think I have not appreciated the calm, for it is not so. If I have become a trifle restless, it is only for want of occupation."

He was ignoring the hand, the dark gaze fixed upon her in a look she found unfathomable, but dismaying in the extreme. "You had occupation. A new baby to nurture, a daughter to learn to love, a household to run. A husband to care for, if that is of any importance to you."

A flare of anger superseded the dismay. "That is unfair! You know you mean the world to me!"

"I thought so, yes."

"Fan, this is mad! But a matter of hours since, we were desperate to be reunited. Don't do this, I beg of you." Again, she held out a hand to him. "Come, my dearest darling."

A defeated look came into his face and he moved slowly to the bed and took the hand. But his hold was slack. If Ottilia had not grasped his strongly, she thought it would have slipped out of her clasp.

"I don't know why I should be surprised," he said in a voice that seemed dead to her ears. "You never will be satisfied with mere domesticity."

Ottilia dragged at his hand, all but forcing him to sit, which he did, perching on the side of the bed. She brought his hand to her mouth and pressed her lips upon it. "I am perfectly happy with my life, Fan. I never meant to belittle what I have."

"But you can't help it, can you?" He let out a sigh and gave a somewhat crooked smile. "Well, you have your wish. We have another mystery, one we must solve."

"I hurt you, my dearest. I am sorry."

He shifted his shoulders, as if he had not the will to shrug fully. "It matters not, my dear one. I still love you."

But it did matter to him. Knowing it, but powerless to retract the words she had so foolishly uttered, Ottilia sought instead for a normality that felt alien now.

"Well, I suppose we must resign ourselves to remaining at Dalesford until we have resolved this business."

"Indeed. We may begin with this captain, at least. When you are well, we can try further afield."

There was effort in his voice and Ottilia's heart cracked. There seemed to be nothing she could say to mitigate the blow.

Better, perhaps, to let it lie for a while. She could only hope the exigencies of working to find out who was responsible for her drop into the Great Ouse might soften the discomfort that had sprung up between them.

CHAPTER SIX

Francis would not have believed, four and twenty hours earlier, that he could harbour resentment against his wife, but he was conscious of a struggle within. His relief was tempered now, and it troubled him greatly. It was not as if he did not know what Tillie was. While he had chafed upon almost every occasion that one of these 'adventures' arose, he could not but be aware of his darling wife's very different attitude. She revelled in them, as much delighted as excited, he believed. Was it the chance to exercise her intellect? However much he might wish to do so, he could not match her in wit, nor in that extraordinary ability to fathom the minds of those she questioned.

He admired her for it, yes he did. Yet the intimation that the life he provided could not satisfy her was anathema. Why it should wound him he could not fully understand. Had not his mother admonished him several times for being disgruntled when Tillie wholeheartedly embraced these events? To him they were a disturbance. To Tillie they were a boon. He understood it, just as he appreciated her talents.

But she was his wife, his helpmeet — or was supposed to be. The role sat uneasily on her shoulders. Plainly, it was not enough. That knowledge hurt, despite all the sensible arguments he had given himself since.

Tillie knew it too. Last night, notwithstanding her condition, she had been particularly loving. Francis grieved that he had found it hard to respond to her overtures. The difficulty was, they were so attuned that he knew Tillie had noticed his reserve, despite his best efforts to conceal it. Besides, when had he ever managed to fool his darling wife? She was too acute. The guilt he saw in that gnawing conscience of hers grieved him almost as much as his own. He felt as if they were papering over an irreparable crack, their very communion, both in words and actions, tentative and dripping with guile. An act, trying to recapture what was natural and real to them both, and failing. There was no other route open to Francis at this moment. The danger to Tillie was pressing, leaving no time to indulge in mending broken fences.

His wife had insisted upon rising from her bed and dressing. Francis's objections were but half-hearted. Tillie would do as she pleased whatever he said. He compromised.

"Very well, but you must promise to rest the moment you feel your strength failing."

"Of course, my dearest. It is only that I do wish to be present when you interview this captain, if you don't object, and I can hardly receive him in our bedchamber."

If he did not object? Lord help him, but she was trying too hard! He delayed his response by concentrating on tying his neck-cloth. When it was done, he nodded to his valet, waiting to help him on with his coat.

"It will probably be best if you are present," he conceded as he thrust his arms into the sleeves, despising himself for the banality of his words, "since you know what this Meggotty let fall."

"Thank you, Fan."

Heart sinking, he glanced to where his wife was sitting on the dressing stool while Joanie did up her hair. Since when did she thank him for giving permission? Since when, if it came to that, did she ask for permission from him? That was not how they were apt to communicate. How in the world were they to get over this? Dismayed to discover in himself a wish to leave her presence, he spoke before he could prevent himself. "I'll go down, as I am ready. Unless you wish me to give you my arm?"

At that, she turned her head and he received a reproachful look. "Yes, if you please, Fan. I am not yet steady enough on my own."

Guilt rode him all over again. "Then I'll wait."

Unable to bear the silence that ensued, he went to the window and gazed out, only for his eyes to meet the far and fatal curve of the river. At a distance, but too reminding to be borne. He set his teeth, looking instead at the nearer prospect that obtained to that side of the Hall towards the back of the mansion: gardens, the woods beyond and the top of his brother-in-law's extensive glasshouse.

"Thank you, Joanie, that will do. No, not the shawl. I am perfectly warm now and the day looks to be fine."

She was done at last. Francis turned and crossed to where his wife stood, shaking out the sprigged petticoats of her high-waisted muslin gown with short sleeves scalloped at the edges. She looked up and gave him a smile. Tentative again. "I am quite ready, Fan."

He nodded and offered his arm. She slipped her hand within it and he led her to the door. As they walked through the long corridor leading towards the stairs, he noted that Tillie leaned on his strength but slightly. However, when it came to negotiating the staircase, she hesitated, gripping the banister and holding tightly on to his arm.

"Don't fret," he said in a more normal tone than he had used recently. "I have you safe." He released his arm from her clutch and put it instead about her, holding her steady.

"That is much better, thank you."

A faint husk in her voice cut him to the heart and he tightened his hold. On instinct, he leaned to whisper in her ear. "We will weather this, sweetheart. We must."

She turned her head and the clear gaze he loved scanned his face, blinking away wetness. "Yes, we must. Somehow."

She said no more but turned her eyes upon the stairway and began the descent. Francis contented himself with the odd murmur to take care, feeling a degree less oppressed.

In the cosy breakfast parlour — a small apartment adjacent to the more formal dining-room, which was entered via the hall by a door opposite to the main downstairs saloon — Sybilla was already at the large, round table, together with her companion and Francis's sister, who at once exclaimed, "Ottilia! Gracious, is this prudent? Should you not be in your bed?"

Francis was spared having to answer by his mother's immediate intervention.

"Don't be such a ninny, Harriet! She will not recruit her strength if she lays about for days. She must give her limbs exercise."

"I am persuaded it is too soon, Mama. She has been through a terrible mishap."

"I don't deny it. But I hold that coddling oneself is never the best remedy."

While they continued to argue, Francis was able to guide his wife to a vacant chair. The round table, an arrangement which made for ease of communication among all present, was already set with platters of bread, baskets of rolls, dishes of creamy butter and pots of honey and jam. Ottilia was served with promptness by the butler, who supplied her with a platter and enquired her preference of several dishes of which she might partake. Francis was able to leave her, serving himself from the collection of silver dishes set upon the large sideboard. He chose a generous portion of bacon and scrambled eggs, together with several slices of cold roast beef before taking his seat next to his wife and looking around for the mustard pot.

"Your appetite is in no way impaired by recent events, I am glad to see, my son."

He was spared having to answer his mother's remark by Tillie choosing to take it up. "Fan is always a good trencherman. He swears by breakfast, do you not, my dearest lord?"

An attempt to introduce jocularity? Then he had best second her efforts. "Indeed. I am forever having to force-feed this woman to set herself up for the day."

Tillie gave him one of her warm smiles and he rejoiced. "Not today, Fan. I protest I am starving."

"Hardly a surprise," commented Sybilla. "You cannot have had enough to satisfy a bird these two days."

"She eats like a bird always, pecking at her food."

"Except when I was pregnant with Luke, if you recall, Fan."

He had to laugh. "True. You consumed the most disgusting combinations and stuffed yourself with roasted cheese and bacon."

Her laugh was far more natural than heretofore and he began to entertain a hope of overcoming this uncomfortable passage. He was not obliged to keep up the effort at normality for his sister, who was pouring tea into her cup from a silver teapot, chimed in at once.

"Gracious, Ottilia, did you have an appetite indeed? I was never a good eater during my pregnancies. I cast my doctor into despair. Except with Gregory. Do you recall, Mama, how I could not stop eating?"

"I recall it with horror, my child. You say Ottilia chose strange foods, Francis. Your sister descended to chewing coal!"

This remark caused a general laugh, Harriet joining in merrily. "Oh, I did, much to Gil's dismay. He found me with black all over my teeth and lips and almost perished from the shock."

Sybilla's tall companion, Henrietta Skelmersdale, silent up to now as she partook of a slice of bread well larded with butter and jam, put her oar in. "I believe, however, that coal is efficacious for one's health." She was sitting opposite Tillie and glanced across, ignoring a snort from her employer beside her. "Perhaps you know, Lady Francis? Your brother doctor might have some knowledge of why this is so."

"I do recall Patrick mentioning that it can be an aid to digestion, which is very much a factor in pregnancy. There now, Harriet. You were only supplying your body with what it needed."

A trifle of the old mischief sounded in her voice and Francis was struck with a riffle of poignancy. There was the woman he loved. Why could he not appreciate what he had without reserve?

Harriet was laughing. "Not according to Gil, I assure you. He swears my strange eating habits while I carried him have passed on to Gregory. He is the most dreadful boy and tries to force his unfortunate siblings to eat insects. Poor little Anne became quite sick once. It was the one time Gil nearly thrashed him."

This prompted another argument between mother and daughter over the efficacy of beating the young, which permitted Francis to slide out of the discussion and check upon his wife, who looked to be toying with the egg on her plate.

"Are you struggling, Tillie? I thought you said you were hungry."

She smiled. "I fear my weakness has overtaken my appetite. Would you pass me one of those rolls instead, Fan?" Then, as he moved to comply, automatically hunting the table for the coffee pot, cream jug and sugar bowl, Tillie raised her voice a little, cutting into the ongoing bickering between his mother and sister. "Give me leave a moment, Harriet, if you will!"

Harriet broke off mid-sentence and looked across, a note of consciousness in her voice. "Of course, my dear Ottilia, what is it?"

"Pardon me for interrupting, but I am anxious to know if you succeeded in sending a basket to my kind rescuers."

"Gracious, did you think I had forgot?"

Tillie produced a deprecating smile. "No, indeed. Pardon my badgering you upon this subject, but I could not reconcile it with my conscience to be backward in any attention to that family. Samuel saved my life, and I am very sure Meggotty preserved it with her care of me."

Harriet waved her hands in the excitable way she had. "Gracious, yes! We must all be eternally grateful to them, but you need not fret, Ottilia. My housekeeper is making up a basket this very morning, and we will send it immediately."

"Oh, that is excellent, thank you, my dear. I hope your people may know where is their cottage."

Francis, in the process of buttering a roll, intervened. "Send it by our steward, Hemp. He knows exactly how to find the place."

This programme being universally approved, he was able to give his attention to locating the honeypot. As he added a measure of honey to the roll in line with his wife's taste as he knew it, he was vaguely aware that Miss Skelmersdale addressed Tillie.

"You look to be rather pale still, Lady Fan. I wonder you are able to manage food at all after what you have been through."

"I am fatigued still. I will rest again later."

The talk faded from his consciousness as he set the prepared roll on a plate before his wife and proceeded to upend a cup, pouring black liquid from the coffee pot. While he served his wife thus, he reflected that these simple acts were the business of his life. How was it he could be content to spend his days in domestic felicity where Tillie craved action similar to that he had experienced in his soldiering days? He had always supposed their tastes to be wholly similar, but he was mistaken. He reached for the cream jug and sugar bowl, hardly aware of what he did. That they had dissimilar notions had not before been of significance. Or perhaps he had merely ignored the difference, deeming it engendered by the interference into their lives of murderous persons. The smart was still with him, it seemed.

Lost in thought, he was recalled by his mother's voice. "Francis! Francis, I say! Are you deaf, boy?"

He shook himself out of his abstraction, setting the prepared cup in its saucer where Tillie could reach it, but he could not keep the irritation from his voice. "What the deuce is it, ma'am?"

"I am asking if you are expecting that captain this morning?"

Tillie cut in. "We are, Sybilla. Which, Harriet," she added with a smile to her hostess, "is truly why I have dressed. I want to hear what he has to say of this gang of robbers."

"A gang?" Miss Henrietta Skelmersdale's eyes danced. "I scent a mystery. How exciting! Do tell, Lady Fan!"

Sybilla turned snapping black eyes on her companion. "There is nothing exciting about this business, my girl. Do you not realise my daughter-in-law's life is in danger?"

Abashed, Henrietta begged pardon. "But you must admit, Lady Polbrook, there is a mystery afoot."

"I have had quite enough of mysteries, I thank you, Henrietta. Francis, when does this captain arrive?"

He glanced at the case clock on the mantel. "He will be here at any moment, I should think. Where is Gil, Harriet?"

"He has gone on an inspection of the estate. His agent called this morning, saying it could not be put off any longer."

"We have kept him from it, then."

"Not at all, Ottilia. It is just that everything has been delayed by the wedding preparations. He said he will be at your service should you need his help, however."

On the whole, Ottilia was glad that her host was from home when Captain Dalby made his appearance. A fourth in the discussion could only make things more complicated. As the captain began by asking after her health, she felt obliged to reciprocate with thanks for his part in her rescue. He bowed, but disclaimed.

"I cannot be said to have done very much, ma'am. If the forester had not accosted one of my men, I imagine we would be still upon a fruitless hunt."

Ottilia gave him a smile, feeling that any conciliatory words on her part could not go amiss. "I must be glad then that you were not put to such trouble, Captain."

"No trouble. Glad to have been of service."

Francis broke in to take this up. "We are hoping you may be able to be of service again, sir."

Captain Dalby raised sandy brows, regarding Francis with a measure of interest out of very blue eyes. "Indeed, my lord?"

Ottilia all but held her breath. How would her spouse approach this? She longed to take the lead, but her consciousness of the delicate state of their relationship kept her silent. He cast her a glance from where he stood at the mantel, as was his wont, and then returned his gaze to the captain, who was standing at a little distance between the two sofas. He was of middling height but muscled, as evidenced by his well-fitting white breeches and scarlet coat, the latter braided in gold. Since he was facing the window, Ottilia, seated in a chair across from him, was able to see his face clearly, a definite advantage. It was a fine face, etched with faint lines that signalled his age. She judged him to be a few years senior to Francis.

The meeting was taking place in a spacious saloon on the ground floor. It was liberally supplied with chairs and sofas, the heavy wood now considered somewhat old-fashioned but comfortable enough. Several windows gave brightness to the place and picked out the landscapes on the walls. Ottilia's preference for such discussions would be a smaller room, since a cosier environment usually made for a better atmosphere for questioning. But all the main rooms of the ground and first floor at Dalesford Hall were large, one leading into the next in the fashion of Palladio.

She hoped the disadvantage of being too great a distance apart would not manifest in this instance as Francis laid out the reason for requesting the captain's presence.

"While my wife was at the cottage, she heard of a gang operating out of Newport Pagnell."

Watching the captain, Ottilia noted the immediate question in his face even before he spoke. "In what way, sir, does this bear upon your wife's misadventure?"

Hope rose in Ottilia's breast. An intelligent fellow, then, this militiaman. She met the query in her husband's eye and gave a slight nod. He looked back at the captain.

"I had not intended to raise this with you at the outset, but perhaps it is as well to be open."

Captain Dalby lifted his chin. "I should be glad of it, my lord. I prefer plain dealing."

A wry look passed over Francis's face. "We were not precisely proposing subterfuge. The matter is, however, susceptible of being disbelieved."

A nod came. "Try me, sir."

Francis gestured towards Ottilia. "Perhaps you should hear it from my wife."

Ottilia met the captain's cool gaze and opted for frankness. "I did not fall by accident, Captain."

"No?"

It was non-committal, but at least he was willing to listen. She drew a breath. "My ankle was seized. I was tugged into the water. I might have saved myself had I not been bending to watch out for fish."

She left it there and, watching to note his reaction, found herself under a steady regard from the bright eyes which gave nothing away. Unable to help herself, she threw a glance at Francis, who gave a slight shrug as his lip quirked. Ottilia was grateful that he did not speak and she likewise waited, meeting the captain's eye.

At last he snuffed in breath through his nose and pursed his lips. "Am I to understand that you suspect a person or persons of being intent upon revenge?"

Startled, Ottilia threw yet another look at Francis and found him similarly surprised, brows flying. He took it up before she could think what to say.

"You know of my wife's exploits?"

The somewhat grim set of the captain's features relaxed into something akin to a grin. "I am acquainted with Lieutenant Colonel Tretower."

"My friend George? Lord above! He's told you of her?"

"We met a few months back when I was seconded to his battalion. His second in command was indisposed, and I served in his place for a while. I cannot now recall how the matter arose in discussion, but the colonel spoke warmly of Lady Fan and her successes."

Ottilia let out a laughing breath. "My dear sir, you have relieved my mind of a weight. I had every expectation you would pooh-pooh the notion that I had been attacked."

He laughed and his whole countenance underwent a change, the pose of efficient officer vanishing for a space. "So I might have done, had the victim been any other lady. When Lord Dalesford enlisted my aid in finding Lady Francis Fanshawe, however, I was only too happy to put my men at his disposal."

Francis was shifting away from the mantel. "Then sit down, man, and let us be comfortable. We have much to discuss. Take that chair, sir, and bring it across and I will do likewise."

When both men were seated within easy talking distance of Ottilia's chair, Francis again brought up the subject of the gang. The captain frowned.

"Why do you wish to know, my lord? Have you reason to suppose there may be a connection?"

"None whatsoever, but we must start somewhere."

Ottilia could not let this pass. "Pardon me, Fan, but you are forgetting that strange experience I had in the haberdasher's."

He frowned. "I thought you said it had not been certain."

"True, but there is the Newport Pagnell connection, don't forget. We were shopping there that day."

Francis looked to the captain. "They are based in Newport Pagnell, this gang?"

Captain Dalby spread his hands. "We are uncertain, but it seems likely. The robberies have, for the most part, taken place in the vicinity of the town."

"Has there been a killing? Meggotty told me it is so rumoured."

The captain became grim again. "A man was stabbed in his own home. We assume he caught these fellows in the act and put up a resistance."

Ottilia's hunting instinct became roused. "Was anyone a witness? Did anyone else in the house hear or see anything?"

Surprise crept into the militiaman's face. "You ask pertinent questions, ma'am."

A wry look from her husband was cast at Ottilia. "That is her forte." And to the captain, "Well? Was there anything?"

He grimaced. "Nothing, unfortunately. The servants were abed in the attics, and the victim had no wife or child. He was a merchant and lived alone. A brother has arrived from elsewhere to take care of the business."

It behoved Ottilia to probe further. "What of the other robberies? Were they all carried out at night? Did no one catch even a glimpse of the perpetrators?"

A gleam appeared in the captain's eye. "Ah, now there we have a faint ray of hope. A servant girl swears she saw a man climbing out of a window. A stocky, thick-limbed fellow, as she described him. It was not full dark, the moon being out, but she spoke of his having a shadowed face, such that she could not make out his features."

"Wearing a hat, perhaps?"

"That is just it, my lord. He had on no headgear." He emitted a cough. "It had not occurred to me before, but when we rode to the cottage, you were accompanied by a black fellow."

"My wife's Barbadian steward, yes. What of it?"

Ottilia's mind leapt. "You think the robber the girl saw may have been black?"

The captain's gaze came back to hers. "It is possible. If so, it would make it a deal easier to spot him. We do not have many foreign individuals of that stamp in this area."

The inference hit Ottilia swiftly. She turned to her spouse just as he spoke, his eyes on her face. "Captain Indigo?"

A spontaneous smile leapt to her lips. "You took the words from my mouth, Fan!"

He laughed. "I hoped I was ahead of you for once."

"Neck and neck, my dearest."

An interrogative sound came from the captain. "May I share in this revelation?"

Ottilia sighed. "It is hardly a revelation. Captain Indigo is a black individual we encountered in Bristol. A sometime pirate from the Caribbean. But if it is he, I cannot imagine he would seek my death. He has no reason to loathe me."

Francis took this up. "Perhaps not, for you were not responsible for sending the authorities after him. Besides, it seems unlikely he would take to robbing houses. That was not his style."

"Nor would he do it himself, unless he was obliged." Ottilia was thinking hard. "He would rather send his bully boys to do the actual robbery."

"Yet you both thought of the fellow upon the instant," the captain broke in.

"Because we are obliged to think about persons who may have been involved in these murders my wife has solved."

"Indigo was not involved, though, was he?"

"Not directly in the killings, as it chanced." Francis turned to the captain. "For my part I would not discount him altogether. He was obliged to flee the city. If he has been evading the law officers, he may not have his associates with him."

Ottilia's mind was roving over the affair at Bristol, when her steward Hemp Roy had sought her help to free the imprisoned slave girl, Dorote Gabon, accused of a murder she did not commit. There were one or two individuals who might have cause to take revenge, but Ottilia did not feel the pirate captain was one of them. Nor was he a man to be operating solo. Her husband's last words caught her attention.

"Perhaps not the associates he had in Bristol, but Captain Dalby speaks of a gang, Fan. He cannot be working alone, if it is indeed Captain Indigo."

The militia captain clinched the matter. "Nothing is certain. But at least it offers a new line of enquiry." He looked to Ottilia again. "Is there any other you might have reason to suspect? Setting aside any connection to the robbers."

"Too many," said Francis, his tone bitter to Ottilia's ears, reviving her troubled conscience. She hastened to intervene.

"To tell you the truth, we have not yet had an opportunity to look at all possibilities. I am better, but by no means back to full strength."

"Nor has there been time since we discovered her whereabouts and brought her home." Francis spoke with finality. "It is a discussion upon which we must embark, but it seemed good to find out more about the rumoured gang at the outset."

The captain looked from one to the other. "What do you need of me? I can hardly suppose the perpetrator is around to be apprehended by this time."

"Not to be apprehended," said Francis. "But I dare not hope that he will not try again once he discovers his failure."

"Good God, sir, do you think so indeed? You don't feel it was a chance taken at a venture?"

Ottilia cut in before her spouse could answer. "Captain Dalby, the man was under the jetty. He could not have been there on a whim."

"It was done by design, then?"

"Just so. Of course, he could not have known I would choose to step onto the jetty. That was sheer luck. But one cannot guess just when he entered the water. Or where he might have been lurking prior to the moment when I went apart to walk by myself."

"Then why not attack you on land?"

Francis took this. "Because she was in full view of myself and Dalesford, not to mention half a dozen servants and the children."

"No one saw a stranger?"

"Apparently not. Where he came from is a mystery, but he must have been there or he could not have taken advantage of the opportunity."

Ottilia thought she saw a trifle of scepticism enter the captain's countenance and did not hesitate to pick it up. "You are starting to think I imagined the whole, are you not? Believe me, I have been tempted to the same thought. But I must hold to my memory, no matter how inconvenient."

This speech elicited a deprecating cough from Dalby. "Hardly inconvenient, ma'am. Yet it is not much to go on."

"That is not the point, man." Impatience sounded in Francis's voice. "What is troubling is the possibility of a further attack. That is why it behoves us to find out who did this."

"I hear you, my lord." Dalby cleared his throat. "If you wish it, I can provide a couple of men to stand guard about the grounds."

Francis snorted. "It would take an army! Have you seen the extent of my brother-in-law's estate?"

Ottilia put out a staying hand. "We must be grateful for the captain's support, Fan." She smiled at Dalby. "My husband will provide all the protection I need. But it would perhaps be of help if you, while in your endeavours regarding these robbers, could keep an eye out for strangers in the vicinity. I dare say you are familiar with the area. Have you lived here long?"

"All my life, bar those years when I served in the army. I shall do what I may, but I cannot promise to notice every stray countenance."

"Of course not."

He continued without acknowledging her reassurance. "We are based in Buckingham, but at present we are obliged to spend a deal of time in the area around Newport Pagnell." He rose and gave a small bow before turning to Francis, who also got to his feet. "I will be sure to bring any news should I discover anything relevant. What is your intention, my lord?"

Francis gave a resigned sigh. "We will be making enquiries of our own. I dare say we may meet in Newport Pagnell."

"Then I will bid you good day for the present. My lady." He saluted smartly and strode to the door. No word was said until it closed behind him.

Francis at once exploded. "A lot of good he is going to be!"

Ottilia gurgled. "At least he did not decry the whole episode."

"I am not sure how much of an advantage that is. It is not as if he will know any of the potential suspects we might name."

Ottilia spoke absently, her mind returning to the meat of the discussion as a new thought entered in. "No, but if it turns out Indigo is indeed robbing houses in the vicinity, there may well be another in his company who does have cause to hate me."

Francis turned a frowning gaze upon her. "Who?"

"The barmaid from the Pyg and Whistle. She had a penchant for black men and Indigo was one of the favoured."

"Are you talking of that girl in Bristol?"

"Cherry, yes. She decamped, if you remember, before we had fully understood her part in those events, thus evading the law. Who is to say she did not accompany Indigo?"

CHAPTER SEVEN

Doro was surprised to see the companion to the dowager stroll into the extensive fenced area known to the Fiske family as the children's garden. Here were set a number of play areas designed to entertain a group of youngsters. There was a rectangular court of shaven grass upon which two of the older boys were playing at battledore and shuttlecock, while the third ran around the perimeter encouraging a hoop along. A swing hung from one of the huge trees that dotted the garden and a seesaw sat idle in the sun. Within a circle designated with rocks and bordered by beds of blossoming wildflowers, Pretty Fanshawe and Lady Anne Fiske were seated, instructing Luke in a game of mancala. Not that the toddler was achieving the purpose of the game. From what Doro could see from where she was seated on a bench fashioned around a large tree, Luke's participation consisted of shunting stones at random from one hole to another, choosing to fill up a hole as fast as the little girls emptied it, along with voluble protests.

Although Doro kept an eye on her charge, she was aware that Hepsie had him under observation. Pretty's nurse was chatting with the maid whose duty was to mind the lady Anne and keep watch over her brothers too. Doro was glad of the agreement she had with Hepsie to provide each other with respite every day for an hour or so, and it was Doro's turn to rest. Luke was an energetic handful but Pretty, in Doro's estimation, was exhausting. She chattered non-stop and Hepsie was hard put to it to keep her attentive to the lessons his lordship insisted must be undertaken.

Relieved it was not her lot to see to Pretty's education, Doro was using this time to turn over in her mind the problem that became ever more perplexing. Why had Hemp not yet spoken?

She was aware he still cared. She knew he had not wished to take advantage of having been instrumental in securing her freedom. Indeed, he had paid the fee for her manumission.

"You owe me nothing, Doro," he'd said when she protested. "It was my pleasure to gift you your freedom. Don't take that away from me."

She had said no more, but the consciousness of being greatly in his debt persisted. Without his intervention, she would have ended on the gallows, never mind the bonus of securing an exit from her life as a slave. The freedom was at first intoxicating, if confusing. When milady bade her think only of her own wishes, she could not dream beyond the fact of having choices. Little by little, as the months passed, she had grown to understand what it meant to order her own life. No undue demands were made upon her and for the first time in her life, she received a wage for her labours. She knew not how to spend the monies that came to her hand every quarter and, beyond the odd trinket or necessary garment, she hoarded the coin, securing it in secret little caches among her belongings. Not that she supposed anyone in the Flitteris household would seek to rob her, but a long habit of concealment was hard to break.

Yet these many months, while she cared for the growing Luke, she had begun to chafe at Hemp's silence. She worried that his reticence had its root in a disgust for the exigencies of her previous life. Did he suppose she had succumbed to the overtures of her former master, thankfully now deceased? Did he consider her too tainted to revive the understanding they'd had so long ago? Was she, in a word, unmarriageable?

If the truth be known, she longed for his touch, his caress, his embrace, the feel she had never forgotten of that stolen kiss of long ago. Only occasionally since her entry into the Flitteris household had he kissed her palm and enclosed her fingers over it in that way he had ever used when they'd parted in the canes in Barbados.

Her thoughts were interrupted by the entry into the children's milieu of Miss Henrietta Skelmersdale. It was rare to see her alone.

Doro did not know whether to be flattered or alarmed when the companion, spotting her, walked towards her. She rose as the woman neared, but Miss Skelmersdale waved her back to her seat.

"Don't disturb yourself, I beg." She gave a merry laugh as she came up. "I have been excluded from the conference, you must know. I seized my chance to take a turn about the grounds and was drawn hither by the children's happy cries." She waved a hand in an arc to encompass the various youngsters. "They seem to be enjoying themselves. How quickly children forget!"

Doro had not retaken her seat. "You mean milady's accident? It is as well. They were severely disturbed on the day."

"I make no doubt of it, poor things, and am glad I was able to do what I might to turn Pretty's attention at least." The companion plonked her large frame down onto the bench and gestured to the place beside her. "Do sit down again, my dear. You need not stand upon ceremony with me, you know."

Doro, with a lifetime of servitude behind her, found it hard to obey this behest. She perched on the bench, feeling far from comfortable. On the day of milady's misadventure, she had been too upset to pay much heed to this woman when she came into the nursery, despatched thereto by her employer, she said. She succeeded, Doro recalled, in making Pretty laugh by a show of clumsiness, perhaps deliberate, in trying to emulate the child's dexterity with a skipping rope.

The companion did not appear to notice Doro's discomfort. She was a tall woman with a strapping figure, in proportion without being at all fleshy, and was possessed of a friendly smile. As befitted her station, she tended to wear modest gowns cut high to show no flesh at the bosom, the one she wore today being of jonquil muslin made up in the prevailing mode with a high waist and elbow-length sleeves.

The opinion of Miss Skelmersdale expressed in the servants' hall, as Doro had heard, was that she was easy with her fellow creatures and had a merry way with her, which appeared to be proving out at this first personal encounter.

"It makes me feel quite at home to see Lady Fan once again involved in investigation, pitiful though it is that she must do so on her own account rather than another's." The companion brought her gaze around to Doro's, a lively curiosity in her eyes. "You have had occasion to command her services, I believe?"

Doro's pulse skipped, but a thread of puzzlement was brewing in her mind. "I did not so command. My — her steward Hemp requested her help on my behalf."

She received a speculative look. "Your —? Friend, is it? Or something warmer?" Doro looked away, embarrassed, and a trill of laughter came from the companion. "I am vulgarly forward, am I not? I fear it is in my nature, my dear, and nothing will cure me. Lady Polbrook deprecates my candour, although she is herself prone to speak exactly as she thinks."

"That is position, madame," said Doro before she could stop herself. "Persons of her station have privilege."

"Oh, pish! You must not allow yourself to be browbeaten, Miss Gabon. I never permit her ladyship to bully me."

Distressed, Doro hastened to disclaim. "No one bullies me, madame. I am treated with great friendliness always by the Fanshawes. Milady is kindness itself."

"I can imagine. She is an original, is she not? I do like Lady Fan enormously."

"Everyone does. She is beloved and with reason."

A pointed look was directed at Doro. "Not everyone, it would seem."

Forgetful of protocol, perplexity growing, Doro stared at her. "What is it you mean?"

"Do you not know? Had you not heard?"

A thump began in Doro's breast, fearful of she knew not what. "Heard what, madame?"

"Why, that her fall into the river was not an accident. Someone dragged her in. Seized her by the ankle, she says."

Appalled, Doro eyed her without realising what she did. "Hemp said nothing of this."

"Perhaps he did not know." The companion let out an odd laugh. "He knows now, I'll warrant. I believe they are discussing this very matter as we speak."

"But this is terrible! That is what you meant when you said she must find things out on her own account?"

"Indeed. Lord Francis has called on the militia captain. It is all most intriguing."

"Intriguing? Milady is in danger!"

"Oh well, yes, but Lord Francis will see to her safety. The question is who might have done this, and it seems your friend Hemp may be able to assist."

A swell of pride entered Doro's breast. "He always assists, if he can. He is very much attached to milady."

"To you also, I dare swear."

Heat rose in Doro's cheeks and she looked away. "Madame, pray don't speak so."

"Why in the world not? I have it from Lady Polbrook that you are friends of long standing, and that Lady Fan expects the two of you to make a match of it. Do you not love him?"

The direct question struck at the core of Doro's buried distress, and she answered before she could think of the wisdom of confession. "He has all my heart. I have loved him from a child."

She felt her hand taken in a warm clasp, but still she could not look at the woman at her side. "Then what is the difficulty, my dear?"

"I do not know. I dare not ask."

Why she was confiding in this virtual stranger, she could not understand. Yet it was balm to open the secrets of her bosom. Better perhaps a stranger than any who knew too well her situation vis-à-vis Hemp Roy and might be watching with surreptitious eyes. Then Miss Skelmersdale surprised her yet again.

"I believe you are a heroine, Miss Gabon."

Doro expelled an astonished laugh. "A heroine? I doubt that. How so?"

A teasing smile was cast at her. "Why, you are a princess in a fairy-tale, my dear, awaiting your prince and the happy ending."

Despite herself, Doro was laughing in genuine amusement. "That kind of heroine, madame? I do not think my prince is ready to wake me up. Perhaps he won't."

She did not add that a jealous little corner of her heart harboured a fear that Hemp's strongest devotion was to milady rather than to herself. Doro saw far less of him than did milady. His duties were not arduous, but they took him from

Doro to dance attendance on the lady of the house. To run her errands, escort her on her walks and drive her where she might need to go if milord was not available. Doro dared swear he shared confidences with milady far more intimate than he did with her.

She could never speak of these fears, never accuse him. She chided herself for thinking so basely of milady, who had been her saviour. But the little demon of jealousy would not be wholly suppressed. And now it appeared milady was herself at risk and Hemp would not hesitate to do all in his power to secure her safety.

"And so he ought," she said aloud unthinkingly.

"I beg your pardon?"

Heat swept through her again. "Do not heed me, madame. I became lost in my own thoughts."

"Have you any notion who might wish to harm Lady Fan?"

The question, seemingly coming out of the blue, threw Doro's mind into high gear. "I know not. Unless it is one who cherishes a grudge." She met the other's questioning gaze, speaking half to herself. "People are apt to resent goodness, if they are themselves prone to wickedness. This I have seen, even among slaves."

The companion pursed her lips. "Need one look for that, I wonder? Lady Fan must have made enemies. I can think of several in the vicinity of her home who objected mightily to being under suspicion."

Doro tapped her fingers together in an absent manner. "I do not think that is sufficient reason to be wishing to harm milady. The person who could do such a thing must hate her."

"What an unpleasant notion!"

"Yes. Hate is terrible. Both for the one who is hated and the one who hates."

Doro found herself under a regard all at once disconcertingly penetrating. "You speak from experience."

It was not a question. Doro bit her lip. "I was accused of killing my master. I hated him enough. My mistress hated him even more than I. Life in that house was a nightmare for all because of it. Hatred breeds unhappiness and cruelty."

"But who could harbour such an intensity of antagonism towards Lady Fan? I will wager that is the substance of this conference. I wish I might have listened at the keyhole!"

The incongruity of this last startled Doro into a burst of laughter, in which Miss Skelmersdale readily joined.

"I am shockingly inquisitive, am I not? If I do not manage to poke my nose into this business, I shall be severely disappointed."

Amusement lightened Doro's heart. She even found herself hoping that the companion might do just that. Then she could ask her for news in case Hemp was sworn to secrecy. He would not break a promise, even to enlighten Doro. Which led her inexorably back to the reflection that she had broken her promise to him all those years ago. The fear that he had not and could never forgive her crept, like a malevolent serpent, into her bosom.

CHAPTER EIGHT

Sunday, perforce useless for the purpose of undertaking an expedition to Newport Pagnell since businesses would be largely shut up, ought to have been delay enough. But Ottilia had been obliged to wait for a further day before Francis would permit her to venture forth. She took care to conceal any sign of weakness. She donned a great-coat dress and had Joanie set out a straw hat ready for her to put on after breakfast. Aware her spouse was eyeing these preparations, she threw him a smile.

"You did say we might go today, Fan."

He was setting a pin into his neck-cloth and looked across once he had secured it. "If you were feeling up to it, I said."

"I am perfectly recovered."

He regarded her with narrowed eyes. "Perfectly?"

She turned back to the mirror, patting the knot Joanie had fashioned in her hair. "Enough."

He made no further remark until he had allowed his valet to help him with his coat. "We'll go down if you are ready."

"Quite ready."

Ottilia turned for the door, determined not to depend upon his arm for support. Although they had discussed at length what steps could be taken to sniff out the perpetrator, she was still conscious of a measure of reserve between them. Hence the need for subterfuge. At any other time she would have argued her case until her husband gave in, but present circumstances made her wary. He was still prickly, apt to go off into brooding silences which Ottilia was loath to interrupt. Conversation between them was confined for the most part to the present problem, which only served to make Ottilia feel distanced.

Francis exited their room behind her but at least took his place at her side. He did not offer his arm and Ottilia felt depression settle upon her spirits. As they approached the stairs, her tongue betrayed her.

"How long will it be thus between us, Fan?"

He did not look at her. "I don't know."

"Not many days since, you said we must find a way through it." She set a hand on the banister rail but did not start down the stairs.

Likewise halting, Francis turned his dark gaze upon her, strain visible about his eyes. "I want to, Ottilia. I don't know how at this moment."

Hurt made her tart. "You might start with calling me by the pet name you are wont to use."

His cheeks darkened. "You might equally use the endearments I am used to hearing from you."

Ottilia swallowed on the prickling in her throat. "Pardon me, pray. I did not mean to carp at you."

His jaw twitched. "Do you want my help to negotiate the stairs?"

Not in this mood. But she succeeded in keeping the words from escaping her lips. "I think I ought to try to manage it for myself."

He nodded and she began the descent, holding fast to the banister and taking it slowly. Francis kept pace beside her, watchful. She noted it and was grateful. At least he still had a care for her welfare.

As she set her foot on the polished wood floor at the bottom, he caught her arm and Ottilia perforce turned to face him. His brows were drawn together, his voice rough as he spoke. "Don't let us quarrel, Tillie! There is too much at stake."

She met his gaze, searching the brown depths. "We have fallen through a crack in the ice, my dearest. We will both freeze unless we can find a way out."

He gave a slight uncomfortable laugh. "I might have known you would pinpoint it precisely." A sigh came. "Let us go in to breakfast. The presence of others ought to help."

She was disappointed. Did they now need other company to be able to converse together with ease? A sorry state. She cursed the slip of the tongue she'd made, a pulled out brick that threatened to bring the walls of her marriage tumbling down.

In the event, it was indeed easier to break her fast to the accompaniment of the usual bickering between Sybilla and Harriet. The topic of the day appeared to centre on Harriet's lamentations that she had nothing to look forward to now that both her daughter and her niece, whom she had sponsored for the last few years since their joint debut, were married and out of her care.

"I cannot imagine why you are fretting, girl," scolded Sybilla. "You may at last attend to the welfare of your younger children and your duties as countess of this estate. I make no doubt you have neglected all."

Indignant, Harriet predictably took issue with this belief. "Nothing of the kind, Mama! My children are my life, as you well know. But Gil will still expect me to play hostess in London when Parliament is sitting. Besides, all the boys will be packed off back to school in due course, so I will only have Anne on my hands."

"Then you may take up embroidery or some such thing. It is ridiculous to be moping about the place merely because you have no young woman to chaperone."

Ottilia let the words wash over her as she consumed a more substantial meal than she truly wanted in a bid to fool her spouse into believing her more robust than she felt. Concentrating, she was a touch startled when Henrietta addressed her from across the table.

"Have you reached any satisfactory conclusion in your deliberations, Lady Fan?"

Momentarily confused, Ottilia blinked. "Deliberations?"

"The day the captain came, I took it you were discussing possibilities?"

A light laugh escaped Ottilia. "You guessed it, did you, Henrietta?"

An engaging grin came her way. "Was I right?"

"We are going into Newport Pagnell today to see if we can find any trace there." Ottilia flicked a glance at Francis as she spoke and encountered a frowning look of warning. Did he think she had said too much? The discussion in question had ranged over her past adventures, Ottilia taking advantage of Hemp's memory as well as her own and her husband's, Sybilla adding her views too. In the event, after much debate, she had felt obliged to discount all but the last two cases, which had taken place respectively in Bristol and at Flitteris. The latter had brought forth one pertinent name, the young man who had come amongst the gentry in company with the unfortunate victim.

Henrietta's question alerted Ottilia to the possibility of canvassing her views on that subject. She hesitated, thinking that the companion had left the area of Flitteris to take up her new post with Sybilla within a matter of months after those events, and had been too busy meanwhile to socialise. Or might she be in correspondence with one of their Flitteris neighbours, Virginia Grindlow, the vicar's niece? If so, Henrietta might be aware of anything new known about the young man that had not reached Ottilia's own ears.

She was just about to enquire when a hasty footstep sounded from outside the breakfast parlour, accompanied by Gil's voice.

"Is Lord Francis in there? Good. Then I will find him for myself."

Ottilia turned her head as her spouse rose from his chair, crossing to meet Gil as he strode into the room.

"What is afoot, Gil? Have you news?"

Gil halted, setting a hand to Francis's shoulder. "News indeed, Fan. There is a body washed up from the river."

He would much have preferred that his wife remain safe in the house, but it was no surprise to Francis when Tillie insisted upon accompanying the party to see the drowned body. His brother-in-law had entered a caveat.

"It is at some distance, Ottilia. You will surely not walk so far."

"How far, Gil? Half a mile?"

"At least. Possibly more."

Tillie had eyed him in that speculative way she had. "Could a carriage negotiate the way?"

Gil had shrugged. "You could take the gig along the lane, but you must still walk to reach the riverbank."

In the end, it was arranged that Hemp would drive Tillie in the gig while Francis walked with Gil, in order to arrive as swiftly as they may.

"Tell your man to stop at the turn-off to the bridge. You will have no difficulty finding the place on foot. I am reliably informed a crowd has already gathered."

Francis left with his host as soon as his wife went up to put on her hat, Gil having directed his butler to inform the steward he was needed.

One of Gil's keepers led the way, taking a route along the path that bordered the grounds and ran parallel to the Great Ouse. Francis's eager questions drew scant information as they made swift progress, but one point was pertinent.

"A female, so Maynard says. Young too."

An echo of the wretchedness that had attacked him when he'd believed his wife had drowned awoke in Francis's breast. Thank heaven she had been found before this discovery. Otherwise this excursion would have harrowed him. Regret for the discomfort that had arisen between them attacked him. He must mend it, and fast. To rid his mind of the sting, he turned his attention back to the present purpose.

"Has this woman been in the water long, did your man say?"

Gil threw him a humorous glance. "Isn't that something our Lady Fan would better determine?"

Francis grunted. "Anyone might be able to tell if the corpse had deteriorated, at least."

"All I know is the woman's gender, Fan, so it is of no use to ask me. We will see soon enough."

Impatience rode Francis. "Surely this fellow of yours," he said with a nod at the keeper in front, "must at least know if she is one of your people?"

"Not necessarily, old fellow. But let us enquire." Gil raised his voice. "Maynard!"

The keeper halted, waiting for the gentlemen to catch up. "My lord?"

"Lord Francis is asking whether this unfortunate is known hereabouts. One of ours, is she?"

The keeper started off again as he responded. "Not that I know of, my lord. Hard to recognise, anyhow. A bit bloated in the face."

These words had the similar effect of throwing Francis back in time as a horrid image of his darling wife in just such a condition flashed across his mind. He had only just succeeded in banishing it when the keeper gestured ahead.

"There, my lord." He gave a contemptuous grunt. "Seemingly we've acquired more spectators."

There was indeed a straggling crowd discernible ahead, those immediately visible in the rear craning their necks to see over the wall of bodies.

"You left someone on guard, I trust, Maynard?"

"That I did, my lord. A couple of gardeners and my own lad who was with me when we were called."

"It's to be hoped they have managed to keep this crew from touching the body," said Francis, his past encounters kicking in. Tillie always made a point of preventing anyone from tampering, if at all possible. For the first time in the last few days, he forgot his dilemma and caught himself wondering what his wife would make of this corpse.

Upon reaching the crowd, he was relieved to have the keeper Maynard's burly form in front to shoulder a passage through the onlookers.

"Make way there! Make way for his lordship!" He shoved indiscriminately at any who did not instantly obey, most heads turning to survey the newcomers. Hands went to forelocks, tugging and tipping in recognition of the great man of the area. Francis took it that in many cases Gil was either employer or landlord. Certainly his presence carved a swifter path through the throng and Francis very soon caught sight of the body lying on the riverbank, its several guardians blocking any from venturing too close.

"It appears a few more have constituted themselves watchdogs, Maynard," called Gil in an amused tone, addressing the men themselves as he came up. "Well done, my good fellows. Give us leave, if you will. Stand off!"

The men increased the circle as Francis and Gil stepped in.

Francis ran a cursory glance over the body from head to foot, and a waft of anxiety made him look at his brother-in-law. "Could Maynard keep an eye out for my wife, Gil? If he does not know her, he may easily spot Hemp."

"Ah, yes." Gil turned. "Maynard, his lordship's lady is coming in the gig via the road. She will be walking down from the turnoff to the bridge, in company with the black fellow who is her steward. Rely on you to find her and see she gets here in one piece."

"Right you are, my lord."

Satisfied as the keeper went off, Francis moved to the body's feet and took a longer examination. The woman looked to be of average height, but her whole body was puffy under the ripped folds of a gown made from some soft material. Muslin? It clung, outlining her limbs and hips. Half torn away, the bodice displayed the outline of a pair of what must have been large breasts, now flattened somewhat from the effects of spending time under water. His gaze rose to the countenance, swollen, but still showing traces of former prettiness. A quantity of dark hair, lank with wetness, fell away from the head, with yet a couple of locks curling up as they dried in the warmth of the day. An oddity struck him. The head lay at a strange angle, not tilted, but slightly off kilter to the shoulders.

As Francis regarded the wreck of a woman, evidently once good-looking, his imagination painted for him another face superimposed on this. Tillie's face, thus disarranged, swollen, dead.

His heart jerked. He blinked several times and the vile image vanished, replaced by the unfortunate whose features were abruptly familiar.

"I think I may know this woman."

Gilbert stepped to his side. "You do? Who is she?"

"I can't tell that. But I believe I have seen her before. She is too distorted. Or my memory is deficient."

As he again regarded the woman's features, he noticed that they were blotched with patches of purple, also visible around her neck and the expanse of flesh above the bosom. What did that betoken? A flickering memory gave him the image of his murdered sister-in-law, his brother's first wife. Strangulation then? Had she not drowned after all? How was the bloating significant? More to the point, when was she killed, and how long had she been in the Ouse?

He began to wish for his wife. Tillie would be able to tell these things. He found himself conceding, with a shade of reluctance, that his wife's talents far exceeded those necessary to run a household and care for his children. Was it fair to expect her to curtail the use of such skills merely to placate his pride? Not that he had done so any time these events turned up. But he could not deny his resentment. The suspicion could not but obtrude that the stance he had currently taken was unjustified. At this moment, he could scarcely remember what had set it off. Then the word slipped back into his mind. *Discontent*. Dismayed that it still had power to wound him, he was relieved when Gil alerted him with a nudge.

"Ottilia is coming, Fan."

He looked round to discover his wife just entering the wider circle designated by the posted guards, Hemp at her back. Guilt stabbed him for his treacherous thoughts and he strode the few steps to greet her with a heartier tone than he might otherwise have used. "In good time. I think you will find this interesting, my dear one."

Her clear gaze met his, an odd expression in her eyes. "Why, is the body known to you?"

He quirked his lip involuntarily. "I might have known you would guess that. I don't recognise her precisely, but she looks familiar." He moved as he spoke, gesturing her to the spot the body was occupying.

"A woman, then."

Tillie's gaze had already turned upon the corpse, running head to foot and back again, as far as Francis could tell. A light indrawn breath and she went swiftly to the head and, shifting the folds of her gown out of the way, dropped to her haunches.

Francis moved to the other side and followed suit, flicking glances from Tillie's concentrating face to the dead woman. He knew better than to interrupt her train of thought, but his brother-in-law was not so circumspect, crowding at the head and bending over the body.

"Well, what do you see, Ottilia?"

Francis looked up. "Give her time, Gil." He noted Hemp standing near the body's legs, his dark gaze likewise fixed upon the corpse's face. "Your thoughts, Hemp?"

"She is familiar, milord, as you say."

A riffle of triumph hit Francis and he returned his gaze to his wife's face. Tillie shifted a little and met his eyes. "I am almost certain it is Cherry."

"Cherry? Ha! I thought I knew her." He stared at the face. "Are you sure it's that girl?"

"What girl?" came from above.

"A barmaid, Gil. She was involved in the affair at Bristol."

Hemp's deep voice came, a rumble of anger within it. "She it was who accused Doro. She has come by her deserts."

Gil snorted. "Merely for accusing that nurse of yours? Is that not a trifle harsh?"

Francis rose to his feet. "There was a deal more to it than that, Gil. If this is indeed Cherry, she has been wanted by the authorities in Bristol for a couple of years or more. Moreover, it is almost certain proof that Captain Indigo is indeed in the area. This woman had become a member of his gang, I suspect."

"Then it seems likely Indigo threw her in the river, milord. Did I not say he is a vile wretch of a human? A pity he did not drown instead."

Tillie, still making her examination, looked up at that. "Cherry did not drown, Hemp."

Francis dropped back down to his haunches and was faintly amused to see Gil follow suit.

"But she's full of water, Ottilia. She must have drowned."

Tillie was pressing her fingers to the body's skin. "That is gas, Gil, not water."

"The bloating, milady, yes?" Hemp was now also on his haunches, watching what Tillie did. "I have seen it with drowned bodies in Barbados."

"Just so." She pushed open the lips and put her fingers in the mouth, drawing out a strand of some brown stuff. "Weeds. She must have dragged along the riverbed." She pointed to abrasions on the cheeks and nose that Francis had not before noticed. "These will have been caused by stones and other obstructions as the current moved the body along."

Francis banished an immediate vision of his darling wife in the place of the corpse, shifted by the unforgiving river. She had been so shifted, he remembered, but thankfully upon the surface.

Gil's voice cut into his thoughts. "Well, if she didn't drown, how did she die?"

Francis spoke his thought aloud. "It looked to me as though she was strangled, Tillie."

"I think not."

"But what of all that bruising?" He wafted a hand over the upper torso and neck.

"That is the pooling of the blood after death. Once she was in the water, she would have hung face down." Tillie set her hands on either side of the neck and her brows came together as she probed. Then she held the body by the shoulders and gave a quick tug. The corpse did not move. "Gil, you are best placed. Pray lift her shoulders a little for me."

Francis watched as his brother-in-law complied, reminded of that odd angle of the head. As the body's shoulders were raised, the head did not lift from the ground, the neck bending in an awkward way, the angle Francis had noticed becoming intense.

"You can set her down." Tillie passed a glance from one face to another and settled on Francis. "This is rather horrible, I fear. Her neck was snapped. It is broken."

Ignoring the exclamation that emanated from Gil, Francis set his gaze back upon the head and neck. "That explains the strange angle of the head."

"Yes, that is just what alerted me, Fan."

"Was it deliberate? Murder?"

"Almost certainly."

"Good grief, Ottilia!" said Gil. "Do you mean some individual did this? Could it not be that she fell and caught her head?"

To Francis's surprise, Hemp took this. "If you know the trick, you can seize the head and snap a person's neck with one jerk and twist."

Gil shot upright. "I trust you don't speak from experience, my good fellow."

Hemp rose to his feet, his tone polite, if not deferent. "If you mean, have I done it myself, the answer is no, milord. I have seen it done." His tone hardened. "There was an overseer on the plantation when I was a boy. He used the method on a slave who tried to escape."

Tillie was rising at last, her eyes darkening as she looked at Hemp. "How cruel! I hope he was not employed there for long."

"He was dismissed immediately, milady. The moment the incident was reported to Master Matt."

Tillie eyed him. "Did you so report, Hemp?"

One of Hemp's rare smiles appeared. "I did, milady."

Francis brought them back to the matter at hand. "Be that as it may, what about this murder, assuming it is one?"

His wife did not answer directly, her attention going rather to Hemp again. "Do you suppose Captain Indigo would know how to break a person's neck in this fashion?"

"All too likely, milady. He left at least two corpses behind him when he escaped incarceration. And he had no weapon then."

They were interrupted, Gil all of a sudden moving away as he hailed a newcomer. "Captain Dalby! Just the fellow we need." He turned to the company about the corpse. "I sent to him before I came to find you, Fan. We may leave the corpse in his hands, if you are done, Ottilia?"

"Quite done, I thank you, Gil."

"And done up, by the look of you, my love. Let's get you back to the house."

Francis moved to a position where he might give her his supporting arm, but she waved him off. "In a moment, Fan. Let me first tell the captain what I have found."

Francis nevertheless set a hand to her waist and was gratified when she leaned a little into him. It did not take long for her to relay her thoughts to the captain of militia, who grunted his satisfaction.

"Then if you are right, we have only to find this Indigo pirate fellow and the whole business will be settled."

Tillie entered a caveat. "You will, I hope, call in a proper doctor, Captain? I am not qualified, you must know."

"Of course, of course. The coroner will expect a doctor's report. May I ask what you intend to do now, Lord Francis?"

Fretting as he became increasingly aware of Tillie's pallor, Francis responded as briefly as he could. "We are not yet decided. If you will pardon me, I must get my wife home. She is not yet fully recovered."

The captain bowed. "I will call upon you, if I may, in a day or so."

"Please do, Captain," Tillie said with that warm smile of hers. "I am anxious to know the outcome. Your doctor and the coroner may not agree with me."

"They will if they have any sense," Francis told her sotto voce as at last he managed to steer her away.

To his delight, she gave one of those irresistible gurgles. "Thank you, Fan, but it is quite possible another opinion will set the matter down as a drowning, pure and simple."

"Could it be that?"

"A post mortem will confirm it one way or the other."

"But you are certain, are you not?"

"As certain as I can be. It is ridiculous after all she did, but I confess I feel sorry for Cherry. Although she will not have suffered. Breaking a neck in that fashion is at least a swift death."

Francis contemplated this as he guided her back to the lane, following Hemp's lead, but the central issue crept back. "This is all very well, Tillie, but we still don't know who pulled you into the river."

CHAPTER NINE

Ottilia could not rest until she had persuaded her spouse to write a letter to Walter Belchamp, the magistrate with whom they had dealt at Bristol, informing him of the situation.

"If his people are still searching either for Cherry or Indigo, or indeed both, which I think very likely, he will be glad to know what has transpired here."

Francis made an objection. "Isn't that rather Dalby's duty?"

"So it may be, Fan, but he does not know the events that occurred in Bristol and we do."

"Can't it wait? I want to see you settled."

Ottilia was seated on the chaise longue in the Fiske family parlour they had used before, and she patted a cushion into the raised back. "I shall be perfectly settled here, Fan, if you will only sit down at the bureau and write that letter."

He threw up his eyes. "Let me see you with your feet up, then." He crossed to the bell-pull. "We'll have Joanie in. She can fetch you a blanket and —"

"A shawl, if you please. I am not lying here swathed in a blanket. Besides, it is far too hot."

"Shawl, blanket, it's all one." He tugged on the bell.

Ottilia shifted her position and lifted her legs onto the chaise longue, wriggling to be comfortable as Francis came over with another cushion.

"Let me put this at your back."

She waved him off. "The one I have is enough, Fan. For heaven's sake, don't cosset me!" She saw with instant regret a shadow cross his face and put out a hand. "Forgive me! I am grateful, my dearest, truly."

He had not taken the hand and moved to dump the cushion onto the chair from where he had taken it. "I neither want nor need your gratitude."

Ottilia eyed his stiff back as he went to one of the open windows and stood looking out across the expanse of lawn to that side of the mansion. Torn between dismay and a creeping irritation, she hesitated over her choice of words. But they came out more harshly than she could have wished. "What then do you want from me, Fan?"

"I want to turn the clock back."

The roughness in his voice spoke to her heart and the burgeoning annoyance melted. "I cannot unsay the words, my dearest dear."

He turned, his gaze piercing her from across the room. "Tillie, I don't wish to feel like this. If I could erase it, make it dissipate, if I knew how, I would do it. I can't find the way back, my loved one."

Hard put to it to keep the pricking of her eyes at bay, Ottilia tried to smile. "You will find it. We will find it, I promise."

She was not entirely sorry to be interrupted by a knock at the door and the entrance of Charles, the Fiskes' footman. Francis at once went forward.

"Ah, good. Will you ask her ladyship's maid to attend her in this room, if you please?"

The footman bowed. "Very good, my lord."

Ottilia jumped in as he headed for the door. "Charles!"

He turned. "My lady?"

She smiled. "Might coffee be forthcoming, do you think?"

Charles gave another bow. "Of course, my lady. It will be here directly."

He withdrew and Ottilia was relieved when Francis headed for the bureau. "I'll write that letter."

Better that than a continuation of their painful discussion. "Thank you, Fan. Charles can see it despatched to the post. Or ought we to send it express?"

He had taken a seat and was hunting through the writing desk drawers. "The ordinary post will get it to Bristol soon enough. The roads should be in good condition after all this dry weather."

Watching as he set a fresh sheet of parchment down on the blotter and selected a cut quill from the brass inkstand, Ottilia found her mind returning to the discovery of Cherry's corpse and the problem of identity. One thing came into question. Could the sometime barmaid be eliminated as a suspect in the attack upon herself? Was she already dead when it happened? One could not definitively state how long she had been in the river. Two or three days at least, and very likely more. Ottilia's own fall into the Ouse had occurred — how many days ago was it? She was losing track. Five or six? It did not seem as if one could eliminate Cherry, then. Where had she been when she was thrown into the water? It was impossible to gauge how far her corpse had travelled with the current before rising to the surface to be found by a passer-by. Even the identity of her killer could not be certain, although Indigo must be a potential suspect.

Could it then have been he who'd waited under the jetty for a chance at Ottilia? But why? He had no reason to wish her dead, had he? Cherry was another matter. Ottilia had foiled her schemes and found her out, leaving her no recourse but to become a fugitive. Then could she have prevailed upon Indigo to act on her behalf? If he was indeed engaged upon a spate of robberies, which was supposition when all was said and done, was it reasonable to think he had also been tracking her movements? Or perhaps Cherry had kept a weather eye out for what Ottilia might be doing? Whoever was responsible for her ducking must have known her whereabouts. Which meant that individual must also have followed in her footsteps.

The thought that, unbeknownst to either herself or Francis, this malevolent creature had been watching where she went, waiting his or her moment, was frankly chilling. She found it hard to believe Captain Indigo would pursue such a course. Not in person, at any rate. Which meant there must be another, or indeed others, in his train, willing and able to act on his behalf. Or was the notion of the involvement of Indigo and his gang too hasty a conclusion altogether? The discovery of Cherry's body could not but point towards it.

If so, Ottilia's endangerment was by no means at an end as Captain Dalby seemed to think. She was loath to speak these thoughts aloud, although it was likely Francis had reached the same conclusion.

"There, that will do."

His voice startled her out of her musings and she looked across to see Francis was shaking a sander over his page.

"What did you write to him?"

"Just what you requested." He was hunting again, this time opening and shutting the little drawers that fanned out above the writing slope. "Where the deuce does Gil keep his wafers? Here is sealing wax, but I don't have my seal. Nor a candle at this hour, come to that."

Ottilia lost sight of his activities as Joanie entered the room on the echo of her knock. She put in her request for a shawl. "Take my hat, Joanie. I won't be needing it again today."

The maid picked up the discarded headgear, curtsied and almost collided with the footman as he re-entered the room with a laden tray. Francis, rising from the bureau, spoke before Ottilia could proffer her thanks.

"Set it down on the side table, and I will pour." The footman did as requested and retreated.

"Thank you, Charles."

"No trouble, my lady. Was there anything else?"

Francis again forestalled her. "You might bring up a decanter and glasses. Madeira, if you have it. Oh, and have this conveyed to the post."

The footman took the folded missive, now sealed with a wafer, and bowed himself out. Francis upended a cup into its saucer and poured the hot black liquid. Ottilia watched him add cream and two lumps of sugar.

"Pray stir it well, Fan."

He did so, silent and frowning as he moved the spoon round and round in the cup. Then he brought one of the occasional tables to a position beside Ottilia and set down the coffee.

She picked up the cup and took a welcome sip of the brew before looking up at Francis, who was still standing over her. "What are you thinking?"

"I was wondering the same thing of you. You went off into one of your reveries."

Ottilia could not resist a tiny poke of mischief. "How do you know when you were busily writing?"

His lip quirked and his gaze softened. "I have eyes in the back of my head where you are concerned, wife of mine."

She laughed, feeling a little of the weight dissipating. "Well, I was cogitating."

"And?"

She gave an involuntary sigh. "I fear we are still in Limbo."

"Meaning we still can't tell who it was that grabbed your ankle."

"Just so." She sipped at her coffee, absently looking into the cup. "Not Cherry in person."

"Clearly."

"No, no, I think she might well have still been alive then. It is difficult to judge the length of time she was in the Ouse. I just meant it was more likely to have been a male. You said as much yourself, remember."

Her spouse leaned and patted her leg. "Move a bit." She made room and he perched on the edge of the chaise longue. The naturalness of the proceeding warmed her heart. "Do I take it you discount Indigo too?"

She met the deep brown gaze. "I can't imagine he would act himself."

"Which means there is another in his train."

"Or it was someone else altogether."

Her spouse uttered a curse. "It seems we are at point non plus." His eyes returned to her. "To be frank with you, I have been wondering what precisely we can do in Newport Pagnell. Have you anything in mind?"

"I have." Ottilia took a restorative sip of her coffee before elaborating. "Retracing our steps from that expedition we made, perhaps. I thought if I returned to the shop where I saw someone watching me —□

"You thought you saw someone, you mean."

"I am persuaded it was not my imagination, Fan. Not in the light of subsequent events."

"You think it might trigger a memory to go there?"

"Just so. At least, perhaps a trifle more detail. Was it a man or woman? Had I seen that person before?"

For a moment, Francis sat without speaking, evidently brooding over her words. Then he let out a sigh. "This is nothing like your usual exploits, is it? Where is the raft of persons you might question? There is no line to point a direction. Apart from Cherry's body and the possibility Indigo is in the area, we are all at sea, Tillie. You could not even look to find out who killed her. Not that it's relevant."

"Oh, but it is, Fan."

She was treated to a frowning regard. "How so?"

Ottilia gave him a smile. "Does it not strike you as peculiar that two women, both known to each other, should be subject to a drowning? In the same place, mark you, and within a period of days. It cannot be coincidence."

His frown did not abate. "But you weren't drowned."

"That was sheer chance. The intent was clear. Although I have no notion how, as far as personnel go, let us say, I dare not suppose the two incidents are unconnected."

"Yet they may be. I am not convinced."

She eyed him. "Is it because you are beginning to suppose I did indeed imagine the hand?"

A slight hesitation supplied his answer, although he at once disclaimed. "Not at all. At least, not entirely."

She bit down on the instant rise of indignation. "What, then?"

He grimaced. "We ought to examine the jetty. The grass is overgrown on the bank along there. It's possible — □

"It is possible some plant or weed caught around my ankle. Is that what you are saying?"

"I'm not saying that." He rose abruptly from the chaise longue, heading for the mantelpiece. Always his refuge, Ottilia reflected in passing. "But we ought to consider all options."

"Including the one that I am a hysterical female with too vivid an imagination?"

He turned on her. "For pity's sake, Tillie, don't put words in my mouth! I never thought that, nor implied it."

"But?"

"But it is just possible you were mistaken. You went through a hideous ordeal, you very nearly lost your life, you were virtually unconscious for some hours, as you told me. Is it unreasonable to wonder if your memory betrayed you?"

Ottilia regarded him as a blast of mingled fury and disappointment swept through her. She dared not answer for a moment or two for fear of her tongue's spite. When she did, she could not keep the huskiness from her voice. "You had no doubts of me prior to this horrid estrangement between us."

He blinked, flinching as if at an unexpected assault. "Of what do you accuse me?"

"You have changed towards me, Francis. Where is the trust we once had?"

His face twisted, in pain, she thought. "It's not gone, Tillie. Nothing has changed."

"How can you say that? We are struggling, Fan, and you know it."

"Outwardly, yes. Inwardly…" Then he was back, throwing himself down next to the chaise longue. He took the cup out of her hands and set it down, and then grasped them in a fierce grip. "My heart is yours, my dearest love, and always will be." He pressed her hands to his lips. "Grant me a little time. I was hurt. I am hurting still. Let me be on this, I beg of you. Just let it be, Tillie."

Moved beyond words, Ottilia pushed up from where she rested against the back of the chaise longue. In the next instant, she was in his arms and balm came in the familiar scent of him, feel of him, sound of his breath in her ear.

She was thus held for an endless moment, the reunion silent but redolent of all she held dear, and hope grew in her bosom. All was not lost. Then the sound of an opening door caused her to spring back even as Francis released her. He rose to his feet as a discreet cough sounded.

"Your Madeira, my lord."

Ottilia was overtaken by an insane desire to giggle. She managed to suppress it, surreptitiously dabbing at her wet eyelids as her spouse was thanking the footman, who set the tray down on the side table and departed. Francis then busied himself with the decanter. She seized her cup only to discover that the coffee inside it had grown cold. She watched Francis toss off the glass he had filled and pour out another. She seized upon the innocuous subject. "Would you refill my cup too, if you please, Fan?"

He did so and brought it across. Ottilia smiled up at him as she took the cup from the saucer. "Why don't you go down and check, Fan?"

"Check what?"

"Whether there is indeed some plant sufficiently strong to have fooled me into thinking it was a hand."

He produced a wry grin. "Placating me, my dear one?"

She bit her lip on a smile, but the mischief would not be suppressed. "It's well to be sure, don't you think? I concede you have a point."

"I thank you. In my turn, I concede that I fully expect to find myself mistaken. It would not be for the first time."

She did laugh then. "If you are, shall we try in Newport Pagnell tomorrow?"

CHAPTER TEN

Having agreed upon a rendezvous with his employers, Hemp set out to find the less fashionable quarter of Newport Pagnell. He had a couple of hours to explore and nose about while milady took a tour of the shops she had been to on a visit to the town before the wedding. He had attended the Fanshawes on that occasion. Thus the environment was not entirely new to him, but he had not before ventured beyond the main thoroughfare. He sought assistance from a street vendor proffering onions from the long bundles hanging from his stick.

"Where may I go to purchase cheap made-up clothes, if you please?"

The onion seller looked him up and down. "Fer the likes of you?"

Hemp produced a sly grin. "For a housemaid. A gift."

He was treated to a suggestive guffaw. "I like yer spirit, friend. You'd best tek a looksee in them shops down St John Street way. There's a market of sorts. Sell all kinds of gewgaws and the Gypsies bring carvings and shawls and that. Oughter find summat what'll please yer lady love."

Hemp thanked him, ignoring the lascivious leer and asking for directions. It did not take long to penetrate the seedier part of the town, not much to Hemp's surprise. He had observed in his travels with the Fanshawes and elsewhere how the rougher parts of any urban environment more or less rubbed shoulders with the areas where the quality walked. Even at Flitteris there were pockets where the seamier side of life was prevalent.

Milord, aware of their existence, had warned him often enough to be sure to avoid any such when escorting milady.

Hemp very soon found himself in a rowdier neighbourhood, peopled by vendors crying their wares: of fish, birds, pots and pans, baskets, a fellow with a tray of pies, and all manner of comestibles. Poky little shops abounded, together with seedy-looking inns and a line of carts down one alley. Hemp turned into it, narrowly avoiding a legless beggar pushing himself along on his behind with the aid of a couple of wooden blocks with leather strap handles.

He halted as Hemp shifted abruptly out of his way, looking up. Slipping one hand out from under the leather strap, he held it up, wheedling. "A penny for a loaf fer the wife and bairns, is it, good sir?"

Not wishing to bring out his bulging purse in this environment, Hemp slipped a hand into his pocket for loose change and brought out a halfpenny. He dropped it into the beggar's hand. "Half a loaf, my friend."

He moved on, hearing a curse from the beggar left behind, and the sound of spitting. No stranger to insults of the kind, he suppressed the impulse to return it with interest. No sense in attracting unnecessary attention. He was drawing enough curious looks as it was, his height and skin colour marking him out. One could not expect to see many of his colouring in such an out of the way spot as Newport Pagnell, although he had seen several in Buckingham when he'd visited the larger town a few days before milady was attacked.

He made the best of his way along the market, pausing to look at ribbons and cheap brooches offered on one cart and oysters on another. Just as he turned from contemplation of a collection of copper kettles, he caught a glimpse of black skin under an old-fashioned three-cornered hat.

Watching with a sidelong look, he tried to see the face, noting that the fellow was stocky and thick-limbed. His thighs bulged under a pair of thickset black breeches and his arms bulked in the sleeves of a loose frieze frock-coat, also black.

As if he felt Hemp's regard, the bull-like head turned. Losing his guard, Hemp faced him, meeting eyes as dark as night, stark against the white surround. The countenance was broad, its power compelling even at a distance.

Momentarily transfixed, Hemp knew the other was likewise frozen. Then the fellow broke contact and slipped between a couple of individuals in conversation at his back. Convinced of his identity, Hemp followed.

As he wove in and out among the idlers, buyers, sellers and vagabonds, keeping just out of sight of his quarry, thoughts chased through Hemp's mind. He had never seen Captain Indigo, but milord's description closely fitted the man. Why he had taken flight after spotting Hemp was a troubling question. Did Indigo know of his association with the Fanshawes? If he was responsible for the barmaid Cherry's death, he would have found it out from her. It was conceivable his interest in the events at Bristol had been piqued after milord had accosted him. Yet his apparent recognition indicated that he had seen Hemp before. Had he been the one watching milady? Or had he merely assumed the presence of another black man in the vicinity might be dangerous?

The latter seemed less likely. Somehow, the pirate had found out that he was involved with the Fanshawes. Perhaps even that he was on occasion milady's guardian. Where was he headed? Merely out of the way of one who might point a finger and alert the authorities? Or…

A belated realisation of potential danger slipped into Hemp's gut, tightening there. He cast a rapid glance left and right, wary of running afoul of any who might be in Indigo's gang. He knew from milord's experience that the fellow was apt to have his bully boys engage anyone of whom he was suspicious, or, as in milord's case, to whom he desired to give a warning.

No one appeared to be interested in Hemp, beyond the usual flicker of attention he drew wherever he walked. Nevertheless, he kept a wary eye open for a possible assault, the more so as Indigo led him into a less frequented maze of alleyways. Hemp was obliged to stop, keeping behind a corner wall in order that Indigo did not see him. Did he know he was being followed?

Peering round the corner, Hemp just caught him turning right at another. He slipped down the alley as noiselessly as he could and paused where his quarry had turned. A quick glance around the edge of the wall showed him an empty street, long and narrow.

Cursing, Hemp walked into it, his gaze hunting the lines of poorly maintained tenements on either side. Had the wretch hidden himself in a doorway? Or was he living in one of these dwellings? There were no shops here, every building seemingly given over to lodgings. The filth in the shadowed roadway gave notice of the likely station of those who inhabited these houses. A thieves den in this milieu would come as no surprise.

Frustrated at losing sight of Indigo, Hemp strolled the length of the street, checking every dark doorway and peering into any windows he found, convinced that he had indeed seen Captain Indigo and that the pirate had known he was followed.

A cursory check down the next couple of streets proved futile. The wretch had vanished without trace. Taking careful note of any landmarks in the street where he had lost him, Hemp made a mental picture of the way the roofs hung, the lamp post on one corner and one facia painted a lighter hue than the dun-coloured frontages of the rest of the dwellings, dulled with the grime of years. It took him some time and several enquiries to find a convoluted route back to the main thoroughfare. Hemp began to doubt he'd find his way back to the street in question, despite taking good note of the areas through which he trod. Even so, he reached the coffee shop where he was due to meet the Fanshawes a little ahead of the appointed time.

Hemp loitered outside, keeping a sharp eye out both for his employers and any sign of having been pursued. He had done so throughout the return journey, but noticed nothing untoward. Yet the consciousness of having alerted Indigo to his presence made him circumspect. He paid no immediate attention to a runty little man who was hurrying along on the other side of the wide road, head down, until something in his stance registered. An image leapt into his mind of just such a stunted individual speeding away from the house in Bristol where Doro had been enslaved.

The name popped into his head. Quin! That rabbity little weasel who had dared to proposition his beloved. Who had been, in his disreputable past, in Indigo's employ when he was terrorising the Caribbean in his piratical role.

About to cross the street and set off after the man, he was hailed from behind by milord.

"There you are, Hemp."

Without preamble, he turned to Lord Francis, pointing across the way. "There, milord! That is none other than that fellow Quin from Bristol. Do you remember?"

"Good God! Is it indeed?"

"I had best go after him, milord."

His arm was seized. "No, don't! There is no time. Her ladyship is fatigued and we must go back to Dalesford."

With regret, Hemp saw the little man slip down a side street. "I can find my own way back, milord. I must follow him. I saw Captain Indigo earlier. I am certain it was he. Quin must be hand in glove with him. Why else would they both be here? That dead barmaid too. All three here, milord? They must be working together."

"Then we'll alert Dalby. We don't need you running your head into trouble and coming home all covered in blood."

Hemp ground his teeth. "If I can catch that weasel, it will not be me who bleeds, milord."

Still Francis held his arm. "Did you follow Indigo?"

"Yes, and I know where he lives. Or at least, in which street. I think I can find it again."

"Then hold hard, Hemp. Better if you go with Dalby and his men."

"By which time, milord, he will likely have decamped, and Quin along with him. He saw me, and he perhaps knew I was following him."

"Damnation!" Hemp chafed as milord cogitated. At last he released his hold. "It makes no matter. We know they are both here, and that is sufficient. Even if you caught him, what good would it do?"

"I'd get him to talk, milord." The undercurrent of rage that had been driving him subsided. He knew it was misplaced, brought on by the memory of how the wretched Quin had insulted his Doro. "It is too late now in any event, milord. He is long gone."

"Then pray go and find where Ryde has left Lord Dalesford's landaulet and bid him bring it to the haberdasher's. I left her ladyship there, and I must return forthwith."

Seated in a cane chair thoughtfully provided by the proprietor, Ottilia gazed at the shop doorway, trying to recreate the image of the person she had thought was watching her that day. With Cherry dead, she found her mind trying to fit the girl to the memory. Disconcerting, since it might well be an inaccurate notion.

Francis was right. To have no points of reference except this vague recollection made it tricky, if not impossible, to know how to pursue her enquiries. She had drawn a blank at each stop along the way, a fact Ottilia considered was likely responsible for the sudden fatigue that had overtaken her, setting her spouse in a bother.

"You've done too much. We'll go home."

"Not before I have been back to the haberdasher's, Fan."

"You've walked enough, Tillie."

She had softened her protest. "It is but a step, my dearest. If you lend me your arm, I am persuaded I can manage it."

In fact, she was obliged to walk almost half the length of the street. This left her so weak that she was glad of Francis's peremptory demand the moment they set foot in the shop.

"You there! Fetch a chair on the instant, if you please. My wife is half fainting."

She had intervened, sotto voce. "I am not faint, Fan. Merely tired."

He paid not the slightest heed, harrying an assistant to do his bidding. In the event, a woman who declared herself the owner came forward — a plump matron with a remarkably sharp gaze.

"Don't stand like a noddy, Cox! Fetch the chair from behind the counter. There now, madam. If you'll sit, Cox will bring a glass of water. Alice, give me one of those fans! I make no doubt it's the heat, sir." This to Francis, as she seized the fan from a thin woman's hand. "Take this, madam."

But Ottilia, contrary to her confident assertion, was indeed feeling faint. She clutched her husband's sleeve and sank back in the chair, closing her eyes. Next moment, a welcome breeze was fanning her face and within a short time, the faintness began to recede. She opened her eyes to find Francis bending over her, brows drawn together as he plied the fan with vigour. Ottilia raised her head, releasing her hold on his sleeve. "Thank you, I am better, Fan."

A hand holding a full glass was thrust before her. "Do take a little water, madam. It will cool you."

Ottilia grasped the proffered glass, becoming aware of anxious, round features in a middle-aged face. "Thank you, Mrs —?"

"Heywood's the name, madam. Do you drink that down."

Obediently, Ottilia sipped, her gaze returning to her spouse's face. Was he angry? The frown cleared as he met her gaze.

"Better?"

She gave him a tremulous smile, grateful not to receive a scold for imprudence. "Much."

He nodded, looking to Mrs Heywood. "Will you be kind enough to attend to Lady Francis while I see to bringing our carriage?"

The proprietor's eyes widened and she dropped a curtsy. "You may leave her ladyship in my care, my lord."

"I thank you. Tillie, I'll be as quick as I can."

She wanted to tell him not to hurry, but she was loath to say anything that might prick him into irritation, his mood being still uncertain. He had grown increasingly disgruntled as they'd trailed from shop to shop without result. Nowhere could Ottilia recall having the sensation of being watched, except here. She sipped her water, largely ignoring Mrs Heywood's tutting commentary, and setting her mind instead to cogitation.

At length she gave up trying to remember the image in the doorway, and upon the instant she had a vivid recollection of a shadow in the periphery of her vision. Was it that which had made her turn, just in time to catch the person leaving the shop? Without effort, the shadow took on form. She had seen a figure! Even as she turned, a face within the hood of the cloak had whipped out of her sight. That fleeting glimpse was enough, however. It had been female. Cherry? She was still alive then.

Ottilia sipped absently, puzzled by the memory. Too slight. The barmaid had been a buxom wench, with a quantity of dark curls. The wisps of hair visible under the hood had been fair.

For an instant she was certain, before doubt set in. If it had not been Cherry, a definite presence in the vicinity, who in the world could have been watching her?

"How do you do now, my lady? Would you care for another glass?"

Jerked back to the present, Ottilia looked up. Mrs Heywood was regarding her questioningly. A glance at the glass told her it was empty. She produced a smile and held it out. "Thank you, no. I am feeling a good deal recovered. I must thank you for your trouble."

The proprietor took the glass, waving aside her thanks. "It's no trouble, my lady." She handed the glass to the female assistant hovering at her back and returned her gaze to Ottilia. "I've a notion I've seen you before, my lady."

"You have indeed. I purchased a silk bag and a packet of pins for my daughter to give as a wedding gift."

"Ah, that would be it, then. I thought you looked familiar, my lady." She hesitated, clearing her throat. "Was you looking for anything particular today, my lady?"

Feeling she ought to make a purchase, Ottilia said the first thing that came into her head. "A fan! As you said, it is such a hot summer and I quite forgot to bring more than a couple. I swear they are falling to bits from overuse. There is the one my husband was using just now."

Mrs Heywood looked gratified. "Ah, yes, though we have quite a selection, my lady." She signalled to the male assistant. "Cox, bring over the box of fans!"

A collection of fans were displayed for Ottilia, from paper, silk or lace confections depicting colourful scenes on the leaves to those of plainer style but with finely carved ivory sticks. A trifle bewildered, Ottilia chose one almost at random, with a green silk ground to the leaves, gilding to the edges and a delicate pattern of trailing vines and flowers.

"A popular design is that, my lady. You'll not be disappointed. Why, I sold one like it only a day ago. That had a yellow ground, but the pattern was very similar. Oddly enough, it was a lady who came in when you were last here, my lady. I remember because she wore a cloak. Green that was too, like the fan you have there."

Ottilia's mind jumped. A green cloak! "How many days ago?"

"Well, it must be a week or more, surely? When you came in yourself, my lady, as I said."

"No, no, I mean, when did she come in to buy the fan?"

"I'm not perfectly sure, now you ask."

Ottilia chafed. "Pray try to remember, Mrs Heywood. It may be important."

She regretted saying as much as a lively curiosity spread across the woman's countenance. "Important? In what way, my lady?"

Inwardly cursing her slip, Ottilia tried to backtrack, reflecting that she must indeed be more fatigued than she knew. "I am not quite sure yet, but it would be most helpful if you could tell me exactly which day she came in."

Looking perfectly mystified, but even more avidly curious, Mrs Heywood put a finger to her chin, stroking as she apparently set her mind to remembering. "Not yesterday, now I think of it. It might have been a day or two before that."

The thin woman, who had reappeared after removing to some inner sanctum to rid herself of the empty glass, intervened at this point, her voice as reedy as her person. "Day before yesterday."

"Are you sure, Alice? I thought it was earlier."

"No. It was day before yesterday." Alice glided to the counter and slipped behind it. "It's in the book, Mrs Heywood." Producing a large ledger from under the counter, she shoved aside a collection of fabric samples and set it down with a bang, throwing it open at a page marked with a leather strip. Half-turning the book, she pointed to an inked entry as Mrs Heywood marched over to the counter. "See? One fan, yellow ground, floral figuring. Eleventh of the month, Monday last."

"Bless me, so it is!" Mrs Heywood read it a couple of times, presumably to be sure, and returned to Ottilia. "Monday it was. The day before yesterday."

Tempted to a tart comment that this fact had been sufficiently established, Ottilia withheld the remark, instead proffering the necessary thanks. "I am most grateful."

Meanwhile, her thoughts were winging to the obvious conclusion. The woman in the green cloak was definitely not the barmaid because on Monday, Cherry was already dead.

"Why is it so important, my lady?"

Would this woman not be satisfied? Ottilia prevaricated. "I had an idea I knew her, but I believe I was mistaken."

Mrs Heywood, it seemed, was not to be put off. "Well, that does seem an odd circumstance. But important? A friend of yours, was it, my lady?"

"By no means," returned Ottilia unguardedly, aware she was making things worse with the snap in her voice. What in the world was the matter with her? Where was Francis to rescue her from this inquisition?

"Not a friend, then."

"No." Tired of the woman's persistence, Ottilia threw caution to the winds. "I wanted to know because I had thought the woman in question might be the one who was found in the river only yesterday, but had clearly been underwater for some days. So it could not have been the same one to whom you sold the fan after all."

Both the assistants were staring, open-mouthed, but Mrs Heywood proved to be made of sterner stuff. "I heard about that, my lady. So you knew the girl that drowned?"

"I have met her." Her reasoning faculties were returning. "Never mind that, Mrs Heywood. Could you describe the lady who came in and bought the fan?"

This brought the puzzlement back to the woman's face, but she did not immediately question Ottilia's interest. "It was Alice who served her. Can you describe her, Alice?"

The assistant had busied herself returning the ledger to its place, but at this she came around the counter and approached

Ottilia's chair. "Blonde, petite, pretty. She had small hands, delicate."

The recital came out staccato and confident. Ottilia regarded the narrow features with appreciation. "You are very observant, Alice. Did you notice anything else about her?"

"Pleasant voice. Soft spoken." Alice sniffed. "Fidgety, though. Kept looking to the window. There was a man outside. Waiting for her, I think."

Mrs Heywood entered a caveat. "How would you know he was waiting for her, Alice?"

"Why loiter if he weren't? I looked after she went out and he weren't there any longer."

Which did not prove anything, as Mrs Heywood was quick to point out. But Ottilia, impressed with Alice's meticulous description, was inclined to trust her judgement. Who the woman was became of immediate concern. But perhaps more importantly, who was the man who'd awaited her outside the shop?

CHAPTER ELEVEN

Sybilla grunted. "You seem to have acquired a plethora of suspects after all, Ottilia."

"Hardly suspects, Sybilla. Mere possibilities. I have no way of knowing if any of these people were anywhere near Dalesford that day."

The exchange was taking place in the bedchamber, Ottilia having been inexorably led thence by her spouse who insisted upon her taking to her bed. She agreed at least to sit thereon, banked by pillows, but without removing her gown or getting between the sheets.

"I am not as debilitated as that, Fan. Coffee, with perhaps a light snack, will set me up."

Francis had allowed this programme to be followed, extracting a promise that she would not rise again before the dinner hour. Having no desire to run the gamut of family concern, Ottilia was content to remain in situ with the window thrown up to let in such breeze as there was. Joanie brought up her favourite beverage, together with a selection of dainties supplied by the cook and augmented with a chunk of her favourite cheese.

"See if you can come by some of the hard yellow type that I like, Joanie. Lady Dalesford will not serve it at her table, but perhaps there is a supply in the pantry?"

"The Cheddar, my lady? That there is, for I've seen it on the table in the servants' hall."

Ottilia's mouth watered. "Excellent. Sneak a slice or two for me, if you are able."

Joanie giggled. "It's an addict you are, my lady, what with that coffee of yours and yellow cheese." She gave her mistress a cheeky grin. "Would you be wanting bacon with that, my lady?"

Ottilia laughed. "I will forego that pleasure. Although now you remind me of it, I might succumb to roasted cheese and bacon when we are home at last."

Her maid gave a pointed look towards her belly. "It's not that all over again, is it, my lady?"

"Another pregnancy? Gracious, no!" Ottilia's mind flitted over the happenings of the morning. Could her fatigue and that near faint have a different origin than her mishap in the river? As Joanie left the room, she ran a hand over her abdomen, but could not feel any untoward bulge. But the possibility lingered in her mind, setting her heart aflutter.

This was no moment to be finding herself *enceinte*. Not with things as they were between herself and Francis. A fleeting conviction that such news would swiftly resolve matters she dismissed at once. No agency outside of settling it together could be contemplated. She and Fan must find their way back without the demands another baby would bring. Besides, she was by no means ready to go through it all again. Luke was not yet two years of age. No, no, it could not be. A ridiculous fancy of Joanie's. Merely because she desired the taste of cheese? She had been hankering for it ever since she was bearing Luke. Nor was she willing to set her tiredness down to anything other than the exigencies of her untoward sojourn in the river. Not very many days had passed since that dreadful day.

She was glad to be interrupted by her mother-in-law before she could run herself into a frenzy.

"What is all this I am hearing, Ottilia? Francis says Hemp saw this pirate fellow in the town."

Having heard at length from Hemp of his discovery during the drive home — Francis having requested him to ride in the landaulet for the purpose rather than on the box with Ryde, who was driving — Ottilia had in turn told the men about the fair woman under the green cloak. She had time only to relay these findings to Sybilla before Francis reappeared.

"I've ordered that you are not to be disturbed by those imps of ours."

Diverted from the goings-on of the day, Ottilia was moved to enter a protest. "But I have not seen the children yet today."

"You may see them in the late afternoon, when you have had time to rest. You don't want Pretty chattering at you, and Luke will only chase about the room and fidget you to death. Besides, I hear from Harriet the whole lot of them are going on a picnic in the woods."

Ottilia bethought her of the present danger, but was forestalled by Sybilla, who had plonked herself in a chair by the bed. "Is that wise, Francis? With some villain after Ottilia? We do not know who may be about."

"They will be perfectly safe, Mama," returned Francis, who was propping up the mantelpiece. "Besides the nurses, they will be hedged about, according to my sister, with a veritable army of servants. You don't imagine Harriet would risk her *precious darlings* otherwise, do you?"

Sybilla gave a snort. "She was always a fearful ninny, my daughter. All children run risks."

"For pity's sake, ma'am! You are the one who raised the matter just now."

Ottilia intervened. "For my part, I am glad of Harriet's caution. I should not care to have anything happen to our little darlings either, Fan."

"Any danger will come to them from their rambunctious cousin Gregory, if you ask me. He is as bad as your nephews, Tillie, if not worse."

She had to laugh. "At least Tom and Ben had a care for Pretty when she was little."

Sybilla became explosive. "Will you stop talking of the children, the two of you? It is of more moment, to my mind, to bend your thoughts to discovering Ottilia's enemies." Without waiting for a response, she turned back to Ottilia. "Who is this fair-headed woman? That is what I wish to know."

Ottilia sighed. "Would I might tell you, Sybilla. That complication serves only to deepen the puzzle."

Francis straightened and came across to the bed. "If there truly was a fellow waiting for her outside the shop, it's possible it was Quin."

"Why Quin, Fan?"

"Because we know he is in the town. Hemp swears he was the man he saw."

"Yes, so he told us, but —□ Ottilia fell silent for a space, thinking this over, aware of Sybilla's interested gaze and Francis's intent one. At length she looked up at him. "I can quite see Quin as part of Indigo's gang, since we know he was once on the pirate's ship."

"What was that *but*?"

"I am not sure. From what Hemp says of him, Quin seems an unlikely escort. Alice said the woman was soft spoken. That does not sound like a girl of Cherry's ilk, and it definitely was not Cherry who bought a fan the day before yesterday."

"What then?" demanded Sybilla.

Ottilia gave a little grimace. "Perhaps not quite a lady, but a woman of better education than our unlucky barmaid."

Her husband dropped to sit on the bed, regarding her with a frown. "What possible motive could an educated woman have to spy upon you, Tillie?"

"She may not have been spying for herself."

"For the fellow outside the shop?"

"It is possible, Sybilla."

"All the more reason to suppose it was Quin."

Ottilia took in a snatch of breath. "No, Fan. You are forgetting one other we had wondered about when we talked over all my experiences." She saw his frown and set a hand on his where it rested on the coverlet. "Percy, remember? The friend of our poor victim at Flitteris."

A gasp escaped her mother-in-law. "That wretched creature? You think he tried to drown you?"

"I don't know, Sybilla. But I am very sure he would take care not to be seen by me."

Francis turned his hand and caught hers. "Because you would be bound to recognise the wretch. Damnation take him!"

"Language, boy!" Sybilla ignored her son's muttered words, which might have been an apology, though Ottilia doubted it, and swept on. "You ought to have him laid by the heels, Francis."

"How, ma'am? We have no evidence of his even being in the vicinity. It is pure supposition."

"That is unfortunately true, Fan. If it had not been for this fair woman, I should be inclined to confine our attentions to Indigo and Quin."

"Have no fear. I have alerted Gil and he has sent to Captain Dalby. I hope he may come here with all speed."

Ottilia agreed but turned her attention to her mother-in-law. "In the meantime, should you object to it if I spoke to Henrietta?"

"Henrietta? What in the world for? I do not see how she can be of use."

Ottilia smiled. "You will not deny she is of use to you, Sybilla. Do you not find her an asset?"

Sybilla flapped a hand. "An intelligent girl, but she talks too much."

"I had thought you would enjoy having someone with you who is of a chatty disposition." She held up a finger as Sybilla opened her mouth to retort. "But that is not the point. Henrietta is friendly with young Virginia Grindlow."

"Who is she?"

"The vicar's niece at Foscot and one of our neighbours at Flitteris, if you recall."

"I cannot be expected to keep a set of names in my head, child."

"Especially when they are strangers to you, Mama," added Francis. Ottilia received one of her spouse's wry grins. "I have trouble myself, what with all those involved in these adventures of yours. What do you want with the Grindlow girl, Tillie?"

Ottilia squeezed the hand still holding hers. "Not her specifically. All those young ones were involved in that business, Fan, and there are sure to have been repercussions. I fear they would shrink from confiding in me, but if there is gossip to be had, I am very sure Henrietta knows it."

Sybilla's companion appeared to be entertained by her inclusion, striding into the bedchamber with a hearty greeting.

"Here I am, Lady Fan. You see that I have obeyed your summons with alacrity."

Ottilia laughed, gesturing to the chair still left beside the bed. "I dare say my mama-in-law phrased it so, but it was a request rather than a summons, Etta," she said, adopting in the privacy of their meeting the pet name she knew the companion preferred. "Thank you for coming."

Henrietta did not immediately take the indicated seat, instead crossing to the open window and taking in a deep breath. "This is welcome. One does not get this breeze coming through in the family parlour."

"Has everyone foregathered there?"

Henrietta turned with a smile. "No, indeed. Lady Dalesford is out supervising this picnic with the children. I don't know where his lordship is. I have been writing letters while Lady Polbrook was occupied."

A promising start. Ottilia pounced on this at once. "Pardon me if I seem inquisitive, but were you by any chance writing to Virginia?"

"Ginny Grindlow?" Henrietta crossed to the bed, lively curiosity in her features. "Now, why, I wonder?"

"I will tell you, but pray sit." Ottilia again waved towards the chair. "You are so tall, you will give me a crick in the neck."

A merry laugh greeted this sally and the companion came around the bed and settled into the chair, flouncing her jonquil muslin petticoats. "Behold me!" She leaned forward. "Do tell, I am agog."

A laugh escaped Ottilia. "The boot is on the other leg, my dear. I am hoping you have been in regular correspondence with Virginia."

"I have, and with Botolf too. Although his letters are mostly concerned with questions regarding matters of the household.

He is perfectly ignorant of such things and inclined to blame me for leaving him to manage."

There was a bone of contention here, as Ottilia knew. When Henrietta's previous employer had died, the estate had fallen to her godson. The small legacy left to the companion had been, in Ottilia's view, paltry, giving her no choice but to accept the post of companion to the Dowager Marchioness of Polbrook. Botolf Claydon had not seen fit to remedy the deficiency either, although he had invited Henrietta to remain as long as she needed. Ottilia allowed herself to be momentarily side-tracked.

"He might have offered you a permanent home."

Henrietta's brows flew up. "As his unpaid drudge? I thank you, Lady Fan, but I am a deal better off with Lady Polbrook."

"You are content, then? You do not find her too domineering?"

The woman's infectious laugh rang out. "If you will have the truth, she is dogmatic, abrasive and often twitty. But underneath it all, she is kind-hearted. I enjoy her company for the most part, and I have seen more life in these few months and visited more places than I did during the whole five years or so I spent with dear Robina. I am perfectly satisfied with my lot, I assure you."

Ottilia smiled. "You relieve my mind. I think she will grow fond of you."

"Oh, I have not yet achieved the privilege of *Sybilla*, but I don't despair."

There was an insouciance about this woman that Ottilia could not but admire. "I like your spirit, Etta. It is rare to find a woman in your situation who is willing to embrace what comes. Even to find enjoyment in it, if I don't miss my guess."

Henrietta gave her a mischievous smile. "Do you ever miss your guess, Lady Fan?"

Ottilia had to laugh. "Frequently."

"I don't believe you. And in this instance, you are perfectly correct. I was writing to Ginny, in answer to her last letter."

Ottilia's senses quickened. "Ah, just as I hoped. But it may not be your recent exchanges that are of most interest."

"What is it you wish to know?"

"Thank you for being direct." Ottilia gave her a straight look. "This concerns my late ducking."

Henrietta's eyes began to sparkle. "I hoped it might. How can I help, Lady Fan?"

Ottilia wasted no more time. "Has there been any local gossip over the months regarding the young man who came into our circle along with Marmaduke Gibbon?"

For a moment, Henrietta looked taken aback. Then her brows drew together. "You think he is the one who attacked you?"

"He is one of the possibilities. Before you ask, I have no evidence, no proof. The name of Percy Pedwardine arises as a matter of elimination of others."

"Aha, I see. You are looking for someone with a thirst for revenge, yes?"

"Just so."

Ottilia waited, half inclined to dismiss the whole proposition since Henrietta did not immediately produce a pat solution to suit her purposes. She had dropped into a brown study, contemplating the intricate pattern of Chinese design on the coverlet. Ottilia was convinced she did not see it as she looked inward.

At length, Henrietta looked up. "Setting aside the talk immediately following those events —

"Yes, I am looking for a later aftermath."

"— there was mention of that fellow's fate."

"Fate? He died?"

"Not fate in that sense." Henrietta nodded in a decisive way. "I think this must be what you want."

"I am all ears."

"Well, the truth is it came via Richenda Vexford. She has spent a good deal of time in London, you must know, enjoying her freedom from her father's strict rule."

"Yes, so I heard. Vexford never properly recovered."

"No, and Richenda has an aunt who had washed her hands of the business of finding her a suitable husband since her brother-in-law was being so difficult."

Impatient of this history, with which she was somewhat familiar, being well acquainted with the heiress who had been the focus of events at Flitteris the previous year, Ottilia intervened. "The aunt is now sponsoring her, I understand. But do you say Richenda had news of Percy?"

Henrietta waved her hands in a deprecating fashion. "Not much. Only that he was no longer seen in fashionable circles after he received the cut direct from a number of people. Ginny wrote that it is thought he was obliged to go abroad."

"But not known for certain?"

"No, but this is the interesting bit." The sparkle returned to Henrietta's gaze. "Rumour holds that he married the daughter of a merchant."

Ottilia felt a prick of gratification. "A rich merchant?"

"That I cannot say, but I imagine so, don't you? He was no doubt barred from attempting another genteel heiress, so… □

"So he eloped with the next best thing?" A petite, softly spoken girl with blonde locks, perhaps? "I don't suppose rumour gave any indication of this girl's identity?"

Henrietta looked regretful. "Sadly, no. Why, is she relevant?"

"She may well be." Ottilia gave the companion a fluent account of her near encounter with the cloaked woman and what she had learned of her in the haberdasher's shop.

Rather to her surprise, Henrietta became anxious. "But this is horrid, Lady Fan! If this escort is indeed that fellow, you may be in the gravest danger. I mean to say, if he blames you for his fall from grace —"

"I imagine that cannot be in any doubt. I was perfectly free with my criticisms to his face, and I encouraged the neighbourhood to tattle. I am very sure, knowing what sort of a man he is, that he will consider himself unfairly stigmatised and I can well understand that he would not hesitate to lay his subsequent misfortunes at my door."

"Lord help you if he does, Lady Fan! He proved himself ruthless."

A fact of which Ottilia was only too aware. She did what she might in the way of mitigation. "There are other suspects too. This is by no means certain."

"How can you say so? If that woman was indeed spying upon you —

"I cannot be sure that she was. I have not seen her again. Nor did I get more than a glimpse at the time. Moreover, it is pure supposition that she might be the merchant's daughter you say Percy has married."

Henrietta eyed her for a moment and then leaned in. "What does your instinct tell you?"

Ottilia let out a laugh. "I do not operate on instinct, Etta."

"Well, but you have these insights. I remember Lady Elizabeth saying as much."

"Any such are based upon observation. One cannot rely upon intuition alone."

"Oh, indeed, but there is evidence too, is there not?"

"Very little." Ottilia put out a staying hand. "However, I am very glad to know of these rumours. The notion that man may have married, whether to his advantage or no, does at least raise the possibility that he — or indeed his wife, if that is the identity of that cloaked woman in the shop — might be tracking my movements."

"With the object of disposing of you? How dreadful, Lady Fan! What if he had succeeded?"

Ottilia tried to smile but it went awry. "Then I fear my death would have been classed as an accident."

"He would have escaped justice," said Henrietta, indignant now. "I do not give much for the chances of this wife of his."

Ottilia could not let this pass. "Be sensible, Etta. If she is the source of the means for him to live, it would not profit him to be rid of her."

"True. He is all about profit."

Ottilia's mind was working. "Which reminds me that there was the uncle in the case."

"The victim's uncle? Who came to take his body?"

"Just so. Mr Edmund Gibbon was little inclined to believe his nephew's friend had anything to do with that affair. I suppose it is too much to ask if rumour spoke of that relationship?"

Henrietta's eyes fairly popped. "Heavens, how came I to forget that? Ginny did write of Marmaduke's uncle. Of course it is only rumour, but it is said that wretched fellow Percy found sanctuary with him for a while, early on. If anyone knows the truth of it all, he must."

CHAPTER TWELVE

Entering the breakfast parlour in company with her husband upon the following morning, Ottilia's gaze went directly to their host, seated beside his wife.

"Gil, the very man we need!"

Gil, in the act of bringing a forkful of beef to his mouth, paused and looked across as Ottilia approached the table. "If you are looking to me for that fellow Dalby, I am happy to say he sent a note to the effect that he will attend you later this morning."

Ottilia took the chair Francis pulled out for her. "That is excellent, but it happens I have another matter in mind."

"What now?" demanded Sybilla, who was seated opposite next to her companion.

Ottilia smiled. "Good morning, Sybilla."

Her mother-in-law waved this away. "Don't waste time, Ottilia." She pointed the spoon, with which she had been digging into a baked egg, at Henrietta. "Was this one of any use to you?"

Not having attended at dinner after all last night, exhausted by a late and extremely noisy visit from her offspring, Ottilia had gone over the discussion with Henrietta only with Francis. She threw the companion a smile. "Henrietta was extremely helpful. She gave me an idea, which —☐ turning back to her host — "is why I wished to consult with you, Gil."

From her place at her husband's side, Harriet chimed in. "Have you made no progress at all, Ottilia?"

"Very little."

"After all this time! You are usually so quick."

To Ottilia's relief, her spouse took this, bristling a trifle. "She has virtually nothing to go on, my dear sister. You could hardly expect her to have an answer already, and it has been only a week."

Exactly a week this day, Ottilia realised, with an inward start. But she had no time to indulge this thought as Harriet took issue with her brother.

"Gracious, Fan, there is no need to take me up in that highty-tighty fashion!"

"Enough, child!" Sybilla cut in. "Francis, don't bark at your sister! Gilbert, your amusement is misplaced." Having reduced her offspring to seething silence, which very nearly set Ottilia off into a fit of the giggles, even more misplaced, Sybilla turned her black gaze on Ottilia herself. "What, if anything, can my son-in-law do for you?"

Ottilia glanced at Gil and discovered he at least had not taken offence at Sybilla's scoldings, for his eyes were dancing. He spoke with admirable smoothness. "I am naturally at your service, Ottilia."

Before she could embark upon her need, Francis answered for her as he rose from his chair and crossed to the sideboard. "She needs the direction of a fellow who may possibly be found in Oxfordshire."

Gil had resumed his meal and he swallowed a mouthful before answering. "Make use of my peerage, if you will. It's in the library."

"He's not a peer."

Ottilia made haste to take it up. "But you may know him, Gil. You are far more often in the capital than are we, and your acquaintance must necessarily be wider. Oxfordshire is the next county to Buckinghamshire, after all. You might even know of him here."

Francis returned to his seat with a platter piled high. "Give Gil the name, Tillie."

"Edmund Gibbon."

Ottilia was amused to see how everyone waited upon Gil's answer, staring at his face. A tantalising aroma from Francis's plate distracted her briefly. A glance showed her an array of bacon nestling beside his favourite beef. She was about to ask to share it when Gil spoke up.

"I can't say I've heard the name."

"Oh. That is disappointing."

Gil grinned cheerfully. "You don't need me, Ottilia. Send someone off to the post office in Oxford. They are bound to know."

Francis gave a laugh. "Genius. We should have thought of that, Tillie."

"Yes, but it was as well to ask Gil," said Harriet. "He knows everyone."

"Hardly everyone, my love."

"He didn't know this fellow," Sybilla pointed out.

Unnecessarily, but Ottilia refrained from drawing her fire by saying so and was glad no one else ventured a retort. She hurried into speech. "I shall write to him at once and send Hemp off to Oxford. He will make sure it reaches Mr Gibbon."

Henrietta, with what Ottilia considered superb tact and timing, changed the subject. "How did the children enjoy their picnic, Lady Dalesford?"

Harriet's eyes lit with enthusiasm. "They revelled in it. Those wretched boys of mine gave me palpitations climbing trees, but Anne and Pretty were as good as gold, helping to set out the dainties Cook provided. Such sweet little darlings they are."

"If my daughter was behaving sweetly, I shall count myself astonished," Francis cut in, but Ottilia was not deceived. The note of pride in his voice was palpable.

The conversation became general and Ottilia signalled to the butler. As he provided her with several slices of bacon at her request, she drew the attention of her spouse.

Francis looked at her plate and then met her gaze, his brows lifted in mute question. She could not withstand a mischievous look. "Succumbing to temptation, Fan. It smelled so good."

He grinned, his manner more relaxed than it had been these many days. "Well, I must say that I am glad, if surprised. Should I take some inference from this?"

No, pray don't, my dearest dear. But instead, Ottilia prevaricated. "Oh, it shows I am recovering, do you not think?"

He regarded her enigmatically for a moment, but to her relief, chose to accept this. "I'm glad of that, at all events."

A sliver of guilt crept into Ottilia's bosom. In truth, she was still feeling fatigued, beset by an unprecedented lethargy. Even the prospect of uncovering the identity of her would-be killer failed to enthuse.

In the event, she ate only half of the bacon, abandoning it for a roll with butter and honey, a sure sign her appetite was still poor. Nevertheless, she rose from the table, determined to get a letter written to Mr Gibbon before Captain Dalby's arrival.

She was just handing the sealed missive to Hemp when Francis entered the family parlour to summon her to meet the captain.

"He is downstairs in the saloon where we received him the other day."

The captain was found to be pacing. He turned as the door opened and returned towards the pair as they entered. "Well met, my lord! Lady Francis, your servant."

Ottilia exchanged greetings, but lost no time in raising the pertinent issues. "We have a little news of our own, Captain, but first pray tell us what you have discovered."

Dalby let out a breath that sounded overwrought. "Very little, I regret to report. Thanks to your identification, at least we know who our victim was."

"Definitely a victim, then?" Francis cut in. "She was murdered?"

"Not a doubt of it. Our doctor pronounced it as strangulation."

Ottilia could not refrain from protest. "Did he not notice that her neck was broken?"

The captain shrugged. "Bunting is inclined to put that down to damage from the body's sojourn in the water. Either way, the need arises to investigate."

With difficulty, Ottilia held her tongue. At least this doctor, however unobservant or mistaken, had recognised that Cherry was murdered.

Francis pitched in. "Have you managed to find out anything to lead you to her killer?"

"Not much. The coroner wants to hold an inquest, but I have asked for time. The body is scheduled for burial, however, now the doctor has done with it."

"Not much means something, perhaps?" Ottilia pursued.

Captain Dalby gave a twitch of the lips, which might have been meant for a smile. "We traced a line back to a certain thieves' den. An informant we use made enquiries there and it appears the girl had frequented the place."

"What sort of den? A tavern?"

"How came you to guess that, my lord?"

"She was a barmaid when we knew her."

"And," put in Ottilia on a deprecating note, "if you will forgive my speaking of such things, she also dispensed her favours among the clientele."

Captain Dalby looked amused rather than shocked. "I see. For lucre?"

"Naturally."

The captain became thoughtful. "You think she may have done the same at this haunt?"

A flash of memory showed Ottilia the girl Cherry tossing her head and talking freely of her side-line to serving in the tap. "To be frank, I should imagine she would choose an establishment a degree above the place you describe. Not one frequented by the gentry, but a tavern where she might hope to earn rather more than a thief would be willing to pay."

Dalby nodded. "That gives me a lead. I will have my men check out taverns of that type." He added on a sour note, "But if that was her means of livelihood, we are no doubt looking at a plethora of potential suspects. Prostitutes turn up dead at the hands of their customers all too often."

Ottilia thought this a less likely solution, but she was spared from saying so when Francis took the point. "You might say so if we did not have a better prospect."

The captain's eyes lit with anticipation. "Indeed? Who might that be?"

"The pirate Indigo, whom my steward saw and followed. He is pretty certain it was our errant pirate captain. Or it might be another man he saw who could well be a member of this gang of yours."

When he had been given an account of the sightings, Captain Dalby grew almost enthusiastic. "This is good hearing, my lord.

Will your fellow remember just where this Indigo went to ground?"

"Hemp thinks he can find his way back there, yes."

"Then I must beg to borrow his services. Tomorrow my men and I are otherwise occupied, but we may make a foray on Saturday if this Hemp is willing to assist us."

CHAPTER THIRTEEN

Francis had not at first intended to make one of the party, but reflection altered his mind. If Dalby managed to apprehend Indigo, he ought to seize his chance to question the man. The militia captain's interest lay in the burglaries as well as Cherry's murder, but all Francis wanted was to identify his wife's attacker. Until they knew who had pulled her into the water, she remained in constant danger. Not knowing where or how a second attempt might be made was beginning to cause him to lose sleep.

While Tillie dreamed beside him at night, Francis spent too many hours running over every possibility of which he could conceive. Bullets flying out of nowhere, carriage wheels loosened on purpose, rope stretched across a path to bring down the unwary walker. Bogeymen leapt from every corner and he took to wondering if any of his brother-in-law's employees or dependents might be suborned into acting on behalf of this unknown assailant. At one moment he would resolve to return his family to the safety of Flitteris at once and bolt all the doors. At the next he would revoke that determination in favour of scouring the area round about Dalesford for signs of a lurking assassin.

Outwardly he remained calm, but he was subject to an unrelenting stretch of the nerves that left him as tetchy as his mother. Or so he reasoned when called to order for snapping at Harriet. The hope of settling the matter once and for all, if only Indigo could be found, drove him to insist upon accompanying the expedition to one of the less salubrious districts of Newport Pagnell.

The apparently unerring accuracy with which Hemp led the militia through a maze of streets earned Francis's respect. He would not himself swear to being able to recall a route so readily, especially one that meandered through a twisting plethora of little alleys, both noisome and shadowed. Not much light was afforded when buildings were set so close together.

Hemp at last halted, holding up a hand and turning to address Captain Dalby, his voice muted. "It is around the next corner, sir."

"Right. Sergeant!"

Francis recognised the voice of command, albeit spoken in a hushed tone.

A heavyset fellow stepped up. "Sir?"

"Send three men to find a way around to the other end of that street and tell them to keep out of sight, but to watch for a signal."

"Right you are, sir."

The sergeant spoke swiftly to a few of the troop Dalby had brought with him, saying these were his best and most trusted men. Three of them slunk off along an alley running parallel behind the street Hemp had pointed out, moving fast and keeping low. Francis was irresistibly reminded of his army days in the Americas when he and George Tretower had led an attack upon a stockade. His attention returned to Dalby, who was giving further instructions.

"When we reach the corner, send all but two to hold the other side. If they can remain concealed in doorways or other shadows, so much the better. You and the rest will come with me."

The militiamen set off and Francis began to follow. Dalby halted and turned on him. "Stay back, my lord." His eyes went to Hemp. "You too. You've done your part."

Francis was moved to object. "But we both know the man. I've spoken with him."

"I have your descriptions. When we have him — if we get him — there will be time enough to involve you."

Francis grunted, exchanging a glance with Hemp, who grimaced. This, however, was not their venture. They had no authority. Francis knew what he would have thought of a civilian interfering in a military manoeuvre. He gave the steward a nod. "Very well. We will await you here."

He watched the red-coated men make their way to the corner of the street. Several broke away and vanished in the other direction. The tension he had not realised was building up began to dissipate as time passed.

"It is likely to be a long wait, milord." Hemp was leaning against a railing, contemplating the sky which was turning an ominous grey. "We ought to look for shelter in case those clouds drop their load."

Impatience tugged at Francis. "Is he not going to investigate? I supposed he would have his men knock at the doors until they found the right house."

"And alert Indigo, milord? He would escape before they had attempted three houses."

"He's got men posted in every direction. How the deuce can the fellow escape? These hovels have no basements as far as I can tell."

Hemp's expression was grim. "He managed to drop out of sight when I followed him here, milord. I was close behind. I should have seen him the instant I turned the corner."

Francis had been watching the stationary militia still visible at the corner, but as he turned his gaze towards Hemp, a movement in the periphery of his vision drew his attention.

A figure was moving along the parallel lane down which the first contingent had gone. It was bent low, stealth in every line of its form. Something in that contour became abruptly familiar.

Francis pulled back out of sight. "You're about to see him now, if I don't miss my guess." He gestured to the lane.

Hemp tsked between his teeth. "Up to us then, milord."

Francis nodded, assessing the end of the lane. Their man was moving slowly, but he would spot them the instant he reached it. The rail gave onto a tiny yard, enclosed at the side, but stopped short of the corner by a foot or so.

"Be ready at my back, Hemp." Francis vaulted the rail, crossed the yard and climbed over it at the corner. He drew the pistol from his pocket and turned it butt end forward as he pressed against the wall.

A glance showed him Hemp had also jumped into the yard and was crouching down in the house doorway. He waited. No way to alert the militia without also warning the quarry.

He could hear footsteps now, treading softly. How the deuce had the wretched man got wind of the redcoats and effected an escape? Francis's pulse was speeding up but the concentration of his old calling gripped him. He had one chance. If he muffed it, Indigo would be away.

The figure lurched into sight and Francis leapt. Two swift strides took him within reach, his pistol arm raised. His victim had time only to turn a terrified gaze before Francis brought the butt swinging against the man's head. At that instant, he realised his victim was not Indigo.

The man fell to the ground and lay senseless. Francis leaned down and seized his coat, turning him over. The face was known to him.

"Damnation! It's the runt." He turned to get Hemp's reaction and found he was gone.

Francis looked about, recalling a vague memory of a pounding noise. Grunts drew his gaze down the lane and he cursed. Hemp was grappling with a burly figure. Francis had just time to recognise it as the one he had originally seen before common sense jerked him into action. He yelled down the street. "Dalby! Here! Bring your men!"

He did not wait for the response, but sped down the lane to Hemp's aid. Just as he came within striking distance, Indigo freed himself from Hemp's bear hug and sprinted away. Hemp gave chase. Hearing the running of many feet, Francis did not waste his energy likewise but waved as the militiamen came into sight, pointing the direction.

"Down there! My man is chasing him. Go! Get after them!"

He heard Dalby give an order and several men in the signature red coat lumbered or sprinted past. Francis watched them go, reflecting that Indigo would have to be a genius to outfox the lot of them.

He went back to where the captain and a couple of his men were standing around his unconscious victim. "Well, we've got one of them at least."

Dalby stirred the body with his foot. "I hope you haven't done for him, my lord."

"He'll have a thundering headache, but he'll live."

"Sergeant, see if he's breathing." And to Francis, "Which is he?"

"The name's Quin. He's a repulsive specimen of a man, but not a killer, as far as I know."

"A thief?"

"Very likely. He's not above taking advantage of any circumstance likely to enrich his pockets. One of these care-for-nobodies out for himself and the devil take the hindmost."

The sergeant rose from his haunches. "He's alive, sir, just about."

"Good." At this point, Quin emitted a groan and his eyes flickered. "He's coming round. Have the men tie him and keep him under guard."

Francis eyed the little man as he became aware of the militia surrounding him. A muttered curse came and he struggled to sit up. One of the men jerked him to his feet.

"Come on, you! You're coming along of us."

"Take him to the lock-up."

Francis stepped in. "Wait! Let me question him first."

Dalby regarded him with a frown. "We'll do that, my lord."

"So you may, but I've enquiries of my own to make." Without waiting for a reply, he stepped up to the little man, who was protesting as one of the militiamen was tying his hands.

"Hoy, let me be! I ain't done nothing."

"Debatable," said Francis. The fellow's gaze shot up. "Remember me, Quin?"

For a moment, the eyes remained blank. Then they widened. "Was it you as thumped me head?"

"It was and I don't regret it. Though I thought you were Indigo."

At that, Quin's gaze shifted off him, darting left and right. "Dunno what you mean, yer honour. Never heard the name."

"Don't be a fool, man! You and he have been working together. For months, very likely. With Cherry."

At mention of the barmaid, Quin shrunk back. "Dunno nothing of that. Ain't never done nothing."

Francis curled his lip. "Indeed? What might you be doing here, so far from Bristol where you belong?"

The fellow's head came up, fire in his eyes. "I don't belong nowhere, specially not there. Give me the boot, didn't she? What was I supposed to do?"

"Elinor Scalloway? No surprise to me. She sacked you, so you took up with Indigo again. How did you find him when the authorities clearly could not?"

"Dunno nobody of that name."

It was clear he was not going to give up his secrets easily. Francis tried another tack. "Why have you been following my wife?"

Quin blinked a couple of times, staring up at him with a blank expression Francis was half inclined to believe in. It was a moment before he responded. "What you say?"

"You've been spying on my wife. Lurking under the jetty, were you?"

"Jetty? What jetty?"

"On the bank of the river that runs beside Lord Dalesford's estate. That was you, wasn't it?"

Quin jerked at his bonds. "Never heard nothing of any lord. Nor I ain't hid under no jetty. Can't swim, can I?"

Francis barked a laugh. "That won't fadge. You were on board a ship with Indigo at one time. Don't tell me you didn't learn to swim."

"I didn't! I'd have drownded if I fell in off of that ship."

Before Francis could pounce, Dalby cut in. "I thought you said you didn't know anything of this Indigo. Now you're admitting you were on his ship?"

Quin's eyes flicked between the captain and Francis. "No, I ain't. 'Twere another ship. Nothing to do with that there pirate."

Triumph lit in Francis. "How do you know he was a pirate if you don't know him?"

"Everyone knew it." Quin wriggled. "In Bristol. It were known."

Dalby cut in, his tone contemptuous. "You incriminate yourself every time you open your mouth. You said you'd never heard the name. Now you know he's a pirate." He let out a disgusted breath. "I've heard enough. Take him away and lock him up."

Urgency engulfed Francis. "I'm not done with him, Dalby. He hasn't yet satisfied me that he had nothing to do with my wife's fall into the river."

Quin's mouth fell open. "River? You ain't meaning that Lady Fan, yer honour, is it? Fell into the river, did she? What, like Cherry and all?"

Dalby seized the fellow's coat, dragging him up so that he was on tip-toe. "You villain! You know all about that girl's murder, eh? Who did it? Was it Indigo?"

"I never!" The little man became frantic, struggling in the captain's grip, his feet scrabbling for purchase. "Never said owt, me! Don't know nothing of that!"

"Then how do you know she was drowned?"

"Heard it, didn't I? Talk of it everywhere. Girl drowned, body found, everybody knows it."

"But not everybody knows her name," snapped Francis. He addressed himself to the captain. "He's all yours, Dalby. See if you can get him to admit he, or Indigo for preference, at least knew of our presence in the neighbourhood. That would be a start."

Dalby let the man go, nodding to the two men assigned to guard him. "Take him! Don't let him escape. Knock him on the head again, if you have to."

A squeal of protest from Quin was overtaken by a sudden medley of grunts and curses issuing from down the lane where the majority of the militiamen had gone after Indigo.

"Looks like our fellows have got your man, my lord."

A muddle of redcoats came into view from a street at right angles to the lane, dragging and pulling at someone who could not yet be seen. Francis caught sight of Hemp walking in the roadway, taking no part in the capture. He looked somewhat dishevelled from what could be seen. In a few moments, their captive became visible, hatless and battling all the way.

"It's Indigo all right, and he's not coming quietly."

Jaded with inaction, Ottilia opted to accompany Sybilla and Henrietta on their daily constitutional — not without opposition from her sister-in-law.

"Are you sure you are well enough, Ottilia? I am persuaded Francis would veto any such excursion."

Predictably, Sybilla took a contrary view. She was apt to gainsay her daughter, whatever opinion Harriet expressed. "She is no namby-pamby obedient wife, child. Ottilia is capable of making up her own mind."

"That is all very well, Mama, but your walks are arduous, as you very well know."

"Arduous? Poppycock! A few turns about the grounds will do Ottilia no harm."

"A few turns?" Harriet threw up her hands. "You walk for an hour or more and cover two or three miles. Pray don't try to deny it, for Miss Skelmersdale told me so."

A scorching look was cast upon the companion. "Jezebel! Reporting on me to my daughter behind my back? I ought to dismiss you upon the instant!"

Henrietta, as Ottilia noted, was hard put to it to keep from laughing outright, for her eyes were imps of mischief. "My dear ma'am, it is nothing of the kind. I merely explained my predicament in having difficulty keeping up with you. But by all means, throw me to the wolves if that is your wish."

Sybilla ignored this, turning on her daughter again. "I'll thank you to refrain from judging my actions, Harriet. At my time of life —□

"You are eminently capable of deciding your own fate," cut in Ottilia, "as am I. Pray don't trouble your head about me, Harriet. I shall dawdle along and stop the moment I feel fatigued."

The lady of the house sniffed, throwing a glare at her mother. "You may count yourself lucky to dawdle. Mama sets a brisk pace."

This time Henrietta jumped in, her tone soothing. "Not today, Lady Dalesford. The Fanshawe children will accompany us, and from what I have seen —□ with an amused glance towards Ottilia — "little Luke's investigations and his sister's determined instructing of him will provoke much delay and give Lady Fan frequent rests."

Ottilia laughed. "Well reasoned, Henrietta. Let us go before Pretty comes looking for me. She is nothing if not impatient."

In the event, with the children scampering ahead, their nurses in tow, the party maintained a desultory pace set by Sybilla herself, who made frequent enquiries as to Ottilia's condition.

"Are you yet tired, my dear child? No, no, do not rush. Let the children run. You look a trifle peaked, Ottilia. Do you wish to turn back?"

Answering with patience and much at random, Ottilia took pleasure in simply being out of doors as well as in the antics of her children. She was enjoying the sun on her face after the grey drizzle that had set in within hours of her last excursion to Newport Pagnell, although the skies were not altogether blue, intermittent grey clouds giving notice of more rain to come. She was even able to put out of mind thoughts of what might be happening at that town in the militia's hunt for the pirate and his associates. Francis had promised he would not run his head into trouble this time.

"I will be perfectly safe, Tillie. With Dalby and his men on the case, I have no need to interfere. Indeed, I shan't attempt it."

Ottilia had eyed him with a riffle of unease. "You say that, Fan, but one does not necessarily have to look for trouble to find it."

He had smiled and, to her joy, kissed her lightly as he was wont to do. "As we know all too well, my dear one. Don't fear for me. I have my pistol and Hemp will be with me."

She had sighed. "That is scarcely reassuring, my dearest."

"When you know how cautious I am?"

"When I know how delighted you are to be up and doing."

He grinned. "Merely because you can't? Fie, Tillie!"

She had to laugh. "Fiend!"

He had left her feeling a trifle less oppressed about the rift. Might she hope he was learning to overcome his disappointment? The reflection raised her mood and had much to do with her determination to leave off the shackles of fatigue.

The party made its leisurely way down to the riverbank, once Ottilia had assured the anxious dowager that she had no qualms about revisiting the site of her fall into the Ouse. On the contrary, she thought it an excellent opportunity to see whether she might dredge up details she had previously overlooked.

She was not so foolish, she assured her mother-in-law, as to venture onto the jetty, but a stroll along the bank, retracing her steps from that fateful day, might jog a hidden memory. Or so she hoped. From a position some feet away, Ottilia peered under the wooden outcrop. Could she have seen anyone hidden there? Her imagination painted for her a head bobbing in the water, but she knew it for her own invention. Any such image was in reality obscured by the outgrowth from the bank and the reeds almost touching the wooden underside of the jetty. Its end was clear of greenery, but Ottilia had to acknowledge it was unlikely her assailant had swum to that point before she set foot on the platform.

Nevertheless, the notion she had most certainly been watched from an unseen vantage point in the gloom below could not but disturb. Ottilia suppressed the uncomfortable sensations, instead raising her gaze upriver where a rowing boat was seen to be more or less drifting with the current. A man was seated with his back towards Ottilia, oars in hand, which he used to keep the small boat steady on its course down the middle of the river.

Ottilia watched its approach. As it came closer, it was borne in upon her that there were two occupants, the other seated opposite, facing the rower. The sun peeked out from behind a cloud just as the boat came abreast of where Ottilia stood. It splashed upon the second figure, a woman swathed in a green cloak. The hood was up, but a face was turned in Ottilia's direction.

Recognition flashed. The woman from the haberdasher's shop! Her pulse riding high, Ottilia tried to make out the girl's features. She received an impression merely, and a glimpse of the eyes. Watching her.

Belatedly, Ottilia switched her gaze to the rower. Too late. The boat was already floating downstream and the man's hat shadowed his face. Ottilia watched until the boat turned into the bend and disappeared from sight.

"Are you fatigued, Lady Fan? You look perfectly white."

"That girl." Unguarded, Ottilia blurted her thoughts. "In the boat. I have seen her before."

"Gracious, where?"

"In a shop in Newport Pagnell." She turned and met Henrietta's gaze. "I think she may be Percy Pedwardine's wife."

"Good heavens!" Henrietta blinked, looking after the boat. "How could you know that?"

"I cannot know. I don't know. It is pure speculation. Alice spoke of a man waiting for her outside when she bought a fan there."

"Who is Alice?"

Ottilia tugged at her scattered thoughts. "An assistant at the haberdasher's. Pardon me, I am in a trifle of shock."

Henrietta's concern was clear in her eyes. "I can see that. Forgive my saying so, but are you not rather leaping to conclusions?"

Ottilia gave a somewhat hysterical laugh. "You may well say so." She drew a steadying breath. "But this cannot be coincidence. She looked straight at me."

"If that is all —□

"Why me? Why not the children playing over there? That would be a more natural sight to draw a woman's attention."

"Well, if you put it like that, I must concede you have a point."

They were interrupted. "What is amiss? Ottilia, why are you looking as if the world has landed upon your shoulders?"

"Am I, Sybilla?" She gave an unconvincing laugh. "Perhaps it has."

She did not know whether or not to be pleased when Henrietta took it upon herself to enlighten Sybilla, as far as she was able. At least it gave her a chance to recover a modicum of her customary sangfroid — much needed at the onslaught of her mother-in-law's response.

"Heavens above, child, will you be starting at shadows? This must be nothing but an irritation of the nerves, Ottilia."

"No, it is not. I admit it may seem fanciful, but I must hold to my observation."

"Yes, that is your forte, is it not?"

Notwithstanding the companion's encouragement, Ottilia felt compelled to explain further, as if she needed to settle it all in her own mind.

"This woman has now been seen three times. Upon two occasions in company with a man who does not show himself. He is too canny to risk exposure. He knows he will be recognised. But the girl cannot be identified, nor associated with him. From my experience of his methods, it would be just like him to use her for his own ends."

Sybilla pursed her lips, also looking along the river as if to verify Ottilia's having seen what she described. "I will vouch for it that the fellow has gall enough. But why then show himself at all?"

"By rowing past the Dalesford estate, you mean, ma'am? That has me in a puzzle too, Lady Fan."

Impatience crept into Ottilia's breast. "He did not show himself. His face was shadowed by his hat. He came, if it was he —▢

"Then you admit there is doubt."

"— to verify for himself that I had survived. Or — and that is where the doubt arises, Sybilla — to see if he might catch sight of me or Francis, having heard of our presence in the vicinity. That assumes he was not the villain of the piece."

Henrietta tutted. "You give him a little too much leeway there, I fear. Why should he care if he did not try to drown you?"

"He cares because, as I said the other day, he no doubt believes I am the author of his misfortunes."

"Poppycock! He brought it on himself."

"True, Sybilla, but he will scarcely see it in that light."

Henrietta's excitement was plain. "It all hinges on whether that woman really is his wife. How are we to find it out?"

Ottilia had no answer and Sybilla chose to take another tack. "Does this mean you will absolve this pirate fellow and his accomplice?"

"By no means. Do not forget that we have a corpse on our hands."

"This barmaid? But you don't know who killed her either."

"It is rather obvious, do you not think? Coincidence ought always to be suspect. Indigo, Quin and Cherry in the same vicinity? The connection positively glares."

Sybilla fell silent for a space. Ruminating? It was left to Henrietta to jerk at the core of Ottilia's discontent. "What do you mean to do next, Lady Fan?"

She sighed. "That is just the difficulty, Henrietta. I do not know. I have never had so little control over a like situation. The principals are out of my reach. I have no one to question. It feels very much an impasse."

"But has not Lord Francis gone to catch this pirate fellow?"

Ottilia let out a frustrated sound. "Even if he does — or rather, if the militia are successful in their mission to capture him — it will not necessarily help my purpose. From my husband's previous encounter with him, the man is altogether taciturn. He would certainly not admit to having laid a plot to encompass my death."

Sybilla shivered. "I wish you will not speak so, Ottilia."

"Well, it is what was intended, Sybilla."

"But the attempt failed. You are very much alive."

For how long? But Ottilia did not say it. She was aware, though nothing had been said, that Francis was in a constant state of anxiety upon this point. Ottilia knew him so well, she was alerted to his thoughts by his moods. He had been as wakeful at night as was she, although she hoped he supposed she slept. Her worry centred more on the state of her marriage than her possible demise at the hands of an assassin. But it was the bugbear under which Francis dwelled every time she became involved in one of these wretched murders. She regretted that it was so. She understood. Even his being part of the expedition today had the power to dismay her with horrid thoughts of her spouse injured, or worse. She ought to solve this puzzle only to allay Fan's fears for her safety. The inherent difficulty of so doing chafed her.

On the whole she was glad when Henrietta became insistent. "Be that as it may, there must be something you can do. What if you went in search of this woman?"

"For heaven's sake, Henrietta, what in the world are you saying? How could she know where to search?"

"I don't know, ma'am. The haberdasher's, perhaps?" Ignoring a grumbling rebuttal from her employer, Henrietta persisted. "It strikes me that if she is so interested in looking for you, Lady Fan, you have only to make yourself available to be found."

Ottilia's mind leapt and she laughed. "How right you are, Henrietta! Thank you. I ought to have fathomed that out for myself. I fear I must still be fatigued for my brain to be so sluggish."

Henrietta grinned in obvious delight. "I count it a triumph to have beaten you to the post."

"Yes, that is all very well," snapped Sybilla, "but you are asking Ottilia to court the very danger we fear by requiring her to expose herself."

Henrietta's face fell. "I had not thought of that."

Ottilia became brisk. "Nonsense. I shall be perfectly safe. Be sure I will go nowhere without my husband to protect me. It is of no use to go to Newport Pagnell, for we cannot know if we have drawn them out. We will visit Buckingham, I think. It is bound to be busier than Newport Pagnell and no one could hope to attack me in the middle of a crowded street."

"But what is the point of it, Ottilia?"

"Well, if I am being observed, my observer may follow me. If that girl appears in Buckingham, I think we can be certain she is tracking me."

CHAPTER FOURTEEN

Francis eyed the sometime pirate through the bars of his cell. The man was hunched against the wall, the bull-like head resting on his raised knees. Ignoring the straw bale covered in hessian placed for his comfort, Indigo had chosen the cold stone floor, as if to emphasize his contempt for the authorities who had him in charge.

It had proved impossible to put any questions at the site of his capture, since Indigo did not cease struggling for an instant. No word came out of his mouth, but he bellowed and grunted his protests, drawing attention from every passer-by as the militiamen dragged him through the streets. By the time the exhausted redcoats had reached the local prison, they had attracted a crowd of onlookers who dispersed only when the prisoner was hauled inside and the massive gates were shut in their faces.

Francis, thanks to Hemp's quick thinking, had just managed to get in ahead of the closure. They had perforce dropped back, leaving Dalby and his sergeant to keep the curious from crowding the struggling redcoats.

"I see the prison ahead, milord. If we don't catch up, we may be excluded." So saying, Hemp began shouldering a way through, his height giving him an advantage.

Francis followed close and they slipped through the gate as the prison staff were shoving the doors to. He caught up with Captain Dalby, who was conferring with an official in the lobby. The battle to get Indigo incarcerated could be heard from a corridor beyond.

"Give me leave, Dalby."

The captain turned his head. "Still with us, my lord?"

"I'm not leaving until I've had words with that fellow."

Dalby cast up his eyes. "Just as you wish. Can't say I'm looking forward to chatting with him myself."

Francis shared a glance with Hemp. "You will find him taciturn. He wastes no words, as I remember. But it ought to be vastly different questioning him in these circumstances. Last time, he had all the advantage and sent his bully boys after us."

The captain blew out a breath. "After his conduct today, nothing would surprise me. I doubt my men will recover for a twelvemonth."

From behind Francis, he heard Hemp clear his throat, drawing Dalby's attention. He glanced from Francis to Hemp. "Something to say?"

"Yes, sir." There was no note of servitude in Hemp's tone. Francis knew his pride and applauded it.

"You would be well advised to hear anything my steward can offer, Dalby. He knows Indigo of old."

The captain's manner altered and he turned to Hemp. "Say on. I am all ears."

A faint, brief smile crossed Hemp's mouth. "It is a small thing, sir, but may be of use. Indigo has shown himself a master of escape."

Dalby uttered a short laugh. "I defy him to get out of this place. It's not one of your fortresses like the one in Buckingham, but it's secure enough."

Hemp's deep voice became a trifle grim. "So thought the authorities in the West Indies, sir. Not only did Indigo escape from his slave compound, when he was captured, he effected an escape from prison. Twice. He evaded the law for years, sailed his ship to England, absconded again from Bristol and has been at large until today."

"Hm." Dalby fingered his chin. "I'd best have him manacled."

From the expression in Hemp's eyes, Francis knew what he was thinking. "I imagine he must have been manacled in the past, Dalby."

"Well, what would you have me do? It's not in my purview in any event, once I hand him over to Stuckey here."

The individual named spoke up. "Don't you worry none, sir. I'll have him so trussed up he can scarce move."

But when Francis at last succeeded in securing his turn at confronting the putative Captain Indigo, the man was neither trussed nor manacled. The cell had stout bars, however, and it was notable he had been given a single occupancy instead of being housed in a dormitory with other felons who had not yet been charged or were on remand awaiting trial.

Though he must have heard approaching footsteps, he paid no heed. The turnkey hovered for a moment until Francis signed to him to withdraw. He shifted along the corridor and set his shoulders against the wall, taking out a toothpick and plying it as if he was settling in for a long wait.

"Indigo!"

The forceful calling of his name brought the man's head up. His countenance was streaked with red where he had bled from encounters with militia fists. The eyes Francis recalled from their previous meeting ran over him, as enigmatic as the man he remembered. He did not speak. Francis opened negotiations.

"It's a while since we last met."

Nothing. With a rise of irritation, he reflected how this was just the way the man had behaved upon the last occasion. He tried a different tack.

"I owed you the beating you've taken today."

A grunt came. "How?"

"You know how. You sent your ruffians to intercept me. I trust one of them still suffers aches from his leg wound."

To his surprise, the prisoner emitted a deep bark of a laugh. "Acquitted yourself good. Didn't expect it."

"I learned a trick or two in the army."

"Soldier?"

"Not for years, but you don't forget."

The bull head nodded. "Long memory, me."

Francis seized on this. "That is what I supposed. Have you been cherishing a grudge against my wife?"

Indigo's head rose the more. "Why so?"

Francis did not hesitate. "Because she found out the murderer and you thought she sent the Bristol authorities after you. Or perhaps it was rather Cherry who was thirsting for revenge. Did you assist her to achieve that ambition, I wonder?"

Indigo did not answer, merely regarding him with a look that might have spelled danger were he not behind bars. Francis pressed on.

"I dare say Cherry was with you from the start. You both disappeared at around the same time. Quin then joined you after he lost his employment. Dalby will no doubt have you both charged with the various robberies that have been carried out in these parts. For my part, there is a more pertinent question."

The gaze was malevolent, but at least Indigo spoke this time. "What?"

What if he took a less accusatory tone? Worth a try. "Someone is threatening my wife's very life. Maybe you. Or Quin. Or another."

"Who?"

"That I don't know. But Cherry is dead. Someone broke her neck and threw her into the river. I don't wish to see my wife served the same way."

Another grunt. "Think I'd do so?"

Should he say outright that he suspected him of killing Cherry? He compromised. "You are capable of it."

Indigo lifted his hands from his knees and inspected them, turning them this way and that, as if he sought to fathom his capacity for himself. Or was it remembrance of jerking Cherry's neck?

It was a moment before he spoke, setting his hands down first and looking directly at Francis. "Want me to find out?"

Astonished, Francis blurted the first thing in his head. "You mean who is after my wife?"

"For a price."

The leap of hope subsided. "What price?"

Indigo jerked his head at the cell walls. "Get me out."

A disbelieving laugh shook Francis. "Have you lost your mind? I have no authority to secure your release. Nor would I do so if I had."

The pirate's mouth twisted in a sneering smile. "Pox on authority. Use cunning. Intelligent, you are. Can work out how. Get me out, I'll find him."

While he had no intention of complying with this outrageous remark, Francis was struck by the offer. Would Indigo make it if he was Tillie's would-be assailant? He had little doubt the pirate could indeed find out what he would give much to know. Indigo was bound to have established acquaintance with those who scraped a living hunting information. But this fellow was as wily as a jackal. He gave nothing away. Francis would in truth feel a deal easier about Tillie with the pirate safely ensconced in gaol.

"Buckingham? Why there, Tillie?"

"Because it will force that girl and her escort to come after me. It won't fadge to go to Newport Pagnell, for that won't tell us if she is indeed tracking my movements. But the extra distance to Buckingham would make it certain. It would be too much of a coincidence to suppose they could go there from choice upon the same day we choose to go. Now that Cherry is dead and both Indigo and Quin are incarcerated, it becomes imperative to lure out the other suspects."

Ottilia had waited to propound her scheme until she had heard her husband's account of the capture, told to the company at large gathered in the family parlour. All three windows were open, letting air into the room, where the chairs and occasional tables were often shifted to where they might be needed on any particular occasion rather than being placed in specific locations. It gave the parlour a higgledy-piggledy look and made for an atmosphere of calm and comfort, singularly lacking today.

Since Sybilla chose to refer to the sighting of the cloaked woman in a rowing boat, Ottilia had no choice but to tell her tale. Harriet's alarm was voluble.

"Heavens, Ottilia, how frightening!" Then, to her husband who had only just come in from a tour of his estate with his agent, "Gil, you ought to have them found and laid by the heels!"

Gil had remained unimpressed. "Upon what charge, my love? It is no crime to row a boat down the Great Ouse."

"Well, but clearly Ottilia is not *safe*. Fan, you cannot be complacent, I am persuaded."

"Far from it, my dear sister. But Gil is right. We must be practical."

"Then what is to be done?"

Sybilla cut in, her tone sharp. "You are not the only one to be concerned, child, but have no fear. Ottilia has the matter in hand. Have you not, my dear?"

Aware of her husband's gaze, in which she recognised a like alarm to that expressed by her hostess, Ottilia opted to play this down. "Hardly, Sybilla." She looked to her spouse. "I had it in mind to show myself abroad. Only with your escort," she added in haste, going on to explain why she had thought of Buckingham.

Francis was clearly dubious. "I am inclined to agree that Indigo may not be our man."

"Just so. Which leaves us with the other alternative."

"You expect to draw him out?"

"Well, the woman rather. I am persuaded our clever Percy won't show himself."

"If it is indeed he. But I take your point."

Ottilia smiled across at him. "I knew you would understand."

He grimaced. "Understand, yes. But don't imagine I am enamoured of such a scheme."

"For heaven's sake, Francis!" Sybilla burst out. "Do you expect her to remain hidden away forever?"

From his expression, Ottilia guessed that he would much prefer that option, but his tone remained neutral. "That would be ineligible, ma'am."

"Then you must allow her to eliminate the threat," stated Sybilla, just as if the entire exercise was not centred upon this goal.

Impatience showed in Francis's face. "I know that, ma'am, but you cannot expect me to favour the prospect of rendering my wife a sitting target."

"What then, Fan?" This from Gil, who was pouring himself a refill from the decanter on a tray set upon the sideboard.

"For my part, you should leave the matter in Dalby's hands. Ottilia must be safe in this house."

She quashed this at once. "I thank you, Gil, but I do not care to wait upon the captain's convenience. Nor is he *au fait* with the history connecting these people to me." She threw a glance at Francis, propping up the mantelpiece as usual. "Fan is reluctant, but I believe he trusts me to know how to act."

Her spouse met her gaze. "I do. I don't have to like it, however."

Francis said no more before others, but when they were alone in their chamber, he spoke his mind with greater freedom.

"I appreciate your impatience, my dear one, but this scheme is fraught with danger."

"Why so, Fan? They cannot molest me in the middle of the street, especially in Buckingham."

"I can't imagine why you should think so. Too sanguine by half. I can think of a dozen ways by which they might, and every one gives me palpitations."

Ottilia moved closer and set a hand to his chest. "I love you for caring so much, my darling lord, only do but think a little."

"Well?"

"Would he wish to cause such a stir in a public place? Whoever it was under the jetty, he took care to remain hidden, and indeed vanished immediately after, presumably under cover of the efforts you made to retrieve me."

Francis grasped the hand and held it tightly. "That is just it, Tillie. Are you naïve enough to suppose that he could not melt away just as readily in the open street?"

She pulled away a little. "Perhaps. I hold that it would be a deal more problematic. Besides that, Fan, we are on the watch for it. That first attack came out of the blue."

Francis did not release her hand, his voice growing a trifle harsh. "And you think I would be willing to leave you, injured or dying, and race after the assailant instead? You must have windmills in your head!"

Her eyes pricked, but she spoke the first thought in her mind. "You are hurting me, Fan!"

His brows snapped together. Ottilia glanced at their joined hands and Francis released hers on the instant. Instinct made her cradle the fingers where he had been gripping too hard. She caught his gaze and read contrition there, overlaid with his still roiling emotion. She tried to mitigate the damage.

"It is easing now. Don't think of it."

His eyes rimmed with moisture but he did not take her into his arms as she half expected. "I cannot live like this."

Her heart cracked. Her voice became husky. "Then let us settle it, my dearest darling. Let us find him out and stop it."

He drew a breath that rasped in Ottilia's ears. "Will that solve it? End it? What about the next time? And the next?"

Aghast, Ottilia stared at him. "You want me to give up altogether. You want me to promise never to investigate another murder."

A bitter laugh came. "You might promise. You wouldn't keep it."

Her temper flared. "I would never make that promise! How could I? I don't seek these things out, Fan. They cross my path."

"Because you have acquired a reputation. Don't I know it!"

He flung away towards the window. About to retaliate, Ottilia was interrupted by a knock and the entrance of Joanie, closely followed by Diplock.

Francis swung round. "Not now! Out!"

Two startled faces looked from him to Ottilia. Compelled, she spoke out. "Give us a few moments, if you please."

The instant the door closed behind her maid and her spouse's valet, she crossed the room to confront him. "Francis, pray let us end this. I do understand how —☐

"No, you don't. You don't understand it at all." The anger was gone from his voice, but the corroding despair was worse. "For near four and twenty hours, I believed you were lost to me. The fear that has haunted me all through our marriage became real. Ironic, as it seemed before I knew the truth, that you died by accident."

"I didn't die, Fan."

He shook his head. "You might as well have done."

A hideous freeze overtook Ottilia's bosom. "What does that mean?"

He drew a heavy breath. "It means that you were killed that day, murdered, just as my deepest fears have pictured you. I know now how it feels. I can't live any longer with that fear. I can't go through that again."

Ottilia did not take her eyes from his face, a dead weight descending upon her chest. "Then you leave me no choice."

"I know it." He sounded spent. "We will go to Buckingham as you wish. Hemp will be the lookout." He moved past her and went towards the door, calling out to the waiting servants to enter.

Dressing felt mechanical, and Ottilia wondered vaguely how she was to get through dinner under the eyes of her relatives. Fortunately, Sybilla, noticing her wan looks, took it for fatigue.

"You have overdone it, Ottilia. I should not have permitted you to accompany me."

"Did I not say so at the outset, Mama?"

Harriet's intervention provoked the usual bickering between mother and daughter, which at least permitted Ottilia to withdraw from making any response.

In a bid, she supposed, to divert his wife's mind, Gil instituted a discussion about their forthcoming plans to visit their newly married daughter at some point in the months ahead, which lasted until dinner was over.

Her mother-in-law's remarks made it easy for Ottilia to plead fatigue and retire before the tea tray was brought in. Francis did not accompany her, for which she did not know whether to be aggrieved or glad. In the event, having rung for Joanie, she was snug in bed and able to have her cry out before her husband appeared.

Ottilia pretended sleep, having no desire to renew the painful discussion. She heard the curtains as Francis closed them on his side, felt the mattress give as he got into bed and the blackness descend over her closed eyes when he blew out the candle.

He settled prone at her side, the little distance between them an ocean. Ottilia felt the tears coming again and struggled to hold them back. Never, since the first night of their marriage, had her husband failed to draw her into his embrace, soothing her to sleep. Or loving her first. The ache in her breast intensified.

Safe to open her eyes, she stared up at the dark of the tester above, willing her tears away and swallowing down the rising sobs. It seemed an age she remained thus, her heart in pieces. She knew Francis was awake. The sound of his sleeping breath was too familiar to be mistaken. His despair was palpable to her, as deep as her own.

Then came a convulsive movement beside her. He had turned. His strong arms swept her up and dragged her to him, holding her blessedly close, his whispers warm in her ear.

"Don't weep, my darling heart, don't weep, for I can't bear it."

But the very words were enough to set her off. She cried into his shoulder, hands clutching about his chest, tight, tight, as if she could never let him go. His embrace cradled her, his hand stroking the tresses released from bondage. Inconsequently, Ottilia recalled that she had forgotten her routine, brushing only desultorily before she set the implement down and clambered into bed, there to weep out her distress as she was doing now.

She hardly heard the murmurs in her ear. That they were words of love was balm enough, calming her at length so that her grip about him relaxed.

Francis released her with one hand, groping under his pillow. Ottilia found a handkerchief thrust into her fingers. She pushed up, made use of it, blowing the bout of weeping away.

She looked down at the shadow of her husband's head on the pillow, her eyes accustoming to the dark enough to be able to make out the shape of his face, the high cheekbones and the stubborn chin. He spoke out of the darkness.

"We will weather this, sweetheart."

Her heart flipped. "Can we, Fan? Truly?"

"We have to. I love you too much to endure any degree of separation."

Ottilia sniffed up the last of the moistures and settled back into his shoulder, snuggling now. "You know you are the world to me, Fan."

He turned his face and kissed her forehead. "It is mutual, you know."

A tiny gurgle escaped her. "I am glad. You do realise I would never let you escape me. Even if I die, I will haunt you forever."

She heard his laugh with a rise of pleasure. "Yes, you would make a mischievous ghost, wretch of a female."

Heart full again, she was silent for a space. But the deep-seated guilt that plagued her rose up. "Fan?"

"Hm?"

"If you want me to make that promise…"

She faded out, but he turned his head and set a finger to her lips. "Make me no promises. Whatever comes, we will deal with it."

"But —

"Hush! Don't say it. Let it lie, Tillie. Go to sleep."

Protest rose up. "I am not Pretty, Fan. You can't command me to sleep."

"But I can persuade you." There was a laugh in his voice, but it faded from Ottilia's mind as his lips sought hers.

CHAPTER FIFTEEN

The prison warder, one of the juniors to the fellow Stuckey who had taken in the captives, did not take kindly to Hemp's request.

"Why d'you want to talk to him? You ain't the law. Nor yet you ain't no lawyer."

Hemp drew on the power of rank. "I am acting for Lord Francis Fanshawe. I am his steward."

The warder, a burly fellow possessed of a belligerence he seemed to consider necessary to his calling, visibly adjusted his ideas at the mention of a member of the peerage. But he thrust up his chin nevertheless. "You are, are you? And what's his lordship want with the likes of that little rat we got cornered?"

Nothing but actual fact would serve, Hemp reasoned. "Milady his wife was attacked a little over a week ago. His lordship has reason to believe this rat of yours could be responsible."

The official champed awhile, ruminating as he ran his eyes over Hemp for the umpteenth time. "Suppose that changes things, do you?"

"I know this fellow of old. We share something of our backgrounds. I am from Barbados and he lived there once. Lord Francis therefore wishes me to conduct these enquiries."

"Ho! He does, does he?"

"He does." Hemp waited, preserving a neutral stance. In truth, the warder had no power to gainsay a lord. Nor was Quin as yet charged with any crime. He and Indigo had only been in the gaol a matter of two days and the law moved slowly in these parts, it seemed. It was politic, Hemp felt, with a man such as the warder was proving himself to be, to refrain from pointing these things out.

At length, the warder gave in. "Well, I don't see as there's harm in letting you talk to him." He moved to a small chamber set off to one side of the hallway that opened to the main dormitory. "You can wait in my office. I'll bring him to you."

Hemp thanked him and passed into the room. It was bare but for a table with a couple of rickety chairs set either side and a small bookcase against the wall, its shelves bulging with untidy stacks of papers and a ledger, plus odds and ends. Hemp spotted candle stubs, an inkpot, a cracked bowl and a stubby club on the bottom shelf. A high barred window gave notice that the room might at one time have been used for a cell.

Presently, a shuffling of footsteps signalled the approach, he hoped, of his quarry.

The warder was heard beyond the door. "In there!"

The ratty little man stumbled in, thrust by an unseen hand. Quin righted himself, took one look at Hemp, gave forth a curse and turned sharp about. As he attempted to exit the room, he ran straight into the thick form of the warder.

"No, you don't. Get back in there!"

Quin snuffled. "Don't want ter talk to him. Don't want to see him neither."

"Ho! And you think I'm interested in what you want or don't want, do you? I say you get in there and answer his questions. Understand?"

Quin shrunk away from the threatening fist, whimpering.

Hemp took a hand. "Thank you. I will deal with him now. Pray close the door."

The warder looked none too pleased to be thus directed, and might have refused had not Quin intervened.

"No! Leave it open! He's a bully, he is. I don't trust him!"

That was enough for the warder, who took to a roar. "You'll do as I say and like it! Sit!" He pointed to the near chair.

Hemp almost felt sorry for Quin as he scurried to obey, sinking into the chair and burying his head in his closed fists, elbows on the table.

"Right then. All yours, mister. If he gives you any trouble, I'll be right outside." The warder left the room and pointedly slammed the door.

Hemp took his seat in the chair across from the prisoner and waited a moment to speak, looking over his quarry. A couple of days in gaol had grimed and wrinkled his clothes, rendering him ragged and a trifle pathetic. Hemp hardened his heart. His silence had an effect. Quin raised his head enough to peer at him from under his brows.

Hemp began. "We meet again, my friend." The pleasant tone availed him nothing.

"What do you want with me?"

Hemp produced a false smile. "I'm interested in your welfare, can you doubt it?"

"Ha! You want to do me fer that Cherry, is it? You and that there Lord Fan."

"As a matter of fact, I'm not interested in Cherry. And it's Lady Fan I serve, as you well know."

Quin sat up straighter. "She knows I never done nothing."

"In Bristol? Perhaps not. But she finds it an odd coincidence that you are here. Following her, were you?"

Quin's shoulders hunched. "Why would I? Never want to see her no more, I don't. Never want to see none of 'em again."

175

"Yet you are presently residing in Newport Pagnell in company with Captain Indigo. And Cherry, I presume, before she was killed."

His victim became agitated. "I don't know nothing of that business. I told that lord of yours, I did."

Time to turn the screw. "He didn't believe you. Nor do I."

"It's the truth, so help me. I never touched her!"

"I don't suppose you did. But it's useless to pretend you weren't here in her train. We caught you with Indigo."

Resentment clouded the little man's eyes and he kept his lips firmly shut. Hemp returned to the more important question. "Did you know milady was at Dalesford Hall?"

"How should I?" The tone was sullen.

"You know of Lord Dalesford?"

Quin's eyes widened for an instant and narrowed again. "Who don't? Owns half the county hereabouts, by all accounts."

An exaggeration, but it was true the Dalesford estates were extensive. The connection of the family to the Fanshawes might well be outside the fellow's knowledge, Hemp conceded. But the coincidence remained. Milady did not trust coincidences. He changed tack. "It's a wide river, the Great Ouse." A shrug was the only answer. "Deep and fast flowing too."

"So? I seen it. Who ain't?"

"A person could easily drown."

Not a flicker. If anything, Quin outstared him. Either he knew nothing of milady's fall or he thought Hemp was badgering him about Cherry. Let him make it clear, then. "Do you know who nearly drowned, Quin?"

The man became sullen again. "Don't know nothing about no drowning."

"Lady Fan."

Quin blinked. "What?"

"Lady Fan. Milady. She nearly drowned in the Ouse."

"She ain't never!"

Was this genuine surprise? "She would have done if she hadn't been rescued." Hemp hit hard. "You didn't expect that, did you? You thought you'd done your part when you seized her ankle and pulled her in." There was that in the man's face which might have been dawning horror, but he did not speak. Was it an act? "Was it Indigo who told you to do it? Or Cherry?"

Quin's head began to shake in negation. "He never said. Nor she neither. You can't pin that on me. I never done it. Why would I? I ain't got no quarrel with her."

"But Cherry had a quarrel with her, a big one. Cherry had to abscond from Bristol because of Lady Fan, didn't she? What's more, the authorities there are after her. They're after Indigo too. He might not blame milady, but Cherry likely did, didn't she?"

"Don't know nothing of that." A sudden look of malevolence crossed his face. "If it'd been you now…"

Hemp was startled into a laugh. "You'd have pulled me in? You'd have caught cold at that, my friend."

"I ain't your friend, not by a long chalk. Nor I never wants to see your face again." With an abrupt movement, he stood up. "You done? Can I go now?"

Hemp rose too, lowering over the table. "Sit down again, Quin."

Quin sat, folding into himself and tucking his hands into his pockets.

Hemp retook his seat and eyed the fellow. He was inclined to believe him innocent, of attempted murder at least. But he had shown himself capable of lying and Hemp did not trust his words, any of them. He sighed in frustration. "Let's put our cards on the table, shall we? Then we'll be done with this and you can go."

Quin sniffed. "Says you."

Hemp ignored this. "I'll start. It's not my business to resolve the Cherry murder. Nor have I aught to do with who committed the robberies in these parts."

"Well?"

"What I want to know is what brought you to Newport Pagnell?"

A fleeting grin passed over the fellow's mouth. "A man got ter live."

"By thieving? Why here?"

Quin shrugged again. "Ask him. Ain't nowise my choice."

Which was as much as to admit he was in a string with Indigo. Not that there could be any doubt.

"How long have you been wandering about the country? All of three years?"

"Nah. Been in Lunnon mostly. Come 'ere weeks back. Better pickings out of the capital, he say."

Then it was Indigo who chose this place. Before milady came here, it would seem. But that did not mean the trio had not discovered her presence in the area. In all likelihood, they would have heard of it since Lord Dalesford was the great man hereabouts and his daughter's wedding had been a fairly public affair. Hemp recalled how crowds of estate workers and tenants had lined the route from Dalesford Hall to the church. It was all too credible that the Fanshawes' attendance was common knowledge.

Short of torturing Quin until he either confessed or demonstrated he knew nothing of the attack on milady, Hemp was at an impasse. His mistress would never approve of such a proceeding. Nor did it appeal. He disliked using violence unless he was driven to it.

Mayhap it mattered little, he reflected. If Quin had indeed done the deed, neither he nor Indigo were at large and milady was safe from harm at their hands.

Having released the fellow into the dubious care of the warder, Hemp made his way back through the open square likely used for exercise towards the main entrance block. When he arrived at the prison lobby, he was about to leave by the main door when his attention was caught by a gentleman with a protruding stomach that gave him a portly appearance, who was in conversation with the porter. Recognition hit. As he waited for a suitable moment, he struggled to recall the name of the justice who had handled the business involving Doro at Bristol.

At length, the porter touched a finger to his forelock. "If you wait here, sir, I'll fetch Mr Stuckey to you."

"I thank you." The man watched the porter take his leave into the prison square and then turned, what time Hemp accosted him, the name rising to his lips.

"Justice Belchamp?"

The magistrate looked up at him with an expression of enquiry which rapidly changed to surprise. "Bless my soul! You are Lady Fan's fellow, if I am not mistaken."

Hemp gave a short bow. "I am, sir. Hemp Roy, her steward."

"Ah, it was your doing she came to Bristol, was it not? Looking to get that girl released."

"Correct, sir." He threw a glance at the door through which the porter had disappeared. "I take it you have come for Captain Indigo?"

Justice Belchamp snorted. "Much good may it do me! Seems the fellow has been raiding houses all about the county. Not to mention becoming a suspect in a couple of murders here. Mere piracy comes a poor second, according to the captain of militia I spoke to earlier."

Hemp gave a wry grin. "Better he is out of circulation either way."

"Yes, if he doesn't escape. I hear from this fellow Dalby that he makes a habit of it. He's evaded my thieftaker for nigh on three years."

Hemp was gratified to learn his warning to the militia captain had gone home. "I am sorry you have had a wasted journey."

Justice Belchamp pursed his lips. "No such thing. I'm glad Lord Francis alerted me. We may at least close the books on the case, assuming that miscreant is properly brought to justice."

"Had you in mind to visit Lady Francis, sir?"

"I certainly shan't leave the area without paying my respects. I must see the warder and confront this Indigo first, however. I'd be glad of directions to Dalesford Hall. Perhaps you can furnish such?"

"I can wait and direct you, if you wish. Are you in your own carriage, sir?"

In deference to her husband's distress, Ottilia made no mention of the Buckingham scheme, even when it came to the Monday morning. She had refrained from speaking of the matter all through Sunday, when nothing could be done, in any event. The entire party had attended St Peter's Church in Gothurst and thereafter spent a lazy day. She was both touched and grateful when her sister-in-law made an unexpected announcement.

"I instructed my housekeeper to make up another basket for that family, Ottilia."

"Heavens, Harriet, how kind! What made you think to do that?"

"Well, with all these dreadful goings-on, I have begun to realise more and more how very much indebted we are to that woman you spoke of."

"Meggotty. She is a treasure, Harriet." On impulse, Ottilia embraced her. "And so are you! Thank you, a thousand times."

Harriet brushed this off. "Well, it is not as if they are outsiders. If that fellow is a forester, he is in Gil's employ. I will make it my business to send them regular supplies."

Ottilia was a little concerned her rescuer might take offence at too much charity, so down-to-earth a woman was Meggotty. She owed her survival to the elderly dame, however, and could not gainsay her sister-in-law's kind intention. She resolved to visit Meggotty when all was over and discover for herself how the gifts were received.

She had been glad meanwhile of the enforced rest of the Lord's day and was feeling a good deal more herself by Monday morning. Yet she hesitated to speak of the planned excursion. She felt it politic and kinder to give Francis the lead.

As it chanced, Captain Dalby arrived soon after breakfast with the announcement that he had turned the whole matter of Indigo and Quin over to the justices of the district.

"It is not my task to bring them to trial, I am happy to say. The justice will have his fellows conduct any investigations among those who have been robbed."

Ottilia could not keep back the question burning on her tongue. "What of Cherry? Do they mean to bring that murder home to him?"

The captain shrugged. "As far as I am aware, the coroner has accepted the doctor's reading. He supposes it will be brought in unlawful killing by person or persons unknown."

Ottilia clicked her tongue. "Unknown fiddlesticks! Is not Indigo under suspicion?"

"That is a matter for the authorities here, my lady. It is out of my hands."

With difficulty, Ottilia held her tongue on a pithy retort. It seemed the captain was washing his hands of all responsibility. She could have kissed Francis when he intervened.

"A trifle convenient for Indigo, wouldn't you say, Dalby? I should have supposed a suspicion of his guilt in that incident might assist the authorities with the householder that was slain in a robbery."

"How so, my lord?"

"To demonstrate a capability of killing. Faced with two counts, a jury would find it hard to do other than convict."

Captain Dalby's brows went up. "You sound, if I may say so, particularly vengeful, sir."

Ottilia saw her spouse's jaw tighten and his eyes flash. "I am merely desirous of ensuring that fellow can do my wife no harm in the future."

"You believe he is responsible for that attack, then?"

"I don't yet know. I have sent my steward to see if he can break Quin into confessing as much."

Astonished, Ottilia threw him a questioning look. Why had he not told her? Yet the realisation he was working to ensure her safety could not but warm her heart. She was the more relieved that she had refrained from pestering him to go to Buckingham today.

Captain Dalby drew in a breath and let it out in a fashion decidedly resigned. "I see you are determined, my lord. What more may I do to assist?"

Ottilia threw caution to the winds. "There is something, Captain Dalby."

He turned to her. "My lady?"

She threw an apologetic glance at her spouse and plunged in. "We have reason to suspect another of causing my fall into the river."

"Indeed? Say on."

Nothing loath, and with a faint hope of appeasing Francis if the Buckingham trip proved unnecessary, Ottilia gave a fluent description of her encounters with the girl in the green cloak. The captain listened with attention, but his response was disappointing. "It is not much to go on."

Francis cut in with impatience. "We know that, sir. But in the absence of any other options, we must follow this one up."

"By all means, but what would you have me do?"

"I can answer that," Ottilia said, seizing back the initiative. "The girl's cloak is distinctive, and we have every reason to believe they are staying in Newport Pagnell. If they are watching me, as I suspect, I mean to draw them out and lead them away from their usual haunt, all the way to Buckingham. Thus we may be certain they are indeed tracking my movements."

"Ah, and you would wish my men to follow, or await you there?"

"I was rather thinking that they might keep an eye out for any such woman and verify whether she is accompanied, and by whom. But —□ with a hopeful look at her spouse — "it is not at all a bad notion to have a militia presence when we do make that trip."

To her mingled relief and pleasure, Francis became enthusiastic. "Excellent, Tillie. I should have thought of that. Well, Dalby, what do you say?"

The captain gave a decisive nod. "I will put my men at your service. We had better liaise on the most suitable day."

Ottilia pressed him further. "Meanwhile, will you have your men be on alert?"

"I will do better, ma'am. I'll post a couple of men in strategic positions to observe any approach to this estate by the said cloaked woman."

"Or anyone else suspicious," put in Francis. "We can't be sure of our quarry being yet identified."

The arrangements made, the captain departed, leaving Ottilia free to express her gratitude. "That was splendidly done, Fan, thank you."

His brow quirked. "A mutual effort, I think." He came close and cradled her cheek with one hand. "I admit I will feel a deal easier to have the militia at our backs."

Ottilia took the hand in hers and kissed his fingers. "You would have protected me without them, my champion."

"Flattery, Tillie?"

"Truth. I have every faith in my knight when he dons armour and mounts his white charger to come to my rescue."

He laughed quite in the old way and her heart rejoiced. "I'll remind you of that the next time you express doubts of my deductive powers."

"When have I ever done so?"

"You don't. You merely outguess me and leave me standing. It's the same thing."

"It is not at all the same thing, you fiendish husband." She released his hand. "Moreover, for this present, I am at sea. If I am wrong about the woman in the cloak being Percy's wife, I am stumped. I shall begin to believe I did imagine that hand tugging me in after all."

Francis gave a grimace. "You might. I won't. Whatever else, I trust your ability to note what happens around you, even in such an extremity." He gestured to the door. "You must be gasping for coffee by now, my addicted one, and I can certainly do with a tot of something soothing."

Ottilia was glad enough to comply, thoroughly encouraged by his words. He seemed altogether more relaxed, and she dared to hope the outburst of the other evening had enabled him to discharge a goodly measure of his distress.

After regaling the company, over coffee in the family parlour, with an account of the interview and what had been decided with Captain Dalby, Ottilia spent a little time watching the antics of her offspring in the children's garden. She then retired to rest in the bedchamber, chagrined to discover her fatigue had not entirely dissipated.

She was called out of this peaceful interlude by her spouse to greet an unexpected visitor, awaiting her in the large downstairs saloon.

"Mr Belchamp! How glad I am to see you again." She went forward with her hand held out.

The Bristol justice took it in his and shook it with vigour, smiling the while. "Mighty pleased myself, my dear lady. Had to thank his lordship and you for writing. I came as soon as I could spare the time. Not that I'm likely to benefit, since Indigo's supposed crimes here supersede my suspicions of his piracy. It is a pity that terrible woman is dead, but at least it saves us from the expense of taking her to court. How do you do, Lady Fan? As much in demand as ever, I surmise."

As he spoke, he was ushering her to a chair. She sat, gesturing him to do likewise. "Not in this instance. My services are not required."

"Just as well," put in her spouse, who had taken his customary stance at the mantel. "She has enough on her hands on her own account."

Mr Belchamp's countenance took on a serious mien. "So I have been hearing. Your steward fellow was telling me."

"You've seen Hemp?"

"Met him in the gaol, ma'am. He was kind enough to direct me and we talked on the way. Sound man, that."

"He is indeed. I am privileged to still have his services. Hemp has no need to remain in our employ."

"Yes, yes, but this attack upon your person is quite appalling, my lady."

It was plain his shock held more of his attention than Ottilia's potential loss of her steward. She allowed the change of subject, although it began to feel tedious to be obliged to repeat her story all over again.

Justice Belchamp expressed a good deal of dissatisfaction at the lack of progress in finding out the culprit and gave it as his opinion that Indigo was just the villain to have perpetrated such an assault.

"Except," broke in Francis, "that it now appears unlikely that it was he."

"Indeed, my lord?"

The interrogatory note prompted Francis to explain how Indigo had offered to find out the culprit if he would arrange his freedom, at which the justice gave a bark of harsh laughter.

"Devil take the man's impudence!"

"You echo my sentiments, Belchamp. It proves nothing, but equally neither Hemp nor myself were successful in provoking his accomplice to confess."

This seized Ottilia's attention. "Hemp had no success at all?"

"Well, it's plain Quin knows just what happened to Cherry, Hemp says, but he is not convinced the fellow had knowledge of what happened to you."

Ottilia was conscious of some slight disappointment. She would have been happy to compound for Quin and Indigo, rather than this woman who may or may not have married the other suspect. One could not help feeling sympathy for any woman caught in the toils of a man with such questionable morals. She could barely repress a sigh. "Which leaves us with that girl and her putative lover or husband."

Mr Belchamp chimed in here. "Is this whom you suspect?"

"Yes, and it is the only other avenue we have to explore."

A gleam entered the justice's eye and he rubbed his hands together in a way Ottilia remembered from their meetings in Bristol. "Ah, but there I think I may be of service to you, Lady Francis."

A rise of anticipation had Ottilia flicking a glance at her spouse, who looked equally interested. "Do not tell me you know of another who might wish to harm me?"

Mr Belchamp set a finger to the side of his nose. "Not as such. But hearing of your predicament has prompted a flash of memory. I admit I have not thought of that business for many months, for as you will appreciate, the calls upon me in the intervening time have been many and various."

"But what did you think of?" Francis spoke in the impatient tone Ottilia knew well. She was no less eager herself and looked a question.

"Yes, yes, I am coming to that, my lord." The justice turned back to Ottilia. "You will recall the mastermind behind those events, I believe?"

"Vividly. What of him?"

"Nothing of him. He has gone the way of all flesh and good riddance. What you may not know is that he had a family."

Francis cut in. "We knew he was married."

"With a collection of progeny. I discovered as much because I was obliged to endure a number of visits from the wife, pleading for clemency."

Ottilia could not refrain from speaking up. "Poor woman. Her situation might well be pitiful. Had she no resources?"

Mr Belchamp blew out his cheeks. "Unfortunately for the wife, her husband's felonious acts meant that his property and effects were forfeit to the Crown. I did what I could for her. Alerted the parish clerk, you know, and so forth. I even secured her a place in a milliners and put the eldest boy to an apprenticeship."

Ottilia's heart was touched and she would have asked for more, wondering if there might be something she could do, except that Francis forestalled anything she might have said.

"Are you saying you think this woman might be a possible suspect in our case here? Why, if you put her to work?"

The justice waved dismissive hands. "Not the wife, my lord, no, no. The son. And very possibly one older daughter."

Ottilia's gaze flew to her husband's and found him with brows raised. She hastened to push for more. "Why in the world might either one, or both, come after me?"

The justice blew out his cheeks. "I don't say they have, Lady Fan, I don't say that at all. But I well remember you were open to all possibilities."

"Just so, but is this even a possibility?"

"Perhaps. Faint, but perhaps."

"How so? Explain, man!"

"I am endeavouring to do so, my lord."

Unable to help throwing an admonitory glance at her spouse, Ottilia sought to soothe. "We keep interrupting you, do we not? Pray go on, sir."

The justice nodded, looking gratified. "The matter would not have come to my attention at all but for the fact that the fellow I persuaded to take on the boy came to me to complain of him." He sniffed in an overwrought sort of way. "One does one's poor best, yet one meets too often with ingratitude." His gaze went from Ottilia to Francis and back again. "I dare say you have guessed at it. The wretch broke his apprenticeship. Absconded. Nowhere to be found."

The pertinent issue struck Ottilia, but she had to be sure. "Do you mean to imply he took his sister with him?"

Belchamp struck his hands together. "Ha! Knew you would catch it upon the instant, Lady Fan." His glee subsided as he returned to his tale. "That is precisely what the mother seemed to believe. I accosted her, as you may suppose. The girl had departed from Bristol, telling no one of her intention."

"When was this?" Francis rapped out.

"Yes, Fan, I should like to know that too."

Mr Belchamp scratched his chin. "When was it now? Some time back. I told you I had not thought of it for some while."

"How long a while, Belchamp? Months? Years?"

"I wish I might remember precisely, my lord, but I don't. At least a year, in any event, that much I know. Perhaps more. It may have been in the autumn of '94 even, if not '95. Yes, now I think of it, the mother was worried for the girl's lack of a good coat to keep her warm in the coming winter."

Ottilia tried a bow at a venture. "I wonder, had the sister a cloak instead, perhaps?"

CHAPTER SIXTEEN

"But this is mad, Ottilia," objected Sybilla, banging the point of her parasol into the ground for emphasis. "Merely because this obscure girl may or may not be wearing a cloak?"

Ottilia, seated beside her mother-in-law on the bench shaded by the canopy of a mature birch tree, put up a finger. "A distinctive cloak, Sybilla." Then she let out a sigh. "Oh, it sounds ridiculous, does it not? Yet I cannot shake the suspicion there may be something in it."

At this, Henrietta spoke up. She was seated on a makeshift stool fashioned out of a cut log in one of the little glades that abounded in the Dalesford grounds. "Does this mean you are ready to discount the woman married to Percy?"

"By no means. Not that we have the slightest proof that she is married to him. Nor, if it comes to that, whether or not he is in the area."

The three women had come to rest after taking the air, Sybilla being insistent that Ottilia take advantage of the clement weather. "We will not go far. I have already taken my constitutional and we may dawdle to suit your pace."

If she could not be up and doing as she longed to be, Ottilia was quite ready to compound for a walk before it was time to dress for dinner. When Sybilla had demanded an update, she had related the discussions of the day.

"In fact," said that dame in a tone of dissatisfaction, "you have very little proof of anything, Ottilia."

"None at all. Except of the woman in the green cloak's determination to spy upon me."

"Poppycock! I submit that is but another instance of your imagination at work."

With difficulty, Ottilia suppressed a retort and was rewarded when Henrietta chose to champion her.

"It is hardly imagination that she fell into the river, ma'am. For my part, I agree with Lady Fan that the coincidences are too many to ignore." Her gaze flicked back to Ottilia before Sybilla could enter into dispute. "The question now seems to centre upon the identity of this woman."

"Also her alleged companion, if indeed he exists."

"There can be no doubt of that, Sybilla, since he was rowing the girl the other day."

The parasol beat an irritated tattoo upon the ground. "I was forgetting that. Very well then. Let us suppose for a moment there is substance to your suspicions."

Ottilia sighed. "I must suppose it, Sybilla. Otherwise, I will be forced to the conclusion my fall was purely an accident, and I know it was not."

Her mother-in-law ignored this. "Supposing it, I say, the task at hand seems to be to find out the fellow in the case."

"If she only knew how, ma'am."

Sybilla pointed her parasol at her companion. "Do not underestimate her, Henrietta. You have only once seen her in action. If — which I must stress — *if* there is a villain to be found, Ottilia will find him."

Ottilia had to laugh at yet another lightning *volte face*, for which her mother-in-law was famed. "I thank you for your approbation, Sybilla."

Henrietta's eyes had danced, but she grew sober immediately. "Have you any endeavour in mind other than this proposed trip to Buckingham?"

"I wish I had, but no." Ottilia looked back at Sybilla. "As to your suggestion of identifying the man, I wrote to Mr Gibbon, but so far no reply has been forthcoming."

"What do you hope for from him?"

"To find out what the brute in whose innocence he insisted on believing has been up to all these months."

"And whether he is indeed married?"

"Just so, Henrietta. If anyone knows, Mr Gibbon must. He may choose to ignore me, of course. He was disinclined to believe my account of that young man's involvement."

If she was truthful, the lack of any reply from Edmund Gibbon was a severe disappointment. He was the only real link she had without questioning the green-cloaked girl. At the least, she had hoped to be able to confirm or deny the possibility that the threat came from Percy. Without testimony from Mr Gibbon as to the man's present condition and whereabouts, she could only speculate, reliant upon gossip she could not substantiate.

It was therefore with some degree of excitement that she read, upon the following morning, a sealed note which the butler set down at her place the moment she had settled into her seat at the breakfast table.

"This was delivered early this morning, my lady. It did not come with the post."

Ottilia picked up the sheet and examined the superscription, which was to *Lady Francis Fanshawe, Dalesford Hall.* "I do not know the hand."

"Open it, Tillie."

She glanced at her spouse and found him frowning. "It is not Justice Belchamp, for I would recognise his writing." She broke the seal as she spoke and unfolded the missive, looking immediately at the signature. "Oh, at last! It is from Edmund Gibbon."

"Ha! Not before time. What does he say?"

Ottilia was running her eyes down the sheet. "Heavens, this is excellent, Fan! He is staying in Newport Pagnell."

"Good God!" Francis leaned across and began to read over her arm. "Significant, I'd say."

"Indeed. He desires me to visit him at the Saracen's Head."

"Why the deuce can't he come here?"

"He does not say."

"What, demanding your presence instead?" Francis snatched the sheet and ran his eyes down the short message. "Impertinence!"

"Yes, but we must go, Fan."

"Of course we will go, but it would have been more polite for him to wait upon you."

Ottilia cared less about this than she did for the highly unexpected fact of Mr Gibbon coming himself instead of writing. "Either he is furious that I suspect his protégé, or he is seeking to exonerate him of all suspicion."

"Well, he can kick his heels until we are ready."

It was plain to Ottilia that her spouse deemed her rank affronted. He was apt to become high-handed and difficult whenever anyone did not treat her with the proper respect. For herself, it was a bagatelle. With the delicate balance affecting her marriage at the present time, however, she was loath to make any attempt to rush him despite her eager need to discover the reason for Mr Gibbon's extraordinary arrival. Convinced the leisurely fashion in which Francis chose to consume his breakfast was deliberate, she was hard put to it to keep her tongue. Instead, she asked for more bacon on her own account and was surprised to find she had appetite enough to finish it, in addition to a roll spread liberally with her favourite honey.

Her thoughts winged ahead to the coming meeting and her impatience was only satisfied when she was at last seated beside Francis in their coach, her husband flatly refusing to make the journey in an open carriage.

"We are not going to make a target of you, Tillie, no matter how warm the day."

As it chanced, the sky was overcast and Ottilia was glad enough to be in shelter when it came on to drizzle just as the coach entered the town. It did not take long for the coachman to locate the Saracen's Head which, as Gil had informed them, was next door to the White Swan. Ottilia was very soon hurrying into its portal, an umbrella held over her by her spouse, who handed it to his groom once they were inside.

"Take this, Ryde. There is no saying how long we will be, so you'd best have Williams drive round to the stables. Rub down the team. We don't want them taking cold."

Wasting no time, Ottilia was already enquiring of the host who had come through a door at the back to greet the newcomers. She was obliged to quash his obvious expectation of serving travellers.

"You have a Mr Gibbon staying here, I believe? Pray tell him Lord and Lady Francis Fanshawe have arrived."

Ushering her to a gilded sofa set to one side of the entrance hall, the landlord bowed himself out, saying he would inform the gentleman. Ottilia looked about the hall, which gave signs of faded opulence. The walls were papered in a once plush red, the wood floor polished with rugs strategically placed, if a trifle worn, and a gilded mirror decorated the overmantel to a large fireplace. Not an inexpensive accommodation. She recalled that Mr Gibbon was a man of reasonable substance, owner of what he had called a *tidy estate*. Had he been moved to assist Percy pecuniarily? Possible, if his illusions had not been shattered.

She was not left long in speculation, since Francis re-joined her just as the landlord reappeared.

"Mr Gibbon begs you to come up to his private parlour, my lady."

"He might have had the grace to come down and greet you himself," grumbled Francis as they followed their guide up the stairs and along a gallery.

The reason for their would-be host's apparent rudeness became obvious the moment Ottilia entered the parlour set aside for his use. Edmund Gibbon was seated in an easy chair by the window, one heavily bandaged foot placed upon a cushioned stool. He looked to be less fleshy than he had been upon the occasion of their last meeting, his veined cheeks marked with lines of suffering. Ottilia descried fewer blond strands in his grey hair, which was tied back but lacked the smoothness she remembered from his appearance at Flitteris during the aftermath of his nephew's death. His coat looked to be looser and his appearance was in general less orderly, although he had left off his blacks and wore a brown frock-coat over fawn breeches. Had grief played a part in this deterioration? Perhaps a combination of that and his evident disability.

He made a low bow over his own lap. "I must beg you to excuse my not rising, my lady." He gestured to the foot. "I cannot do so without the assistance of my valet."

"I am indeed sorry to see you in such a case, sir," said Ottilia, walking forward and leaning to shake hands. "I hope it is not the gout?"

"You might be forgiven for thinking so, but no. I had the misfortune to take a toss from my horse. Broke my ankle. It is taking an inordinate amount of time to repair itself."

"Unfortunate indeed, sir. What does your physician say?"

The man fetched a heavy sigh. "He bids me to patience and warns me not to put weight upon it if I don't wish it to take even longer."

Ottilia eyed him. "Have you done so?"

"Impossible not to, if I don't wish to be carried or wheeled everywhere." He seemed to remember his duties as host. "But will you not be seated, my lady?"

"Thank you." She took the chair indicated, which stood at no great distance from his own.

Francis, having taken up a stance at the mantel, chose to gesture at the man's injured foot. "I wonder at your coming so far in this condition."

Mr Gibbon's face changed, a look of anxiety overspreading it. "I had to, my lord. The possibility that young man might be here brought me hotfoot — though that is an inappropriate allusion, now I hear myself."

Ottilia let this pass, fastening upon the pertinent point. "Do I understand you to be anxious to find Mr Pedwardine?"

"Most anxious, ma'am. I have been so these many months."

Her spouse took the question in her mind before Ottilia could voice it. "Then you don't know his whereabouts? We were hoping you might know precisely where he is and what he has been up to."

"So I understand." He cast a glance at Ottilia. "Your letter dismayed me, ma'am, but it gave me hope."

Hope? Had he not yet come to believe in the truth of that episode? A question she would do better not to ask at this juncture. "When did you last see your nephew's friend, sir?"

Another sigh came. "He surprised me at Christmas. I thought he was abroad still." A faintly reproachful look came Ottilia's way. "I dare say you know why he was obliged to leave the country."

Ottilia noted her spouse bristling and hastened to respond. "I had heard of his departure."

The attempt at an innocuous comment availed her nothing. Francis spoke his mind with some heat. "If you think to lay the blame for that on my wife, sir, I'll thank you to keep your tongue. Pedwardine brought it on himself."

Mr Gibbon dropped his gaze, his hands restless in his lap. "He behaved foolishly."

"Foolishly!"

"Hush, Fan, I pray you." Ottilia put out a staying hand. "Let us find out if Mr Gibbon can add anything to our store of information."

Francis threw her an impatient look but thankfully refrained from further derogatory comment. Ottilia breathed again, returning her attention to their host. "Why do you wish so particularly to find him, sir?"

"To lend him my support, of course." Mr Gibbon held up a hand as if to forestall any adverse response. "It is for my nephew's sake. No matter what happened, he was Marmaduke's closest friend. I could not reconcile it with my nephew's ghost to ignore his plight."

While she could appreciate this point of view, Ottilia could not avoid the thought that Marmaduke's ghost might well prefer a different attitude. "Did you perhaps give him pecuniary assistance at Christmas?"

"What else could I do? The boy was at a stand. I told him he might rely upon me at need, and he promised to write and give a comfortable account of himself. But I have heard nothing."

"You did not hear that he had married?"

Mr Gibbon stared. "Married? No! He could scarce support himself, never mind a wife."

"The boot," said Francis, "is evidently on the other foot."

"I do not understand what you mean, my lord."

"By all accounts, he has married the daughter of a merchant of means."

"It is only rumour, sir," Ottilia put in, "but it is the appearance of a woman who may or may not be in his train that prompted me to write to you."

Once again, she went over the various showings of the girl in the green cloak, adding, "Unfortunately, I have had no sight of the man who accompanies her other than in the rowing boat, when his face was shadowed."

Mr Gibbon became eager. "But his form? His height? Could you recognise nothing of that?"

"Sadly, no. My attention was focused on the girl. It was only at the last moment that I looked to the man, by which time it was too late to make out much of his appearance."

"But you believe the couple are here, in Newport Pagnell?"

"Just so." She did not reveal the plan to draw them out by encouraging them to chase after her to Buckingham. It occurred to her to wonder whether this visit might have been spotted by either one of the couple. Unlikely, since she and her spouse had travelled in a closed coach and not shown themselves abroad. She was relieved when Francis chose another tack.

"Do we take it the fellow was unencumbered with a wife when he visited you?"

Mr Gibbon spread his hands. "I could not say for certain. He came alone."

"No doubt you would not think to ask him."

"Why should I, sir? In his situation, he was scarcely in a position to be offering for any woman."

"Not one of his own station, I grant you."

Their host shook his head in a bewildered fashion but said nothing. Ottilia took up the next probe on her mind. "What do you mean to do now, Mr Gibbon?"

"I have not thought. I confess I had hoped you would be able to give me Percy's direction."

"When I was asking you for information concerning him?"

"Well, I supposed by this time you would have found him for yourself, my lady."

"I am sorry to disappoint you. However, I must tell you that I am somewhat hampered by the possibility that he intends to accomplish my demise."

Shock overspread the man's features. "You cannot mean that!"

"Why would she not mean it?" Francis was in again. "If you were not so stubborn in your refusal to believe in the facts, you might suppose it too."

Mr Gibbon's chin came up. "Never, sir! Never, do you hear me? I have known Percy from his boyhood. If you tell me there was an accident, I might accept it. But to deliberately — ☐ He broke off, shuddering. "I utterly refuse to believe such a thing of him."

Ottilia's heart sank. Neither time nor Percy Pedwardine's social disgrace had changed the man's view. A flashing thought made her speak before she could weigh the wisdom of her words. "You are thinking of making him your heir, are you not?"

Deep colour flushed in the man's face. "What if I am? My estate is not entailed. I may do as I please."

Ottilia said nothing and a glance at her spouse saw his eyes roll. Then Mr Gibbon looked across at Francis, the high colour receding. "Although if what you say is true, I will have to see this woman for myself before I put the matter in hand."

To weigh the suitability of a merchant's daughter to take up the position of the squire's wife? "If she is the woman I have seen, I understand she is soft spoken, sir." Not that Ottilia was advocating any elevation for that reprobate, but his wife, if it was she, had nothing to do with his past misdeeds.

"You give me hope again, my lady."

With some acidity, Francis spoke. "If this is your mind, Gibbon, I wish you will discover the wretch in short order and inform him of your decision. That might at least turn his mind from thoughts of revenge upon my wife."

"What revenge? Why do you say this?"

In as few words as possible, as Ottilia expected, her spouse gave an account of her fall into the Ouse. She was not in the least surprised to hear Mr Gibbon ascribe the whole episode to her imagination and deny, with a good deal of vehemence, that his young friend would indulge in so petty a proceeding.

"Petty? He tried to murder her!"

"Of which you have no slightest proof, my lord. No, nor reason to blame the boy. When I find him, he will tell you so himself."

Ottilia exchanged a glance with her spouse, knowing that as little as she would he believe a word that young miscreant said. There was plainly no point in continuing the argument. Instead, she thrust her scheme into the open.

"It is possible we will find him first, sir, if a plan to lure this woman in the green cloak to follow us to Buckingham proves fruitful."

A light drizzle having made a visit to the children's garden ineligible, Doro followed the lead of the Fiske children and carried her charge along a tunnel formed by arching trestle frames covered over with climbing plants, which ended at a large glasshouse in the grounds of Dalesford Hall.

"I did not know this place was here," she remarked to Hepsie, who had been dragged hither by Pretty. The child had become devoted to Lady Anne Fiske and was apt to insist upon doing whatever her "cousin" did.

"Nor did I," Hepsie returned, her eyes upon her nurseling, who was racing along a row of plants in tubs in a bid to keep up with the bigger children. "The Fiskes' nurse told me they are allowed to play here. Hide and seek is a favourite, she says."

"I can see there are many places to hide."

As Luke was wriggling and making largely unintelligible remarks indicative of his wish to join his older sister and cousins, Doro set him down, following as he toddled as fast as he was able in the wake of the others.

Hepsie, keeping pace beside her, laughed. "He is like his mother. Determined and persistent."

"Yes, but he has his father's temperament. I do not think he will grow up to be as kind as milady."

"She will teach him to be, mark my words, Doro. She has influence even on his lordship, have you not noticed?"

Her counterpart in the nursery had told her Pretty's history as they became better acquainted. She knew, as did the whole household, that the little girl was adored by her adoptive father and even now did not acknowledge milady as a mother, but Hepsie had explained how the child would never have been brought into the family if it were not for milady.

"It is true, but…" Doro faded out. She must not speak of her suspicion that all was not well between milord and milady. Joanie, with whom Doro had struck up a friendship, had confided that there had been words exchanged, that milady was not herself.

"I don't know what is amiss, Doro, but it's not like my lord and my lady to be at outs."

Prompted to observe milady more particularly when she took Luke in to visit his mother, Doro noted a tell-tale wanness in her features. She was not as talkative with the children, watching them play rather than engaging them as she usually did.

Doro tackled Hemp. Even if he would not speak of their future, he at least made a point of finding time for them to talk when both were off duty. It had been almost like the old days, strolling under a sky just verging on the turn to darkness on a warm night. But Hemp was not forthcoming. "It is not our affair, Doro."

"Even if we care enough to worry over milady?"

She saw him shift his shoulders, but he kept his gaze on the bank of trees at the other end of the vegetable garden where they were walking.

"I care about milord also."

"But not as much as you care about her," Doro said before she could stop herself.

He turned then, his gaze fixing on hers. "She is my friend, Doro. I told you that at the outset."

"She is your employer, Hemp."

"No. Milord employs me to serve her, but I would be her friend without payment."

Her ever uncertain temper flared. "Yet you don't care if she is unhappy!"

He snapped back. "Of course I care! If you must have it, she is not unhappy. Whatever is wrong, it is a temporary setback. Where two people love each other as deeply as these —□ He cut himself off abruptly, looking away.

Doro's heart beat a little faster. She dared not speak, hope lifting in her breast. But when Hemp spoke again after a moment, she was disappointed.

"Rest assured, milady and milord will find their path again."

With that she had been obliged to be content, afraid to open her lips on her own account. But she worried nonetheless, refusing to believe that the threat to milady was the only reason she was distrait.

The children had scampered ahead and Gregory, the eldest, was in the throes of arguing his case to be first to hide while his siblings demanded he ought to seek. The woman who accompanied them intervened. A matronly and authoritative figure, Peggy had been with the family for years, originally as nurse to Lady Elizabeth and continuing in an undefined role as nurse general. Her word was law as Doro had learned and she it was who settled the matter, addressing the most vociferous boy.

"Master Freddy, that is enough now. You will have your turn to hide. Turn your back, close your eyes and start counting."

Thus adjured, the child groaned his protest, but obeyed and began counting down from twenty at the top of his voice. The rest scattered, shrieking as they rushed to find a suitable hiding place.

"Lukey hidin'!" piped up Doro's young charge, tottering after Pretty, who had raced off hand-in-hand with Lady Anne.

"Come, Luke, we will hide together."

This programme clearly did not recommend itself to its recipient. Luke immediately set up a wail which brought his sister running back. She snatched him up before Doro could intervene.

"Come on, Lukey! You can hide with Pretty."

"Wait!" Doro's cry came too late. Pretty vanished as she ran off along a high table of seedlings which took her below Doro's eyeline.

Hepsie seized her arm to stay her as she made to follow. "Leave them, Doro. Pretty can take care of him."

"I never let him go out of my sight, Hepsie."

"They will be hiding, in any event. Look, Freddy has almost finished counting."

Doro tuned in to the loud voice and found the boy had reached number fifteen. The conservatory had gone silent, but for the odd muffled whisper.

"Nineteen, twenty. Coming, ready or not!" intoned Master Freddy, removing his hands from over his eyes. He began his hunt, producing a running commentary as he went. "Where are you? I know all the places where you hide, you know, you can't fool me."

As he continued in the same vein, Doro left Hepsie and the Fiske maid, who had engaged her in conversation, and began a search on her own account, troubled by Luke's absence from her line of sight. The glasshouse was high and larger than she realised, she discovered, as she attempted to follow in the direction Pretty had gone. Apart from the long trestle tables set in rows, there were pots of huge plants which blocked the way, making it difficult to spot any of the children.

"Got you, Harry!" yelled Freddy, somewhere off to Doro's left. Master Harry complained bitterly at being found, but then joined in the hunt with his brother.

Rounding the end of a passageway, Doro caught sight of a stranger standing just within the glasshouse in front of a side door. She stopped short. Who was this woman? What could she want? She was not dressed in the garb of a servant, a green cloak falling away from a round gown of striped and figured dimity, fair head visible where a hood had tipped back.

Doro started forward with the intention of asking the woman what she wanted. Then, before she knew what was happening, the woman darted out of sight. There came a shriek. She reappeared, holding, to Doro's horror, little Luke.

CHAPTER SEVENTEEN

As the woman hurried for the door, Doro ran, rescue the only thought in her head. The woman disappeared through the door and Doro cried out, speeding up.

Before she reached it, she saw Pretty running out, yelling, "Come back! Come back! Lukey! Lukey!"

Somewhere outside the sound of her racing heartbeat, Doro heard a cacophony break out behind her as she made it to the door and ran out.

"Got you, Anne! Hey, where you going?"

"Someone catched Luke!"

"Who? Freddy, did you?"

"I never!"

"Come on, don't stand there! Get after them, quick!"

This last was Master Gregory's voice, and Doro glanced back to see him hurtling through the door. She had no time to waste on those who followed. Ahead of her she could see the green cloak streaming as the woman ran along one of the gravel paths, Pretty in pursuit, shouting her brother's name.

Doro heard a chorus of pounding steps behind her and the thought flashed through her mind that the woman could never escape this many pursuers. Despite being obliged to take more care on the damp ground, Doro was gaining on Pretty, but the runaway had succeeded in building a frighteningly long lead.

Doro's breath was coming hard and fast as she longed for Hemp. None could escape him if he were here.

Then young Gregory shot past, calling out, "I'll get him, don't you worry!"

But Doro kept on even as she began to labour. She caught up with Pretty, seeing Gregory already well ahead, his young legs strong and sturdy as they thumped along in pursuit.

The kidnapper looked back, slowing slightly. Had she seen how many were after her? Next instant, she flung down her burden and sprinted away.

Luke tumbled over and over where he fell. A scream tore through Doro's breast, but did not leave her throat, her breath too short to allow for it.

Gregory stumbled to a halt as he reached the toddler, bending to pick him up. Doro found her voice. "Leave him! I will get him. Go after her!"

Needing no further urging, Gregory yelled a "tally-ho" hunting cry and set off again. Doro, her heart shattered, sped to the prone little figure of her charge.

To her relief, he was conscious, dirtied but apparently otherwise unharmed, his expression more of astonishment than distress. But no sooner did he catch sight of his nurse leaning over him than he set up a wail, reaching towards her.

Doro scooped him up and held him to her bosom, crooning in the mother tongue she no longer understood herself.

"Is Lukey all right, Doro? Did she hurt him?"

She looked down to find a tearful Pretty prying at Luke in a bid to discover his condition. Doro hushed her. "He is all right. I don't think he is hurt."

"But he's crying, Doro!"

"It is the shock." She returned to her crooning, relieved to see Hepsie hurrying up to take charge of Pretty and soothe her alarms.

The other children crowded round, Freddy and Harry demanding permission to chase the horrid lady as their brother was doing. The Fiske nurse general objected mightily. "No, you don't, Master Freddy. No need for you all to disappear. Ah, and here comes Master Gregory in any event."

The eldest of the Fiske children was limping back, out of breath and red in the face. "She got away," he told them as he came close. "I couldn't keep up."

"Never mind, Master Gregory," said Peggy. "You did well. Your papa will be proud."

Doro smiled at him. "Thank you. I don't think she would have dropped Luke if you had not managed to get so close."

"I'm sorry I didn't catch her. Uncle Fan will say I should have."

Before Doro could reassure him, one of his brothers saw fit to pour scorn. "I would have caught her. I wouldn't have given up."

Lady Anne delivered a blow to his arm. "Be quiet, Freddy! You never even caught up with Doro."

"I nearly did."

"Quiet, all of you!" the redoubtable nurse general cut in. "Master Gregory did well, and his lordship won't say nothing mean, you can be sure."

"Of course he will not," Doro said, smiling at the boy. "Milord will thank you. But try to remember what she looked like, if you please. Milord will wish for a description."

Nothing loath, Gregory launched into one immediately. "Fair, she was. I didn't see her face much, but she's not that tall and quite slim. She was panting by the time I lost sight of her. Disappeared into the trees. I didn't think I'd find her easily in the woods, so I came back."

"You will tell all this to milord, if you please."

Doro caught a glance from Hepsie, who waved her hand in an arc encompassing the whole party. "We'd best get them inside. You don't know who may be lurking. Besides, it is coming on to drizzle again."

Only now did Doro realise that the rain had fortunately stopped, holding off for the duration of the chase. The children were herded towards the glasshouse, not without a good deal of excited chatter.

"If any are lurking on our grounds, I'll tell Papa," vowed Master Harry.

"I'll get a stout stick," said Freddy, "and bash them the minute I see them."

The discussion was pursued as the whole party moved through the glasshouse and made their way back to the mansion, the claims of what the boys would do to any intruder becoming wilder as they tried to outdo each other.

Doro, beginning to dread the inevitable interview with milady and milord, carried the now quietened Luke up to the nursery, where Pretty took up his entertainment in the hopes of making him forget his ordeal.

While Hepsie rang for refreshments for the children, Doro found herself with too much time to grow ever more anxious. She had neglected her duty. What milady would say when she learned of her son's near loss made palpitations rise in Doro's chest. Worse, how angry would be milord? She wished desperately for Hemp, to whom she might unburden her worries, but she dared not leave Luke for one moment.

A craven wish to resign her duty came upon her. Only she had no alternative to this life, despite her freedom. And on that score, Hemp was silent.

"This is the outside of enough!" Francis paced as he spoke, only half aware that he trod almost the whole length of the carpet in the family parlour and back again, swinging away from misplaced chairs at which he was much inclined to kick, were he to give rein to his emotions. "When it comes to attacking my children, we have reached the limit of my tolerance." His gaze swept the room and found his brother-in-law. "Have you sent to Dalby, Gil?"

"I did so the moment Gregory told me his tale, Fan, never fear. My groom ought to reach him within the hour."

"A lot of use his men proved to be! Did he not assure me he would post them in strategic places, specifically to keep an eye out for that woman? And what happens?"

His mother, still pale with shock, took this up. "If she had succeeded! I dread to think of Ottilia's distress."

Francis very nearly hit back that his own distress was as great as any his wife had exhibited, but he managed to hold his tongue. Truth to tell, he was more furious than upset. "I ought to have taken them all home days since."

Gil came up and set a hand to his shoulder. "I sympathise with the sentiment, but only consider, Fan. If you go home before these individuals are found and stopped, you will never know a moment's peace for fear of their following."

"You are very right, Gilbert," said Sybilla before Francis could respond. "You must settle the business first, Francis. At least we know they are here. If you leave, they could be anywhere and you will not know it."

He let out an overwrought breath. "I just want it over."

Gil kneaded his shoulder. "Of course you do. So do we all."

He was tempted to throw off the sympathetic hand, such was his impatience. Instead, he reached and grasped it. "I thank you, Gil."

The other laughed. "What for? It's little enough I have done."

"For everything. For giving us what security you could."

A snort emanated from his mother. "Security? When that creature can enter his grounds without let or hindrance?"

Francis released the hand, turning instead to his mother. "That is not Gil's blame, ma'am. The grounds are extensive. No one could offer complete protection."

"I shall have a damned good try — saving your presence, ma'am. I've instructed Maynard to set every able man to patrolling the perimeter."

"Excellently done, Gilbert," said Sybilla with another of the lightning changes of face which she claimed as the privilege of age. "I hope Harriet has forbidden the children to leave the house."

Not much to Francis's surprise, Gil shifted his shoulders, looking dubious. "She will undoubtedly do so, ma'am, but to no avail, I suspect. Nothing could keep my boys from venturing forth. Indeed, Freddy and Harry have both declared their intention of joining the guard. I left Gregory arguing the point."

Francis eyed him. "I trust they won't, Gil. I should hate your children to be endangered on account of some villain's campaign of revenge upon my wife."

Gil grinned. "Not a chance, Fan. They might go outside, but they won't be permitted anywhere near the men. You don't know our Peggy. The only person in the place who can keep those brats of mine in check. That's why we've kept her on all these years."

This remark prompted Sybilla to express her views on the proper way to bring up boys. Francis ignored the tirade. His mother's increased tetchiness arose from anxiety, as he knew too well from his own. Aware he resembled her closely in this, he was apt to keep a guard upon his tongue. But his son's kidnap had revived all the painful despair he had succeeded in damping down, at least to a degree. Interrupting his mother, he voiced his frustration aloud. "What did she intend by it? What could she gain?"

"This woman?" Gil's brows drew together. "Ransom? I imagine you'd pay handsomely for Luke's return safe and sound."

"Yes, but that isn't the issue. Or it has not been up to now. They meant to harm Ottilia."

"Harm enough to cause her panic and distress," snapped his mother.

It did not satisfy. "I don't see that. An inevitable outcome, of course, but it can't be all."

Gil was pouring wine, but he paused with the bottle poised over a glass, glancing across. "You need your Lady Fan to fathom it out."

Francis said nothing. The sobriquet was presently anathema, too reminiscent of the whole reason for this debacle and the current difficulty within his marriage.

His brother-in-law came across and pressed a glass upon him. "Get this down you, old fellow. Nothing more soothing than port."

Francis took it with a faint smile of thanks as Gil took a second glass over to Sybilla. The liquor slid down his throat and burned a little in his chest, warming a region which had turned to ice without him noticing. An image of Tillie jumped into his head, frozen and silent in her chaise longue after the loss of their first son in childbed. Realisation leapt. To see that again? Had Luke been lost to them, could he have endured the closing down of his wife's lively mind? On that occasion, he had engineered her involvement in the affair at Weymouth in the hope, fortunately realised, that it would turn her thoughts and bring her back to life. It flashed through his mind that his present outrage was already embedding a desire in him to shut her down forever. Guilt and dismay engulfed him. What was he trying to do to the woman he loved?

He was vaguely aware that a conversation continued between Gil and his mother, but these tumbling thoughts occupied his attention to the exclusion of all else. The opening of the door startled him. The sight of his wife entering the room threw him into an odd state wherein he felt he stood outside himself and watched a stranger. That man set aside a glass, walked directly to the woman and enfolded her in a loving embrace. "Never be other than you are," he said. The woman looked up, surprise in her face. The warm smile slammed him back and he felt the body held against him, the breath that feathered his face as she spoke. "Luke is none the worse for his adventure."

Francis sighed out an overwrought breath. "I am glad." He did not know if she had taken in his earlier words; he hardly knew if he had uttered them aloud. Something had changed. He hoped it would hold. She was speaking again and he forced his attention back as Tillie gently withdrew herself from his arms.

"The same cannot be said for Doro. She is distraught. She pleaded with me to release her from her post, saying she is not worthy to fill it. Nonsensical, of course. She could not have foreseen this happening and there were any number of persons in the glasshouse who must take part of the blame, if blame there be. For my part, I said I could not thank her enough. She acted promptly and saved Luke."

"With the help of everyone else, I gather. Gregory in particular." Francis cast a glance at Gil as he spoke. "We are indebted to that boy."

Tillie's smile returned as she swept across. "Indeed we are, Gil. Doro told me the whole. Gregory very nearly caught the girl, and she would not have dropped Luke if he had not managed to get so close."

"I'm very glad to know my son is useful for something," returned Gil in his insouciant fashion, but the pride in his voice was unmistakeable.

Francis had an abrupt vision of himself at some years' distance, father of a boy of Gregory's age. Would he be similarly proud of Luke? Another source of guilt slithered through him. He gave more attention to his adoptive daughter than to his son. He must remedy that.

The combination of too many anxieties proved overwhelming. Sybilla was asking after Luke in more precise detail, freeing him to move. He looked about for his glass, picked it up and went to the side table where the tray with decanter and glasses was set.

"Refill, Fan?"

He had not even noticed his brother-in-law come up. Gil was already holding the decanter. Francis nodded and held out his glass, watching the dark red liquid rise.

Gil set down the decanter and eyed him in a critical fashion. "You'd best sit down before you fall down, man. You look done up."

Francis was thankful he spoke in a murmur and he replied likewise. "The shock has caught up with me. Don't tell my wife."

Gil tsked, edging him towards the nearest chair. "She's not blind, Fan."

Finding a chair behind him, Francis sat, glad of Gil's figure close enough to conceal him from his wife's too probing gaze. Or Sybilla's. The last thing he needed was his mother parroting her customary scolds. That these were a shield for anxiety he knew, but it made them no easier to bear.

"I ought to have called for brandy," observed his host.

"This is doing the trick, I thank you, Gil. I will be better in a moment."

"You've a little more colour, that I will say."

Francis made no answer. His chest felt constricted, his breath tight. Was he about to suffer an apoplexy? Tillie would know. Could one inherit a tendency? His grandfather had died by that route.

Presently, soothed by the port, his breath began to ease and his ability to think coherently returned. Inevitably, his mind centred on the now urgent necessity to settle this business once and for all. He looked up at Gil. "I must decide what to do next."

"What have you in mind?"

He did not have to think far ahead. "Buckingham. Dalby promised to let us know which day he may free up his men. I hope it may not be too long delayed."

Gil's brows drew together. "You mean this scheme of Ottilia's to lure these individuals into following you?"

"I can't doubt they will after this."

"What do you hope to gain by it?"

Francis blew out a breath. "I have no notion. Either they will show themselves or make a covert attempt on Tillie's life."

"That's what you expect?"

"I don't know what to expect. But we must do something."

A movement behind Gil caught his eye and made Gil turn. Francis saw his wife coming towards them. She began speaking before she reached him.

"I have been talking it over with Sybilla, Fan, but I cannot agree that this was done only to cause us distress."

Francis got to his feet. "Gil thought ransom."

Tillie spared Gil a glance. "I think not, Gil. If money was their object, they would have said so before this."

"What then, Ottilia? I was saying to Fan that he ought to consult you on the matter."

She produced a smile. "I am scarcely infallible, but I do have a notion."

Francis cut in. "Let's have it then."

"It strikes me that each time I have seen that girl, her approach becomes bolder. I wonder now if she meant to keep Luke at all?"

"What, you suppose she means only to frighten you?"

"She must know I do not frighten easily. Besides, don't let us forget the possibility that she and her paramour — or someone, for we cannot yet be certain who — did try to drown me."

Francis sighed in frustration. "You've lost me, Tillie. I am in no mood to guess what you would be at. Be plain, I beg of you."

His wife glanced from him to Gil and thence to his mother, sitting forward in eager fashion. It was a thing Tillie did when she had some notion to put forward she thought the rest would deprecate. Francis became alert. Had she made one of her periodic leaps?

"Well?"

Tillie's clear gaze came back to his. "I believe she wants to goad me into finding her out in person."

"To what purpose?"

"She wants to talk to me. She has questions, perhaps. Or, if she bears a grudge, she desires an opportunity to inform me of it. Disposing of me may not be enough."

This brought Sybilla into play. "It is more than enough for me. Francis too, I imagine."

Tillie turned, sweeping across the room. "I am not making myself clear, Sybilla." She took up a stance that was Francis's norm, setting a hand on the mantel. "How sweet is this revenge if the person upon whom you perpetrate it does not know why?"

Francis moved in. "That won't fadge, Tillie. In the first instance, the attempt to murder you came out of the blue. No one sought to tell you why they were drowning you."

She looked at him, but her eyes had that odd faraway look they took on when her mind was working behind them. She spoke slowly. "I am beginning to believe that assault was perpetrated by someone other."

Gil took the question from his mind. "You mean there are two villains in the case?"

"Two or more. One individual, whether or not involved with someone else, tried to drown me. That was an act carried out with stealth, to make it appear an accident. This girl has been too visible to be guilty of that. Why show herself? Why supply herself with witnesses who may testify to her interest in me if she was looking for an opportunity to try again? No, it cannot be the girl in the cloak who tried to kill me."

Once again, her logic confounded Francis. He spoke the first thought in his head. "Then what is the point of luring her to Buckingham?"

Tillie turned, moving to him. "Don't you see, Fan? We must provide an opportunity for her to come up to me in person."

"I don't like it."

"Nor I," chimed in Sybilla. "Who is to say she will not have a dagger handy and strike at you?"

A light laugh escaped Tillie. "Thank you for that disquieting thought. Even if she has, I am sure both Francis and Hemp, or either, will be able to foil any such attempt."

"Then you must be sure not to go apart with her."

"Certainly, Sybilla. I can promise that. Or not unless she agrees to be searched for weapons."

"I see a flaw in this plan of yours, Ottilia." Gil returned to his earlier theme. "Two villains, you said. How if you draw the other into this net at the same time?"

A cold hand clutched at Francis's heart. "For pity's sake, Gil, must you?"

"It's a possibility, Fan, assuming Ottilia is right that another perpetrated the first attack."

His mother opened fire. "That settles it. You can't go, Ottilia."

Tillie turned on her. "I must, Sybilla." She echoed Francis's own earlier words. "We must do something. Otherwise we will be at sea, waiting for who knows what further attempt. I cannot allow Luke, or indeed Pretty, for she is not immune, to be targeted again."

Francis was in wholehearted agreement, much as he disliked the scheme. Before the point could be further argued, however, a knock at the door produced the butler.

"Captain Dalby, my lord."

Gil started forward. "The very man we need. Come in, Dalby. Lord Francis is planning this Buckingham affair."

CHAPTER EIGHTEEN

Primed by Ottilia, Hemp resolved to find an opportunity before the day was out. To do what he felt he must had become imperative, which had made the interview with his friend and employer both poignant and difficult. The accident that had befallen Ottilia had seared him with grief. Relief when she was found alive and safe was succeeded by a corroding fear of potential loss on his own account. His Doro, whom he had released from all obligation to him these many months, could as easily fall victim to some mischance. Today's unfortunate contretemps might indeed have ended badly for her. He seized the excuse when Ottilia requested him to intercede with Doro.

"She is determined to resign her place, Hemp, which is perfectly absurd. No blame attaches to her. We must persuade her that she is invaluable, as indeed she is. Luke would miss her dreadfully, and I cannot contemplate losing her."

He had not spoken for some moments, aware that the words hovering on his tongue would wound. His intentions towards Doro would inevitably lead to his exit from the Fanshawe ménage. Ottilia must have seen something of his reluctance in his face or in his hesitation, for her brow furrowed.

"What is it, Hemp? Will you not speak to her? She will listen to you."

There could be no further delay. Hemp drew a breath. "Perhaps it is time."

Her face changed, shock and sorrow entering in. He ought to have guessed she would understand on the instant. Her voice grew hushed, thickening. "Now? At such a juncture?"

He tried to smile. "I do not mean immediately. The present trouble must be settled first."

"The present trouble and a good deal else! Hemp, this is too soon, too precipitate."

"But long overdue." He saw wetness standing in her eyes and his chest tightened. "I have left it for too many months, milady. I should not have let it lie."

Ottilia's speech became hurried. "Fix your interest with her, by all means. I am in agreement with that aspect. It has indeed been too long delayed. But need that mean you will leave us? You have not yet settled where to go, nor discussed the future with your intended bride. Surely —□

"Milady!" Hemp cut her off with regret, but the more she said the harder it became. "It will be the worse for waiting. If Doro agrees, we must be wed soon. Once man and wife, we can no longer remain in your employ."

Ottilia had gazed at him with a look of pain in her eyes. "Why? Who says so? By what rule do you make that out, Hemp?"

He laughed then, mirthless. "No rule, milady. You know my ambition. I had only myself to think of before, but now that ambition centres on Doro. I want to make a life for her, milady, one that is our own, where we may grow together, as you and milord have done. Have children of our own, I hope."

In her turn, Ottilia remained silent for a space. Hemp could see her thinking. Seeking an alternative? He was determined, however.

At length her warm smile appeared. "I do understand. I will not pretend it does not distress me to lose your constant presence. Doro's too. I have grown fond of her."

Capitulation made him generous. "It will not be forever."

"I hope not indeed. You will always be welcome visitors in our home."

"Perhaps you and milord will come to us also."

"If you have a lodging house, we will certainly come. With frequency. You will grow quite tired of us, I dare say."

Hemp smiled. "Never, milady." He paused, but the words would not be kept inside. "I will — *we* will miss you deeply." He saw a shadow cross her face. "It will not be as swift as all that, milady. The arrangements cannot be made all in a bang."

"No, and you must find somewhere for your proposed business and make the purchase. These things do not happen overnight." Ottilia surged with fresh energy. "First, however, pray do what you can to allay Doro's alarms. Until you marry, or after, even, I would have her continue to nurse Luke. I shall have to find another, and perhaps you might remain until he has weathered a transition?"

Having gained his point, Hemp found himself willing to make concessions. "You are right, milady. It will take a little time to arrange the future. I had not considered Master Luke's needs. Of course Doro must stay until he is resettled."

Ottilia gave him one of those mischievous looks he had seen her throw upon her husband. "What is more, you have yet to woo Doro and gain her consent."

Hemp's laugh was hollow. Now that he had decided to come to the point, he was conscious of a sliver of anxiety. Had he waited too long?

He left his mistress apparently cheerful, but he was not deceived. His own sneaking regret at the coming parting mirrored what he knew she felt. But the time had certainly come.

The evening proved fine, and he drew Doro out for their customary walk once the meal in the servants' hall was over.

Easier to begin with the mission entrusted to him by Ottilia. But he had no need to bring it up, for Doro began upon the matter as soon as they were out of earshot of the house.

"I failed milady, Hemp. I dare not trust myself with Master Luke."

A flicker of irritation threw Hemp into speech. "The child is not your master, Doro. You are his nurse."

She waved this away with an impatient hand. "It is what the servants call him. I do not address him so to his face."

Hemp grinned. "No, you call him some name culled from your Gabonese heritage."

A tiny smile appeared. "My blue magic heritage, my witch language."

He laughed. "I have never called it that."

"The other slaves did. I do not even know what I say, but Luke likes it."

"He likes your crooning." Hemp hesitated. A way to approach his object beckoned. "He would be happy with an English tune, I suspect. From another's voice."

Doro halted, those extraordinary eyes of blue, which had attracted him from the first and held him forever captive, staring into his. "You do think I must give him up."

"I did not say that."

"It is what you think. It is a poor nurse who cannot keep her nurseling safe."

Hemp met her accusing stare with a rise of anxiety. The moment was upon him. Yet he prevaricated. "I neither thought it nor said it. Nor does milady blame you."

Doro swung her gaze away. "I know it. I blame myself."

Hemp took her by the shoulders, urging her to look at him again. "There is no need. You did all you could and Luke is unharmed."

223

"But he might have been taken. I am not fit, Hemp."

He drew a breath. "You are fit for better, Doro. For a mother. For a wife." Her expression was changing, but he could not tell its portent. "My wife. If you will have me."

For an agonising moment, she did not speak. Then she shifted out of his hold. "Why do you ask me now?"

"I have waited too long."

"Is it to offer me a way out? Because I am ashamed of doing badly?"

Dismayed, he broke into rapid speech. "No, Doro, no. I have been thinking of it these many days, ever since the attack upon milady. That made me realise, made me see. The longer I held off, the more chance to lose you."

She did not soften, though he thought he saw a light of something — hope or desire? — in her eyes. "You might have spoken at any time these many months, Hemp. Why did you hold off?"

"You know why." It came out as a protest and he altered his tone. "I hoped you might understand why. I did not wish you to feel beholden. This was your first taste of freedom, Doro. How could I mar it by pressing you to put yourself under my power, my command?"

The hint of amusement was in her face. "Is that how you see marriage, Hemp? Have you no eyes? It is not thus with milady and milord."

"No, and it would not be thus with you, my wild termagant."

"Then why did you wait?"

His breath became tight in his throat and he looked away briefly. But it had to be said. "I was afraid you would refuse me. I believed you needed time to become used to me again."

The brilliant eyes were shining and she set a hand to his cheek, touching it with delicacy. "I have loved you from a child. Do you think it has been easy for me? To be in your vicinity, to revive the memories? Pinpricks, Hemp. How could I know if your love had survived? I feared I had killed it. Then when you did not speak…" She faded out, but not before he caught the huskiness in her voice.

There was no hesitation then. Hemp captured her to him, cradling her as he looked down into the depths of those eyes. "Never. I tried, God knows, but you are too deeply embedded in my heart, my blue magic queen."

As she surrendered to his kiss, the intervening years fell away. When he released her lips, he sought her hand, kissed the palm and closed her fingers over it in the way he had done each time they'd parted all those years ago.

Doro's laugh was delight and magic all over again. "*Mon roi*."

"*Ma reine*," he whispered. How long since they had addressed each other thus? His heart soared. He had won her at last.

For a while he was content to walk, murmuring words he had kept inside, exhilarating in her responses. Then Doro brought him down to earth.

"Hemp, we must not tell milady yet. We must wait until all this trouble is over, until she is safe."

"I have already told her." The words slipped out and he regretted them at once, for Doro stopped dead, pulling her hand out of his.

"You told her? Hemp, how could you?"

"I had to. She asked me to dissuade you from giving up your post, and I told her it was time to settle things between us."

"You could have waited. How much did you tell her?"

"That I would ask for your hand. That once we are wed, we will go our own way. Milady was distressed but —□

"Distressed! Of course she was distressed. She cannot wish to lose you, Hemp."

"I know that, but —"

"Today of all days! How could you add to her sorrows? You call yourself her friend, yet on a day when she nearly lost her son, you tell her you are leaving."

The temper he knew too well was unleashing. Hemp tried to stem its growth. "Nothing of the sort. Milady understood."

"She understood? What else did you expect? That she would harangue you and beg you not to go? Milady always understands, but to deliver a blow like this? It is unkind. Insensitive, Hemp."

Knowing she was right did nothing to ease him. He tried for mitigation. "I promised we would remain until Luke has become used to another nurse. Besides, it will take time to arrange our departure. I must find a suitable place to live." He took her reluctant hands and held them fast. "I want you to choose, Doro. I want us to visit Weymouth and other places where we might settle, but this we must do together and we cannot until we are married."

Doro was not appeased. "All this is well, and you might have told me such plans. But not milady. Not now."

Disappointment flooded him and he released her hands. "It is too late. Scold me if you must, but I cannot undo it."

The blue gaze flashed. "You can. You must tell her we are in no hurry. You must say that I do not wish to leave Luke until he is older, until he does not need me so much."

"Not an hour since you were insisting you could not remain."

"I did not then know you had acted as only a man will act, without sense."

"I thank you." Hemp gave a grunt. "This was supposed to be the happiest day of my life."

Doro emitted a laugh that sounded hollow. "That day is yet to come. Be content. We have a lifetime in which to quarrel."

She left him then. For several moments he seethed, until it was borne in upon him that he had achieved his object, and Ottilia's too. The rest could wait.

For all her eager words, when the expedition finally set out for Buckingham, Ottilia was conscious of a nervous flutter as the phaeton bowled along under Francis's guiding hand, with only his groom up behind. The open carriage was essential if they were to lure the prey into following. Yet the sensation of setting herself up as a target sent a shiver of apprehension down Ottilia's back, despite all her spouse's careful precautions.

Hemp had gone ahead on horseback, his task to remain out of sight until and if he were needed. He would await them in Market Square, conspicuous by his colour but apparently unattached to the Fanshawes. Backing him, half a dozen militia were to be stationed at strategic intervals, using hidden vantage points from where they might observe and leap into action if required.

Captain Dalby, accompanied by others of his men, was riding at some distance behind, well out of sight. Francis had no wish to put off their quarry by a show of soldiery.

"Dalby won't come after us, in any event, until he sees that we are followed indeed."

"How will he know, Fan? He has not seen those two."

"He will advance if any carriage takes to the road which contains a male and female. We are taking no chances."

A number of further objections entered Ottilia's mind, but she did not voice them. This was her notion, after all. Nor did she truly believe the woman in the cloak meant to harm her.

Not directly. She had made herself too visible. Unless she was a fool, she must know her conduct was suspicious. Taking Luke had been, Ottilia was persuaded, an impulsive act. Why release him otherwise? Having snatched him up and found herself outnumbered, she had abandoned the attempt to carry him away. That might argue a fear she would be caught, but she was not caught. Luke was a lightweight, no burden to a young woman as capable and strong as this one appeared to be.

She had been reluctant to wait even one day when Captain Dalby appointed Thursday, but she had curbed her impatience, realising that the girl was unlikely to make a second attempt within four and twenty hours. Besides, it was essential to the scheme that their quarry should be watching, and perhaps she might have been discouraged by the debacle with Luke. Waiting might ensure she was once again upon the hunt.

"Are you fretting, Tillie?"

She glanced round in time to catch a frowning look from her spouse before he returned his attention to the road. "A little, perhaps."

"Shall we abandon the scheme? We can go back, if you wish it?"

Ottilia straightened her spine. "No, we must go on. It is worse to be waiting for anything they might think to do next."

He did not answer, his gaze steady on the way ahead. For a while, Ottilia watched the muscled motion of the horses' rumps and backs as they trotted. The pace was lulling, the day warm. Her anxiety eased and with it, her mind. A recollection surfaced. "I forgot to tell you, Fan. Hemp has made up his mind to speak to Doro."

He flashed her a look of surprise. "About time."

"He says he has waited too long."

"I could have told him as much."

Ottilia, dismay rising again, paid this no heed. "He says they will marry and then leave. I have persuaded him to wait until Luke has become accustomed to a new nurse."

A scoffing sound came from her husband. "He will scarcely rush off in an instant, Tillie. He has not yet found a lodging house to purchase. Assuming he still holds by that scheme."

"Oh, yes." Ottilia touched a hand to his thigh. "I said we will visit, wherever they may be."

His glance was searching. "Are you distressed?"

She hesitated. "I am trying not to be. It was always inevitable. We are fortunate that Doro's advent delayed his departure."

"You are thus fortunate. Hemp is a good fellow. He has proved himself useful. But he is not indispensable to me."

"It is not that, Fan. I may do without his services, but —"

"He is a friend. I know. You need not argue the case."

Ottilia bit her tongue on a retort. Francis had ever cherished a spark of jealousy where Hemp was concerned. As things stood between them now, it was likely a discomforting reminder. She had wondered once or twice whether her spouse suspected that, in other circumstances, she might have thought of Hemp as more than a friend, absurd as such a supposition was in her eyes. Fan was all the man she wanted, had ever done, almost from the first moment of their meeting. He ought to know that. He did know. Was it a masculine thing that he must needs look upon any man for whom she felt an affinity as some sort of rival? It was not affection in the way Fan thought of it. Rather it was a meeting of two minds, two souls, perhaps.

"We are on the outskirts of Buckingham. Not long now."

Ottilia's mind snapped back to the matter at hand, the rest fading as the purpose of this morning's excursion came to the fore. "I hope this expedition will not prove to be in vain."

"I hope it might."

"Fan!"

She was spared a glance. "You know very well what I mean."

Ottilia ignored this. "It hangs on whether they have spotted us."

"What do you propose to do once we are in the town?"

"Walk about, what else? Pretend to be interested in the shops. I would be glad to see some of this famous lace they produce locally."

As the church spire came into sight, Francis prepared to change direction at the next turn as Gil, long familiar with the town, had directed. The phaeton was very soon passing through a more populous area, with loungers on corners, clerks going about their business and a row of buildings to one side. Francis negotiated his way down Castle Street and Ottilia was granted a sight of the medieval-looking gaol as they entered Market Square.

"Ah, there is the White Hart," said her spouse, spotting the inn recommended by their host for their temporary accommodation. He brought the vehicle to a halt in front of the large building. The groom leapt down from his seat behind and went to the horses' heads. Ottilia watched her spouse descend into the road and prepared to alight herself, waiting for him to hand her down.

"We will leave the phaeton to you, Ryde. Take good care of my brother-in-law's horses, won't you?"

"I'll bait them here, my lord. They'll need the rest."

"Very good. We will find you here once this business is done with."

He came around to Ottilia's side as he spoke and held up a hand to assist her to get down. She released his hand as she reached the flag way and shook out her figured muslin petticoats, conscious of the pitter-patter of her pulse as anticipation mounted.

She had every expectation that something would happen, but what? She had looked at and discarded any number of possibilities since the inception of the idea. Now that the moment was upon her, she could not but wonder if she had gauged them with any accuracy.

"Ready?"

Ottilia took the proffered arm and glanced up at her spouse. "Let us proceed."

It proved harder than Ottilia had anticipated to pretend disengagement as she sauntered at Francis's side. Her instinct was to dart glances at every person who came within her vision, directly or on the periphery. These were enough to be distracting. She might ignore street vendors with their trays, but any female figure drew her immediate attention. To no avail, as one was a stout dame carrying a basket and accompanied by a young boy, trudging with obvious reluctance beside her; another was clearly a maidservant by her dress, and a third was too elderly to be her quarry, with an escort of similar age.

Ottilia disciplined herself to look instead into shop windows as she passed. She paused at one, signalling with a tightening grip on his arm that Francis should stop.

"This place looks intriguing," she said in a spurious tone of interest, affecting to examine the multitude of wares set upon shelves beyond the glass. In one cursory glance, she spied trinkets of all kinds, such as seals, tweezers and toothpick cases, smelling bottles, snuff boxes, tea chests and inkstands. In reality, she was trying to see any possible reflection in the glass of persons in the square behind. Failing, she instead murmured to her spouse. "If you look bored, Fan, you may check the street. A green cloak, remember?"

He turned away from the window, taking a nonchalant pose as if divorced from his wife's examination of the articles within. "Nothing to see yet."

Ottilia sighed. "We will move on, then."

This same procedure she repeated at a milliner's, a pawnbroker and silversmith's and a printer with a multitude of sample pamphlets and advertisements in his window. There was no sign of any lacemakers in this thoroughfare, and Ottilia came to the conclusion they most likely worked from home. The best one could hope for was to find samples in a haberdasher's, not that she had so far seen one.

By this time, they had traversed more than half the length of one side of the square and Francis had reported spotting Hemp twice.

"No sign of the militia. I begin to think this trip is going to prove abortive."

Ottilia was fast coming to the same conclusion. "Let us cross and go back down the other side."

"Don't you think you had better make some kind of purchase? We will attract undesirable attention if we don't at least enter one of these infernal shops."

Ottilia cast a searching look at the establishments opposite. "We might find something for the children. After that horrid experience, they both deserve a treat, do you not think? Assuming we can find a shop devoted to dolls and games."

"We can ask, can't we?"

"An excellent idea, Fan. That will make us appear genuine."

Her husband stopped the next passer-by, who stated that there was no shop in the town specifically catering for the entertainment of children, but recommended that his questioners try Mrs Skinner's place, which might be found between the clockmaker and the dealer of teas on the other side of the square.

"All manner of goods may be obtained at Mrs Skinner's. Musical pipes and such, books, slate and chalks, if these are of use to you. Brass figures I've seen in there too, and shoe buckles, pins, pretty gewgaws. You know the style of thing, I dare say, sir."

Ottilia put her oar in. "Does she sell dolls or games, do you know?"

"I should not be at all surprised, ma'am. In fact, I remember spotting a small doll or two. Might have been a china figure, though. But games? There's a good chance she'll have a pack of cards at least."

Francis thanked him and offered Ottilia his arm again. "It seems we must cross after all."

"Yes, although I am not sanguine that we may find anything suitable in this Mrs Skinner's."

In this she was proved wrong. Mrs Skinner's was found to be at first a tiny shop, squeezed between two others. But upon entering down a long corridor, the premises opened out into a fairly large space in which several counters, piled higgledy-piggledy with goods, were placed around the walls with crammed shelves behind. Ottilia gained an impression of a jumble of colour and odd shapes. Mrs Skinner, learning of their need, was quick to produce a wide selection of items that might suit. Ottilia straightaway forgot the purpose of the Buckingham visit in examining the various articles proffered, since several of the proprietor's choices, along with some of her own finds, would be bound to give pleasure to Pretty and Luke. Her spouse becoming equally enthusiastic, a half hour passed in amusement and discussion until Francis unearthed a recorder for Pretty.

Ottilia had to laugh. "Dear me, Fan. She will drive poor Hepsie crazy attempting to play that thing."

"Yes, but it will give her something new to learn and may content her until she can begin upon a pianoforte."

He turned to Mrs Skinner to request some simple music for a beginner and Ottilia, with a silent prayer of thankfulness that the nursery was at the top of Dalesford Hall, returned to her examination of a cherrywood spinning top she was considering for Luke. She was doubtful his small fingers would be dexterous enough to manipulate it, but her son was a determined little man and she hoped he would persist. No doubt Doro would encourage him and Hemp, in all likelihood, would be happy to teach him the trick of it.

These purchases made and packed up by the helpful Mrs Skinner, Francis held the door as Ottilia exited the shop and ran straight into the girl in the cloak, who was standing directly in her path.

"Lady Fan, is it not?"

Ottilia was startled only for a moment. Recovering, she answered with a touch of satisfaction. "Ah, so you did wish to accost me?"

Without preamble, the girl spoke, her voice both gentle and genteel, though a trifle breathy. "I hope your little boy is none the worse?"

Taken aback by this blunt admission, Ottilia hesitated, leaving space for her husband to cut in, his tone gruff.

"No thanks to you. What did you mean by it? How dared you sneak into Dalesford's estate and steal him away?"

The girl, seen now to be equally fair of face with the pale locks visible beneath the hood of the cloak, cast a glance at

Francis in which deprecation mingled with indignation. "I did not mean any harm. I would not have hurt him."

Seeing wrath gathering in her spouse's face, Ottilia set a staying hand on his arm, addressing the woman. "I believe you. You wished for an opportunity to talk to me, is that it?"

The girl glanced in one direction down the square and then in the other before she answered. Searching for her spouse? Making sure she would not be disturbed? Or was she checking that he was in position? The thought made Ottilia shiver a little and she was about to make a tart comment to hurry the girl when the pretty features turned once more in their direction.

"I thought you would look for me if I had your child. I promise you he would have been quite safe with me."

Ottilia lost patience. "That is past. Will you come to the point, if you please? Give me your name and tell me what you want of me."

The girl's gaze strayed to Francis, who was looking even more like a thundercloud with this repeated mention of Luke. "I will tell you, but alone. I don't wish to speak before him." She nodded in his direction.

Predictably, Francis snapped back. "Too bad, madam. I am going nowhere."

Ottilia abandoned her promise not to go apart with the woman. She would get nowhere if they continued in this vein, and she was by now too intrigued to let the matter rest. "If you keep us within sight, Fan, perhaps I may walk a little way beside her?"

"Certainly not. I'm not letting you walk alone with this woman."

"We are in full view, Fan," Ottilia said, with a meaningful look meant to convey that Hemp and the militiamen were no doubt close enough to keep watch.

He grunted, throwing glances up and down the street just as the girl had done, as if he sought to locate her guardians among the persons walking or standing about, of whom there were now rather more than before they had entered the shop. After giving the girl a somewhat menacing look, he capitulated. "Very well, but if there is the slightest hint of mischief, this tête-à-tête ends upon the instant. Understood?"

"Then pray keep a little behind us, Fan."

"Out of earshot," insisted the woman, a pair of eyes spattered with green flecks fixed on his face.

"You are in no position to make demands, madam."

"Fan, pray."

The softly uttered plea had its effect. Francis stepped back a pace and waved them on. Ottilia turned down the square in the direction of the gaol, a gesture inviting the girl to join her. She did not speak as they began to walk, calculating when it might be politic to begin.

As it chanced, the girl spoke first. "He will not hear us now."

Ottilia threw her a glance, repeating her original question, though she took a more gentle note. "What is your name, my dear, and what do you want of me?"

The girl now stared straight ahead as she walked. "I will not give you my name, not yet."

"Then will you tell me who is the man who accompanies you?"

"He is not relevant."

Irritation burgeoned again. "Why don't you let me be the judge of that? Do I know him? Or does he know me?"

The girl became insistent. "I tell you he does not matter."

"I doubt that, but let us move on. You wanted to have speech with me. Why?"

The girl walked in silence for a space, as if, having gained the access she wished, she knew not how to begin.

Ottilia applied a spur. "My husband is not a patient man."

She received a direct look. "But you have that attribute, by all accounts."

"My patience is not inexhaustible, I assure you. Come now, what is the matter?"

Out it came, the tone low and vibrant. "I want to know of my husband."

"*Your* husband?" Startled, Ottilia halted, her gaze flying to the girl's face.

"Do not stop! I don't wish him to come up with us."

"Who?" Ottilia began to feel bewildered. "Your husband or mine?"

"Yours, of course. Mine is … my husband is waiting for me elsewhere."

"Then there is a man in the case. I thought you said he was irrelevant."

"To this discussion is what I meant."

"If he is your husband, he must be relevant indeed, since you are asking about him."

"But not in connection with the present time."

Ottilia let out an overcharged breath. "I wish you will cease prevaricating. What is it I am supposed to know of your husband? Or that you think I know?"

"Was it he?" The tone was tense, and a glance showed the girl's hands caught tightly together.

Ottilia's mind was flying now. Was it Percy she meant? Caution made her proceed warily. "Was what he, my dear?"

"Was he — his friend who died — was he involved?"

Confirmation. Ottilia turned her head and found the girl now looking at her with dread in her eyes. Pity flooded her. The wretched man had clearly imposed upon an innocent girl. She fenced a little. "How did you find out about that business? I presume Percy did not tell you?"

The name had a profound effect. The girl's eyes flashed. "I said no names!"

Ottilia became tart. "I am not a mind reader. Do you know how many of these horrid crimes I have been obliged to solve?"

The girl ignored this. "You have not answered my question."

Deliberately. How to proceed? "I cannot, if I do not understand your circumstances. Or indeed your intentions. I really think you must tell me something of your background before I answer."

"I have told you all you need to know."

"You have told me precisely nothing. Let us cease shilly-shallying. Answer me this one question. Are you indeed married to Percy Pedwardine?"

If she spoke, Ottilia did not hear it. Instead, a loud report exploded on her eardrums. A flitter of wind passed across her face and then blood spurted in her vision.

CHAPTER NINETEEN

Shouts and cries erupted about Ottilia as she stood there, dazed. Her gaze caught that of the woman in the cloak, the other's eyes registering shock. Then the woman toppled, falling to the ground. Arms caught Ottilia as she swayed a little. Francis was there, shouting into her face words she could not hear.

The moment replayed. Report. Wind. Blood. With awful clarity, Ottilia recognised what had happened.

"He missed me. The bullet took her instead."

"For pity's sake, Tillie, are you hurt? Answer me!"

The words were a jumble to her ears but she could detect a note of urgency, demanding a response. "Fear not, Fan. I am alive, I think."

He caught her hard against him. "Thank God!" He released her almost at once. "Here, sit!"

From somewhere, a straight chair had appeared. Ottilia was pushed into it. She sat, but her gaze sought the fallen woman. She was scarcely visible for the persons crowding about her where she lay on the ground. Ottilia recognised Hemp, methodically checking a pulse.

Her attention caught on Francis, who was speaking again. Her hearing was beginning to return, though his voice was faint to her ears.

"The militia have gone after him. Whether they will catch him, who knows?"

"Is she dead, Fan?"

"I don't know. It looks like it."

Ottilia felt curiously light-headed but her mind remained clear, her thoughts clean. "He meant it for me. He could not have meant to kill her, could he? No, for it passed so close. His aim was inaccurate."

"I didn't even see the villain."

"Was it Percy?"

"I tell you I didn't see him. It was all so quick. Too sudden."

Ottilia's ability to make out detail began to revive. The press of persons was dispersing a little, or at least drawing back, and she could make out the figure on the ground. Hemp was still kneeling by her. As Ottilia watched, he took out a handkerchief, spread it open and laid it over the wound in the woman's head. An image pressed itself upon Ottilia's senses. Behind the spray of blood, a face half shattered. She could not have survived.

Ottilia became aware that her spouse was dabbing at her own face. "What are you doing, Fan?"

"You are covered in her blood."

Her hearing must have improved because she could make out the tone. Flat, redolent with underlying horror. It became imperative to soothe. "I am alive, Fan. That poor girl took the bullet meant for me."

Francis was intent upon his task, wetting a corner of the handkerchief with his tongue and swabbing at her cheek. "She is no innocent. She lured you to the spot where he was waiting. I should never have agreed to this venture."

Ottilia reached up and stayed his hand. "Leave it, Fan. I will wash when we return home."

His eyes were fierce as they met hers. "Your gown is ruined, do you know that?"

She was betrayed into a slight, hysterical laugh. "A small price to pay." But she looked down and found her gown was indeed spattered with the woman's blood. A little shudder shook her. "That is not pleasant."

"Pleasant? Dear God! You are in shock and no wonder."

A figure in a red coat appeared. "I've sent for a doctor, my lord."

"A trifle late in the day, isn't it, Dalby?"

The captain's reply was stiff. "To certify the death."

Ottilia's heart kicked. "Then she is dead?"

"I imagine she was killed instantly, ma'am."

Not instantly. There had been time for realisation. Time for shock. She had known what had happened to her.

Looking across, Ottilia saw that Hemp had risen. He caught her glance and shook his head. Confirmation. A wave of pity flooded Ottilia. A victim twice over? If she was cheated into marriage, she had paid dearly for her mistake. The questions the girl had asked echoed in Ottilia's head. *Was it he? Was he involved?* Had she heard the rumours after they were wed? Had she taken the chance when it offered to find out the truth, even as she drew Ottilia into the trap? Or had she not known what her husband intended?

She became aware of the ongoing conversation between Francis and Captain Dalby.

"Nothing yet, my lord. All the men are hunting the area."

"Did you see him? I had my eyes on my wife and paid no attention, I fear. Did he run away?"

"He was cleverer than that, my lord. After the shot was fired, he must have waited for the commotion and slipped away unseen."

Ottilia spoke the thought in her mind. "That is in keeping with his style."

"My lady?"

"Percy Pedwardine," she answered. "It is he. It must be he."

"Did that woman say so?"

"Not directly. She would not give me names, but when I taxed her with his name, she became agitated. Besides, who else could it be? She asked me if he was involved in his friend's death. That is all the proof I need. There is no other it could be."

Dalby looked dubious, but Francis backed her up. "You may take it my wife has it right. We have suspected that villain from the outset."

Except, Ottilia reflected, that she had come to the conclusion that the girl and her paramour were a separate issue from the attempt upon her life. A distinctly disturbing thought entered her mind. Could the bullet have been intended for the wife? Was Ottilia herself only a scapegoat?

Her ears buzzed. Just as she was deciding they were not quite recovered, she lost consciousness.

Ottilia was lost in a dream. Floating in water, the girl swimming at her side. She knew who it was because of the cloak streaming behind.

"He will not drown," the girl said. "He always comes up again."

They were walking in a forest, the man some way ahead. Ottilia began running, the desire to catch a glimpse of his face paramount. He must have heard her steps, for he turned his head.

She woke in shock, his name on her lips. "Quin?"

"Lie still, my dear one. Hemp has gone for brandy."

Ottilia blinked up into her husband's face. "How could it be Quin? Has he escaped?"

Concern entered his face. "You are talking nonsense, Tillie." He snapped his fingers. "Come back to me!"

The dream receded and Ottilia's senses and vision coalesced, presenting her with a strange scene. She was lying on a hard surface but for something soft under her head, Francis standing by and leaning over her. Above was a white-painted ceiling, to one side were shelves, at her feet a set of faces she did not know. "What is this place?"

"It is a linen draper's. Rickward here kindly allowed me to bring you in."

She noted a chubby countenance in the man at her husband's elbow. She spoke with automatic politeness despite her bewilderment. "Thank you. But why?"

"You swooned." A grim note came. "Small wonder."

Events flooded back. "The girl! He shot her."

"He shot at you. Thank the Lord he missed."

Realisation returned. "He did not miss. He meant to kill the girl." Francis said no word for a moment, but Ottilia's mind was beginning to work again and she pressed on. "You will think I have lost my senses."

"I wasn't going to say so."

Ottilia brought a hand up and grasped at his coat. "I am better. Help me up, Fan."

He took the hand and held it. "I'd rather you waited for the brandy."

She looked from one side to the other. "What am I lying on?"

"The counter."

"Well, it is decidedly uncomfortable. Pray help me up."

He rolled his eyes but complied, setting a hand under her back and lifting. Ottilia's head swam as she sat up, but she managed to swing her legs off the counter. She caught at her husband's shoulders for support, steadying her head on his chest as she waited for the giddy sensation to recede.

He held her, a low murmur reaching her ears. "Steady, sweetheart. You've had a violent shock. Take your time."

But urgency was burgeoning. "What happened to the girl?"

"Dalby is taking care of all that."

She pushed away, sitting up. "Is she still out there? Has he taken her away as yet?"

"Hardly. The doctor sent for the coroner and Dalby is finding an undertaker."

Relief swept through Ottilia. "I want to see her."

His brows drew together. "Why in the world, Tillie? We know how she died. There's no need."

She could hear the note of irritation under the apparent calm and knew it was borne of latent anxiety. Ottilia met his gaze. "Indulge me, Fan. Help me down, if you please."

His lips tightened but he did not speak as he assisted her off the counter. His hands held her strongly as she stood. "I won't let go until you're stable on your own feet."

Ottilia managed a smile. "Always my rock, my dearest."

He grunted but deigned no reply. Ottilia looked for the shopkeeper and discovered him hovering. "I must thank you, sir. It was kind of you to let me clutter up your counter."

The fellow bowed over a protruding paunch. "Only too happy, my lady. Shocking thing. Never had such an event happen in these parts."

"I am so sorry we have caused such a commotion."

"No, indeed. No such thing, my lady. Not your fault. A maniac methinks. Firing off pistols in the open street."

Ottilia did not disabuse him, reiterating her thanks before returning her gaze to Francis. "I am ready."

"Are you sure about this?"

"Perfectly."

She took his arm, leaning on it but slightly as he escorted her out of the shop. The body was lying at a little distance from the entrance, the green cloak forming a partial macabre shroud. The feet had remained more or less where the girl and Ottilia had been standing, the head pointing into the roadway. One hand was thrown outwards, while the other had fallen across the woman's breast. The face was covered and Ottilia recalled Hemp placing his handkerchief there. It was bloodied now, soaked through where it had come into contact with the wreckage caused by the bullet.

Arriving above the body, Ottilia let go of Francis's arm and sank down beside the unfortunate girl. An image of the girl's face, animated, imprinted itself on her memory. The striped dimity gown, not then blood-spattered, had been cut low over breasts now flattened, with full petticoats that had risen up with the fall, exposing her ankles.

Ottilia clicked her tongue. Had no one thought to give the girl back her dignity? She leaned down, smoothing the petticoats over the exposed stockings. Then she moved to the head, reached for the edge of the handkerchief, drew in a steadying breath and pulled the cloth off the face. Someone must have closed the girl's eyes. Where her skin was clean of blood, the waxy look of death was visible. But the wound inevitably drew the eye. It was a pitiful sight. Ottilia could not prevent the horrid thought that the face thus ruined might have been her own.

She thrust it away, convinced she had not been the intended target. The shooter must have been too close to miss. A flame of anger rose inside her. Typical of the man, to seek to obfuscate the deed by using her to draw attention away from his real intention.

Ottilia re-covered the face. Then, with fastidious precision, she used the cloak to shroud as much of the girl's body as she could. She should not be left as a raree-show for the curious.

They loitered still, crowding on the other side of the street, held back by Captain Dalby's men. Ottilia watched the faces and knew her motions had been taken in, the staring eyes directed at her instead of the body.

She looked for her spouse and found him standing a little way off, talking in low tones to the captain. He had noticed her search, for he left the militiaman and came across.

"Have you seen enough?"

She held up her hand. "Yes, I thank you, Fan." He helped her to rise and Ottilia met his gaze, a swell of emotion in her bosom. "May we go home?"

Before he could reply, the deep voice of Hemp sounded. "Drink this first, milady." He handed her a glass with a small quantity of brown liquid inside. Ottilia took it and sipped. "Ryde is bringing the phaeton, milord."

"Then we'll wait. Fetch that chair for her ladyship, Hemp."

Ottilia made no objection to being encouraged to sit again. The fiery liquid was warming, and the rising distress began to recede. Vaguely she heard her husband conferring with Hemp, then again with Captain Dalby, but the words washed over her without making sense. She was recalling the dream.

"No sign of your assailant," Francis said as he manoeuvred the phaeton through streets crowded with hurrying persons. Word of the shooting had no doubt spread, bringing all and sundry to the centre of the town to stare and point. Tillie's bloodied gown was thankfully concealed by a short military cloak thoughtfully loaned by Dalby. None of these gawkers would connect her with the gory sight they were no doubt hoping to see. Dalby had expressed his impatience to have the body removed.

"Which will not, I fear, release myself and my men from this hideous debacle, my lord. We must hunt down the perpetrator, if it takes all night."

Francis had doubts they would find the wretch at all. If it was whom Tillie seemed to believe, he would doubtless give the authorities the slip just as he had done at Flitteris. Once again the deed would not be brought home to him.

"That devil will once again escape his just deserts," he said aloud, weaving past a cart containing an overload of eager young lads squashed in together.

"Not necessarily."

Tillie's condition still worried him. She was shaky, though she tried to conceal it. For himself, he doubted he would ever recover. The horror of the moment kept replaying in his mind, together with the hideous conviction he'd had at that instant that his wife had been shot. Only when the girl had fallen did he realise Tillie had miraculously escaped death by a hairsbreadth. He kept silence on his own feelings, not wishing to add to her distress.

That she was distressed he knew, and not because of the near miss upon her own life. She was upset for the girl, and Francis did not know why. Naturally he would not wish her dead, but her antics had brought his darling wife too close to the brink. A vile trap had she devised, and Tillie had fallen into it.

Nothing of his thoughts would he permit upon his tongue, instead focusing on the aftermath. But Tillie's last remark demanded refutation.

"I can't imagine why you think that villain might be caught. Who is to know he pulled the trigger, even if they find him?"

Tillie turned her head and he met her gaze for a moment, clear as it ought to be, he was relieved to note. "They will find him. Not in Buckingham, perhaps. They were staying in Newport Pagnell. The authorities will track him down there, if only to inform him that his wife is dead."

"But they don't know she is the fellow's wife. If she is."

"I think there can be no room for doubt now, Fan. Her attitude made it obvious when I mentioned Percy's name. Did you by chance tell Captain Dalby of that?"

Francis blew out a breath. "I can't recall. He was focused upon the coroner and having his men continue the search."

Tillie tutted. "Then I must send to him. Mr Gibbon also. Perhaps we ought to tell him in person."

Francis balked. "You will do no such thing. You're staying safe at Dalesford, wife of mine." A little trill of laughter made him curse. "What the deuce is so funny?"

"Pardon me, Fan, but to me it is inconsistent. If he meant to fire at his wife, as I believe, I cannot any longer be in danger. Not from him, in any event."

"Well, I don't share your view. Even if you are right, it makes no odds. It was too close run, and I won't let you show yourself abroad again."

She was silent and Francis inwardly cursed. He had not meant to sound harsh. He moderated his tone. "Tillie, the danger is not past. Do you forget Belchamp's offering?"

He received a frowning glance. "Of a girl and her brother. I do not forget, Fan. But that was to substitute for the girl in the cloak and we have identified her now, poor child."

"Poor child? When she meant to lure you to your death?"

"But did she? Did she know? Or did she genuinely want to discover the truth about her husband? I can well believe he fooled her into believing he had some other scheme afoot. One we shall likely never know."

Francis struggled with his demons. "Nevertheless, the danger is not past. If you don't desire to drive me insane, you will oblige me in this, Tillie."

He felt her hand on his thigh and her voice came quietly. "It shall be as you wish, my dearest."

He let out an overwrought breath. "I thank you. We'll talk it all out when we get back to Dalesford."

He meant to be conciliatory, but his wife did not reply. Francis kept silence, not wishing to reopen hostilities. But when they had left the town and he was guiding the vehicle along the main road that ran alongside the Great Ouse, a burgeoning thought chased away his distress and he gave it voice.

"What did you mean about Quin?"

Her gaze was trained upon the road. "I dreamed of him. When I was unconscious. It woke me to recognise him because I was expecting to see Percy."

Francis sighed in relief. "Is that all? I'm not surprised the whole business is jumbled up in your head. Rest assured. Quin is safe in gaol."

Tillie's head turned and he caught one those faraway looks on her face. What the deuce was she puzzling at now? Her voice when she spoke was vague in tone.

"Yes … but I think it is well to pay heed to such oddities. The mind has a way of alerting one to something that has passed one by. Have you not experienced it so?"

"I can't say that I have. Moreover, I don't understand what you mean. How alert? Of what possible use to puzzle over a dream? I know you make those impossible leaps of yours, but you are not in general an advocate of following unsubstantiated hunches."

She became eager, turning to him, her eyes alight. "We dismissed Quin, don't you see? He was adamant he knew nothing of my fall into the Ouse and you thought it was genuine."

"It was. He clearly knew about Cherry's death, but he had no knowledge of your near drowning." Yet even as he spoke, replaying the brief discussion he'd had with Quin when he'd caught him that day, Francis felt doubt creep in.

"Or he managed to convince you."

"Not only me. Hemp tackled him also."

Tillie blew out a breath. Frustration? "I must talk to Hemp. He did not tell me what was said."

Francis was conscious of a rise of irritation. "You are throwing the whole affair into question again, Tillie. We will get nowhere if we go round in circles."

"I am only following logic, Fan. It cannot be coincidence that my brain throws Quin at me just when I have made a reckoning that the wretched Percy did not mean my death, but that of his wife."

"You are being ridiculous. I suppose it is to be expected."

A trill of laughter came. "You think me addled by shock? Well, perhaps you are right. But you must allow me to follow my instinct, if you please."

He was silent for a space, seething. He had driven a mile or so before it occurred to him to wonder why in the world he was infuriated. The answer came swiftly. He wanted an end to this. His wife's determination to pursue it was anathema. Which made no sense. Gil had said it all. If they went home without a solution, there could be no peace for either of them. On the thought, he put the question in his mind.

"Are you now suggesting it was Quin who hid under the jetty and pulled you in?"

He expected hesitation or prevarication, but there was neither.

"Just so, Fan. I think he did it, egged on thereto by Cherry, in all likelihood. After all, she had the strongest motive to be wishing me out of the way, since I am undoubtedly responsible for her becoming a fugitive from the law."

"Not Indigo, then?"

"It would not surprise me if that episode had become Indigo's motive for disposing of Cherry. If she was acting on her own, she might be considered a liability. From what you have said of him, I cannot imagine Indigo keeping anyone about him who was not immediately under his control, can you?"

"A trifle flimsy, it seems to me."

"What is flimsy?"

"The motive. I grant you Cherry's vengeance, but if that was why Indigo killed her, why didn't he kill off Quin while he was about it?"

"Because Quin is biddable? Hemp was able to intimidate him with ease."

The bridge to cross the Great Ouse was coming up ahead and Francis thought over her words as he negotiated the turn. Relief that they were almost back at Dalesford Hall was tempered by the horrid certainty that his darling wife was going to persuade him into going against his better judgement. It was always hard to withstand her when she had the bit between her teeth, and he was by no means persuaded of her being right. If she was, the danger was past. Quin was incarcerated. If Percy had the intention to kill his own wife, that now accomplished. Yet he could not shake a conviction that Tillie was too sanguine. The day's debacle proved there was nowhere to be considered entirely safe.

Arrived at Dalesford, it became immediately clear that Hemp, on horseback and thus able to weave more readily through the throngs of ghoulish sightseers in Buckingham, had arrived back ahead and raised the alarm.

"I've been watching for you," announced Gil, pounding down the steps and hastening up to the phaeton. "Ottilia, we are all in an uproar for your shocking misadventure."

Before his wife could answer, Francis intervened. "She is in need of rest and a change of clothes, Gil. Be a good fellow and send at once for her maid to come to the bedchamber."

"Yes, yes, I will do so directly. Let me first help you down, Ottilia."

Tillie gave him her warm smile and took the hand he reached up to her. "Thank you, Gil. I am a little fatigued, but otherwise well enough."

Impatient to alight himself, Francis called to his groom, who had leapt from his perch and gone to the horses' heads. "Ryde, come and take the reins! You may drive them round to the stables and see them bestowed."

Gil, in the act of guiding Ottilia to the ground, intervened. "My grooms will do that, Fan. Let your fellow take a rest. Well-earned, I don't doubt."

Francis had handed the reins to Ryde, who touched his hat. "Begging your pardon, my lord, but I won't rest until I've seen them properly rubbed down and settled."

"Quite right, Ryde." And to his wife, "I am coming, Tillie."

To his chagrin, Gil undertook the task of escorting her up the stairs and into the house. Francis followed with hasty steps, but before he could take over at his wife's side, his mother and sister came out from the large saloon to one side in which they had presumably been waiting for this return.

"Ottilia, my child, what a horrible thing to happen!"

"Thank heaven you are in one piece, Ottilia! I was never so shocked in my life! Oh, dear lord in heaven, you are bloodied!"

Francis jumped on this. "For pity's sake, Harriet, be quiet! It is not her blood."

Both women reached his wife and Tillie took his sister's held-out hands. "I am unharmed, Harriet. I escaped injury entirely."

His mother pitched in. "Not entirely, by what that steward fellow of yours told us. Did you not swoon?"

"No wonder, Mama! In Ottilia's place, I should have had hysterics."

"Give her space to breathe, both of you." Francis moved to his wife's side. "Lean on me, my love. I will take you up."

"You'd best carry her, Francis."

Tillie had left off Gil's arm and taken his instead. "By no means, Sybilla. I am well able to walk. Forgive me. I must change my dress. We will tell you all presently."

"No, you won't," said Francis, *sotto voce*. "You must rest."

He was glad to note his brother-in-law had accosted the butler, who hurried off, hopefully to fetch his wife's maid. His relatives' voices followed them up the stairs as he led Tillie thence.

"I should think she ought to be laid down upon her bed after such a happening."

"So she may, but if I know my daughter-in-law she is a good deal more resilient than you suppose."

"Shall we repair to the family parlour?" Gil called up as Francis reached the landing. "Meet us there, Fan, if you will. We are all anxious for a proper account of events."

He paused on the landing, turning to look down, and found the whole party now upon the stairs. "I shall do so once Ottilia has her maid with her." Turning back, it was borne in on him that his wife was leaning rather more heavily into him. "Sweetheart, are you able to make it? Shall I carry you after all?"

She pushed herself upright, with an effort, he thought. "I will do, Fan. I confess I am a trifle more debilitated than I supposed."

"I'm not surprised."

He received a deprecating glance. "Delayed shock, I fear."

"Then let us get you secured." With which, he captured her under the shoulders and knees and swung her up into his arms.

She caught at his coat, throwing one hand about his neck. "I could have walked, Fan."

He was moving swiftly and ignored this. "Hot water is what you need. A bath would be best."

"I haven't the strength for a bath, my darling lord. Joanie will help me wash it all off."

The maid came running down the corridor, having evidently come up via the servant's stairway at the back, just as Francis was approaching the door to their allotted bedchamber, fortunately situated on the first floor.

"Open the door, if you will."

The maid did so and Francis carried his burden into the room and set her down on the bed. Tillie landed in some disorder and he was obliged to steady her with a hand on each shoulder.

"All right?"

She nodded. "Thank you, Fan. I will manage now. You go."

"Are you sure? I'll stay if you need me."

"No need. The others are impatient to hear all." She smiled at the hovering maid. "Joanie will do all that I require."

The girl dropped a curtsy. "That I will, my lady. I'll look after her, my lord, don't you worry."

"Very well." Francis leaned and dropped a kiss on his wife's brow. "Rest, Tillie. Everything else can wait."

He felt his hand caught and the clear gaze met his, apology in its depths. "Thank you, my dearest. I cannot think how I would manage without you."

He grimaced. "Fortunately, you don't have to."

He did not add the thought in his mind, that it was rather he who might today have been obliged to manage without her. The notion caused a painful twinge. On impulse, he brought the hand that held his to his lips and kissed it. She smiled and released him.

Francis turned and walked out of the room, closing the door behind him. All at once, the enormity of the day's events came home to him. He leaned against the door, breathing hard. His heart was pumping, as loud in his ears as the shot that had nearly done for Tillie, or so it felt.

A voice spoke, startling him. "I thought as much." Gil, holding out a glass. "Here. Take it. Drink."

"Brandy? You are a lifesaver, Gil." He downed the golden liquid in two swallows. In seconds, the expected warmth radiated through him and the discomforts under which he was labouring began to ease.

Gil nodded towards the bedroom door as Francis straightened. "How is she doing?"

"I've left her in the care of her maid. She's more affected than she knew."

"One might suppose it." Gil looked him up and down. "You seem a degree better, but if you are not up to giving us an account as yet, take your time. I'll keep the women in check."

"No, I will do." Francis held up the glass. "This did the trick."

Gil took it from him. "That's why I came to find you. Right then, *en avant*, my brother."

Francis drew a breath. He was not looking forward to a plethora of impossible questions and exclamatory comment. Better him than Tillie, however. He could at least shield her in this, even if he could not guarantee to keep her alive.

CHAPTER TWENTY

With her maid's assistance to untie the strings, Ottilia succeeded in divesting herself of the stained round gown. It dropped to the floor and she stepped out of it, but Joanie did not immediately bend to pick it up, instead regarding Ottilia's upper body and tutting the while.

"It's got through onto your stays and your shift too, my lady. Nor I don't doubt it's all over your skin there and all."

Glancing down, Ottilia found the silken shift and the ribbed corset were both marred by stains in a fainter red than that on her ruined gown. An urgent need to be rid of the blood came over her. "Untie my stays, Joanie, quickly."

"Let's get this under-petticoat off first, my lady, or we'll never do."

Ottilia's skin crawled but she stood obediently still while Joanie wrestled with the ties. The instant the under-petticoat fell, she turned to give access to the strings of her stays, almost fell in her haste and had to put out her hands to steady herself on the bed.

"Take care, my lady!"

Thanks to the maid grasping her about the waist, she kept her footing and was able to push upright again, impatient for the stays to fall away. The moment they did, Ottilia seized the stuff of her shift and dragged it over her head, throwing it aside. Naked, she looked again down her person. The blood had indeed soaked through onto her skin, leaving welts of colour across her bosom and shoulder.

Ottilia shuddered and abruptly sat sideways on the bed as a wave of nausea attacked her. Then Joanie was there, holding up a wrapper.

"Put this on, my lady. There's hot water on the way. We'll soon have you clean again."

Ottilia paid no heed, gasping out her need. "Basin!" She put a hand over her mouth, feeling the retching start up in her stomach.

"Oh, lordy me, she's going to be sick!" She heard Joanie's rapid steps across the floor and back again. "Here, my lady, take this!"

Ottilia saw the empty wash basin and seized it just as her stomach erupted, spilling its contents into the receptacle. Several times her stomach heaved before the urge to empty it began to ease. Her head was swimming and she was relieved to find the maid was still holding the bowl. Ottilia let go, wiped a hand across her mouth and sank onto the bed, oblivious both to her unclothed state and the mutterings of her maid.

Presently, she felt the softness of the wrapper being laid over her person and was vaguely aware of a knocking at the door.

"That'll be your hot water, my lady. Not before time." Joanie bustled off and Ottilia heard a whispered colloquy off in the distance of her mind. Then the maid was back and a hot damp cloth was being applied to Ottilia's face. The girl spoke again, to someone else, it seemed. "Help me lift her legs, Doro. That's it. She'll be more comfortable and I can wash off that horrid blood too."

Ottilia could do nothing to help, although it passed through her mind that she ought to do so. Her legs were raised and hands turned her, lifting her head to the pillow. She sighed for the added comfort and the dreadful fog in her brain began to lift.

"Doro, could you bring his lordship's basin over? Can't use this one now. Leave the jug!"

Blessed warmth plied across Ottilia's bosom. Relief swept through her. Joanie was cleaning away the blood. She gave herself up to the maid's ministrations, paying scant mind to the whispered discussions going forward.

"I came myself when Hemp told me. Hepsie is minding Luke."

"I'm glad you did. I don't think I'd have managed on my own."

"We should get her between sheets, no?"

"She's best lying where she is. Give me the towel. When I'm done, we'll put the quilt over her."

This penetrated. Ottilia opened her eyes and found both Joanie's and Doro's faces leaning over her. "Not the quilt. Too hot."

Joanie registered consternation. "Beg your pardon, my lady. I thought you'd fainted."

"Very nearly. Water? To drink, I mean."

Doro set a hand on her leg. "I will fetch it, milady."

"Thank you."

She retreated out of Ottilia's line of vision, but Joanie called after her. "Best order coffee too. If I know my lady, she'll be asking for that next."

A faint gurgle escaped Ottilia. "And cheese, Joanie. Don't forget the cheese."

The maid left off towelling to call out, "Cheese too, Doro! The Cheddar. And toast."

An assenting voice called back and the door opened and closed. Ottilia caught Joanie's eye as the maid turned back to her. "I was joking."

"Well, I weren't, my lady. You can dip the toast if you don't want to eat the cheese."

"You are very good to me."

"I should think I ought to be, my lady." Joanie was plying the towel. "There, that'll do. You look more yourself now." She peered into Ottilia's face. "Though you are pale still."

Ottilia ignored this, struggling onto her elbow. "Pray bank the pillows behind me, Joanie. I wish to sit up."

"Are you sure you ought to, my lady?" But she was obeying the injunction nevertheless, seizing an extra pillow from Francis's side and plumping it up before setting it at Ottilia's back.

She pulled up on the bed and sank into the pile, what time the wrapper the maid had just replaced slipped down.

Joanie tutted and tugged it back up. "I'll fetch your big shawl."

"The cotton one, if you please. Not the wool."

Ottilia lay quiescent for a while, longing for the water to quench her thirst and clear her mouth of the foul taste of vomit. The notion crept into her mind that she had been more unnerved by the shooting than she had supposed. Delayed shock indeed. Although it was unlike her to be sick without due cause. She had swooned at the scene, but that was to be expected. Wasn't it?

Joanie returned with her printed Indian cotton shawl, having unearthed it from the press she and Francis were using. The maid helped her to put on the wrapper at least around her upper half, and spread the shawl over the rest like a sheet.

"Your hair is all over the place, my lady. I'd best unpin it." She did so and then applied the brush to smooth Ottilia's soft brown locks. "We'll leave it loose for now, my lady."

It mattered little to Ottilia, her thirst paramount. Fortunately, Doro returned in short order, armed with a jug of water and a glass on a small tray. Joanie pounced on it.

"Just what we need. I'll dip your toothbrush, my lady, and lard on the toothpowder. Fill a glass for her, Doro."

Ottilia was so thirsty, she was ready to forgo brushing her teeth. She was obedient to Joanie's urging, however, when the maid presented her with the means to freshen her mouth, spitting into a small bowl kept for the purpose, and at once feeling the benefit of the proceeding. Doro spoke as she once again set her lips to the glass.

"The coffee will be here directly, milady."

Ottilia blinked at her. She had not quite taken in Doro's presence until this moment. "Should you not be with Luke, Doro?"

"Hepsie is taking care of him, milady. I had to come after what Hemp told me. Also he wanted me to find out how you are."

This evidence of her steward's affection caught at Ottilia's heartstrings and she was obliged to sip at the water through a tightened throat when she wanted to gulp it down. Her brother's voice in her head told her this was the better course. "Never allow a patient to drink greedily, especially if they are nauseous," had been Patrick's dictum. One of them. She had absorbed so much. Yet when it came to her own well-being, she was inclined to be less than scrupulous. Small wonder Francis was often infuriated.

"I suppose I ought to rest more," she said aloud.

"That you ought, my lady. Special as you've had such a nasty happening." Joanie spoke from across the room, where she was evidently dealing with the various basins and the discarded clothing. "What do you want doing with these, my lady?" She held up the soiled garments. "I doubt as I'll be able to get them stains out."

Ottilia was about to tell her to throw or give them away when a thought occurred. "Have I enough gowns without it? I do not know how long we may be obliged to remain here."

"We'll manage without, my lady, never you fear."

Doro intervened before she could say more. "Give them to me, Joanie. I have a way of removing such stains. We had no choice but to preserve our clothing in Barbados."

Half inclined to reject this offer, Ottilia held her tongue. Because she did not wish to wear the clothes again was no reason to be unkind. Instead she thanked Doro, who brushed it aside.

"May I tell Hemp you are somewhat recovered, milady?"

Except that she did not feel much recovered at all. A sensation of malaise possessed her. Unusually. Was she so poor a creature now to be laid low by such an event? When she thought of all she had seen and done, all she had undergone when undertaking these adventures, it struck her as peculiar she should be thus debilitated by the events of the day.

"I am a degree better," she conceded. She set aside the empty glass on the bedside cabinet and voiced a fresh need. "However, now I fear I am indeed hungry."

"Did I not say so?" Triumphant, the maid came across to the bed. "I knew you'd need a snack, my lady. It's just like when you were pregnant with Master Luke. Swoons and growing quickly fatigued and hungry as a hunter you were."

All at once, Joanie's eyes popped and she threw a hand to her mouth. Ottilia caught the inference. "No. It cannot be, Joanie."

"Well, I don't know, my lady. Seems to me it's quite like the last time."

Aware of Doro joining the maid at the bedside, Ottilia's mind was working. It was days since she had considered the possibility she might again be pregnant. She had been resistant then, given the unsatisfactory state of affairs between herself and Francis. At this moment, however, it did not appear either quite so far-fetched, nor so disastrous a turn, should it prove to be the case.

"When did I last have my flux, Joanie?"

The maid set her arms akimbo, a frown appearing. "Must be all of three or four weeks, my lady. Before we came here, in any event. Maybe more."

"Then I am due, am I not?"

"Any day, I should think."

Then Doro spoke, her beautiful dark features showing anxiety. "Five weeks, milady. I remember because Luke was rebellious when he could not visit you."

Ottilia's breath caught. "*Five*? Joanie, could it be five?"

The maid became agitated. "Might be, my lady. I'd have kept proper count if we'd been at home at Flitteris. I always note it down so I'm ready for when it starts, but I didn't think to bring my little book. Nor it hasn't been that long since your flux began again after giving Master Luke suck for the last time."

Ottilia blew out an overcharged breath. "We are getting ahead of ourselves. Today has been difficult. We may as easily put it all down to that."

At this point, a knock at the door announced the arrival of a footman with Ottilia's refreshments. Doro brought in the tray and set it down on the side table, while Joanie continued to regard Ottilia.

"Begging your pardon, my lady, but have you checked for a bump?"

"No, and I could not be showing yet. I have not felt my clothes too tight." Even as she spoke, she set her hands to her belly and smoothed across the expanse of it. "No, there is nothing."

"Well, we'd best keep an eye on it, my lady."

Dismay crept into Ottilia's breast. She did not know whether the prospect was welcome or not. Doro came across, bearing a platter with slices of toast and cheese and a cup from which the welcome aroma of coffee reached Ottilia's nostrils.

She took it, sipping gratefully. A bite of the toast with her favourite cheese did much to restore her equilibrium.

"I had better get back to Luke now, milady."

Urgency engulfed Ottilia. "Wait, Doro! Not a word of this to my husband, if you please. Nor anyone else. Not yet. Not until we are certain." Both servants regarded her in silence. Ottilia became tart. "Don't look at me like that. I have my reasons. I want you both to promise. Don't speak of it, and don't tell him I was sick, Joanie." At the consternation in her maid's face, she added more gently, "I don't wish to worry him. He has enough to plague him at this present."

Both maid and nurse at last consented to keep the matter secret. But Ottilia felt guilt rising. It was not for fear of worrying Francis that she wished to keep him ignorant, although that was a consideration. As sure as check, he would point blank refuse to allow her to pursue her enquiries any further. Moreover, if she truly was again pregnant, she would wish to tell him only when this business was all over and she had succeeded in recovering that ease of communication between them that was so much a part of what she valued in her marriage.

She missed it. How much became clear when she could not take pleasure in the prospect of possibly presenting him with another pledge of her affection. Nor, to say truth, could she contemplate with equanimity the thought of the months stretching ahead with the attendant necessity for rest, quiet and relative inaction. She needed time to adjust to the notion herself before burdening her husband. If, that was, it proved true that she was bearing another child. Yet the thought, once instilled, refused to go away.

"What do you mean to do now, Francis?"

The question, coming from his mother hard upon the heels of his relation of the day's events, caught him off guard.

"I have no notion, ma'am."

His sister, who had paled at the tale, took it upon herself to champion him. "Gracious, Mama, how should he know? He has scarcely had time to think of it. One could not expect poor Fan to be troubling his head with what comes next when Ottilia has been as near death as makes no odds."

Sybilla snorted. "Do you take your brother for such a poor creature? I will wager Ottilia herself is already making plans." Francis came under the beam of her gimlet eye. "I am right, am I not?"

For once, he had given in to the effects of the day upon his person and taken a seat on the sofa instead of assuming his usual pose at the mantel. He was thus able to avoid that eye with a glance at Harriet instead. "We did mention possibilities on the journey back."

His mother grew impatient. "Well, what? Speak up, boy!"

That brought his head round. "We made no exact plans. Tillie has got some notion in her head about that fellow Quin."

"Isn't he safe in gaol?" asked Gil, seated in a chair opposite.

"Yes, but she is thinking of the first attack."

Harriet shuddered. "I wish you won't speak of that. I truly thought we had lost her forever."

"Yes, my love, but there is no need to be reminding Fan of that." Gil's gaze returned to Francis. "Does Ottilia intend to question the fellow again?"

"She hasn't questioned him. I did so briefly when we caught him, and Hemp had another attempt in the gaol. We both decided he knew nothing of the business."

"But Ottilia thinks otherwise," cut in his mother on a note of relish that could not but irritate.

"She said she dreamed of him while she was in a swoon."

Sybilla delivered herself of another snort. "Typical. However, you will allow her notions, however outlandish, too often turn out to be correct."

Francis knew it, but he chose to ignore this. "Everything hinges on whether that reprobate meant to hit Ottilia and missed, or if he deliberately aimed at his own wife."

"But you don't even know that it was this particular reprobate," objected Gil. "Nor that the unfortunate victim was married to him. Didn't you say she would not give Ottilia her name?"

Francis flung up a hand. "Don't ask me, Gil. Tillie is convinced by the woman's reaction to her mentioning the name of Percy. I cannot say for certain either way. Unless the militia succeed in running him to earth, I dare say we may never know."

"But you cannot leave it to chance, Fan," cried his sister. "Who is to say this terrible man will not try again?"

"Bravo, Harriet." This from his mother, for once praising her daughter, who looked gratified. "Well spoken, my child. And do not imagine Francis does not realise it."

He did, with a vengeance. Everything in him urged flight. Yet the sometime soldier inside him knew he must stand his ground and pursue the business to its end, whatever that might prove to be. "I have no choice, ma'am."

"Quite so, my son. You must make a plan."

He rose. "In due course. I must go and see how my wife does."

He left the room on the words, relieved to escape. He had no plan, no notion of how to proceed. Dalby and the authorities had the task of identifying the victim as well as locating her killer. The captain had promised to send word the moment he discovered anything to the purpose. It might be politic to wait for that. Whether he could keep his wife from pursuing the matter beforehand remained a question.

But when he opened the door to their bedchamber, he entered to silence and the sight of Tillie lying against a bank of pillows, her eyes closed. He went softly forward, noting she was wearing her wrapper and was covered with a large shawl.

At the bedside, he stood looking down at her, affection building in his breast. Free of the bloodstains, her hair falling about her head, she was altogether the woman he adored. There was an innocence about her as she slept. As if nothing of the terrible events had touched her.

Although she was more pallid than usual. A glance at a discarded tray told him she had been provided with coffee and something to eat. He gave silent thanks for Joanie's care of her. The servants to a man were apt to cater to her every whim. She had the knack of endearing herself to all with whom she came into contact. Except those whose machinations she exposed.

How had he found and secured this treasure? As the thought filtered into his mind, his wife's eyelids fluttered open. He saw her catch sight of him and recognition flashed.

"Fan!"

He could not look away from her face. "I did not mean to wake you."

She smiled. "I was dozing only."

On impulse, he walked around the bed, shrugging off his coat as he went. He threw it over the nearest chair, sat on the bed and tugged at his boots.

"What are you doing?"

"Joining you." Divested of the boots, he got onto the bed, banked more pillows and settled beside her. "Come here, wife of my heart." He gathered her to him and held her close, affection swelling in his bosom. Turning, he planted a kiss on her forehead. "Now you may rest better."

A gurgle rewarded him. "Infinitely better, my dearest dear."

For a while he was content to remain silent, cherishing the feel of her in his arms, the warmth of her body against his and the joy of her aliveness. His fears receded.

"Fan?"

"Hm?" He felt her hesitation and squinted down, trying to see her face. "What is it, Tillie?"

She shifted, pushing up onto her elbow so that he was able to meet her gaze. "I was not going to tell you."

He put up a hand and smoothed the hair that fell about her face. "Tell me what, sweetheart?"

There was a rueful look in the grey eyes. "I think I may be with child again."

For an instant the words did not register. Then they hit and he sat up in a bang, spilling her from his hold. "You are pregnant?"

Tillie struggled up too, clutching at the shawl that threatened to fall away. "It is by no means certain, Fan."

"Have you reason to suppose it?"

He saw her draw breath. "The fainting. Twice now. Moreover, I was sick just after you left the room earlier. My appetite, too, is building." She touched a hand to his chest in the way she had. "But it may all be attributed to these events. It may mean nothing."

He felt as if he was reeling. "What of your monthlies?"

"We were trying to work it out, Joanie and I. We could only account for four weeks, but Doro thinks it was five."

"Doro?"

"Yes, she came when Hemp told her what had happened. She helped Joanie. I made them both promise not to mention it, especially not to you."

This salient point penetrated and a shadow crossed his heart. "Why weren't you going to tell me?"

His hand was seized and held tightly. Her gaze became luminous. "Because I knew you would curtail my activities."

It was true, but he held off saying so. Nor had his wife finished.

"Also, Fan, because I did not want to tell you while we are estranged."

Protest rose up. "We are not estranged, Tillie."

"A little distanced, then."

"No. Not now, my dear one."

A gasping sort of breath escaped her, although the threatening tears seemed to have receded. "You say that, but you know it has been difficult for us both."

He did not want to pursue it. "We will weather it, sweetheart."

She was still grasping his hand and shook it. "You keep saying that, my darling lord. Pray let us weather it now. I cannot bear it any longer."

It was his turn to blow out a difficult breath. "How do you propose we do that?"

For a moment she only regarded him. Questioning what she should say? Or how to say it? He waited. When she spoke, she said the last thing he might have expected.

"Why did you fall in love with me, Fan?"

He gave a self-conscious laugh. "What an odd question!"

"Indulge me. It is to the purpose."

"Well … because you are — you were brave and clever." The memories leapt up. "Because you made me laugh when my life was turned upside-down. Because you were utterly unpredictable and I never knew what you would be at. Because you brought mayhem into my life as well as warmth and love. Because you giggled like a little girl…" He faded out, the smile tugging at his lips as it all came back to him.

Tears were trickling down her cheeks. Francis put out a finger and brushed them away. The smile he loved appeared and her voice was husky.

"What was I doing when we met?"

The question puzzled for a space. Then he took her meaning and let out a sigh. "Solving Emily's murder."

"Just so. I am as I am, Fan. For all that I love you and always will, I cannot change. Not in the essentials."

"I don't want you to change." He kissed her lips and settled back against the pillows. "I was following some dream of my own, I think. I don't know why it affected me so."

She had changed position as they talked, sitting almost on her haunches. She continued to regard him from there. "You had only just recovered from thinking me lost to you. It is no surprise you took it badly. Moreover, I spoke out of turn. It was unkind, Fan, and I am sorry for it."

It was the truth for all that, but he withheld the words. For the first time in days, he felt freer, more able to be generous. "No regrets, my dear one."

She gave her infectious chuckle. "That is too much to ask. You know my conscience will plague me."

"I can't help that. You were obviously born with it."

"Fiend!"

He could not help grinning. "There's the woman I married." He reached for her. "Settle down. If you are enceinte, you need to rest."

"I knew you would say so." But she re-joined him, cuddling him in a way that warmed his heart all over again.

"Fan?"

His breath stilled. "What now? No more revelations, I beg of you."

One of her gurgles came. "None, I promise. I forgot the gifts we bought for Luke and Pretty. Are they lost, do you think?"

"I confess I forgot them too in the commotion. Dropped them, I think. But they are not lost. Some kind person retrieved them and returned them to me. Hemp took them in charge. I dare say they are in the phaeton. Ryde will find them."

"That is a relief. At least we may salvage something from the wreck of the day."

She fell silent then and Francis cradled her, conscious of a wish he might erase the whole affair. If another child was on the way, the well-being of his darling wife became a priority.

Presently, however, the press of the aftermath, the difficulty still to be overcome, grew too insistent in his mind to be ignored. An echo of his fears rose up. He dismissed it. A new determination settled in his breast.

"The family want to know what we mean to do, Tillie. Have you a notion in your head?"

CHAPTER TWENTY-ONE

Mr Gibbon was denied. Instantly suspicious, Ottilia persisted.

"It is extremely urgent that we have speech with him," she told the waiter who had delivered the message. "Pray go again and tell him we will wait if we must, but see him we will."

The servant at the Saracen's Head appeared dubious, but he went off towards the stairs, what time Ottilia turned to her spouse.

"Unless he is indisposed with that ankle of his, there is no reason for him to refuse us."

His brows drew together. "What are you thinking?"

"That he has seen his protégé, of course. Or he does indeed know where he is."

"But Dalby believes the wretch has bolted."

"Would he go without trying for succour?"

"If you are right that his mission was always to dispose of his wife, I imagine he would get as far away from the scene of the crime as he could. Especially if he discovers Dalby found out his hidey-hole."

Armed with a full description of the murdered woman, the men of the militia troop had the previous day enquired at every hostelry in Newport Pagnell where one might secure a room. One trooper had at length struck lucky. The captain and his second-in-command had searched the room where the couple had been staying. There were signs of a hasty exit. Clothes strewn about, a portmanteau containing female apparel half packed and torn papers in the grate, none of which yielded any pertinent information. Nothing that might identify either party by name had been found.

"They would have remained unknown," the captain had stated, "if not for the vigilance of the landlady. She had written the names in her register. They were down as Mr and Mrs Gibbon."

Ottilia's mind leapt and she exchanged a startled glance with Francis. "He stole his friend's name!"

Captain Dalby became intent. "Which friend is this?"

"One in whose journey into the afterlife I believe he was instrumental, although I could not prove it." But she was alight with triumph. "Yet it is all the proof we need in this instance. I may assert without doubt that the man you seek is Percy Pedwardine. What is more, Mr Gibbon senior is staying in this very town."

The captain expressed himself as confused and Ottilia was glad when Francis took it upon himself to explain. "Gibbon is the uncle of this man's friend. He is here in search of the fellow. Or he was — we must trust he has not left the place. My wife had written to him to ask if he knew the young man's whereabouts and it brought him at speed to Newport Pagnell."

"Do you suppose Gibbon found him?"

"That we don't know."

"I had best seek him out at once."

Ottilia cut in without ceremony. "Pray let me go instead, Captain. He knows me. If I fail to discover anything useful, you may go in horse and foot."

To gain the captain's agreement, Ottilia had been obliged to promise an immediate visit. Fortunately, she had recovered sufficiently from the debacle of two days ago to be able to undertake the task at once. Not without resistance from her careful spouse.

"Are you sure you are enough rested?"

"Fan, it is a mere mile or two. I will not wilt for such a little journey. Besides, if we wait, we cannot go tomorrow and must hold off until Monday. Too late for Captain Dalby."

He had perforce allowed it, but opted to travel by coach instead of the phaeton. "Until we know the villain is indeed gone, we'll err on the side of caution."

Even now, as they waited for the message to be delivered to Mr Gibbon's room, Francis showed his anxiety.

"You'd best sit down, Tillie." He urged her towards a long sofa placed for the convenience of patrons who were detained in the square hall. "You don't feel sick, do you?"

She allowed herself to be guided into the chair, but nevertheless entered a protest. "I am perfectly well, Fan. Pray don't fuss. Besides, I am more likely to be sick in the morning."

"You weren't, were you?"

"Today? I did a feel a trifle nauseous, but I was not sick."

He was frowning down at her. "This becomes more convincing by the moment."

She smiled up at him. "Let us not be putting the cart before the horse, my dearest. I dare say we will know one way or the other in a week or two."

He said nothing more, but continued to survey her with a searching air. Ottilia suppressed a sigh. The renewed closeness was too precious to risk with a show of impatience. Yet the prospect of months of coddling could not but make her jib a trifle.

Fortunately the waiter reappeared before Francis's anxiety could intensify.

"Begging your pardon, my lady, but Mr Gibbon says he is not receiving today."

A gust of rage swept through Ottilia and she pushed up from the sofa and rose abruptly. "Well, that is a great deal too bad, but I do not propose to accept his dictum. You need not show us up. We know the way."

With which she swept to the stairs, the waiter on her heels. "But, my lady, indeed Mr Gibbon was adamant."

To Ottilia's relief, Francis took a hand. "Leave it, man. We are going up."

"But, my lord —☐

"You need not be alarmed. I will make it clear to Mr Gibbon that you were overborne. You will take no blame. Come, Tillie." He offered his arm and Ottilia began to ascend at his side.

"Thank you, Fan. I was ripe for murder myself."

"I could see that." He gave a laugh that did much to allay her ruffled feathers. "If we are to have tantrums, I'll wager you are indeed pregnant again."

"Be quiet, you fiend! I only lost my temper once or twice the last time."

"Yes, well, at least I am forearmed upon this occasion."

"I wish you will stop. We can't be sure of anything."

"Are you afraid I will jinx it?"

She had to laugh. "No. I'm afraid you'll start plying me with bacon and shoving cushions behind my back."

"I shall, if I think fit. Moreover, I will demand the attendance of my esteemed brother-in-law in his capacity as medical man. At least I can be sure you will mind Patrick's dicta."

Ottilia would have argued the point but there was time for no more as they were already traversing the corridor that led to Mr Gibbon's temporary accommodation. Arrived at the door to the parlour, Francis rapped smartly on the wood and opened the door. Ottilia swept in ahead of him and stopped short in mingled shock and triumph.

Edmund Gibbon was seated in the same comfortable armchair, his injured ankle again resting on a stool. Standing before the window behind him was none other than the errant Percy.

Ottilia saw chagrin in his face, quickly disguised with an expression of spurious amiability.

"Lady Francis! But what a pleasant surprise."

Mr Gibbon had looked across upon their entrance and now directed a violent glare upon Ottilia. "How dared you enter unannounced? When I had expressly sent to say I was not receiving? What does this mean, ma'am?"

Francis appeared at Ottilia's side, bristling. "You'll keep a civil tongue in your head when you address my wife, sir. I've had occasion to tell you so before. Don't try my patience!"

Percy took this, that glib mockery of a smile Ottilia remembered curling his lip. "Will you offer violence to a man in my dear friend's condition, my lord Francis? I would not have credited it."

Francis strode a step or two towards him. "What you might credit, Pedwardine, is of scant interest. Your presence, however, interests me very much indeed."

"Does it so? I wonder why."

"You'll soon find out."

It behoved Ottilia to intervene. They did not want to antagonise the wretch this early. "Give me leave, Fan, if you will."

He flicked a glance at her and she saw how he smouldered. But he gave a curt nod and rocked back on his heels, folding his arms. "My wife has a good deal to say to you."

"To me?"

The air of innocence grated. She was not surprised at her spouse's snapped response. "To both of you."

She moved forward. "I will address myself rather to you, Mr Gibbon, to begin with."

He had begun to look a trifle less belligerent, his gaze going from Percy to Francis and back again while they exchanged blows by way of words. Was he seeing a different side to the man? She looked at her spouse. "Would you pull up a chair for me, Fan?"

He fetched a straight chair with a cushioned seat from those surrounding the table in the centre of the parlour and Ottilia took it with a word of thanks, aware that both men watched her. She took a covert glance at the younger as she settled herself.

He had not the appearance of a man who had recently disposed of his wife. Not that one could expect as much. No trace of grief was visible in the remembered pleasant countenance framed by dark hair, and his garb was as neat as ever it had been, which argued he was by no means as purse-pinched as Mr Gibbon supposed. He wore a country frock-coat of fashionable cut over a striped waistcoat, buckskin breeches, polished top-boots, and a neck-cloth intricately tied. Yet was there a wary look in the eyes?

"Now we are comfortable, Mr Gibbon, let me tell you that I came here in hopes you might be able to direct me to your friend Percy." Ottilia smiled, as falsely as had her quarry. "To find him thus engaged with you will save me endless trouble."

Mr Gibbon stared her out, frowning under heavy brows. "Well?"

"He does not look like a man bereaved, do you not think?" She flicked a glance at the other and saw him stiffen.

The older man grunted. "It is nigh on two years. Even I have learned to live with the loss of my nephew."

Ottilia raised her brows. "Oh, he has not told you?"

"Told me what, ma'am?"

"I am not talking of your nephew. Two days ago your protégé here had the misfortune to lose his wife."

The young man said nothing, but Mr Gibbon stared at Ottilia in an uncomprehending way for a moment before swinging his gaze to the young man.

"Thought you said she was waiting for you at your lodging, my boy."

To Ottilia's mingled annoyance and reluctant acknowledgement of his brazen stance, the reprobate tried to bluff it out.

"I did and she is. I cannot imagine what Lady Francis means by it." He turned on her a gaze redolent of confusion. "Where you had your information I do not know, my lady, but I fear you have been duped."

Ottilia heard her husband swearing beneath his breath and hastily took this up. "I was certainly duped. Not by any informant, however. By the pretty creature now lying in the morgue with a bullet in her face."

Mr Gibbon exclaimed and apparent horror spread over Percy's face. "Good God, ma'am, you shock me! Who could do such a thing?"

Francis started forward. "You unmitigated villain! How dare you pretend to ignorance? Your shot very nearly caught my wife!"

"Mine?" He threw a hand to his chest as if to underline the accusation. "You suggest I could do such a thing?"

"You not only could, you did, you lying cur!"

279

Mr Gibbon seized the stick resting against his leg and banged it down upon the wooden floor. "Enough, sir! You bade me be civil to your wife. I demand the same courtesy to my young protégé here."

"He deserves no courtesy. He has fooled you, Gibbon. Twice now. If you will continue to allow yourself to be gulled and very likely fleeced in due course, then I have done." Francis turned for the door. "Come, Tillie."

Ottilia threw up a hand. "We will not give up so readily, Fan." Wasting no more time, she turned to Mr Gibbon. "At least allow me to tell you what occurred. Then you may judge for yourself, if you will."

He lifted his chin. "Very well. Say what you have to say and then go."

To her surprise, Percy made no attempt to stop Ottilia as she launched into her account, merely regarding her in that supercilious way he had, a faint smile all the recognition she received.

"As soon as the girl accosted me, I knew her for the one who had been attempting to attract my attention. She would not give me her name, but —☐

"Then how could you think she was Percy's wife?"

"I am coming to that, sir. I mentioned Percy by name, at which she became agitated, saying there must be no names. She asked me outright if he had been involved in his friend's death. That made her identity certain."

"To you? It does not do so for me. I never believed in that fairy-tale."

"Yet the question could not point to any other. Why ask me otherwise?" Mr Gibbon champed a little, but made no retort. Ottilia was encouraged by his casting no glance at his so-called protégé. "To clinch the matter, I asked if she was married to

Percy Pedwardine. At that precise moment, the fatal shot was fired. She dropped dead right in front of me."

Francis had been standing near the door during this, but he strode back. "That shot was fired across my wife's bows, so to speak. It is with me yet a question which of them he meant to injure."

Ottilia kept a surreptitious eye upon her quarry as she watched for Mr Gibbon's reaction. Had his cheek paled a trifle? Gibbon was plainly discomposed, fidgeting with the knob of his cane which he was still holding, the fingers of his other hand tapping on his knee. Percy did not speak. Cunning? Was he waiting for the other's response to see how he might wriggle his way out?

At length Mr Gibbon ceased to fidget and directed a fierce look towards Ottilia, bypassing Francis altogether. "A distressing tale told well. You attract this sort of attention, my lady, by all accounts." He cleared his throat in a noisy fashion. "I am sorry for the young woman, whoever she may be, but I don't propose to take that matter any further."

This proved too much for Francis. "For pity's sake, man, what more proof do you need? If it will make you see sense, you'd best know the couple were staying at the Raven under your name. As Mr and Mrs Gibbon. How do you take that?"

The elder man's chin came up. "It is a common enough name."

"Faugh!"

As her spouse turned away in disgust, Ottilia addressed herself to Percy. "I ought not to have been surprised to see you here. Were you perhaps disturbed in the act of packing your effects?"

Francis turned back. "I had not thought of that. Do you say he scarpered, leaving all behind as Dalby found it?"

"And ran for protection to Mr Gibbon here." She waited, but no word came from her victim. "Have you nothing to say, Percy?"

"Don't answer her, my boy."

"But that would be rude, my dear sir." His tone was soft. "Lady Fan means well. She seeks to save you from my evil machinations and that is praiseworthy."

Ottilia felt her husband's rising choler and cut in swiftly. "Just so, Mr Gibbon. When we met you the other day, we still supposed that Percy meant to revenge himself upon me. But when that bullet missed me, I realised our mistake." She directed her gaze back to Percy. "If you intended my death, why not accomplish it there and then? Whether or not you encouraged your wife in that belief is another matter. You certainly gave her to understand your vengeful feelings towards Lady Fan for bringing about your expulsion from Society. Oh, you told her nothing directly, I dare say, but you are clever with words, are you not, sir? Easy enough to point your way with subtle suggestion. Whether your wife heard of young Mr Gibbon's demise from you or from rumour I cannot judge, though I suspect the latter. You could not wish, by relating that episode, to jeopardise your standing with the woman who brought you wealth."

The smile did not waver. "Say on, Lady Fan. Your imagination was ever fertile."

Ottilia ignored this. She checked to note whether Mr Gibbon was still paying attention. Let him hear it all. If she could shake his blind faith it would at least put doubt in his mind.

"Did your wife grow a little too interested in that affair for your liking? Was it because you saw how she sought me out that you became determined upon this course? Or had you it in mind all along? The poor girl had not the position to regain you the entrée to the circles you wished to re-enter. Moreover, as her husband, you are no doubt master of all she owned."

At last Mr Gibbon spoke. "What are you at, madam? Would you condemn a man for seeking to better himself by marriage?"

"Not at all, sir. Unless he seeks also to rid himself of the merchant's daughter who enriched him."

"Pah! Percy is not so high in the instep. A faradiddle!"

"Have it as you will." She rose, ready to admit defeat. A thought occurred and she determined to make one last throw. She sent a smile as spurious as his own towards Percy, and turned back to the elder man. "It might profit you, sir, to request your protégé to produce his wife for your inspection."

Mr Gibbon bridled. "I have every intention of meeting the young woman, not that it is any concern of yours."

"I've warned you, Gibbon!"

Ottilia put out a staying hand. "No matter, Fan. We will be leaving in a moment." She looked again at Gibbon. "You will ask him, will you not? Do not let him fob you off."

Percy stepped in. "He will ask me and I will bring my wife to see him."

Ottilia looked at him. "I make no doubt you will produce some woman whom you will present as your wife. Whether she will be the woman you married, I take leave to doubt."

CHAPTER TWENTY-TWO

Summoned to the family parlour by Lord Dalesford, Hemp found it occupied only by its owner and Mr Belchamp, the Bristol magistrate. Relieved none of the ladies of the house were present, Hemp eyed the obvious agitation in the visitor's face with a sinking heart. What now?

"Mr Belchamp here asked for you," Lord Dalesford told him, "when he learned the Fanshawes are in town."

The magistrate tutted. "If I had only known as much, I might have found them there."

"Unlikely, sir. Milord and milady had the intention of seeking out Mr Gibbon. Unless you know the gentleman?"

"Never heard of the fellow."

Lord Dalesford cut in. "Never mind that now. They are pursuing this business of the shooting."

Belchamp's eyes popped. "Shooting? What shooting, pray?"

His lordship waved at Hemp. "You'd best tell it. You were there."

When Hemp had given a brief account, he was obliged to wait while the magistrate blessed himself and expressed his horror and astonishment. At length he ran down and Hemp took his chance.

"Why did you wish to find milord and milady, sir? May I assist?"

Belchamp's brows snapped together. "I doubt it, but I asked my lord Dalesford if I might speak with you since you are acquainted with the whole affair."

"Which affair, sir?"

"That business in Bristol. Indeed, now that I hear what happened in Buckingham, I must confess myself doubly anxious. There seems to be no end to the difficulties that beset our Lady Fan."

Undeniable, but that brought them no further forward. If milady was in yet more immediate danger, Hemp needed to know it. "Sir, if I may, what news have you that causes you so much anxiety?"

"Yes, I am wondering that too," said Lord Dalesford, bending a frowning gaze upon the magistrate. "Cut line, man. What is amiss?"

Belchamp put his fingers to his temples briefly as if to alleviate an ache. "I can hardly bear to speak of it, my lord." His gaze returned to Hemp. "I have just come from the prison. Those villains have escaped."

Hemp's mind was abuzz. "Indigo?"

"Both of them."

"You mean those fellows the militia caught? Good grief!"

"How, sir?"

Belchamp threw up his hands. "No one seems to know. The gaoler went to give that damnable pirate his meal and found the cell empty. Later, they discovered the other man missing too."

Sifting possibilities, Hemp voiced the obvious one. "Bribery? Someone must have unlocked the door."

"That is the curious thing. It was locked."

"Then Indigo obtained the key somehow. I warned the warder he was cunning."

Lord Dalesford directed a frowning gaze at him. "What do you mean?"

"Indigo escaped captivity at least twice over in the Caribbean. How he does it, I do not know, milord, but I can't say I am surprised he has again outfoxed his captors."

Lord Dalesford moved to the fireplace and set a hand on the mantel, directing his attention back to the magistrate. "What is being done to recover him, do you know?"

"I don't, my lord. I came away the moment I learned of it. Lady Francis must be warned."

Hemp was of his opinion, but he saw no point in chasing after the Fanshawes. "We will inform her the moment she returns, sir." He turned to Lord Dalesford. "In the meantime, milord, may I suggest alerting your keepers?"

"I'll do more than that. We'll have every able-bodied man out patrolling the grounds."

Belchamp entered a caveat. "What need of that, my lord? I cannot think those two will remain long in the vicinity."

Hemp nearly laughed in his face. "They will, if Indigo fancies himself to have a reason to revenge himself upon myself and milord."

"What, and risk recapture? I cannot think it."

"But you did think to warn milady, sir."

"Because she was nearly concerned in those events. Now I consider it more rationally, it seems to me unlikely that she could be in danger from Captain Indigo. He must wish to remove himself from the vicinity, I would have thought. He vanished from Bristol fast enough."

Lord Dalesford came away from the mantel, frowning now. "I seem to recall Fanshawe saying his wife spoke rather of the other fellow than Indigo. I forget his name."

"Quin?" It was news to Hemp that milady was again interested in the rat. "He was dismissed as a suspect."

"Well, apparently she has changed her mind. It is no use asking me. I was not privy to Ottilia's opinion on the subject. Until today, she had been keeping her room since the last incident."

Which was precisely why Hemp had not heard of this latest turn. Doro had naturally seen Ottilia when she took Luke in to visit, but she was altogether close-mouthed, claiming she knew nothing. But Hemp knew his inamorata too well. She was concealing something.

The magistrate let out a harrumph. "For my part, I am grieved beyond words. I thought those two were safely incarcerated and I was planning to return to Bristol. I would come back for the trial, of course. But now it appears there won't be one, if both men are once more at large."

Hemp bethought him of the other couple of whom the magistrate had spoken, so Francis had told him. "Have you had any news of that girl and her brother? I understand they also disappeared from Bristol."

Belchamp slapped his own forehead. "If I had not forgotten! I have had word, as it chances. My secretary sent an express. They were spotted by one of my thieftakers."

"Not here then, sir?"

"No, no. In Lyme. She has hired herself out as a cook-maid, it seems, in a bakery. The lad is working in a local tavern."

Hemp breathed out. "No danger is to be apprehended from them, then."

"I imagine not. They have assumed some other name. I suppose one must wish them well."

Lord Dalesford was looking puzzled. Hemp hastened to explain. "These were children of the fellow responsible for the affair at Bristol, milord. It was thought she might have been the girl who came after milady and seized Master Luke."

"Well, that seems to explode that theory, then."

"Indeed, milord."

"Which leaves us with no real clue as to who began this whole shambles by pulling Ottilia into the river."

Hemp was now in little doubt, but he refrained from saying so. He had been a fool to allow himself to be duped. Had he forgotten how slippery was the rat? The only question now was whether he would make another attempt.

The magistrate declined Lord Dalesford's invitation to await the return of Lord and Lady Fanshawe. When he had gone, Hemp sought out Doro. After an abortive run up to the schoolroom, where the Fiske children were at their desks along with Pretty, under the charge of the formidable Peggy, he at length found Doro seated on the grass adjoining the yard outside the kitchen, aiding her nurseling's inexpert attempt to create a crude figure with a lump of pastry dough donated by the cook.

Luke, intent upon his task, made no objection to Hemp joining the party as he squatted beside the pair.

Hemp kept his voice low as he addressed Doro. "There has been a development."

Her blue gaze met his with instant consternation. "Milady?"

"Not directly." He did not immediately relate the particulars of Justice Belchamp's visit. "I need you to cast your mind back, Doro."

"To when?" Her attention returned to her charge. "You need another leg, Luke. See?" She ripped a piece off the dough and put it next to the one already in place. "There. Make it stick there."

"You remember Quin, Doro?"

Her eyes came back to his, a quick flash in them. "How could I forget?"

He ignored this. "You told me how he was always sneaking about the house. How you found him where he had no business to be."

"He did it all the time. I never knew where he might appear, that rascal."

"This is my point, Doro. If he could glide about that house without being seen, he could as easily slip into the river here and hide under the jetty."

Doro's gaze had returned to Luke, but at this she whipped round, staring at him in undisguised horror. "You think he did it? But you believed him when he said he knew nothing of it."

"I think I was mistaken. I should have remembered how adept a liar he was. How cunning. Always with an eye to his own advantage."

Doro's shoulders jerked in a shiver. "He made my skin crawl." She lowered her tone. "But you and milord caught him."

Hemp did not hesitate. "He has escaped. Indigo also."

"No! Does milady know?"

"Not yet. Justice Belchamp came to warn her." He related Lord Dalesford's plan to have men patrol the grounds. "It is best if you keep Luke inside, Doro. We don't want to run any risks."

Her gaze went to the little boy, who was still struggling with the second leg. "I will take him as soon as he finishes making his man. I don't want to alarm him."

"Don't delay," Hemp murmured. "Make some excuse."

She nodded and he rose. He had agreed with Lord Dalesford that he would start along the drive in the hopes of meeting the coach as the Fanshawes returned. Accordingly, he did not go back inside, but set off from behind the house, taking a shortcut across the greensward towards the main drag, avoiding the sweep that ran around to the front of the mansion.

There was no sight or sound of any approaching vehicle by the time he reached the lane that ran alongside the river and led into the main driveway. But a coterie of men were to be seen about one of the keepers, who was evidently giving instructions. In a moment they scattered, each taking a different route. Hemp walked up and hailed the man whom he recognised as Maynard, the fellow who had come to inform Lord Dalesford of the woman's body, which had turned out to be that of the barmaid Cherry.

"Ah, you're Lord Francis's man, aren't you?"

"That's right, sir. I'm hoping to catch them as they arrive back."

"Well, they've to come along this road, that's sure. No other way in for a coach."

"That is what I supposed. I'll keep on along it."

"You do that. I've to find the gardeners and have them stay on the move and keep their eyes open."

So saying, he went off in the direction of the drive towards the house. Hemp kept on his way, unable to help casting glances into the trees on the estate side, towards the river and across to the opposite bank. He cursed, thinking he ought to have asked exactly when the escape had occurred. Had the fugitives had time to reach this far, assuming they had not, as Belchamp supposed, taken off from Newport Pagnell altogether?

He passed a couple of patrolling men on his way, and the bridge was in sight by the time the welcome sound of hooves signalled the approach of a vehicle. In a moment Hemp saw a coach drive onto the bridge and he halted, keeping a wary eye out for any sign of the escapees. Presently, the coach turned into the lane and he recognised Williams seated on the box with Ryde beside him. He hailed the coachman, signalling to him to stop.

"What's afoot, Roy?" demanded this worthy as he brought his horses to a standstill.

"I've news for milord and milady. I'll get in and you can proceed." So saying, Hemp went to the door to one side just as Lord Francis poked his head out of the window.

"Oh, it's you, Hemp. I wondered why we'd stopped."

"Let me come in, milord. There is urgent news."

Hemp set his hand on the handle, but the door swung open. He climbed in, negotiating the height without difficulty. He closed the door, rapped on the roof and sat down on the forward seat facing his employers as the coach moved off again.

Ottilia spoke before he could answer the questioning look on both faces. "This is unprecedented, Hemp. You look decidedly troubled."

"With reason, milady."

Lord Francis thumped his own knee. "Well, let's have it, then. It's not as if we haven't had enough to bear already this day."

The note of sarcasm was not lost on Hemp but he saw milady set a quietening hand to her husband's arm, registering a silent resolve to find out what had occurred at their meeting with Mr Gibbon. But that must wait.

"Justice Belchamp has been here, milord. He wanted to warn milady at once. Indigo and Quin have both escaped."

Lord Francis uttered a curse but Ottilia's eye gleamed and she struck her hands together. "Then I was right."

Hemp hazarded a guess at her intent. "You mean that Quin was the one who pulled you into the Ouse?"

Her countenance lit as she smiled. "Just so. How came you to guess that, Hemp?"

Her husband grunted. "I'm not sure I subscribe to this notion, but go on."

"At first it did not occur to me, but I did think Indigo might choose to revenge himself upon you, milord. Or, more likely, myself, for he knew well it was I who followed him to his lair and must be responsible for bringing the militia to the place. Indigo may well blame us both as having been instrumental in his being incarcerated."

"I shouldn't think he'd trouble himself. In his place, I would get as far from this vicinity as I could."

"That is what Mr Belchamp supposed too, milord."

Ottilia was watching him. "But you don't agree, Hemp?"

"Not now, milady. Indigo I know to be capable of anything and he is a vengeful wretch. But Milord Dalesford mentioned that you had changed your mind about Quin, milady. Even then I was not convinced."

"Nor I. And I'm still not," stated Lord Francis.

"What persuaded you then, Hemp?"

"I asked the justice about the other two he had mentioned, who had departed from Bristol some months ago."

"The sister and brother?"

"He had news of them in Lyme, where they have both taken employment under assumed names."

Lord Francis emitted one of his habitual disbelieving snorts. "I don't see how that leads you back to Quin."

"Failing Pedwardine, milord, it left one option only as to the person who hid under the jetty. It would be typical of Quin. I recalled how Doro told me he was apt to sneak around the house back in Bristol. Also I had forgotten his tendency to palter with truth. I now believe he duped me when I questioned him, milord."

"He's cunning, I'll give you that."

Ottilia cut in. "You are sceptical, Fan, and I do not blame you. But I do remember how Quin was somewhat under Cherry's spell, even in Bristol. I can well imagine that to be in close proximity with her, even assuming she had become Indigo's mistress, must have increased his ardour."

Lord Francis looked to Hemp. "You may as well know my wife thinks Quin did the honours at Cherry's bidding. I am not convinced. Nor do I see why he would wish to try again since the girl is dead."

"Oh, he might well, Fan. As long as I am alive, he is in danger of being held responsible both for my attempted murder and for Cherry's death too, if only as an accomplice. Quin knows well how persistent I can be. Why not take his chance now to silence me?"

Shock held Hemp silent, but Lord Francis shook his head. "I don't see it, Tillie. I submit he's too canny an individual to add another charge to the list. He's a wanted man and free again. I'll wager he is even now upon the road." Ottilia forbore to argue further, and Lord Francis blew out a breath and gave a grimace. "Nevertheless, we'll take no chances."

It was no hardship to Ottilia to obey her husband's injunction to remain within doors. For two days she was plagued with morning sickness, followed within an hour or so by cravings for bacon and cheese. She felt unnaturally fatigued and began to partake of Joanie's conviction that she was indeed pregnant.

"Because if you aren't, my lady, you ought to see a doctor."

The last thing Ottilia wished for was to have a physician poking about her abdomen or prescribing Epsom salts for a suspected colic. "Not yet, Joanie. Let us wait a little while."

So far she had managed to conceal the vomiting from Francis, although he had remarked upon her appetite for bacon at breakfast. She relied upon her maid for the cheese, knowing Joanie would not fail to supply it along with her morning coffee.

"I have told his lordship, by the by. But he does not know of my sickness these two days, so pray don't trouble him with that."

The maid tutted, setting a filled cup upon the bedside table. "Well, I hope he don't ask me outright, my lady, for I'll blurt it out to him, sure as check."

Ottilia nibbled at the sliced cheddar on her plate. "Don't fret. I shall go back to the parlour when I have done. My mother-in-law is growing suspicious of my absences, I fear."

She had made many an excuse to disappear after spending a little time in the family parlour after breakfast and had not attended church with the rest on Sunday. Fortunately, Sybilla adhered to her regime of walking daily and Harriet had domestic affairs to attend to, which allowed Ottilia to come up to rest without being obliged to answer difficult questions.

Since Francis was now privy to the possibility of her being with child, he was in any event encouraging rest. Not merely on that account.

"At least I know you to be safe in our bedchamber, my loved one. No one could venture there."

"Not that we have seen a sign of any assailant. I begin to think we are needlessly worrying, Fan."

But her spouse would have none of that. He remained sceptical of the possibility of Quin coming after her or Indigo coming after Hemp or himself, but he was by no means convinced of Percy's innocence.

"If anything, your accusations have given him even more cause to resent you, Tillie. After all, we can't know how accurate were your suppositions since he admitted nothing."

Ottilia put forward no argument, although she was herself certain Percy would be found to have absconded, very likely in company with Edmund Gibbon.

Nothing had been heard from Captain Dalby, even though Francis had sent a report to him giving the gist of the outcome of their visit. He received a note back immediately, informing them in turn of the escape of which they had already learned that same day from Justice Belchamp. No further word had come from him. Ottilia could only guess at what enquiries he might be pursuing.

She was conscious of a sense of calm that seemed likely to prove spurious. Could it all end there? Should they be thinking of a return to Flitteris and normality?

Her hostess, when she put this to the ladies of the party on returning to the family parlour, proved surprisingly recalcitrant.

"Oh, no, no, Ottilia. You cannot go home yet."

Sybilla, engaged in critiquing the design on an embroidery frame upon which Henrietta Skelmersdale was working, for once agreed with her daughter. "Harriet is perfectly correct, my child. You must see this through to the finish."

Ottilia grimaced. "Yes, but I rather think we may have reached the finish."

Her mother-in-law shoved the embroidery frame at her companion. "Take this, girl." She then returned her attention to Ottilia. "It is not like you to admit defeat. What is amiss with you, child?"

Guilt leapt up. She was wont to take Sybilla into her confidence, but on this occasion she wanted to hug the news she might indeed be increasing again to herself and Francis. She prevaricated. "Nothing is amiss. It is just that we seem to have exhausted all the options."

"Francis does not appear to think so."

"Nor Gil," chimed in Harriet. "He is not keeping the men patrolling for nothing, Ottilia."

"Yes, I know, and we are grateful. But we cannot impose upon Gil's generosity for much longer. Nor yours, Harriet."

"Poppycock! Do you suppose my daughter and her husband are not delighted to have you remain?"

Ottilia had to laugh. "I suppose both are far too kind and polite to say otherwise."

Harriet hastened into speech. "Don't be silly, of course we are only too happy. Besides that, Anne has become very fond of Pretty. They are fast friends."

"What you mean is that Pretty is dazzled by Anne and wishes to copy her in everything. Oh, don't mistake me. I am very happy she has made friends with her cousins. It has made me realise I must take pains to find her companions when we do go home."

"But that will not be until this whole affair is thoroughly settled. You must promise now, Ottilia."

"Very well, Harriet, since you insist."

Rather to Ottilia's relief, Henrietta chose to change the subject. "Speaking of those two girls, Lady Dalesford, did you know that Pretty's nurse — Hepsie, is it not, Lady Fan? — well, Hepsie says the girls are inclined to look upon Luke as a live doll for them to play with."

Ottilia broke into giggles. "Pretty has done so from the first. I am sure she believes I brought Luke forth solely for her entertainment."

As she spoke, she found herself wondering how her adoptive daughter would react to another baby joining the nursery party. She was moved to chide herself. She must not become too attached to the notion. Patrick had warned her it might prove difficult, if not impossible, to conceive again. Moreover, false pregnancies were not unknown. Worse, the shadow of her first loss could never be completely suppressed. She had brought Luke to term successfully, but there was no saying she might do so again.

Before she could sink herself into melancholy — *yet another sign, drat you, Ottilia!* — the distant sound of heavy footsteps pounding up the stairs broke into her thoughts and brought the continuing conversation among the other ladies to a dead stop.

Sybilla was the first to recover. "What in the world —?"

The rapid steps were approaching the door. It opened and Gil appeared in the aperture, somewhat out of breath.

"They've been spotted."

Ottilia's mind snapped into action. "Where and who?"

"The pirate and another fellow."

"Quin?"

"I don't know, Ottilia. Someone is with him, that is all I was told. They were seen moving through the woods in the direction of the glasshouse."

Harriet leapt to her feet. "The children! I must make sure they are safe."

"Don't fret, my love. Peggy will have them in charge."

But Harriet was hurrying to the door as she spoke. "Heaven send she has not permitted them to venture out of doors!"

She was gone on the words and Gil turned back to Ottilia. "Fan has gone off with your steward fellow. He enjoined me to instruct you to return to your bedchamber where you will be safe."

Ottilia balked. "I will be safe enough here, Gil." She threw a mischievous glance at her mother-in-law. "I defy Indigo to attempt anything with Sybilla here to defend me."

Her mild attempt at humour was rejected with scorn. "Don't be ridiculous, child! Do as Francis asks. Gilbert, you ought to have a man stand guard outside the chamber."

"I shall do that, ma'am. Charles is a sensible fellow. I will send him along, Ottilia. Meanwhile, I must return to the downstairs saloon. We have instituted it our headquarters."

He left the room directly and Ottilia could have screamed. She threw up her hands. "I have a very good mind to go down to these headquarters myself."

"You would be foolish to do so, Ottilia. What could you do, after all?"

"I don't know, but I should much prefer to be in the thick of things."

"Don't I know it. In general, I agree with you, but in this instance, I must urge you to err on the side of caution."

Before Ottilia could reply, Henrietta entered the lists. "You are the target, after all, Lady Fan."

Ottilia sighed. "I was forgetting that." Her quickened interest damped, she hesitated a moment. "What will you do, both of you?"

Sybilla rose. "I propose to retire to my own room. Henrietta will accompany me and we will lock the doors until all is over."

Ottilia tried one more throw. "We could all remain here and lock this door, could we not?"

"We are too close to the main entrance. It is better to retreat out of the way of any potential battleground."

Ottilia could not think it likely that any fight, should there be one, would reach within a hundred yards of the house, but she was outnumbered. Moreover, there was little she could do without knowing what was going on in the woods. Nor where Francis and Hemp were headed. There seemed to be nothing for it but to acquiesce. At least she would gain her spouse's approval, even if she was not to be included in dealing with Captain Indigo and his cohort. Assuming Quin was the man with him.

Accordingly, she followed the dowager out and parted from Sybilla and Henrietta when she reached the corridor that led to her chamber. The footman had not yet put in an appearance. Ottilia opened the door and entered the bedchamber.

She went immediately to the open window and looked out across the grounds which approached the rear of the Hall. From this aspect she could see an enclosed garden, the walls of the glasshouse poking up through foliage and the distant woods beyond. Looking to one side, the line of the river was just visible.

"Excellent," she said aloud. If Indigo had been seen in the woods, it was safe to suppose she might catch a glimpse of whatever might be going forward, when or if Gilbert's men came up with him.

For quite some time she kept vigil at the window, without result. No movement disturbed the peaceful scene. No untoward sound either, beyond the background noise one might expect. The unintelligible chatter of a couple of maids engaged in emptying buckets into the bushes; a flutter of leaves as the wind passed through them; the scrabbling sound of some animal not within sight; and the clink of utensils from the kitchen premises invisible below.

At length, growing weary of standing, Ottilia left her post, turning her attention to the room. Too restless to settle upon the bed, she moved to the standing mirror and checked her reflection. As she straightened her gown and prinked at her hair, she received an indefinable impression that she was not alone in the room.

Ottilia turned abruptly, flicking glances from one side to the other and across the four-poster. No one else was visible. An odd instant of panic took her and she threw a brief look back at the mirror, half expecting to see some other face than her own looking back at her.

"You are being absurd," she chided herself aloud.

Had she heard some sound from without? The footman! Crossing swiftly to the door, she wrenched it open. There was no reassuring solid body standing there. Where was Charles? Gil had promised to send him to guard the door.

For a moment, Ottilia was both chagrined and questioning. What was happening that the footman should be kept from his designated duty? She crushed a temptation to investigate, whisked back into the room, shut the door and leaned against it, once more studying the empty space.

Nothing stirred. No sound above the ordinary. She must have been mistaken. She was not usually given to flights of fancy. Another instance of the effects of pregnancy? It began to seem more real that she was indeed enceinte.

She was just beginning to relax again as she moved into the room, when a noise sounded near at hand. A breath. Slight, as if some person was trying to prevent themselves from coughing.

"Who is there?"

The words escaped her involuntarily. No answer was forthcoming. She stood stock still, the rhythm of her pulse going awry, her breath catching in her throat.

Should she retire from the room? If she did, she had better take the key and lock it from the outside. Or was she being altogether hysterical?

With deliberation, she let her breath go, trying for calm. If only the footman had arrived she could call out to him. Perhaps he was there. Though she would have heard his steps, would she not?

Her gaze pierced about the room. There was nowhere for anyone to hide. Then she recalled the very first time she had become involved in the aftermath of a murder. She looked intently at the curtains at the back of the four-poster. No bulge rewarded her searching stare. Moreover, the bed looked to be almost flush against the wall. No one was hiding there.

A sudden conviction gripped her and she spoke aloud before she could consider the wisdom of her words. "You are under that bed, are you not? Come out, if you dare!"

For several agonising minutes, nothing happened. No sound, no movement. Yet her senses prickled with certainty. Ottilia began to edge back towards the door, treading as softly as she could.

Then from beneath the bed came the unmistakeable noises of someone shifting position, coupled with a grunt of effort.

Ottilia raced for the door and seized the key in the lock. It proved recalcitrant and she struggled to extract it. She cursed herself for delaying, for not trusting her intuition. The intruder was no longer troubling to conceal his motions as he squeezed out from what must have been, judging from the noise, a tight fit.

Ottilia's fingers were shaking as she wrestled with the key. It came out at last and she seized the door handle.

"Hoy!"

The yell from behind her was accompanied by a whizzing sound. Next instant a blade embedded itself in the wood of the door within a few inches of Ottilia's face. She froze.

CHAPTER TWENTY-THREE

The quarry had vanished from sight by the time Francis, accompanied by Hemp, arrived at the spot where he had been seen. The fellow left on guard looked to be considerably nervous, casting glances to and fro. He jumped when Francis spoke from a few yards behind.

"You there!"

The man spun, raising the stout stick he held. Attired in homespuns, boots and a short jacket, the garb of an outdoors servant, he visibly relaxed as a youthful countenance showed recognition.

"Begging your pardon, me lord, I thought you was that great black feller." He cast an apologetic glance at Hemp as he spoke. "Saving your presence, Mister Roy."

"One of the under-gardeners, milord," Hemp murmured.

Francis nodded acknowledgement, but proceeded to the business at hand. "When did you last see them?"

Puzzlement entered the lad's face. "Them?"

"There's a little fellow with him, isn't there?"

The gardener shook his head. "I ain't seen him, me lord. I catched a glimpse of the black fellow just, afore Mr Maynard and the others went after him."

"Went after him where?"

"Into them woods." He pointed to the thicket adjoining the lane. "There's been no sign since, me lord, and that were all of twenty minutes gone."

Francis cursed under his breath. "We are behindhand, Hemp."

"True, milord. If they have not returned, Indigo must have evaded them." He eyed the temporary guard. "You've heard nothing either?"

"Nothing, Mister Roy. I were told to stay here in case he come out this way."

Francis caught Hemp's glance. "What do you think?"

Hemp was frowning. "We might do better to get in closer to the house before we enter. If he's making for it, we might stand a chance of catching him further along."

"Good thinking." Francis nodded to the guard. "You'd best stay here. Yell at the top of your voice if you see anything." He added, as he set off with the steward, "I don't hold out much hope. He'll likely be paralysed with fright if Indigo surprises him."

A laugh grunted out of Hemp. "A good thing he was not given a pistol, milord."

"Good God, yes! He'd be firing at shadows." As he trudged back the way they had come, keeping a wary eye out, he voiced the question in his mind. "What I want to know is where the deuce that rat of a Quin has got to. The messenger spoke of two men."

A derisory note entered Hemp's voice. "If I know Quin, he has too great a regard for his own skin to risk himself here. He'll be laying low somewhere."

"Yes, but who then is the other?"

"Indigo may have associates of whom we know nothing, milord. He had his bully boys attack you in Bristol."

"We had the impression he was in a string only with Quin and Cherry, though." He glanced at Hemp as he spoke and discovered a shrewd look in the steward's face. "Well, what?"

"Someone must have aided and abetted Indigo's escape."

"Damnation! I hadn't thought, but it makes sense. Very likely he didn't carry out all those robberies alone either."

Hemp made no reply and Francis fell to brooding. He had half convinced himself that the threat to his wife had been averted with the elimination of the girl in the green cloak. Now it seemed he had underestimated Indigo. He spoke his thought aloud. "I think you are right about Indigo, Hemp. I can't believe he has come for my wife. As you said, his quarrel must be with you and me."

"We will give him the chance to have a try at one or other of us, milord. You have your pistol?"

"Of course. You?"

"And my dagger."

"Good. Between us, we should be able to take him down."

As he spoke, he was scanning the trees. The sun winked on something, causing odd flashes of light through the foliage. Francis halted. "We must be near the glasshouse."

"It's catching on the windows?"

"That's what I suppose."

"Doro said there are numerous places to hide in there."

Francis shoved a hand in his pocket and brought out his pistol. "Then what are we waiting for?"

He took a line into the woods and started off but was checked by Hemp's voice. "A moment, milord."

"Well?"

"We ought to proceed with caution. If he is hiding there, we don't want to advertise our approach."

Francis cursed, but noted the wisdom of this. He had been ready to charge in, his eagerness to be rid of the threat undermining his common sense. Moderating his pace and treading with more care, he made his way between the trees. Hemp was doing likewise, but at a little distance, taking a separate line. Francis had a fleeting thought that the man would have made a good soldier. Was it instinctive to put in the possibility of catching the enemy in a pincer movement?

The massive windows began to manifest in the gaps as they drew closer to the glasshouse. Francis took extra care, using the trees for cover. There was no saying they might not be seen by anyone hiding within. He noted Hemp was doing likewise.

Within some twenty feet of the huge structure, he paused. A brickwork break between the windows of the building signalled a possible entry point. Hemp also stopped and an idea occurred to Francis. He caught Hemp's eye and mimed that he should enter by a different door. Hemp nodded and held up an open hand, digits spread wide. Five minutes? Francis gave him the thumbs-up and watched him slip noiselessly towards the lower end of the glasshouse.

The wait, as he made a rough count of the passing seconds, began to press upon his nerves. He was inevitably reminded of the discomforts endured in the moments before the start of a battle. With action came relief. He was glad at length to draw a conclusion on his count. Five minutes must have passed. He hoped Hemp was in position.

Creeping forward, he made his careful way to the break where there was indeed a door. Fortunately, this side was somewhat camouflaged by large plants he could just make out on either side of the door. He grasped the handle, turning it with care. It scraped on the flags as it opened into the interior. Francis held his breath.

After a moment, he became certain he could not have been heard. The silence in the building, bright with entering light, was thick, the atmosphere airless. A steady trickle of water, presumably a method of irrigation, came from somewhere. Otherwise nothing stirred.

Had Hemp yet entered? Was he hunting, treading catlike along the passages between the long trestles upon which trays of seedlings and early growing plants were stationed?

His gaze pierced in several directions, looking for places where a man of Indigo's bulk might find concealment. The perspective from where Francis stood showed two or three spots worth investigating. A large pineapple plant, a bank of young leafy trees, and several full shrubs standing close to two of the huge glass windows all offered potential hiding places.

He took a firmer grasp of his pistol and set out, treading as softly as possible, in the direction of the shrubs towards what must be the rear of the structure. He had not covered more than a few yards when a grunt sounded, followed by a thumping noise.

Francis whipped about, trying to see through the vegetation that stood between him and the emanation of an ensuing scuffle. Had Hemp found the brute?

A confusion of shifting feet, growling and another thump was followed almost on the instant by an almighty crash and splintering glass. Abandoning caution, Francis doubled back and took one of the alleys that ran between the trestles. Within seconds he was rewarded with the appearance above a trestle towards the front of a dark head. At this distance he could not tell if it was Indigo or Hemp, but a second crash told him a fight was in progress. Francis hastened towards the commotion, now growing louder with intermittent grunts and curses sounding from either throat.

As he came within sight of the battle, it became obvious that one of the trestles had overturned, causing sections of the glass surround of the building to break. He could not at first see the combatants, but presently they staggered into sight, fists flying as one gained advantage and shoved until the other pushed back and the mêlée cannoned into another trestle table. It too overturned, the men falling with it, crashing into the underside. Wood splintered. Plants flew in all directions. The two men, battling all the way, rolled onto the flags that made up the glasshouse floor.

Francis held back, finding it almost impossible to make out which man was which as the two bodies hugged and struggled while fists made contact wherever they were able.

Somewhere in the background he could hear shouts and running feet, but his concentration remained focused on the tussle. Pistol at the ready, Francis waited to be certain he was not aiming at Hemp.

The two men rolled again and suddenly Hemp had taken control. How he did it Francis could not tell, but in a violent movement, with the advantage of his height, he managed to get his legs astride the pirate's body. The thickly muscled Indigo humped upward, trying to free himself, his hefty limbs thumping on the ground. But Hemp did not wait. Fists curled, he pummelled his opponent's face without mercy, the thick bull-like head batting from side to side as he was hit over and over.

Francis sidled past, clambering over the legs of the upended trestle table. "Hold, Hemp!" As he called out, he dropped to his haunches beside the pirate and set the opening of the barrel to the man's cheek as the barrage of thumps ceased.

"Move and you're dead, my friend." Indigo's dark eyes swivelled. Francis cocked the pistol and saw the fear flash. "Your game is done, Indigo."

The pirate went still, letting fall his arms from the vain attempt to hold Hemp off. He was panting, his chest rising and falling even under the weight of his opponent's body.

"You can get off, Hemp. I doubt he'll dare move."

Hemp raised his eyes and Francis saw his face had not escaped injury. He was bloodied at the lip, cheek and below one eye. Fellow feeling made Francis grimace. "You're going to feel all that in due course."

Hemp, as spent as the pirate from the effort it took him to begin to get to his feet, gave a grunt. His voice was hoarse. "It will be worth it, milord."

Hemp had hardly risen to a stand when a number of men came charging down the various alleys. Francis recognised their leader.

"In good time, Maynard. Have you some kind of rope? We need to truss this villain up."

The keeper was staring down at the pirate's prone body. "That's a welcome sight, my lord. Here, Jim, you got the twine. You and Nobby come and tie this feller up, tight as you can."

Francis remained where he was, keeping the pistol ready, although he was obliged to remove it from Indigo's cheek as the men rolled him so they could bind his hands behind his back.

Once this exercise was complete, they hauled him to his feet and Francis was able to release the hammer and put his pistol away.

"Tie that twine around his body too. Make sure he can't move his arms."

He watched the men as they began this operation and then moved to the keeper, who was wringing Hemp's hand.

"Just saying, my lord, as Mister Roy here done a good job on him. If he ain't swole up proper by tonight, I'll eat old Rowley's hat."

Hemp's grin was more of a grimace. "I fear I may expect a like result myself."

"Ah, but you won the bout. There's the difference."

Francis bethought him of the words of the young guard they had met. "Maynard, wasn't it two men that were seen?"

"Oh, aye, it were, my lord. We've got the other. Caught him in the woods. He's been marched off to the cellars. Reckon we'll shove this one down there and all."

But Francis remained dissatisfied. "What was he like, that other? A small man?"

Maynard scratched his chin. "I'd not call him small exactly, my lord, though he's nowhere near as hefty as this 'un." He cast another admiring glance at Hemp. "I can see as you're big yourself, but I'd not have cared to take him on by myself, I can swear to that."

Francis paid this sally no heed. He turned instead to Indigo, who was looking as sullen as a battered face could show. "Who was your companion?"

Indigo gave a grunt. "Nowt to you."

Francis curbed a desire to plant him a flush hit. One did not strike a bound man, no matter the provocation. Even one as vile as Captain Indigo. "What I want to know is where is Quin."

Indigo managed a shrug. "Not his keeper."

"But you did engineer his escape along with your own."

Indigo said nothing. The black gaze stared with malevolence, in no way cowed by his situation.

"Stubborn to the last, eh? You made an error of judgement when you thought to exact revenge here. You should have gone while you had the chance. Well, never mind. Take him away, Maynard."

He watched the cavalcade as the two men who had tied up the prisoner marched him off towards the front of the glasshouse. Then he turned to Hemp and gave a wry grin. "If you must be a hero, we'd best get you patched up."

Hemp let out a laugh and then winced, hissing in a breath. "Don't trouble, milord. Doro will enjoy scolding me while she does the honours."

"Well, get that butler to dose you up with a tot of brandy. You deserve it." He set a hand to Hemp's shoulder and squeezed. "My thanks, friend. I'd best let Dalesford know."

"Also that his glasshouse is a wreck, milord," said Hemp on a rueful note.

Francis glanced around, taking in the damage, which was extensive but confined to one area. "I dare say my brother-in-law's carpenter and the gardeners will speedily set all to rights. The windows too. What I must do is send for Dalby. Then I don't doubt my wife will be happy to hear that all danger is past."

Ottilia was transfixed only for a moment. Instinct and calculation came to her aid. The dagger's handle was well within her reach. She grasped it and tugged. It came away and she turned, holding the weapon in front of her like a sword.

Quin was just coming out from the other side of the big bed, but he halted, staring at the dagger in her hand.

"A miscalculation on your part, Quin." Her voice was a trifle shaky, but Ottilia felt all the growing confidence of having the advantage. She made a threatening gesture with her weapon. "Step back, if you please."

His face showed chagrin but he backed a couple of feet. Ottilia gestured with the dagger to indicate he should retreat to one side so that the bed was between them. He obeyed and she moved to the relative safety of her side. If he made a sudden spring over the bed, she would have time to get out of the way.

Still, the possibility was troubling. She glanced past him and saw the dressing table set at the far wall for her use. "Take a seat on that dressing stool."

Quin flicked a glance behind him and then back at Ottilia. She waited, hoping he would obey. She did not want to have to use the dagger, but she would have no hesitation in sticking him with it if he tried to come for her.

He seemed to realise his position was untenable. With a sour look, he retreated to the stool, drew it out and plonked down in an insolent manner, folding his arms. "Now what, my Lady Fan?"

Ottilia let her breath go, but remained where she was. "Now we will talk."

His chin came up. "Got nowt to say."

"Indeed? Yet I believe you owe me an explanation at least of your presence in my bedchamber."

He scratched his chin, but said no word. This was not going to be easy. Ottilia lowered the dagger slightly, glancing at it as she did so. Recognition flashed. It was one with those which had featured in the affair at Bristol, made by a fellow at the plantation in Barbados. It gave her a curious feeling of power to be in possession. She eyed the intruder again, who still had not answered. Ottilia tried a different tack.

"You make a habit of hiding under things, I think. It was you under the jetty, was it not?"

His gaze became fixed, as if he must prevent himself from showing anything in his face. "Don't know nowt of that."

"Oh, I think you do, Quin. You were watching from some vantage point. You saw me walking alone and slid into the water. I expect you thought to seize me from the bank, but by sheer luck I stepped onto the jetty. I made it easy for you, do you not think?"

His features were rigid. "Don't know nowt about no jetty. Nor I never grabbed anyone by the leg."

Triumph lit in Ottilia's breast. She spoke softly. "Did I mention I was seized by the ankle?"

Instant consternation. Colour came and went in his cheeks. He sputtered slightly as he got words out. "It were him. That bully o' yourn. He said it."

Ottilia became tart. "Do not let us shilly-shally in this foolish way, Quin. Why did you do it?"

For a few breathless instants, she thought he had himself well in hand. His lips were compressed, his eyes narrowed, squinting with some inner effort. Then he drew in a heavy breath and sighed it out. "I never meant no harm. A ducking is all. Nor it weren't my notion, not by a long chalk. Never wanted ter do it, only she made me."

Gathering interest overcame Ottilia's caution and she held the dagger more loosely, moving a step towards the bed. "Cherry?"

Now he had capitulated, it seemed whatever Quin's design had been in infiltrating her very chamber was overborne by the urge to exonerate himself. "It were her as wanted you to suffer. When she learned as you was here, she come on to me to do you a mischief. For her sake, she said."

Ottilia could well imagine Cherry's methods. "Do I take it she offered to reward you with her person?"

Quin sniffed. "Wouldn't let me do nowt without I done her bidding."

"She wanted me dead?"

He shrugged. "It were her notion as you oughter get a ducking. To learn you, she said."

An echo replayed in Ottilia's head. *That'll learn you.* She had indeed heard someone speak!

The intruder's voice took on a whine. "I thought that were all, I swear, missus."

A chill crept down Ottilia's spine. Quin's words indicated that he had misunderstood the barmaid's intention. Cherry might not make her desire clear, and Quin could well suppose a dip in the river would prove relatively harmless. But Cherry would have known that a woman's petticoats would drag her down. A canny woman she had been, while Quin's intelligence was wanting. It would not occur to him to calculate that the speed of flow of the Ouse was strong, that even a person who could swim might find themselves in difficulties. He had been under the jetty, where he could hold onto struts. One other consideration too.

"Did you think my people would save me?"

"A wetting was all," he reiterated. "When I saw as you never come up, I took meself off, didn't I?"

Just as she had supposed. "You told Cherry?"

"Course I told her. She were right pleased. 'That's the end of Lady Fan,' says she. 'End of me too,' says I, 'if they knows as I done it.' Cherry said nobody would find out. Said if you was gone, there weren't no one as could work out as it were me."

Which, presumably, was why he had ventured into her bedchamber. To rid himself of the possibility of the crime being brought home to him? Not to mention the barmaid's murder. Had he intended to stab her with the knife, perhaps while she slept? Easy enough to slip away in the night hours, never to be seen again. If Indigo had not been spotted, her life would not have been worth a moment's purchase.

Her conviction increased as a frown descended and he eyed Ottilia with hatred, venom in his tone. "Dunno how you found me out. That Roy feller believed me. You a witch woman like that Doro?"

Ottilia ignored the entirety of this address, pushing aside the horrid notion of her intended fate. She had questions in need of answers. "What happened with Cherry that she ended up in the Ouse herself?"

He grew sullen. "Heard you was still alive, didn't she?"

"And then? Did you quarrel?"

Quin became defiant. "It weren't my blame, I tell you! I never touched her."

"Did Indigo?"

Was it scorn in the little man's eyes now? "Him? He cared nowt 'cepting as Cherry warmed his bed fer him when he wanted. Only let her take up with him fer that. Didn't care as she plied her trade elsewhere, long as she give him his."

Then had Indigo not killed her after all? Ottilia spoke with deliberation, determined on extracting the truth. "Cherry did not drown, Quin. Her neck was broken."

He wriggled in the chair. "It never were. Fell into the river, she did."

"She was thrown into the river, Quin. She was already dead."

He was kneading his hands between his knees, his gaze shifting first one way and then another. Ottilia recalled his doing so before, when he wished to escape her questions in Bristol. She applied a goad. "Come, Quin, of what use to conceal the truth? I examined Cherry's corpse. I know her neck was broken. Her body showed none of the usual signs of drowning."

All at once, he leapt from the stool, his voice rising. "I never done it, I tell you! It were an accident!"

Ottilia backed a couple of steps, raising the dagger again. But she kept her tone neutral and quiet. "What precisely happened?"

"We was argufying is all. She were mad as fire 'cause you ain't died. Insisted as we found where you was dragged out, fer the tale were told all over."

"So you were down by the river when you quarrelled."

"It were her blame! I never done nowt. Took to hitting of me, she were that mad. I shoved her off and … and she fell." He dropped back onto the stool, throwing his hands over his face.

"Did she hit her head? Is that how she broke her neck?"

The hands dropped. Despair was in the man's face. "I dunno. I don't hold with violence, me. I didn't think nothing at first, only she weren't moving. When I went to look, I seen her head were all twisted like."

Ottilia began to grow suspicious. This did not fit the facts as she had discovered them. "You are lying, Quin."

"I ain't, I swear it."

She persisted, speaking with deliberation. "Cherry's neck had been snapped. There was no sign of injury to her head, which there would have been if the fall had caused a broken neck. She would have had to hit her head on something hard, like a rock or hidden tree stump, perhaps."

"I'm telling you like it was." The protest was querulous now.

"I can believe Cherry was stunned by a fall, perhaps. But someone — you or Indigo — took her head in his hands and twisted it until her neck snapped. It can be done very easily by a strong man who knows the trick of it."

Quin jumped up again. "I ain't strong. Never been. Nor I don't know no tricks of that kind. I'm a peaceable man."

Ottilia eyed him. "Then you must be covering for Indigo. Did he threaten to do the same by you if you spoke out of turn?"

Before Quin could respond, the door opened. To her horror, Ottilia saw Doro enter, Luke in her arms. Instinct took over.

"No! Take him away at once, Doro! Leave! Go!"

She was moving as she spoke, but Quin was quicker. He leapt up and flew across the room, reaching the door just as Doro was trying to exit. Before Ottilia knew what had happened, her little son was in the enemy's hands, Doro knocked to the floor.

CHAPTER TWENTY-FOUR

A yell tore out of Ottilia's throat as she scrambled to the rescue. About to thrust at Quin with the blade, she was brought up short as he shoved Luke in front of him, holding him up as a shield.

By a miracle, Ottilia managed to deflect her aim. The point of the dagger just missed her little boy's face. She pulled back her arm. The dagger went spinning. Ottilia seized her child, wrenched him out of the hands that held him and hugged his small person to her bosom, heedless of the commotion behind her as she hastened as far away from the door as she could get.

Luke, at first stunned by the speed of events, began to wail. Ottilia shushed at him, huddling against a wall. "Hush, my darling, hush. You are safe with Mama. Hush now, my little man."

Soothed by her voice, his cries became muted and Ottilia, who had fetched up to one side at the head of the four-poster, was able to give her attention to the struggle that was going forward on the other side of the room.

Quin had evidently dived after the dagger, but was impeded by Doro. She had somehow succeeded in getting herself up from her fall, for Ottilia saw she had seized Quin's foot and was climbing up his body, thumping at his person as she went. From her lips came a stream of invective in a foreign tongue. Doro had reverted to the language of her lost childhood.

Ottilia looked to the open door. Where was the footman? Had Charles never arrived at his post? She wanted to run for the door and call out for help, but to reach it she must circumvent the struggling pair on the floor. Her first care was for her terrified boy, still whimpering and clutching her about the neck. Nor was any shout she made likely to be heard above the cacophony being made by the combatants, for Quin was making quite as much protest as was Doro. Nevertheless, she opened her throat and called for help.

"Charles! Anyone! Come, quick!"

Then, in an instant, it was over. How Quin got free, Ottilia could not tell. He struggled up, Doro clinging to his person. He turned, the dagger in his hand, and slashed at the incubus that hampered him.

Blood spurted. Doro let go, fell back and lay still.

Ottilia cried out and started forward. At the same moment, Quin leapt over the nurse's body and made for the door. He disappeared through it, but Ottilia no longer cared. She hurried to Doro, dropping down beside the prone figure.

"Luke, darling, I am going to set you down. I must help Doro."

She prised the child's arms from about her neck and set him on the ground. His attention went directly to his nurse and he stood watching as Ottilia pulled up the hem of her own gown. Seizing folds of under-petticoat, she bunched them and held them to the wound across Doro's upper chest from which she was losing blood, her bodice already stained with red.

Relief swept through Ottilia as she realised it was a surface wound. Thank heaven he had sliced rather than stabbed. Doro had not quite lost consciousness. Her blue eyes rolled open and closed several times.

"Lie still, Doro. I must hold this steady to staunch the blood."

Doro spoke, her voice faint. "Where is he?"

"I don't know. Have no fear. He cannot get far."

Even as she said it, Ottilia became aware of sounds in the corridor indicative of a struggle. Shouts, curses and the thump of several sets of footsteps, coming at a run.

One of these sounded familiar to Ottilia's ears and hope lit in her breast. Seconds later, Francis crashed into the room.

"Dear God, what happened?" He barely halted, his gaze falling on Ottilia, then Doro and Luke.

"Pick Luke up, Fan," Ottilia said as he reached them. "The poor little mite has had a dreadful time of it."

He did not hesitate, but swung the child up into his arms, holding him secure. "Hush, Luke. Papa has you safe."

Ottilia lifted her improvised compress and examined the wound. "It is bleeding but sluggishly now, thank heaven." The nurse made to move, but Ottilia set the bundle back and held it there. "Stay, Doro. We must wait until I can fashion you a proper dressing. Fan, pray ring the bell. I need Joanie."

"Ring the bell? There's a veritable army outside this room." He made for the door, Luke held on his hip. "Hi! Someone fetch my wife's maid. At once." He came back into the room. "Did Quin do this?"

Ottilia looked up. "Yes. Have they caught him?"

"He ran directly into the footman and Gil. Between them, they were able to overpower him."

"Where in the world was the footman? Gil said he was going to have him guard the door. Not that it would have prevented the fracas. Quin was hiding under the bed."

"For pity's sake! There I was thinking all was over because we had Indigo."

"You caught him?"

"Hemp did. He fought him and won. Nearly pummelled the life out of the fellow."

At this Doro's eyes, which had been closed again, flew open. "Hemp did? Is he hurt, milord?"

"Not as badly as you."

Hardly were the words out of his mouth when Hemp himself charged into the room. He halted at the door. "I heard Doro is injured." Ottilia was about to answer when her steward spotted his inamorata. "Doro!"

Unable to move out of the way, Ottilia sought to reassure as Hemp came forward, squeezing to Doro's other side, his back to the corner of the bed, and dropping to one knee. "It is a surface wound. Already the bleeding is reducing."

But Hemp was unheeding. "That rat of a villain! I'll kill him!"

An empty threat, Ottilia supposed, but she had no need to say so. Nor would her words have been heard. Doro was gazing up at Hemp with adoration in her eyes, and he had taken hold of one hand and was kissing it with a degree of passion Ottilia had never before seen him display. She wished she might absent herself from the ensuing low-toned conversation between the pair and exchanged a glance with her spouse. Francis raised his brows in acknowledgement, a wry twist to his lips.

Then Joanie arrived, accompanied by Hepsie, who had, as she explained, hastened down from the nursery. The tale must be all over the house by now, Ottilia reflected. She gave her requirements to her maid, who hurried off to fetch water, clean cloths and gauze.

"Let me take Master Luke, my lord."

Ottilia looked to her spouse and saw his reluctance. "Give him to Hepsie, Fan. Pretty can entertain him and he will very soon forget all about it."

Francis murmured to the boy before handing him over. A pang smote Ottilia as she watched how Luke settled readily

321

into the nurse's arms, seeming to realise he must accept a substitute in place of his Doro. She could not withstand a plea. "Take good care of him, Hepsie. He has had a shocking fright. I will come up to see both children when we have settled everything here."

"He will be quite safe with me, my lady, never fear." She cast a sympathetic glance at Doro, still engaged in low-voiced conversation with Hemp, and then bore Luke off.

At first bereft, Ottilia very quickly recovered as the room began to seem overfull of persons. First, her mother-in-law arrived. "Gracious heaven! And I supposed you would be quite safe in your bedchamber, Ottilia."

She was accompanied by her companion, who had barely exclaimed when Harriet turned up, voluble with dismay until Francis drove them all out again as Joanie arrived and had difficulty making her way into the chamber for the press of persons.

"For pity's sake, let Ottilia deal with Doro first. Then she must change her dress. You can ask your questions at a later time."

Once Doro had been lifted by Hemp and settled on the bed, Ottilia cast both Hemp and her spouse out while Doro's wound was dealt with. Between them, she and Joanie succeeded in drawing down Doro's upper garments and laying bare the wound.

"Ah, the bleeding is but sluggish now, my dear. Rest easy. We will have you sorted in a trice."

Warm water and a clean cloth very soon cleared the skin of disfiguring stains. "The basilicum powder, Joanie. Did you bring it?"

The maid, in the act of removing the basin she had been holding ready, tutted. "I've not forgot, my lady, but I must get it from your dressing case."

"Hurry, if you please. It's beginning to ooze again."

While Joanie set down the basin and rummaged for the tin of powder, Ottilia used the towel to dab at the long red line that crossed Doro's upper chest. "He just missed your bosom, Doro, mercifully. If there is a scar, it will be slight."

Doro managed a smile. "I do not mind it, milady. As long as Luke is safe, that is all that matters."

"He was shocked, poor little man, but he will suffer no lasting damage. You kept that villain from attacking him again and I have not even thanked you."

"Do not thank me. If he had harmed Luke, milady, I could never forgive myself."

Rather to Ottilia's relief, Joanie intervened at this point, holding out the tin. "The basilicum, my lady."

Ottilia took it with a word of thanks. She knew not how to respond to Doro. Such a risk she had taken in tackling Quin. If he had caught her in the throat…

She banished the horrid notion, setting herself to cover every inch of the wound with basilicum, both to staunch the blood and prevent any infection from entering the wound. Gauze strips served to keep it covered, kept in place with a bandage she was obliged to wind around the nurse's back before pinning it in place.

"There, that will keep it secure. We will look at it again tomorrow, Doro, to make sure it is healing well. I hope you may be able to leave off the bandaging in a day or two, once the wound has sealed." She smiled at the girl as she assisted her to sit, setting her legs to the floor. "Fortunately, the human body is extraordinarily successful at repairing itself."

Joanie helped Doro to adjust her bodice and slip her sleeves back into the gown, what time Ottilia went to the door to call Hemp to carry away his wounded betrothed. He was ready and waiting, wasting no time in springing to the task.

As he left, his inamorata in his arms, Ottilia moved back into the room to find her maid regarding her severely, arms akimbo. "Now, we'd best see to you, my lady."

Ottilia sighed. "I am not injured, Joanie."

"No, but you're blood all over. There's another gown ruined."

Ottilia lifted the gown which had fallen back over the under-petticoat she had used to staunch the blood. "Don't fret, my dear. It may have caught a spot or two, but the gown will be readily cleaned."

Joanie was busy undoing the strings that held her round gown together. "Not that petticoat won't be, my lady. It's fair wrecked with wrinkles and we'll never get it back to proper white."

"Never mind it, Joanie." She shrugged out of the sleeves and the maid pulled the gown over her head.

"At this rate, my lady, you'll have nothing left to wear," Joanie grumbled, setting the gown aside and beginning to untie the strings at the waist of the damaged petticoat.

All at once, the exigencies of the past hectic period overcame Ottilia. "Joanie, I have to sit down." She fairly staggered to the bed and plonked down, setting her hands each side and holding fast to the edge in a bid to prevent herself from losing consciousness as dots began to swim in her vision. But it was to no avail. The world went spinning and she knew no more.

CHAPTER TWENTY-FIVE

Despite her protests, Hemp insisted on carrying Doro along to the room allotted to her, which she shared with Hepsie. Dalesford Hall was so vast, the servants were housed not in the attics, but in a wing that had been part of an earlier building and was situated to the far side of the mansion. The rooms were serviceable, if not large, and well appointed, though with mismatched and old-fashioned furnishings. Doro's chamber was on the first floor, reached from the newer part of the house by a series of long corridors. Since she and Hepsie alternated the duty of sleeping in the nursery, it was no hardship to be assigned to the same chamber and Hemp was in the habit of escorting her there after their night-time walks. He thus knew the way and she was very soon set down upon her bed.

"Now you may rest."

"Not yet." With care, Doro traced a finger along the dressing that covered the wound. The dagger had carved a long cut, but Doro had not been able to see the damage for herself. "It will mend fast, milady says."

There was concern in Hemp's face. "It must have stung to have it cleaned."

"A little, but I don't feel it much now. I am well recovered already."

His tone became urgent. "Nevertheless, you ought to rest now. Lie down, Doro. You have had a horrible attack and you may experience shock. I will bring you a tisane."

Doro reached out a hand to detain him. "Don't go. Not yet."

He had begun to move towards the door, but paused. As he looked down, Doro subjected his countenance to a more thorough inspection. "You are as much injured, if not more than I. Milord said that pirate hurt you."

Hemp brushed it aside with a wafture of one hand. "It is nothing. I am more worried about your injury."

"It has been well tended, but yours has not." Doro patted the bed. "Sit, Hemp."

He hesitated. "I ought not. It is not seemly."

"As if I care for that. We are betrothed. Sit, I tell you!"

He grinned, wincing a little. "That's my Doro."

She ignored this as he sat down beside her. Doro lifted a hand to his face, touching wounds at his lip and cheek. "Have you even cleaned these wounds?"

"To tell true, I was expecting you would insist on nursing them for me."

"I will presently. We will have water and clean cloths brought to this room. The housekeeper is very kind and she will send it. Ask when you go down to the kitchens."

"If you insist."

"I do insist. Are you hurting?"

He shrugged. "It's nothing, I promise you."

She slapped at his arm. "Nothing? When your eye is half closed and your cheek begins to look like a watermelon?" He laughed and hissed in a breath, grimacing. "See?"

"Witch."

"I will be a true witch if you do not stop trying to be a hero."

His dark gaze roved her face, growing serious. "You are the heroine, my queen. What possessed you to tackle Quin?"

She growled as the memory stirred. "He dared to threaten Luke. I could not let him get by with no punishment."

Hemp's hand came up and a little shiver shook her as he stroked her face. "You lost your temper, you wild thing."

Doro could not help a tiny smile. "You know how it is with me."

"Too well."

He leaned in and Doro accepted his kiss. Chaste as usual. He had not shown her the passion she knew dwelled inside him, not since the night they'd settled their future. She might long for it, but if he knew her, she knew him the more. He would think it dishonoured her to kiss her deeply before they were wed. The thought had scarcely formed when Hemp seemed to take it from her mind.

"This has decided me, Doro. We must marry very soon."

She smiled at him. "With that I will not argue."

"And you must encourage milady to find a replacement as soon as may be. Once Luke has learned to —⬚

She interrupted without ceremony, all the loyalty and gratitude she felt towards Ottilia rising to the fore. "No!"

Hemp drew back a little, his chin coming up in that haughty look he wore when he was thwarted. "What do you mean, no? We are agreed, Doro, so I thought. Once Luke has become used to another nurse, we may leave and make our own life together."

Doro seized his hand and held it tight between both her own. "We will do so, Hemp. I want that too. But not yet. We cannot leave milady quite yet."

"Not yet, I grant you, but soon. As soon as we may manage."

His voice was growing more frustrated and Doro searched this way and that for a valid excuse. She had given her word to milady, but how was she to persuade Hemp without revealing the truth?

"We do not only have ourselves to consider, Hemp."

"Who then? Milady? She has agreed."

"Then, yes. But now … things have changed."

"You mean because of this? She is no longer in danger."

"It is not that."

"What then?"

Doro sighed out a breath, capitulating. "I am not supposed to tell you this, but if you will be so stubborn, I have no choice."

His brows drew together. "Doro, what in the world are you talking about?"

She eyed him for a moment. It was no use. "Milady may be with child again."

Shock in his face. "What?"

"It is not yet certain, but the signs are there. Hemp, I cannot leave her if she is in that condition. We will have to remain until the birth, and then until the new nurse has become accustomed."

Hemp blew out a breath. "I don't see that we need wait so long. She will find a new nurse for Luke and that woman can take care of a new baby too. Also there is Hepsie."

Trying not to fly into a pelter, Doro opted for persuasion. "That is so, but you are asking me to abandon the woman who saved my life, who engineered my freedom. I cannot do it."

He was silent for a moment, his frowning gaze regarding her in a considering way. "But you will not hesitate to wed me?"

"I have said."

Again he paused. "What if I find a place where we may choose to live?"

Doro snapped. "You will find? I thought you wished me to choose, or at least that we will choose together."

He shrugged. "If you will not come away, what can I do? We cannot leave until we have somewhere to go."

For a moment she regarded him with rising choler in her breast. Then a certain look in his face she recalled from years gone by alerted her. "Hemp Roy, you are a devil man."

He drew back. "This from a witch woman?"

She wagged a finger in his face. "I know your game of old. You are trying to provoke me that I shall give in to you. Sneak behind my guard, would you?"

"Riddle talk, Mademoiselle Gabon."

"You are the riddler, with your stupid threats of going without me. You know well we have no need to be settled on a place. Such possessions as we have we may leave at Flitteris while we search."

He grunted. "You have an answer for everything." He got up. "I will fetch that tisane."

Doro caught his hand. "I don't wish for a tisane."

"Then what do you want? I have given up trying to read your mind, blue magic queen."

She gave him a smile tinged with mischief. "I would like tea, if you would be so kind, my king."

He produced one of his rare smiles and lifted the hand to his lips. "I am yours to command. As if you didn't know."

"And do not forget the things I need to clean your wounds."

He emitted a groan. "A termagant is what I am marrying."

Doro laughed and blew him a kiss as he looked back from the door. With affection in her breast, she watched him leave the room. She would have her way, but in due course she would make it up to him. Thanks to Ottilia, she had a lifetime for the purpose.

The next thing Ottilia knew was the frantic voice of her husband.

"Tillie! Wake up, my dear one!"

She struggled to open her eyes, but the room was going round and she closed them again.

"Tillie! Fetch some brandy, girl!"

Brandy? Why did she need brandy? Despite herself her eyelids fluttered open. The dizziness began to recede. Ottilia discovered she was on her side but her legs still hung over the edge of the bed. Francis was squatting beside her, anxiety in the beloved face.

"Thank the Lord, she is coming round!"

Ottilia stared at him. "Did I swoon?"

"With a vengeance. Joanie was beside herself. She couldn't rouse you even with your vinaigrette. At least she had the sense to call me in. She's gone for brandy."

The rapid fire of words only vaguely penetrated the fog in Ottilia's head. She hardly knew she spoke. "Were you outside?"

"I was waiting for you to finish with Doro. I would have come in when Hemp took her off, but Gil arrived and we were conferring. I wouldn't have done so had I known you were ill."

He kissed her hand and Ottilia only now realised he was holding it. She gave his fingers a squeeze.

"I am not ill." Even as she spoke, her mind was clearing, the events of the past hour or so returning to her memory. She tried to sit up, but Francis prevented her.

"Stay put, my loved one."

"But I am decidedly uncomfortable. Help me, Fan."

He rose and drew her to a sitting posture. Ottilia held onto him, letting her head fall against him as she waited for the sudden dizziness caused by sitting up to recede.

"Tillie?"

"I am all right," she said into his clothes, her voice somewhat muffled. "Just let me rest a moment."

"Sniff this, Tillie."

Her little silver box appeared under her nose, already open, its acrid aroma overwhelming. She turned her face. "Not that, Fan, pray."

The box vanished. Francis instead supported her shoulders, but she felt one hand release, instead stroking her hair. Her cap had come off and her locks were loosened from their moorings. Realising as much, she spoke her thought aloud.

"No surprise the pins would not hold after all that."

A laugh sounded above her. "You are talking nonsense, wife of my heart."

She pushed away, feeling more recovered, and looked up at him. "Nothing of the kind." She released her hold and flicked at loose strands of hair. "See? What with rushing hither and yon, I have come undone."

"No surprise to me." He sat down beside her and set an arm about her, holding her steady. "You have been coming undone ever since I met you. I count myself astonished it has taken so long for you to arrive at the same conclusion."

Delight entered Ottilia's breast and she broke into gurgling laughter. "You fiend of a husband, how dare you?"

He turned her face towards him and kissed her. "How do you feel?"

"Disorientated."

"No, I mean truly. In yourself."

"I don't know, my dearest dear. What do you want me to say?"

He drew in a breath and sighed it out. "If you must have it in plain words, I am anxious for why this faint came about. Harriet has an excellent doctor, and —□

"No doctors! I am perfectly well, Fan."

His tone became peremptory. "No, you are not. I grant you, these fainting fits have come after severe upsets —□

"There you are, then. That is a valid explanation."

"All well and good, but these past weeks have taken a toll on your health and if you are indeed pregnant —□

She interrupted again. "It is too soon to be certain. No doctor can say any more than I whether or not I am enceinte."

"The signs are there. Have you been sick again and not told me?"

Guilt flooded Ottilia's bosom. She gave a grudging response. "Yes, but I didn't want to worry you."

Francis let out an exasperated sound. "You're worrying me now, wretched female."

Much to Ottilia's relief, the entrance of her maid obliged her husband to abandon the argument. She accepted the glass from Joanie and sipped the brandy at his command. Her mind roved over the late incident. Events had moved so fast, she realised an omission.

"Fan, I have not told you all I learned from Quin."

He gave a grunt. "That sneaky rat? I ought never to have sent you in here. For safety forsooth!"

"You could not have known, my darling lord."

"I might have suspected some trickery. Especially after that odd dream of yours."

She laid her free hand on his unquiet one. "I did not recall it either, Fan, and it seemed trivial at the time."

"Trivial! Hardly, in the light of subsequent events. What did he intend? Why was he hiding under the bed?"

Impossible to avoid the answer, however much Ottilia might wish to conceal her own realisation. "Pray don't get into a fuss, my darling lord, but I believe he would have crept out in the night and plunged the dagger into me." The look of horror on her spouse's face made her grip his hand. "I dare say you would have known nothing of it until the morning, my dearest."

He vented his feelings in a volley of cursing and ended by holding her in so tight an embrace she was obliged to protest. When he was at last induced to release her, she set a hand to his chest, her tone rueful.

"Do not let us waste time upon what cannot be helped. It did not happen, after all. Far more important is that Quin admitted to pulling me into the water."

"Villain! He makes a habit of hiding, I take it. It was he under the jetty, then?"

"Yes, but he was not the true villain of that piece, Fan. Do but let me tell you all."

He listened while she related the tale she had extracted, not without exclaiming at the perfidy of the barmaid Cherry. As she talked, Ottilia forgot to sip her brandy and was only reminded when she came to the end of her revelations and moved to set down the glass on the bedside cabinet.

"You've not finished that, Tillie. Drink it all." Francis rose as he spoke and she was treated to a wry look. "You are going to need fortifying, quite apart from recovering from your ordeal at Quin's hands. Gil came to tell me Captain Dalby has arrived."

Ottilia, in the act of sipping the remainder of her brandy, almost choked. Her mind leapt to the still unsolved parts of the puzzle. "Oh, what news?"

Francis glanced at the maid, who was busy tidying away the items left from the late fracas. He lowered his voice. "He has seen Pedwardine. When you feel up to it, you'd best dress again and we'll meet him."

"Assuredly. He won't vanish for a while, will he?"

"No chance of that. He is waiting for his men to take off Indigo and Quin."

Ottilia became brisk. "Then I had best get ready immediately." She looked round and saw her maid was about to dispose of the gown she had been wearing. "Joanie, don't put that gown away."

"But it's dirty, my lady."

"Then find me another directly."

Francis helped her as she set aside the now empty glass and made to rise. "You need not rush."

"I need to indeed, Fan. I must speak to Indigo before he is taken away."

The pirate, trussed up like a pig on a spit, was being held in a little-used pantry off the kitchen area. Quin was evidently imprisoned elsewhere.

"Gil did not want them together for fear of them conferring to concoct some sort of mutual defence," Francis told her. "He's down in a cellar with the other fellow that came with him."

Ottilia glanced through the doorway to which the butler held the key. He had opened it at her spouse's command and was waiting in the narrow passageway. All she could see within was a bare wooden cupboard to one side and two booted feet secured at the ankles. Indigo was evidently sitting at his ease. Ottilia had never before met him and curiosity overtook her as she followed Francis into the little room.

Her first sight of the pirate startled her with an impression of power, despite his being tied hand and foot. Thickset with a head like a cannon ball, he possessed a pair of dynamic eyes, the dark pupils stark against their white background, which met Ottilia's gaze with a fearless insouciance she could not but appreciate. His face was broad and flat, just now decorated with cuts and disfiguring bruises further darkening his skin in places.

Ottilia's medical instincts came to the fore. "Has not anyone thought to tend to his wounds?"

Francis gave her a look as if he questioned her sanity. "Clearly not."

"Then they should."

"Well, don't expect Hemp to undertake it. This is his handiwork."

Resolving to instruct the butler to see that someone, the footman Charles perhaps, at least cleaned the prisoner's wounds, Ottilia turned her attention to the questions still posed by Quin's unreliable testimony. She addressed the pirate directly. "I am Lady Francis Fanshawe."

A deep voice on the pitch of a growl answered her. "Know who you are."

Ottilia raised her brows. "Indeed? You've seen me before, then?"

The dark gaze, malevolence within it, glanced at Francis. "Two and two make four."

Her husband threw up his eyes. "You'll get nothing but cryptic answers from him, I warn you."

She nodded but spoke rather to the man himself. "I am glad to find you can add up, since it is my habit also and I fear the tale Quin saw fit to tell me does not tally."

Indigo's brows lowered. "Tattled, huh?"

"I asked him about Cherry's death."

His head dropped a trifle, as if he sought to hide what he might of his features. Not that she could read his expression. He was adept, one imagined, at concealing his thoughts. She persisted.

"Quin tried to make me believe it was an accident." She waited but no response was forthcoming beyond a hard stare. Ottilia flicked a glance at Francis and found him frowning, whether at her line of questioning or with displeasure at the pirate's attitude she could not tell. "Quin said that Cherry broke her neck when she hit her head, but that is what does not add up."

Indigo's chin came up in an arrogant fashion and he eyed her with a strange sort of interest. "You say how."

"Certainly. Cherry died when someone took her head in his hands and gave it a mortal twist to one side, thus snapping her neck."

Was it surprise in his face? He had not expected to be found out, then. She drove a nail into the coffin. "Quin does not have the strength to make such a kill. You do."

His dark features were motionless. His stare was thick with an emanation of fury. Ottilia silently triumphed. Instead her spouse gave it voice.

"It looks as if my wife has hit the mark, Indigo."

The pirate turned his head and, with deliberation, spat on the floor. "Girl was a whore. No loss."

Ottilia's ire rose. "She was used, Indigo. Suborned into committing those crimes."

At this, Francis broke into protest. "For pity's sake, Tillie! She plotted your death. Quin admitted as much."

"He also said that he had not known her intent. At that point, he did not think of disposing of me forever." She turned suddenly on Indigo. "Did you know it? Or did you kill her because she had become a danger to you? She was making your position untenable. You knew if I had been targeted, and lived, that I would pursue enquiries which must inevitably lead to you. I dare say Quin confessed all to you when he found out

I had survived and that Cherry had intended I should drown. He became frightened, for he knew even better than you that I would not rest until I found out the culprit. Thus you decided that Cherry had to go. Collateral damage, Indigo?"

He did not answer, but there was hatred now in his gaze.

"My God!" The curse, said softly in a stunned tone, came from beside her. "All the while we were on the wrong track altogether."

"I fear so, Fan."

"You asserted the two incidents were connected and I could not see it."

"It escaped me too, what with the distraction of our other unfortunate victim." She was still regarding Indigo, whose gaze did not waver from hers. "Yet I fear that is not all, is it, Indigo?"

He spoke then, guttural, with a challenge in his eye. "What more?"

"My husband thinks you came here to revenge yourself on him or my steward, but that is not so, is it?"

"What, Tillie? What are you saying?" Her husband's tone was urgent.

Ottilia kept her eyes locked with the pirate's hard gaze. "I said Quin knows how persistent I am, did I not? He was afraid I would find a way to prove either one of you guilty of doing away with Cherry. He whined as much to you, I suspect, and you decided to act. Left to himself, I doubt Quin would have had the courage to enter these grounds. Only he feared retribution at your hands more than he feared to do your bidding. He was afraid if he did not make a further and final attempt upon my life, you would serve him as you did Cherry."

"Do you mean to say," her spouse said in hollow accents, "that they were *both* here to try for you again?"

"I suspect Indigo's part was to cause a diversion to enable Quin to get into the house. Why would he allow himself to be seen otherwise?"

"You unmitigated scoundrel!" Francis took a hasty step towards the pirate, but Ottilia set a staying hand on his arm and he hesitated, his breath rasping. Then he gave a harsh bark of laughter. "You did not bargain for Hemp Roy's fighting skills, I'll warrant."

"I am quite sure he did not. Once he had given Quin sufficient time to find a hiding place, he and his associate would have melted away again."

Seeing her husband was bereft of words, Ottilia gave Indigo a spurious smile and adopted a conversational tone. "You are going to hang in any event, you must know. Robbery with violence in Newport Pagnell. Not to mention a householder's death. Piracy and wrecking back in Bristol. Heaven knows how many other crimes might be laid to your account, even if we discount your activities today. You are doomed, Indigo."

The pirate showed yellowed teeth, emitting a grunted laugh. "Wish me to confess? Whistle for it, you can, Lady Fan."

Ottilia let out a sigh. "I didn't think you would. I doubt silence will save you. Yet I am satisfied. You have given me all the assurance I require." She turned for the door. "Come, Fan. I have done."

CHAPTER TWENTY-SIX

Captain Dalby listened to Ottilia's account with interest, but at the end he was regretful. "Unfortunately, I have nothing to proffer to the coroner by way of proof."

"Despite the fact your medical man gave Cherry's death as strangulation?"

"I mean, my lady, I can't bring it home to Captain Indigo. We have his other crimes, however. Not that we have proof as yet that he committed the burglaries."

Francis intervened. "But you know he entered Dalesford's grounds for some nefarious purpose, even if we cannot prove precisely what that was. Not that there can be any doubt after what my wife has said. Moreover, you are bound to discover some witness who can recognise him. For pity's sake, don't let him get off all charges!"

"I certainly will not if I can help it, my lord. It is a pity he would not confess to this murder."

Ottilia re-entered the lists. "I am satisfied Indigo did it, and can only trust he will not this time be permitted to escape."

"Have no fear, my lady. He will be chained and guarded day and night."

An idea occurred to Ottilia. "If you can persuade Quin he stands in no danger from Indigo's vengeance, you might get him to testify that the wretch did indeed murder Cherry. I am certain he witnessed the killing."

Ottilia and her spouse had located Captain Dalby in Gil's study where he was partaking of a glass of sherry. The earl greeted their arrival with enthusiasm.

"Ottilia! I am glad to see you up and about. Are you much hurt?"

"Not at all, Gil, I thank you. Fatigued, perhaps."

"No surprise there." He took her hand and held it between both his own, becoming serious. "I owe you an apology, my dear."

"How so?"

"You were missing a protector and it is my fault. I was about to send Charles up to guard your door when I learned my rascal of an older son had defied Peggy and gone off hunting for birds' nests. Since virtually every other man jack was out looking for the intruders —□

"Giving that blasted runt every opportunity to enter the house," cut in Francis in bitter accents.

"— it fell to myself and the footman to hunt down Gregory," went on Gil, unheeding. Ottilia doubted he had even heard the interjection. "It took us an age to locate the boy and no sooner had I led him back to safety than Fan and your steward arrived with news of Indigo's capture. So you see I am wholly to blame that you were left to fight off that villain by yourself."

He was evidently upset by his lapse and Ottilia set herself to soothe. "My dear Gil, don't think of it again. In your place, I should have done the same. I hope Harriet was not in despair over it."

"Never told her," said Gil with candour, "and I'd be obliged if you did not mention the matter either. Gregory may be depended upon to say nothing since he won't want to endure his mother's alarms."

Nor, it would appear, did Harriet's husband. But Ottilia refrained from pointing this out, giving an assurance she would keep mum.

"Yesterday afternoon. I could not get there the same day you visited Mr Gibbon."

Deflation hit Ottilia. "Then I fear it is already too late. If he is still in Newport Pagnell, I will own myself astonished."

Francis re-entered the lists. "You will have to chase after him and take those people with you."

"The devil! I must first see to securing these wretches here. At least they will not escape my clutches."

Ottilia bethought her of one point in which she could assist. "If you do mean to pursue the other, we can furnish you with Mr Gibbon's address. Not that I imagine Percy will remain with his benefactor for long. He is far too astute to stay where he might be in danger of discovery. I dare say that once his coffers are replenished, he will take himself off to some other country."

"And find another heiress to marry, no doubt," put in her spouse on a sour note.

Ottilia had no argument to make on that head. She bade the captain farewell and steeled herself for the inevitable repetition of the shenanigans in her bedchamber for the edification of Sybilla and Harriet.

With matters resolved, before their approaching departure, Ottilia found opportunity in the next days to visit Meggotty, armed with a further basket of provisions. The elderly dame greeted her with acclaim and a demand to know what had been happening.

"For if the rumours which have reached my ears are even half true, I'd've been out of my head worrying over you, dearie, and that's a fact."

Ottilia hastened to reassure her, delivering herself of an account, judiciously expurgated, of the past hideous weeks.

Samuel's wife Bridget, who was the only other member of the family present, exclaimed with horror, but Meggotty maintained the phlegmatic attitude that had carried Ottilia through the exigencies of the aftermath of her rescue.

"Well, what's done is done, and if them ruffians is took and come by their deserts, there ain't no need fer any weeping and wailing, dearie. Not as you're one to do any such, as I know."

"No, indeed, Meggotty. It is a waste of energy, and I have need now of all my strength."

"Have you, dearie?" The redoubtable dame's gaze swept Ottilia's person where she sat with her hosts on one of several rickety chairs set around the kitchen table, partaking of a glass, fortunately small, of home-made cowslip wine. "Will you be setting me to wondering why?" Meggotty gave a cracked laugh. "Or do I guess at it?"

Ottilia smiled. "I dare say you have already guessed. I believe I am with child again."

Bridget, round-eyed, took to blessing herself. But Meggotty gave a wry grin. "A right good thing as Samuel fetched you out of that river then, dearie. Nor he never suspected as it were two of you as he brought home."

"I am the more relieved that he did, Meggotty," Ottilia said, laughing.

"Well, you don't look a penny the worse for it, dearie, that I will say. Not as you wasn't none too clever when you left us that day neither. But I can see as you're better, never mind all them goings-on."

Ottilia was happy enough to encourage this theme, not wishing to dwell upon the horrid events. She remained for the best part of an hour until Francis, who had elected to wait outside, signified his impatience at last with a rap upon the kitchen door.

"I must go, Meggotty. We are leaving for home very shortly and there is still much to do in preparation."

The redoubtable dame then plied her with a great deal of advice for a successful outcome of her pregnancy, which in other circumstances Ottilia would have stigmatised as a collection of old wives' tales. She thanked her kind hostess with every appearance of gratitude, however, and reiterated her thanks.

Meggotty would have none of it. "Nowt to thank me for, dearie. You'd have done the same fer me, or anyone, if I ain't mistaken. Nor it ain't likely I am at my time of life. You take good care now, you hear? And if you visit these parts again, as I don't doubt you will, seeing as them at Dalesford is family, you be sure and come to see old Meggotty, and welcome you'll be, dearie, no mistake."

Ottilia promised to do so and thanked her again, waving from the phaeton until the cottage and her kind benefactor were no longer visible. She turned at last to Francis.

"It had not before occurred to me, my dearest, but without Meggotty's care, I dare say none of these events would have occurred."

"I might wish they had not, but they are vividly in my remembrance and will be for some time."

"Well, but only think, Fan. I would have expired before ever anyone knew anything of my whereabouts, and all set down to accident. A compelling instance of the strange workings of fate, do you not think?"

"Finally," came from Francis in heartfelt accents as the cavalcade at last drew away from Dalesford Hall en route to Flitteris Manor. "I have never been so relieved to be going home."

Ottilia turned from waving her farewells out of the window and settled back against the squabs. "You did instruct Williams to hold a steady pace, I hope, Fan?"

"Have no fear. None of the coaches are going to be doing much more than a snail's pace."

An unexpected addition to the party heading for Flitteris had meant the occupation of three coaches rather than only two. Sybilla, her companion and her dour maid made up the first coach, followed by the Fanshawe children, their nurses and Ottilia's maid in the second, herself and Francis bringing up the rear in the third. Diplock had opted to take the perch up behind rather than travel with noisy infants, Hemp having given up that seat in favour of riding alongside the middle coach to be near Doro.

"Williams knows you don't travel well," Francis pursued, "but I warned him in particular on this occasion, yes. As he's in charge of this whole expedition, his word goes. Tell me at once if you feel sick and we'll stop."

Since the start of the journey had been postponed until the travellers had partaken of a protracted breakfast, followed by the lengthy process of gathering everyone together and bidding all the members of the Fiske family farewell, Ottilia trusted she might well have done all the vomiting she needed for that day. As on each of the last few days while they prepared for departure, she had been nauseous first thing but well again in time for the early meal of the day. She was now in no doubt that she was again enceinte, the growing certainty fostered by Joanie's conviction that her belly was already thickening.

She did not yet feel her clothes too tight, but since it was now three weeks since her near drowning in the Great Ouse with no sign of her flux, Ottilia had to conclude she was already seven or eight weeks along. She still did not know how she felt about the prospect of another seven to eight months of curtailed motions and the malaise engendered by pregnancy. Her husband was bound to cosset and coddle her, which would undoubtedly become irksome, much as she enjoyed his solicitous attentions.

As if he read the subject of her ruminations, Francis spoke again, interrupting her thoughts. "You will have to tell my esteemed mama soon."

She repressed a sigh. "Not before I have seen a doctor."

"I thought you didn't wish to see a doctor. And you can't abide Lister."

Ottilia glanced round. "I can stand him on matters of which he necessarily has some knowledge. If only he was not so arrogant as to dismiss me as a mere female, incapable of rational observation."

Francis laughed and reached for her hand. "Which proves he knows little of you, my dear one. In any event, I will be writing to Patrick as soon as we get home."

She cast up her eyes. "I might know you would bring my brother down upon me in the shortest possible order. Though if I know Patrick, he will refuse to attend me until I am at least three or four months in." A thought occurred and she gave it voice. "I only hope Sybilla does not take it into her head to remain until the birth."

An explosive sound came from beside her. "I can't think what possessed you to invite her to come back with us in the first place."

Indignant, Ottilia turned on him. "I did no such thing. She invited herself, declaring that she had as well remain with us for the remainder of summer rather than return to the dower house to be incensed by the antics of the hussy she is obliged to call her daughter-in-law."

"Not that I've ever heard her refer to Violette as such. I could wish she was on better terms with Randal. She might at least leave us in peace now and then."

Ottilia returned no answer. Fond as she was of her mother-in-law, after the exigencies of these last weeks she had been looking forward to a period of renewal of her connubial life. The brush with death, together with the horrid estrangement from her beloved, however brief, had struck home. She might not settle quite, but she could at least build upon the life of domesticity Francis coveted. Besides, her apparent condition would not permit of her indulging in untoward activity.

She rested her head on Francis's shoulder, tucking her hand more firmly into his. "I hope you are satisfied that I am no longer in any danger, my dearest dear."

"I won't ever dare to be so satisfied." He pulled an arm free so he could set it about her shoulders, cuddling her to him. "I mean to cherish every moment you are still with me, however." He turned his head and Ottilia felt him drop a kiss on her brow. "We must promise to try our hardest not to fall out over trifles."

"It wasn't a trifle, Fan."

"Let us dismiss it as such. If you want the truth, I believe those hours when I thought you had drowned took me to the depths. I was too raw to be tolerant."

Ottilia could not speak, instead bringing his hand to her bosom and holding it fast. His voice came again, in a soothing murmur. "Don't fret, my loved one. We won't fall into such dispute again — ever."

She found her voice, husky though it was. "How can you be sure?"

A laugh sounded in her ear. "I can't. It is but a heartfelt hope."

She brought his hand to her lips and kissed it, then set it down in her lap, though she kept it firmly held. "You said at the outset it would never be all roses, Fan. I have never forgotten that."

He released her hand and she felt his fingers take hold of her chin, turning her so that she met his gaze. "It is, has been and will be a veritable garden, my darling heart. We have only to deadhead the bad blooms."

Ottilia sighed with satisfaction, at last ready to accept the worst was over. She rested her head on his shoulder again, preparing to enjoy this blessed time when they might be quite alone and revel in each other's company.

In a very short space of time, however, the idyll came to an abrupt end. Ottilia sat bolt upright, putting her hand to her mouth, her plea coming muffled.

"Knock on the roof, Fan! I am going to be sick."

A NOTE TO THE READER

Dear Reader

I am fortunate to have close friends who enjoy Lady Fan and when we met for coffee the other day, one of them threatened not to read any more if Ottilia did not survive or suffered too much. I did rather put her through the mill in this book, I'm afraid.

To say true, I hadn't intended the story to be quite so eventful and dangerous for my heroine. The fall into the river, yes. But the other incidents — not to mention the upsetting difficulties in Ottilia's marriage — took me completely by surprise. A telling instance of how the Inner Writer can confound the expectations of the analytical writer.

It was also interesting for me to expand the extended family with the younger Dalesford children popping up, together with renewing acquaintance with their parents Gil and Harriet. Building the family tree surrounding my central couple is both fascinating and a nightmare. It becomes really hard to keep track.

Some writers make use of aids where they can record all these individuals and interactions. I wish I was that organised. I do have a few documents where I've tried to gather everything together, but it's time-consuming and I would far rather be writing the next story. I need a secretary or a research assistant who can comb through all my bibles and pick everything up. As it is, I find myself doing exactly that when a new book gets underway.

I'm looking at Lady Fan 10 now, and as it involves Ottilia's two nephews, I've had to figure out how old they are now. To my astonishment, the elder Ben turns out to be going on fifteen already! Would you believe, we have been following members of this family for seven years? That's in story time, not our time. Is it any wonder I can't remember which from what or who?

My hope is that I can keep going long enough to see Pretty and Luke grow up. I've got plans in mind for Pretty's future, but that's some way off yet. Sybilla's new companion, Henrietta, is knocking at the Inner Writer's imagination too. And there are the two French offspring of Randal, Marquis of Polbrook, who seem determined to edge their way into a story at some point. Characters have a way of insinuating themselves into the mix without my say-so.

The upshot of all this is that I do hope you have enjoyed this latest adventure and will want to read more of Lady Fan and her insatiable thirst for detection for some time to come.

If you would consider leaving a review, it would be much appreciated and very helpful. Do feel free to contact me on **elizabeth@elizabethbailey.co.uk** or find me on **Facebook**, **Twitter**, **Goodreads** or my website **elizabethbailey.co.uk**. You might like to browse all things Lady Fan at **ladyfan.uk** too.

Elizabeth Bailey

Sapere Books is an exciting new publisher of brilliant fiction and popular history.

To find out more about our latest releases and our monthly bargain books visit our website:
saperebooks.com